Of Forges & Fury

ALSO BY T.C. KRAVEN

Of Death & Desires

Of Prophecies & Pomegranates

A DARK FATES NOVEL

T.C. KRAVEN

DIVERSION
BOOKS

Diversion Books
A division of Diversion Publishing Corp. www.diversionbooks.com

For more information, email info@diversionbooks.com

First Diversion Books Edition: April 2026
Trade Paperback ISBN: 9798895150610
e-ISBN: 9798895150627

Design by Neuwirth & Associates, Inc.
Cover design by T.C. Kraven
Chapter-header illustrations by Artywings

Printed in the United States of America
1 3 5 7 9 10 8 6 4 2

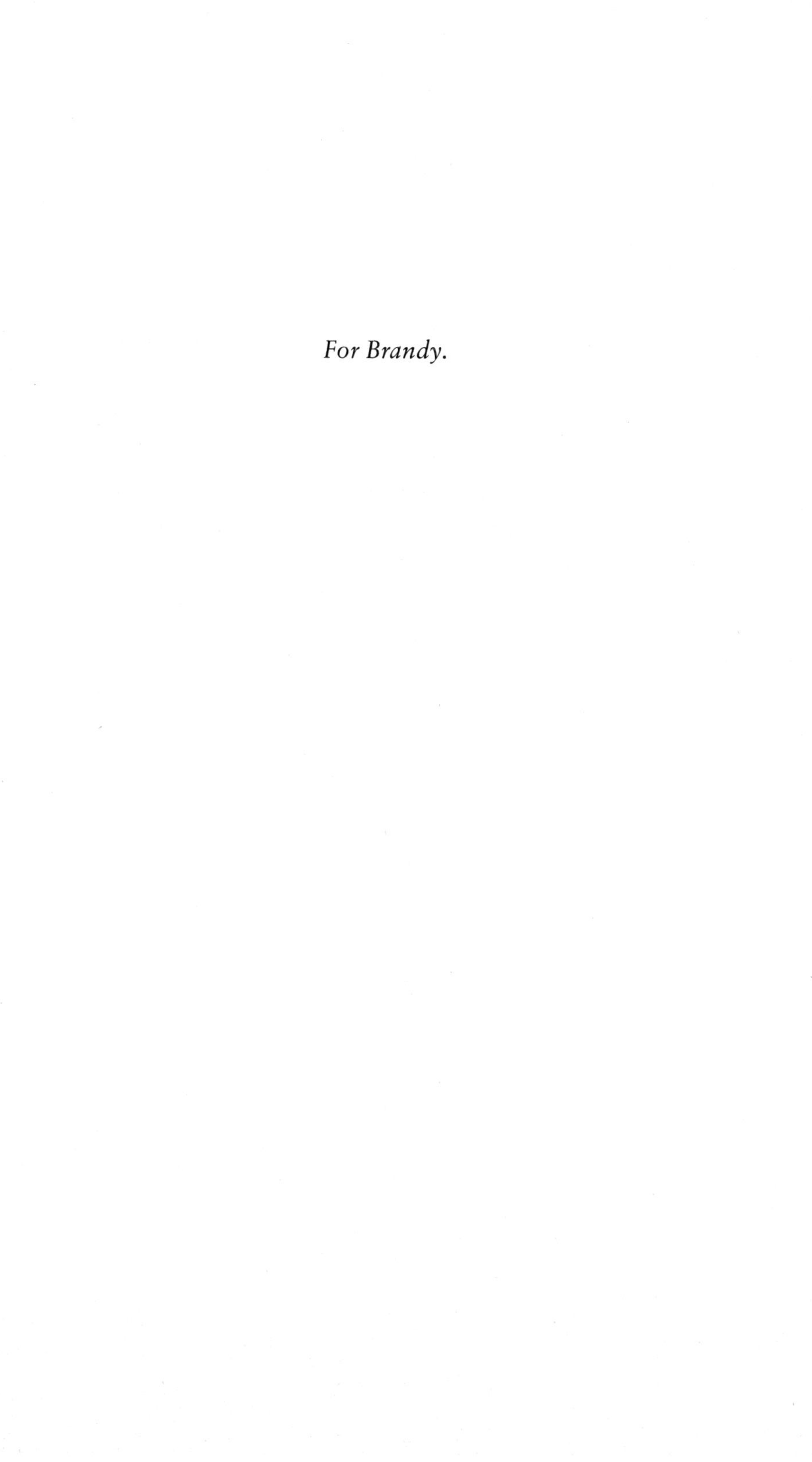

For Brandy.

The Divine

OF THE DARK FATES

HADES

GOD OF THE UNDERWORLD, BORN OF OLYMPIAN ESSENCE

PERSEPHONE

GODDESS OF SPRING, BORN OF DEMETER + ZEUS

DEMETER

GODDESS OF THE HARVEST, BORN OF OLYMPIAN ESSENCE

HEPHAESTUS

GOD OF THE FORGE, BORN OF HERA, BONDED TO APHRODITE

APHRODITE

GODDESS OF LOVE, BORN OF OLYMPIAN ESSENCE, BONDED TO ARES + HEPHAESTUS

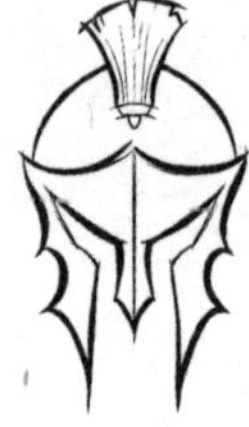

ARES

GOD OF WAR, BORN OF ZEUS, BONDED TO APHRODITE

HERMES

MESSENGER GOD OF THIEVES, BORN OF ZEUS + A MORTAL LOVER

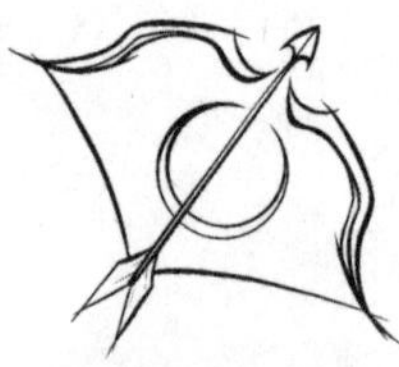

ARTEMIS

GODDESS OF THE HUNT, BORN OF ZEUS + LETO

APOLLO

GOD OF MUSIC, BORN OF ZEUS + LETO

NICK

WOODLAND NYMPH

HELIOS

TITAN OF THE SUN,
BORN OF
HYPERION + THEIA

ZEUS

GOD OF GODS,
BORN OF OLYMPIAN
ESSENCE,
BONDED TO HERA

DIONYSUS

GOD OF WINE,
BORN OF
ZEUS + SEMELE

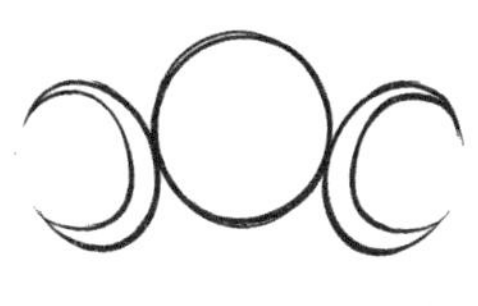

HECATE

GODDESS OF
WITCHCRAFT,
BORN OF
ASTERIA + PERSES

THANATOS

GOD OF DEATH,
BORN OF
NYX + EREBUS

HERA

GODDESS OF
MARRIAGE + BONDS,
BORN OF OLYMPIAN
ESSENCE,
BONDED TO ZEUS

POSEIDON

GOD OF THE SEA,
BORN OF OLYMPIAN
ESSENCE,
BONDED TO ATHENA

ATHENA

GODDESS OF
WISDOM,
BORN OF ZEUS,
BONDED TO POSEIDON

Playlist

1. “Desire”—Meg Myers
2. “Beggin’”—Måneskin
3. “Pencil Fight”—Atomship
4. “Wide Lovely Eyes”—Nick Cave & The Bad Seeds
5. “Habits (Stay High) Hippie Sabotage Remix”—Tove Lo
6. “Such a Simple Thing”—Ray LaMontagne
7. “Apocalypse”—Cigarettes After Sex
8. “If You Could Only See”—Tonic
9. “Little One”—Highly Suspect
10. “Good Looking”—Suki Waterhouse
11. “Polar Opposites”—Modest Mouse
12. “Sex on Fire”—Kings of Leon
13. “Big Empty”—Stone Temple Pilots
14. “War Pigs”—Black Sabbath
15. “You Know I’m No Good”—Amy Winehouse

16. "Killshot (Slowed + Reverb)"—Magdalena Bay
17. "Ride"—Lana Del Rey
18. "Matador"—Luvcat
19. "Trouble"—Cage The Elephant
20. "The Weakness In Me"—Melissa Etheridge (cover)
21. "Send the Pain Below"—Chevelle
22. "Landslide"—Fleetwood Mac
23. "Nothing's Gonna Hurt You Baby"—Cigarettes After Sex
24. "Real Love Baby"—Father John Misty
25. "Breezeblocks"—alt-J
26. "Glycerine"—Bush
27. "Black"—Pearl Jam

Scan the QR code
to access the Spotify playlist:

CONTENT WARNING

This book contains heavy themes, including but not limited to: PTSD, attempted SA (not on page), death, depression, war flashbacks, violence, explicit sexual scenes, scarification, kink and BDSM themes (bondage, somnophilia, edging, minor impact play, denial, use of sex toys, DP, DVP, and sub/Dom/switch dynamics).

AUTHOR'S NOTE

The third installment in the Dark Fates novels encompasses many heavy themes, but the one I hope sticks with you, my muses, is the right to *choose*.

Ares, Aphrodite, and Hephaestus are possibly my favorites to write because, as a polyamorous person, I want to see more of that dynamic represented in media. Every book in the Dark Fates seeks to normalize and highlight different lifestyles and kink, but the most consistent thread is choice. These three had their autonomy stripped from them, and *Of Forges & Fury* is their crucible to take that power back. To defy crushing expectations, even when those judgments come from those who love us, a feat sometimes greater than standing up to overt bigotry.

Just because your love looks different from what we've been conditioned to expect doesn't invalidate it. As long as all parties are *safe* and *consenting adults*, live your life in the way that makes you shine.

And when they try to dim that light, you keep on shining.

Choose yourself, damn the rest.

Welcome back to the Dark Fates.

T.C.

"There is a fine line between love and war.
You're our line, Hephaestus."

—ARES

Prologue

Once, they were free.

Ares, the sharp sword of Zeus, wild and glorious in his brutality. Hephaestus, the warm, steady heart of creation, patient as the forges he commanded. Born of opposite realms— of fire and fury. One raised with spite, one with adoration, both of divine possession. Between them, the thread that bound curled around Aphrodite of the seafoam, of starlight and desire; the radiant Goddess of Love who never asked to choose.

But the God of Gods and the Queen Mother did not take kindly to love that defied their designs, and when those desires threatened loyalties, Olympus answered defiance with chains made from magic that could shackle the gods, forged from anger and spite and desperation. In Bonds that broke and took.

Unseen and unbreakable, but poisoned at the root, the three were bound, eternal shades caught in torment. The victims of jealousy, pride, divine punishment as pawns in an endless war between a scorned Queen and her faithless King. The God of War was cursed to crave what would never be his alone; the God of the Forge condemned to wait, to ache from hope and longing; and the Goddess of Love, the heart that beat between them, was trapped in a cruel loop of loving them both too deeply but never fully belonging to either. To watch helplessly as the gods she cherished tore themselves apart.

Ares gave her passion, Hephaestus devotion, but neither was enough to soothe the wounds the broken Bonds caused between them. Through centuries, through empires, through the Fall of Olympus, they loved and suffered greatly for it. Their love was not tender; it was a ruinous, twisted thing with barbs and hooks that sank too deep, that scarred flesh and made tinder of bones.

And when the agony grew too great, Aphrodite fled, desperate for time and distance to heal what the Fates would not, praying to the cosmos her absence would soften the blade of cruelty between them. But the torment held fast. On the heels of an ancient power awakening, she returned to New Orleans to attempt what even Olympus could not: to break the curse and free the gods she loved, even if that meant she walked alone forever. The Goddess knew that love—true love—was not about possession. It was sacrifice.

And from sacrifice, the gods may once again be made whole.

Aphrodite

CHAPTER 1

"*He's slipping!*"

I heard Hygieia's voice as the air rippled around me, felt the pull to Hephaestus by the searing pain just under my ribs. I stumbled on shaking legs, breath stuck in a stitch and hair tangled from the portal as I tried and failed to right myself. My eyes widened with panic the closer I got, knees buckling under my own weight as the pain doubled, *tripled*.

"Hephaestus," I whispered, horrified. "No, *no, no, fucking Fates, no!*"

Hygieia hovered over Hephaestus, hands glowing purple as magic surged into the husk of the God of the Forge, but her power flickered, no match for the decay racing over his skin.

Hades grabbed me gently as I tried to get to Hephaestus, holding me back as he cried out, vomiting blood and bile on the floor. I fought through pure instinct, kicking and bucking against the God of the Dead.

Hephaestus's chest rose in shallow, rattling gasps. He choked on bloody poison, the massive crater in his chest seeping and gushing not blood— not *only* blood—but a darkness. An abyss of foul, devouring ichor that hissed and smoked anywhere it touched Hephaestus's flesh, practically eating away at him with every heartbeat.

I could hear his heart's weakened gallop as he paled, and even though I was lost to the pain rocking through the Bond, I fought Hades with everything I had, twisting until I broke free.

"Aphrodite—" Hades called, trying to stop me, but I was already there, pushing Hygieia aside.

"It's beyond saving. If you touch that magic—" the Goddess of Mental Health warned, but I was past caring.

"I don't give a fuck, now move," I growled, climbing up on the bed to straddle Hephaestus's waist. The wound was pure carnage: savagely torn skin and bent armor. *Fates, what had happened to him?* I cradled his face, ignoring the sizzling rot that crept toward my fingers, and panic seized me at how cold he was. His eyelashes fluttered open for just a second, only barely, and his unfocused gaze found mine, clouded, pain-drenched, but he knew me.

"Come on, baby, don't do this. Not today." I sniffed. Steeling myself and sucking in a breath, I sunk my hands deep inside the wound on his chest. How long had it been since I'd heard his laugh? Seen his smile? Fuck, this couldn't be it, I couldn't let it. I didn't know if a healthy Bond could have healed him, not to mention one in the same state as ours, but I had to try. Even though we had spent decades apart, I couldn't exist in a cosmos without Hephaestus.

I dug deep inside myself, harnessing the connection that flowed from his body to mine through all the points our flesh touched, and yanked, *hard*. Leashing that tether, I wrenched with all my fucking might, cried out when my hands flared bright with pure golden light, radiant and divine in a way I hadn't felt in centuries, but I didn't question it. Power seeped into his chest cavity while the ichor screamed against it, recoiling, resisting as though it were sentient. It knew I had come to rip it from the host it was trying to consume, and that spurred me on, the rivers of blood and rot that expelled from him and slipped over my arms and thighs. I flooded my essence into Hephaestus with an open heart, an open Bond, love woven into every thread.

Beneath me, Hephaestus's body arched, his lips parted on a groan as the skin started to knit back together, covering bone and muscle and viscera with healed and new flesh. The drain of wielding that much divinity hit me like a freight train, but the wound wasn't closed, not even halfway there, and I owed this to him. I owed everything I had to give into saving his life.

Tears clouded my vision as the pain took hold, my hands raw and burning, coated in poison that I willingly drank from him. It fought me back, angry at me for depriving its meal, tearing at me from within. It seeped into the space beneath my fingernails, the pores of my skin, cutting down to my very shade. I cried out as I gave a final push, legs shaking, fingertips blackened from the rot.

Just a little more.

His eyes cracked open again, more focused as I fed his power.

Almost. Just a little more.

My name fell from cracked lips, his voice hoarse and raw.

Almost there.

My vision tunneled, gravity the heaviest force in the cosmos. I tried to pull back my hands, but I couldn't. Something was wrong. Something was terribly wrong.

The rot.

I had taken it from him. There were voices around me as my eyes rolled back, but I couldn't bring myself to care. I saved him.

I heard his voice, far away but still here, and then the world was shaking, my back bowing and breaking under the weight of it all. I thought of Ares, of how much I missed him too. I'd been without either of them for so long, but now that I was here, with Hephaestus, his Bond demanded I think of him. Crave him in the same selfish way I craved Hephaestus.

I let go, succumbing to the darkness, dreaming of how it all began.

*

ANCIENT GREECE
THREE THOUSAND YEARS AGO

The formal dining hall of Olympus Mons glittered and sparkled. The massive white columns of marble shimmered with veins of gold, and the pillars stretched toward the domed ceiling painted with constellations from the cosmos that shifted slowly across the sky. All around us, floating totems cast warm flame over the feast on the long table carved from precious stone, the planks laden with golden platters piled too high for just us. Beneath all the grandeur, there was a current of anxiety, pressure that pushed in from all sides, nearly suffocating. The summons to Olympus had arrived just a few days ago, and I'd been a twisted bundle of nerves over it, knowing my punishment would be severe.

I took a sip of wine, let the bitter and sweet wash some of my nerves back as Hera and Zeus made polite conversation. I knew them both too well to find comfort in their nonchalance as I tracked the way the Queen Mother's voice curled venomously sweet around her responses. As for the God of Gods, I could nearly feel the undercurrent of Zeus's displeasure filling the silence between sips. It was a special kind of torture: the unknown, the pit of snakes writhing in my gut awaiting judgment for my defiance. Across the ambrosia glazed with honey, the roasted figs bleeding nectar, and goblets of Dionysian wine sat Hephaestus.

I watched him curiously across the table. He'd grown since we'd last seen each other. To my knowledge, he had only ever been to Olympus once before, when we were both made new and learning the ways of the cosmos. He had been kind to me then, a boy who radiated warmth with a shy smile. Now that same warmth filled the space between us, the boy grown into a god of quiet mystery.

His hands clutched a goblet, calloused fingers tracing the metal beneath his touch, and I watched it warble, responding to the God of the Forge. Hephaestus was beautiful, in a striking sort of way, and I knew that beauty. Knew the weight of it and what it could cost. A strand of his pale hair fell across his furrowed brow, his shoulders rising and falling just a little more rapidly than would be normal.

So he was nervous too.

It was no secret the disdain Zeus held for Hera's son, the one she made all on her own to defy him. It was rumored that he had ordered her to kill Hephaestus, to toss him from Olympus, and that was why he had been raised in the depths of the Underworld.

He looked up through his bowed head, catching me staring, and a small smile quirked the side of his lips that felt too natural not to return. He felt like a pocket of steady calm, the eye in this hurricane that spun around us, coiling around the perfectly staged dinner we were both trapped in.

Hera cleared her throat from the end of the table, drawing both of our attention to the goddess. She was a vision in deep indigo and ivory. Her fair hair, the same color as her son's, adorned with sapphires and an elegant spray of peacock feathers. Her beauty was cold and ornamental, and yet I yearned for her approval. For her acceptance. I had known her since my own creation, but that was so long ago that the memories weren't clear, and somedays I wondered if I had dreamt them up in the first place.

Her eyes assessed me, pierced right through to my shade, and I straightened in my seat, smoothing down the fabric of my pink chiton. Did she know why her husband was displeased? Fear choked me at the very thought.

There was another set of eyes on me, ones that hadn't left or given me a moment's peace since I'd crawled out of the surf and my divine existence had begun. But I studiously ignored the God of Gods. He had ordered me to diffuse a bad situation, and though I had been initially successful, another incident had set my power off, reigniting the blood lust on the field. I had displeased him, but the alternative would have meant something far more nefarious. It was a dangerous blade, spurning Zeus, or ending up on the wrong end of Hera's wrath. I didn't know which scared me most—Hera was famous for her vengeance, taking her scorn out on those who dared to touch what belonged to her.

Even if Zeus touched them first. Even if he took what wasn't freely given. Would Hera believe me if I told her? I wanted to tell her.

"I am sure that you are aware of the meaning of this summons." Her shrewd eyes pinned me in place. I swallowed.

"I didn't try to, I swe—" I began, but her gaze turned to stone, and the defense died on my lips.

Zeus's fist toppled a carafe of wine. "Choose your words," he whispered, the implication clear.

I couldn't look at him, but I couldn't meet Hera's eyes either. Instead, they fell on Hephaestus, and there was concern in his amber gaze as he studied the tremble in my fingers. He kept me there, with him, steadying me. His fingertips traced over the base of his goblet a few times, and I swore I could feel the warmth of him stroking along the back of my hand.

I exhaled, reminding myself to breathe.

I humbled myself under the weight of their egos, choosing my words as carefully. "I only meant that I could not control my power. It was a mistake; I tapped too much, and that caused a surge. I did not mean to offend."

"They had surrendered, but your error caused them to rally. We lost the city because of your greed and wanton thirst for power,"

Zeus spat, voice cruel and spiteful. I flinched, swallowing down my rage and the tears threatening to undo me. My body then froze, and I retreated deep inside myself, curling in protectively as my mind went back to that day, back to that tent, when the God of Gods had attempted to make good on the eons of restrained lust he'd been holding.

When my power had swelled within me, pulling from every living being within the city walls, and protected me. Until Ares had arrived, who nearly ruined us all in his rage.

Zeus continued his tirade, attacking my character, accusing my hubris, voice full of vitriol and disgust, but I could only see Hephaestus. Only hear his voice when he whispered, "That's enough."

The God of Gods barked a laugh and slunk back in his seat, arrogance dripping from him. He knew I wouldn't tell her. Knew she wouldn't believe me if I did, and there wasn't a chance in the Hells she would believe anything that came out of Ares's mouth.

"We have summoned you both because we feel there is a match to be made of this mess. Athena is meeting with the Thalesians, and we will figure out a peace accord. In the meantime, your power, or lack of discipline with it, needs to be tethered. The two of you will wed, in the hopes of tempering this," Hera announced, and my blood ran cold as Hephaestus jerked his eyes to his mother.

"What?" he asked, voice low, but I couldn't move. Couldn't think.

"Love has become a weapon, so it is time we sheath it. What better way than to wrap it in the brilliant embrace of the forge?" Hera's voice turned calm, the kindness and adoration nearly palpable as she spoke to her boy. She was nearly a different goddess for him, for the God of the Forge, so lovingly made. Hephaestus took one look at me, and whatever he saw on my face told me I wasn't hiding my true feelings well.

"Do you want to do this?" he asked, the genuine care and concern in his voice so unfamiliar in these halls. Kindness was not a virtue espoused by many of the inhabitants of Olympus Mons, and certainly not by Hera and Zeus.

Hephaestus waited patiently as I opened my mouth to speak, but words would not come. We both knew it mattered not what we wanted. The edict came from Olympus, and defying that . . .

"You may yet learn some humility living in the shadows of the forge, with a god who could never match your beauty," Zeus taunted. Hera shot daggers at her husband, but before she could respond, the double doors at the end of the hall groaned open beneath the God of War's hand.

"Ah, Ares," Zeus boomed, lifting his goblet, "you're late."

They stared at one another as Ares approached, confidence in every step he took, but I could see the tension rippled over his broad shoulders. My heart shredded in my chest as something foreign and new bloomed behind my ribs. I hadn't seen him in hours, but the change felt sudden. Visceral.

"I wasn't told it was dinner," Ares replied, voice rough. He pulled out a chair next to Hephaestus, a place setting I'd missed.

Dread coiled in my gut at the mirth I could see dancing in Zeus's eyes. To betroth me to Hephaestus and invite Ares to witness was a cruelty beyond measure, a delight only a god as vicious as Zeus would enjoy. He may not have been able to prove why Ares had come to my aid, but he was punishing us for even the thought of it, pushing his son to the brink in hopes he would betray our secret in a fit of rage.

"The eastern kings have agreed to lay down arms, if Olympus intervenes. They want your word, Father. A seal of unity," Ares said.

"Let them wait. Tonight is not for war." Zeus waved a dismissive hand, his attention still on me, watching, waiting, wanting to see the look on my face when Ares found out the news. Of the

gods, he was the only one who'd suspected, and after the way Ares behaved when he'd found us in that tent, I had no doubt he knew. This was Zeus acting out his pettiest, cruelest intentions, either hoping to force Ares to lose his temper enough to implicate us, or to simply watch the misery we suffered for his own amusement.

Zeus had forbidden Ares from taking a divine lover centuries ago. For whatever reason, we weren't sure, but his word was law, and Ares and I had broken his command. This was our punishment.

"Everything is for war. It is why I exist," Ares answered. The God of War leaned back in his seat, all sharp lines of restless energy, my predator in polished armor. He looked so handsome sitting there, the want living in the space between us, the little bit of distance nearly too much. I ached for him as his eyes—those warm, brown eyes—never left my body. They touched parts of me covered with my chiton, where bruises that fit his fingers perfectly rested, then lower, to where he knew I would be dripping with him, with the evidence of stolen passion that had nearly ruined us both hours before. His gaze flicked to my lips, his own curving into a smirk that held far too much heat and not nearly enough discretion.

My heart thundered in my chest.

"And yet, tonight, we celebrate something far more . . . civilized," Hera commented, voice icy.

Next to Ares, Hephaestus said nothing, but his jaw was tight enough to crack teeth. I couldn't meet either of their gazes.

Zeus rose, goblet in hand. "You arrived just in time, son. A toast. To Olympus. To peace. And to the joining of divine houses."

Ares's jaw slowed, chewing the grape he'd plucked from the platter nearest him. His eyes shifted slowly, taking it all in. I saw the moment it registered, when Hera lifted her own glass and began to speak, but I couldn't make out her words. I was too focused on what he might do, on the slow rise of his chest, that quiet fury more dangerous than any outburst.

"And let it be known that Aphrodite is no longer untethered. Love belongs to the forge now."

I flinched as silence swallowed the room. I wished it would swallow me too, that the stone beneath my feet would open and I could fall straight back through the clouds to the Upper Realm.

Ares laughed once, quiet and dangerous, and that terrified me most. Hera and Zeus drained their cups, caring little that the three of ours remained untouched.

"Are you not pleased with your news, Aphrodite?" Hera asked sweetly, suspiciously kind as she waited. I sucked a small breath in then shifted my smile toward her, as measured and pleasant as I could muster. The Queen Mother never forgot an offense, and in her eyes, I had committed many.

"I am honored to be bestowed such a blessing," I replied, lifting my glass to my lips. Above the rim of my goblet, I watched anger and emotion mist Ares's eyes and prayed to the Fates that he would keep his composure, keep his life.

I would figure out a way around this. I just needed more time.

Hephaestus

CHAPTER 2

My chest ached as a soft pressure settled over my body. Hands—two hands, perfect and delicate—pressed against me. Coaxing, giving. I felt the tingles spread over my flesh where our skin connected, and my lungs relaxed, breathing deep with ease for the first time in decades.

Aphrodite.

I struggled to open my eyes, the desperate need to see her beautiful face a gnawing ache that chewed at me from the inside.

I was hurt. She had come.

Affection in my chest split past the pain, and I cursed the darkness that paralyzed me, pinning me under as my divinity failed to heal what had been ravaged by poison and rot. Where it had failed, she wouldn't.

Aphrodite shifted, panting as she pulled the damage from me, using our Bond as it was intended. The power share, the accelerated healing—all perks of the sacred Bond. If only ours didn't come with so much pain. I hadn't felt her body on mine in so long, and she felt so fucking *good*. She panted, knitting me back together, giving and giving and—

Too much. An insatiable hunger ripped through our Bond, nearly bowing my back from the force of it.

There was a bite to the pull of our entwined magic. A starving, insidious leeching of life determined to wrench back every second of the last near-century it had been starved tenfold. I grew stronger as the Bond worked on healing my wounds, but it was taking from her, far more than it should have been able to. Far more than she could survive.

My eyes flew open, only to watch in rapt horror as Aphrodite's beautiful face contorted into a grimace above me. Fingernails dug into my skin, my chest, as she pushed, drawing blood from the effort to remove herself.

But the Bond had been neglected for so, so long. It was ravenous as it drew on her power. I put my hands on her shoulders, shoving with all my strength, but the magic held her locked around me.

"*Help!*" I rasped as Aphrodite's eyes rolled back, jaw slack on a mangled scream that set the hairs on the back of my neck on edge. Panic built in my chest, and I fought to break the hold as she convulsed and seized. Black streaks of corruption crawled up her arms and chest, tracing her veins. The wound in my chest was almost healed, but the Bond took and plundered, unrelenting.

Hades's shadows wrapped around Aphrodite's body as she sagged against mine, wave after wave of pain tearing through her. Hades pulled his hand back, wrenching his shadows and, with them, the Goddess of Love, breaking our connection. Aphrodite let out a blood-curdling scream, arched back in midair, reaching for me. Begging through broken sobs and tears.

Hygieia held me back as I lunged for her, the Bond in my chest snapping tight. It was unnatural to let Aphrodite be in pain. I could take it, could fix it, but the Goddess of Mental Health pinned me with her full weight and power. My mind fogged.

Hades kept a light touch on Aphrodite, only allowing her to be physically in contact with the shadows. She floated, suspended in midair, soft tendrils of her long blonde hair lifting and swirling around her.

"What's happening to her?" I demanded, frantically.

Hygieia instructed Hades to lay Aphrodite on the opposite bed, and he complied, setting her gently between the sheets.

Aphrodite's hands sought my touch, a clear instruction. *Stay.*

"Where is her Bondmark?" Hades asked.

I gestured to her torso, and he commanded the shadows silently to lift her shirt, to expose no more than necessary.

I balked at the sight. Our Bondmark was bruised and oozing, the lines puffed out like an infected tattoo, the skin around it red and angry. I reached over my shoulder to feel mine but found it smooth, not painful to the touch at all.

Hygieia grabbed a pair of gloves to slip her hands into before taking her place next to Aphrodite. She pushed her hair back, ran a small touch across the mark. Aphrodite cried out, the sound slicing me to the bone.

Hygieia and I both winced.

"How long has it been since you've been together?" she asked.

I ran my fingers through my hair. "About eighty years," I answered.

Hygieia let out a hiss and turned back to Aphrodite, shaking her head with an impatient tsk. "None of you have *any* damned sense. I should never have let her in here," she scolded, working deftly. Magic flowed from her hands, now stripped of gloves and moving fast over Aphrodite's flesh.

"You can't neglect the Bond and then *demand* from it. That's not how it works." She was frustrated, too preoccupied on soothing the Bondmark to notice Hades shift uncomfortably, but I caught it.

I pushed myself out of the bed and made my way over to him.

"I should tell you; Ares has passed into my realm," Hades told me. "I expect whatever she's feeling, he is, too, considering he shares a mark as well. He's on a trajectory to come straight here."

I nodded quickly, eyeing Aphrodite's frail form. It was good that he was coming, right? She might need him. Something in our Bond was corrupted. Perhaps he could take her pain away, and I could see enough reason to know this was about more than ego or infidelities.

Ares

CHAPTER 3

War song reverberated in my chest, the mandate of my power swelling, reaching out to collect the tribute of battle from the sand and decay and blood. The sun above baked sweat and ash into my skin, but I smiled as I watched the enemy line crumble, the rush of panic and chaos permeating the battlefield. Men screamed and cried out in a myriad of languages my divinity translated automatically, but even if they hadn't, in the end, all warriors—righteous and wicked alike—begged for the same thing.

Time.

More time to live, to right wrongs, the fear of death and the beyond debilitating even in the face of excruciating pain. The guilt wouldn't come later—the weight of the unnecessary lives lost over territory, bigotry, or greed—because *these* men? These were righteous deaths. The depths of their depravity rivalled the corruption of the government who sent us to occupy lands for resources they coveted, through state-funded propaganda, fearmongering, and the oxymoron of the Peace Through Force testaments.

No, I took my marching orders from one of *our* kind. From a sect of Otherworlders embedded into the armed forces who rooted out extreme evil and passed judgment based on a person's shade, not the color of their skin nor what they could offer. And these men? They did not represent the good people of their home country. These men used fear and brutality to oppress innocent lives, wielded force and torture to restrain and bleed their own dry, and today, that bill came due for them.

My fingers twitched against the metal of my rifle, and, not for the first time, I ached for the old ways—the delicate balance of a good and sharp blade. My tattoo itched against the rough scrape of my uniform, begging to be set free, for the violent dance of melee combat rather than the distance fired metal afforded. I sniffed as the smoke choked the air, the stench of burning flesh and iron heavy around us. The violence fed me, sustained me in a way nothing else ever had. A flash of memory sent crystalline blue eyes across my mind, and my chest tightened under my battle rattle.

Almost nothing.

I shook my head, forcing my mind away from roads too painful to get stuck down, returning my thoughts to the wreckage around me, to the sounds of screams and peppered gunshots that rained down like a symphony of macabre comfort. Blood and glory and ruin. The sand beneath my boots was soaked in it, drenched deep brown and crimson with every step, and I lapped it up. I fucking *reveled* in it.

Pain cracked across my ribs, sharp and sudden. Too divine for a bullet, too well hidden behind plate metal to come from anywhere but deep inside. I hissed as the pain lanced through my side, and I felt that distinct bite. Something older than the land I stood on, piercing deeper than the wounds the scars on my body commemorated.

Her.

My knees locked up beneath me, and I stumbled, back bowing as another shock wave thundered through my body. My eyes shot skyward, taking the blinding haze of the sun and the distorted sky, all smoke and blood and war forgotten. The Bondmark I shared with Aphrodite ached and pulsed, shooting stabbing pains deep down to the marrow, expelling ragged breaths from my bones.

Aphrodite was in danger; I could feel it vibrating through every cell in my body, singing to me to find her. Go to her. Fix her and kill whatever fucking thing dared to touch her.

"Sir!" Tullis, a Roman demi-god, shouted above the din, her pale eyes wide in alarm, sweat-plastered strands of blonde stuck to her temples. But I was gone before she could take a step to steady me. For the first time in my existence, I turned from the fight, from the battle and my soldiers, because the call to Aphrodite was stronger than the bloodlust that fueled me.

Words left my lips in the old tongue, words I hadn't invoked in decades, as my divinity frantically searched and sought out hers.

The world shifted. The desert blurred in the smoke, melting into shadows and silence. Extreme heat cooled so rapidly, the metal of my weapon began to steam as the stench of burning flesh gave way to the scent of cold stone and rushing water. It took me only moments to regain my bearings, but it didn't take a genius to work out that I was a long way from Iraq. Beneath it, maybe, but none of that mattered as the stench of something familiar and foreign all at once overwhelmed me.

It took too long to realize it was fear, and it was coming from me. I'd smelled it on the aura of every life I'd ever taken, but there were less than a handful of times I could recall being the source.

Panic washed over me as my feet picked up pace, the invisible tether behind my ribs yanking me along the Asphodels. Shadows curled around me, and the whispering voices of the dead tempted me into the River Styx that flowed through the heart of the

Underworld. But I ran at a full tilt, the spear of pain still burning in my side, urging me deeper into the Hells.

She was here, somewhere, and in danger. Or dead. Fuck. Fates, the thought choked me as it formed, and I stumbled, tripping over the mangled vines and roots of dark flora that sprouted across the lands. The sound of my boots as they sunk into cold earth warred with the pulse screaming in my eardrums with every step, past the Questing Road, the Moonlit Path, the Elysian Fields.

If she were dead, I would know. Wouldn't I?

More pain lanced through me, expelling a grunt from my lips as I pushed harder, repeating the mantra.

If she were dead, I would know. If she were dead, I would know.

I knew Hades had felt the moment I trespassed in his realm; I felt the ripple of power pulse from the broken barrier as I passed through the Gates, and I braced myself for the punishment that usually came with breaking the edict he'd laid down the day he'd expelled Zeus from the Asphodels. But the patches of my exposed skin that should have been frostbitten remained unharmed, and that could mean only one thing.

The Spring Queen had returned.

I rounded the cave where the beast Cerberus made his home in time to see the path to Aphrodite blocked by a legion of ghostly shades, pale specters of power that served at the beck and call of the God of the Dead. They were formidable opponents; warriors of great bravery and renown that kept their afterlife in New Elysium, which I had built many years ago with Helios. There would be no honor in the destruction of their shades. With them, I knew, the guilt *would* come, but I didn't falter. My steps were sure and swift as I continued my trajectory to the palace, weapon drawn and barrel trained. A normal bullet wouldn't do damage to the shades, but fused with my furious power, I'd dispatch them with little effort.

Aphrodite was in there; I could feel it with every fiber of my divine being, and if the dead tried to stop me?

I'd kill them all again.

Hephaestus

CHAPTER 4

The door to the room nearly blew off its hinges, and it was as though the pep talk I'd given myself about this being a *good* thing flew right out the damned window.

Ares pushed through, massive eyes wide and searching until they fell on Aphrodite. He charged forward, every inch of his six-foot-three frame radiating rage and energy. Blood boiled in my veins as dark brown eyes pierced through me, full of hatred just as they always had whenever they fell on me. His clear judgment and subsequent dismissal caused my own temper to rise, to meet his disdain inch for inch as his turmoil permeated the air around us.

He stopped short of her bed, oversized muscles bulging through his uniform, barely restrained the fury rolling off him.

"What did you do to her?" he snarled, and I felt my anger amp, rising to the bait.

Always a fucking fight with him.

"*I* didn't do anything to her. I didn't even know she was here until I woke up, and she was on top of me," I snapped back through gritted teeth.

Ares's nostrils flared at the innuendo, and an immature, sadistic lick of satisfaction bloomed over my chest. There was a time when I'd felt badly for the situation we were all trapped in. I'd *empathized*. But that was before I'd realized what a truly unsanctimonious prick he could be. No, his penchant for being an asshole burned that bridge long ago.

The God of War's longing for her was violent, a flame that only seemed to burn hotter the more he tried to smother it, nearly consuming them both anytime they were together. It usually ended with her heartbroken, and I'd found myself hating him for it, for her tears, for the pain she wore for him. Worse still, I hated myself for not having had the strength to walk away all those years ago.

Not that we'd really had a choice.

He bowed up into my space. His lip curled in disgust, in challenge, and all I wanted to do was punch him in that stupidly chiseled jaw of his.

Tension coiled through the room, the temperature rising with every labored breath we exchanged, the atoms in the air buzzing. Waiting. We were so close that I inhaled his exhales, he mine, but neither of us were willing to back down. I knew I should. Aphrodite was laying between us, but I couldn't take my eyes off him for even a moment, and that pissed me off too.

Ares's brown irises darkened to pitch blacks as they flicked between my own, and all the while, the heat rose, oppressive. *Stifling*. There was something about the God of War that chipped away at my calm, the way he burrowed under my fucking skin. Ares set me on edge like no other.

"Don't . . . don't fight." The words, broken and exhausted, swelled between us, and like magic, the tension deflated as we both looked at *her*.

The reason for the war we'd waged for thousands of years.

The reason the air filled my lungs every day.

The most stunning goddess to walk this realm or any other.

Aphrodite.

My fists flexed at my sides as I tried to keep a lid on my composure, my relief that she was conscious stealing my breath.

Aphrodite's eyes flitted in and out of focus, and she lifted her frail hand aimlessly toward me, or maybe him—it was impossible to tell from where we stood at the edge of her bed.

I watched Ares's chest heave with the same restrained effort, his serious brown eyes sweeping over her face, her body, then back and forth between the two of us, as though he had realized I was closer to her than he was. Assessing our proximity. Calculating.

Sizing me up in case of a fight.

I was a threat to him, *to her*, still in my armor, bloodied from the now-healed wound in my chest and caked with the ichor of the Underworld's grime. My eyes narrowed, body bristling under his scrutiny, under the way he sliced through my defenses, searching for weaknesses. An unsettling shiver threatened to work down my spine, the same as it always did anytime the God of War's eyes lingered too long. He may be a skilled tactician, but he had no idea how far I'd go to protect Aphrodite. I had contemplated how to kill Ares before, or rather, how to seriously maim him, in the darkest times. Aphrodite's love for him had kept me at bay, but if he fucked around, I was more than happy to let him find out.

I kept my eyes locked on his challenge. The air crackled around us, again thickening with our power as it rammed together in the small space between us, mixing in a haze of mutual hatred and barely controlled rage.

Then the delicate scent of springtime wafted through the room as Persephone entered, the goddess stopping to whisper something to her husband before continuing on. Hades made a face, tugging her back to his chest, but she only gave him an exasperated smile and ushered him out of the room with an "I'll be fine. Go."

The God of the Dead shot us both icy looks, the implication clear that, if we caused harm to his wife by way of a brawl, he'd string us up by our toes in the Styx. Still, neither of us moved an inch.

"Boys, enough," Persephone admonished. "This isn't the time, and you won't be spilling any blood in my palace. *Sit down.*"

Her words were calm, but an undercurrent of power bolstered her tone, and I marveled at the change in her. Persephone may have looked delicate and kind, but she was the Queen of the Underworld, and days ago, I watched her squeeze the life out of the powerful sorceress Minthe and discard her corpse in the Styx without hesitation. This goddess was my friend, a confidant, but she had somehow reconciled her new sense of self with her old power, and I knew better than to test the Queen of the Underworld.

I rolled my shoulders in submission.

Ares tore his gaze from mine with a huff and brought his hand to Aphrodite's cheek, slick with the sweat that beaded and slid down from her hairline.

"What happened to her?" he demanded, tone clipped. He looked stiff and bulky in his uniform, a muted beige camouflage offset with a bulletproof vest, speckled with blood spatter. His combat boots wreaked havoc all over the floor, and I could see the trail of sand strewn across the stone surface. The nameplate embroidered over his breast pocket read ENYALIUS as it peeked through the bulk of his armor. A dark maple leaf, signifying the rank of major, rested on both sides of his collar and in the center of the cap he wore. The muted black of the M16A3 slung across his chest lay in chilling contrast to the light colors camouflaging his form, and the scent of sweat and ash made it clear he had just come from a firefight. I could smell the residue of expelled bullets and blood on him, and I wondered, for a moment, how many shades had been dispatched to the Asphodels bearing the mark of Ares.

Hades may have been the God of the Dead, and Thanatos the God of Death, but Ares was the *swift* of death. Major Ares Enyalius, he was now, but he had gone by many names over the eons. The Bane of Mortals, the Slayer of Men, the City-Stormer, the Armor-Clattering, the Arm-Bearing. *The Breaker.* After the fall of Olympus, he'd strapped himself to whichever military-industrial complex would have him and kept his reputation for bloodletting flying across new territories, taking breaks only as long as it took to return and fuck up our lives.

". . . So, essentially, Hygieia thinks Aphrodite asked too much of the Bond when she healed Hephaestus. But it's just a guess," Persephone finished, and I startled, too lost in my own thoughts to recall what she'd just said. I worked to keep a neutral expression on my face, begging the Fates to help get us through this interaction without bloodshed. I just needed to know how much longer he'd be here and how we could get him gone.

Deep brown eyes burned into me again as Ares swept his cover from his head, and I watched the almost-too-long black strands slide to slightly frame his face. A face now etched with fury and the promise of retribution because whatever Persephone had said sent him raging like a bull all over again.

"You let her fucking heal you? Now she's sick because you couldn't wait a few days to heal up? If it wasn't Poisoned Ambrosia, you'd have been fine." His cover twisted between his fingers as he wrung the fabric, voice low and deadly. But his breathing . . . there was something hidden beneath the arrogance in his words, in the flare of his nostrils as he wound himself back up, and it called to my blood, called to the deeper parts of me I rarely let out of the cage to put him in his fucking place.

I stood up to my full height and turned to him, letting out the weight of my power, stepping right up into his space. "Listen, fuckface, I didn't *let* her do anything. I was unconscious, and I woke up to her forcing the Bond. As soon as I realized what she was doing, I attempted to separate us, so back the fuck up."

Anger laced my tone, so out of character that at the end of the bed, Persephone's eyes went wide with shock. I hated that she was seeing this side of me. Hells, I hardly recognized it myself, but Ares had a knack for bringing out the absolute worst in someone, even me. *Especially me.* The air crackled around us in anticipation.

Beneath us and the oppressive swell of our divinity, Aphrodite whimpered, and it was like a bucket of the Styx was dumped over me. I sighed heavily, letting out low and steady breaths as I consciously worked to rein in my power. This wasn't going to help her; I knew she needed calm with how our chaos affected her heavily, as the bearer of two Bonds. I swallowed back the emotions I felt swirling in my chest and tucked my tongue behind my teeth, reaching deep to settle my temper.

She asked for peace. I could give her that, even if he couldn't.

"Thank you for coming," I said, begrudgingly. A look of pure shock passed over Ares's face as his hand fell to his side, fingertips grazing over the exposed skin of Aphrodite's wrist. He stilled, swallowed hard, surprising me, too, as he pulled back the violence that lived just beneath his skin.

For her. Only ever for *her*.

The color began to return to Aphrodite's cheeks, and I cursed myself internally, the crushing weight of wretched guilt heavy on my shoulders. This was my fault, no matter how much I didn't want to give Ares the satisfaction of being right. My Bond had taken while his gave to her now, freely, tenderly.

We all watched in silence as a power gentler than I'd ever imagined him possessing flowed through the tips of the God of War's fingers, invigorating Aphrodite, pouring into her divinity, her essence.

Persephone glanced between us before putting her hand on my bicep and giving it a squeeze. I was grateful for the way she'd come to know me, better now than she ever had before. Persephone knew what this was costing me, to see Aphrodite like this, to know it was his power saving her life.

"I was in the Middle East on a recon mission that went a little sideways. I felt her calling to me through the Bond and thought I'd been shot. It'd been so long since I felt it at all that I wasn't sure I had. I felt the pull tugging me here, and I thought . . ." Ares's voice wavered, and pain flashed over his face as he rubbed steady circles with his thumb on the back of her hand. It was jarring to see the worry and weariness etched in the lines of his face, all traces of anger and arrogance replaced while he looked at her lying there. ". . . I left my squad in the middle of a firefight."

A gasp left me faster than I could rein it in, my head jerking up at his words. Never in all my lifetimes had I *ever* heard of him leaving a battlefield for anyone other than victory. War was the calling of Ares, and he could put none above it, not even Aphrodite. His very nature of bloodlust kept their relationship volatile and served as the root of all our problems because he may love her, but he wouldn't, *couldn't*, choose her when the hounds of war called to him.

The pattern of destruction had become so predictable, it was nearly like clockwork, the torment and longing that echoed between us. Even when she was with me and we were happy, his Bond demanded attention, demanded Ares. I'd watched helplessly as she tried to fight it, but the magic of a Bond could break worlds.

We never stood a chance.

And because I could never bring myself to hate her when she ripped my heart from my chest—because I loved her and wanted her to be free—I let her go. I couldn't hate her for what I knew she couldn't help, but we all knew his love wouldn't sustain, and when he inevitably left her in pieces, broken and aching for him when his bloodlust overrode his own need, I let myself hate him enough for the both of us, knowing she never could. Again and again, we loved and lost, locked in a viciously never-ending cycle.

But he was here now, breaking our pattern, changing the rules. An unease settled into me as I looked past the bravado and courage Ares projected. I really allowed myself to *see* him: stubble peppered his jaw, and his dark eyes were alert but unsteady. He looked tired, *drained*, but having just left theatre, he should have been brimming with raw energy and power. The whole of his attention was on Aphrodite, and I watched him trace over the sculpt of her brow and the Cupid's bow of her lip with his gaze.

Persephone kept speaking, but it was as though Ares had tuned her out—tuned out the world, maybe—as he worked to get the Goddess of Love back to good, and it was moments like this that tore at me. It was easy to pretend he was a selfish asshole who loved and left her, but this . . . In all our years, I had never seen *this*.

I could feel his power as it moved through her, soaked up by their Bond. It reminded me of the first night we'd met, all those years ago, in golden halls that hid the rot of Olympus, before our paths were irrevocably altered, destined for heartache and ruin.

Before we hated each other.

Before I'd known they were in love.

"So, the thing is, in order for us to try and figure a way out of this, we need your blood. A vial from each of you," Persephone finished, studying us both closely. Ares stiffened, and I couldn't blame him. Our blood was ancient. *Sacred*. Just giving someone access to it was not something any of us made a habit of doing.

Ares's jaw set, and he leveled a stony look at her. "Absolutely not."

Persephone frowned, the crease between her eyebrows deepening. "I understand you're hesitant—" she began but Ares cut her off.

"I'm not hesitant. There will be no harvesting of Aphrodite's blood without her consent. I will not give you something so valuable with no way to ensure it's only being used for the purpose you claim." His voice was gruff, borderline rude.

Persephone rested her hands on her hips, pursing her lips. "If you could see for yourself that the vial was used up in front of you, would that change your mind?"

Ares paused. Considered. "For my blood, it would be sufficient, but not Aphrodite's. Only she can consent to that." He brought Aphrodite's hand to his lips and pressed a small kiss to her palm. "I don't speak for Hephaestus."

Even though he jerked his head toward me, there was far less animosity in his tone than usual. It made me feel even more out of sorts to find us on a united side. For once.

Persephone inclined her head in understanding before turning to me. "Heph?" she asked.

I dipped my head once. "For mine, yes. But I agree with Ares about Aphrodite's blood; not without her knowledge and consent."

The words burned my throat to say. Ares lifted his eyes to mine in a silent thank-you, or as close to one as I would get. Many years had passed since either of us held a civil conversation with the other, and though I trusted Persephone and Hecate, who no doubt would be performing the ritual, I couldn't offer up Aphrodite's blood like that.

"*Right*. Well, come with me then. Aphrodite gave Hecate her blood weeks ago, apparently for this very purpose."

"What purpose?" I asked, confused.

Persephone bit down on her lip, nervous.

"Seph," I pleaded.

"I . . . I only found out a few minutes ago, Hephaestus." Her green eyes full of pity. "Aphrodite asked if Hecate could find a way to break the Bonds between you. We've all been busy with, you know, Minthe almost killing us all, but now that's handled . . . Hecate and Hermes are working on setting up the ritual to try to produce a vision."

My knees buckled as pain ricocheted through my body, the shock of her words nearly knocking the breath from my lungs.

Ares's eyes went wide as he looked at me, alarmed. "Did you know?" he asked, tone rife with pain and panic that mirrored my own, but I shook my head, just as blindsided by this information as he was.

A piercing ache speared through me. *Break the Bonds.*

"If you insist on being a part of what's to come, to keep an eye on your blood, then that's fine." Persephone's tone was kind and gentle as she delivered the news ripping me to fucking shreds. A slash of betrayal sliced through my chest, right over the wound above my Bondmark. I shouldn't be hearing this from the Goddess of Spring. No, Aphrodite had been in the city for weeks, I'd known it, and apparently so had Hecate. And yet . . . Aphrodite hadn't come to me. And as fucked up as this was, Ares deserved to hear it firsthand as well.

Persephone snapped her fingers lightly, and a small tendril broke free from the dark shadows in the corner of the room to slither over the stone floor like a playful snake. It danced up over her skin and settled onto her outstretched palm. Persephone smiled and brought her hand close to her mouth, speaking into it.

"We're on our way; they both insist on being present," she whispered into the darkness.

I watched as the little shadow darted away, zooming out the door and through the palace, a message no doubt on its way to Hades.

Ares's hands shook slightly, and I knew he was feeling the same uncertainty and anguish I was. She hadn't told him either, and that meant she was looking for a way out of the Bonds from *both* of us, not planning to choose. Leaving us both.

Bile rose in my throat, the tether that connected us stretched taut as my own emotions overwhelmed the Bond. Aphrodite groaned, and I scolded myself, knowing the magic between us was still raw, that she felt my pain, too, but hearing this news gutted me.

Persephone held her hand out again, and the shadows descended, whispering and rustling as they formed a long, obsidian athame in her palm. Her fingers clasped around the solid blade, the other hand producing two glass vials from her jeans pocket. She looked at me expectantly, and I extended my hand, mind still reeling and turning her words over.

Persephone pressed the shadow edge to my flesh and pierced gently, sliding the blade across my palm. The split skin bloomed crimson, welling up until blood flowed freely into a single line that dropped into the vial. Knowing its purpose felt like I was volunteering to sign my own death warrant, giving my blessing for the love of my life to undo the vows we'd spoken into the cosmos.

The vial was full in seconds, each drop damnation. Persephone slid a finger over my wound, knitting it back together with ease as she stoppered the vial with a cork and turned to Ares.

He hesitated for only a moment before thrusting his hand out, palm up for her to take. Ares made no commotion when the blade sliced into him. Still, I noticed the way he stared at the red droplets as they pooled in his palm before Persephone turned his hand to the vial. It was the same dull, devastated look he'd worn that night at Dio's Name Day, when we'd fought for the first time. I'd suspected then something deeper sat between the God of War and my betrothed, but blinded by love and my good fortune at a match that seemed to return my affections, I'd brushed it away. Like a fucking moron.

Satisfied that she had collected all she needed, Persephone turned and walked to the door, calling out a cryptic "If you're coming, we should go now. They're close."

With a last look at Aphrodite, I turned to follow, Ares close on my heels, no doubt in search of answers we were both terrified to learn.

Ares

CHAPTER 5

ANCIENT GREECE

The Wild Wood pulsed with magic and music, and I bristled at the pull that had dragged me out to this ridiculous display of revelry. For centuries, the summons for the God of Wine's bacchanals had gone largely untouched, but I had known they would be here, and after weeks without even a whisper from Aphrodite, I could feel the desperation to hear her voice as it overtook my better sense. I stared around from my dark corner, observing the gathered.

Time suspended, holding us somewhere between dusk and moonrise, the veil between divine and decadent thinned to nothing more than a memory. So many gathered together, and the weight of our power was nearly too much to contain, putting me on high alert. While I had known and interacted with many of those in attendance, I was never truly welcomed.

The sharp tang of that truth cut through the haze of honeyed wine on my tongue, souring my tastes to match my mood. I glanced over the tops of the bonfires as they stretched to the heavens, cracking and flitting through the dusk, casting golden light over gilded masks of dancing maenads as they spun barefoot in the moss. Satyrs leapt through the crowd, flutes in hand, tipsy with mischief and drunk on the power of the gods that flowed freely from them.

They showed for him, my kindred, in a way I had never experienced. Not to celebrate a war, or some deed he had accomplished, they simply were here for him.

Glad that he walked the cosmos.

A pang of loneliness twisted from a deep, dark pit inside me, but I washed it down with more wine as I let my gaze drag me by my hair to the one part of the clearing I had been studiously avoiding, even though it held the only reason I'd accepted the invitation from the God of Wine. There were so many around us, but all I could see was her. Golden hair braided with ivy, her chiton clinging to every lush curve of her body as though she had poured it on. She was stunning, in all ways, but it wasn't her beauty that stalled my breath, caused my hands to tremble, my eyes to sting. It was the way she smiled.

Unburdened, she laughed at him, her radiant grin a match to his shy one, blue eyes sparkling into browns in the dancing light. The way she walked, the way she looked and talked to him. It had been silence between us since the night she'd ripped my heart from my chest.

This must end.

She had not given me any choice, any say. Her words haunted me: every breath, every time I closed my eyes.

"You're staring," Helios said, bumping my shoulder as he raised his goblet to his lips.

"Fuck off," I tossed back. The Titan of the Sun knew not enough to have him in the line of Zeus's ire, but more than he should, and we both knew how dangerous that could be.

"Oh, come on. You've never attended any sort of celebration, and now you've dragged us both down to the Wild Wood? Or

was asking me to attend your subtle way of trying to get into my armor?" he teased.

"Maybe it's just that for the first time in a long time, there seems to be peace settled in the Upper Realm, and I wanted a drink," I gruffed.

"Ah," Helios acquiesced, taking a sip of his wine. "Perhaps, that's exactly it. There has nothing to do with a certain goddess and a certain god celebrating a betrothal."

"Stop it," I hissed.

Helios sighed. "When are you going to stop doing this to yourself? You knew that this was an inevitability and proceeded to have congress anyway." His eyes were kinder, his expression somber as he looked me over.

"I know." I spat through gritted teeth then turned, watched as she laughed again at something he said.

He returned her smile in that quiet, unsure way he seemed to have, his cheeks rosy from the drink or her touch as she swiped a lock of his hair back. I hated him. I hated him for all the ways that everyone else seemed to love him, for being kind and revered amongst the others in a way that I never had been. Warm—a warmth I could never touch. And the way she was with him, the way she opened for him.

"I hate him." I didn't mean to say it out loud, but the words left my lips anyway.

Helios turned, eyeing me, assessing if I was about to fly off into a rage, and he must have decided that I was restrained still, because he made no move to block my eyeline. "I don't know him. The others think well of him, but if you hate him, then I hate him. He must be a prick."

His lightness had me smiling, despite myself.

Dionysus clapped then, twice, calling the attention of the gathered. The music around us lowered, nearly stilled as he spoke.

"It is time for my favorite part of the evening: the tributes! And as it is my Name Day, I have decided I would love my very unusual guest, Lord Ares, to present his first."

All eyes turned to meet mine, pinning me in place as many realized, for the first time all evening, that I was even in attendance. All eyes, except one pair. The only pair that mattered. I didn't have to look at her to know that she would be looking at him. Anger burned through me, licking up my insides. The well of rage that lived just below my surface pricked to the top of my skin.

"Well?" Dionysus asked expectantly, jovial smile still firmly on his face as I then recalled that, in my haste to see her, in my inexperience at being invited to social gatherings, I hadn't actually gotten the God of Wine a Name Day tribute.

Fuck.

I only knew battle and war, and unless he wanted a brawl in the middle of the Wild Wood . . . I caught an idea and stepped forward, the weight of their stares uncomfortable.

"Happiest of name days, Dionysus," I managed. I thought I had been polite in delivering the words, but the silent laughter that shook Helios's shoulders, coupled with the uneasy, raised eyebrows of the crowd, told me otherwise. I pulled the sword at my hip, eliciting several gasps, but I just lightly tossed it back and forth and turned, pointing it at Helios.

"Fancy this challenge?" I offered, and with a grin, the Titan of the Sun drained the rest of his dredge and pulled his own.

"Of course, I would never miss the opportunity to spank you, young one." He wiggled his eyebrows, and the tension immediately broke.

There it was, that gentle flirt that we always seemed to fall back into. Harmless, both of us knowing that nothing would ever happen between us, but Helios was beautiful and charming. He put the others at ease, so it made it easy to focus on him and our friendship and the fight. Swords clashed, his body moving, mirroring mine, our feet dancing, and I lost myself in it. The anger of it, I let it out. I let it go, and it was, for a moment, as though all would be well. Around us, cheers erupted. Cheers from deities and beings that had only ever looked on me with disdain or fear, and though I knew it was because of Helios's easy demeanor, I could pretend that some of it was for me.

I spun as he did, meeting a blow behind my back, and then at once I dropped, swiping out my leg to take out his ankle. He landed unceremoniously onto his back, armor clinging, a laugh expelling from his lips as I straightened and pointed my sword down at him from above.

"That's certainly one way to school me, old man," I teased.

He laughed, loud and easy, and even though I had no doubt I was going to be the winner, the cheers felt good. I reached down, helped pull him back to his feet. Helios clapped me twice on the back, grabbing my armor, shaking my body, giving me a smile to let me know that it was alright. I was perhaps a little too high on the excitement, the thrum of tasted battle, as I turned to Dionysus and bowed to him, offering my tribute.

And then, instead of stopping while I was ahead, I turned, reveling in the unfamiliar glow of divine praise.

"Any other takers?" I asked, circling the gathered, arms wide, the smile on my face nearly painful from the stretch. Satisfied there were none, I bowed my head once more to our host and moved to re-sheath my sword.

"I'd love a try."

My blood roared, veins bulging from the sound of his voice as I turned to see Hephaestus, God of the Forge, smiling warmly, turning the weight of his attention on me. Unease, something hot and unsettling, prickled under the collar of my armor. And then came the rage.

I looked at him, a small smile on my lips, vicious and sinister, as Aphrodite stepped in front of him, calm, but I could hear the slow panic in her voice as she pushed lightly against his armor and said, "Perhaps another night. I am tired."

Hephaestus looked back at her, gaze faltering between us, as though torn. Then, he smiled and gave her what she wanted with a nod of his head to her and an apologetic smile to me.

"Ah, of course, we should retire."

But the thought of them going back to shared chambers, to these rooms they had spent what felt like lifetimes in, until their wedding day ripped a volcano through me. Had they kissed? Had she fucked him? Did she love him? Jealousy burned white-hot through me. Vicious, visceral. I fucking hated him for it all. I had to stop them somehow.

"The goddess is right to caution you away. This is not a challenge for beginners," I called, tone a little mocking and laced with natural hubris I could not leash if my life depended on it.

Hephaestus stopped, turning back, eyeing me in confusion and lifting his brow as though he couldn't understand if I had insulted him, or if it was just the nature of the drink. Aphrodite did. She understood my words and tones better than any, and with fear in her eyes, she pulled harder against her betrothed, and that stoked the fire inside me higher, her protection of him.

He took a step toward me, something tugging between us, something magnetic. Two inevitabilities on a crash course for one another because, even though he had been betrothed to her, I could see he already loved her. Of course he did. She was impossible not to adore, to covet and cherish.

His lips tugged up in a smirk as he leaned down and pressed a tender kiss to the side of her cheek, cupping her face with reverence that sent a spear through my rib cage. "Darling, it'll be quick."

Another collective gasp rang out through the crowd, and my chest inflated, blood rushing in my ears at the fucking hubris he showed, defying the God of War, challenging me.

I rolled my shoulders back, cracked my neck. "Your weapon," I spat, gesturing my sword toward him.

In a blink of an eye, a maul appeared in Hephaestus's hands. His muscles flexed as he lifted it gently, calmly, and we started to circle one another. Tension built between us, and I felt the call of battle, the deep well of bloodlust, as it ignited in my veins, and with Aphrodite so close, it was as though her essence clouded my judgment, my space, my senses.

I assessed him, his strong shoulders, big chest—a result of time in the forges smashing metal for the gods. That led to strength. His blond hair was tied back in a little strap, his armor leather, plain, nothing flashy. Nothing about him demanded attention, yet I could not look away.

I lunged, quick, deliberate. A thunderclap reverberated through the clearing as his maul met my sword. The clash, unbearably loud, our power the weight of it. It fueled me more, his meeting my challenge. Oh, how we moved, how we fought. Lighthearted at first, toying with each other, but it turned deeper, faster, and I could feel him catching on to the power behind my blows, to the weight behind them.

Confusion knit his brow together as he matched me blow for blow, and that pissed me off even more. Who was this god? I had always known of him to be left in the shadows, discarded from Olympus, hidden from Zeus. A deformed thing. My father's rage and ire often fell on Hephaestus, and I had heard over the millennia of how much of a weak disappointment the goddess's son was. But in front of me, moving, fighting, the cause of the sweat breaking out along my brow . . . this was not weakness.

The fight got more intense. The blows harder, the parrying requiring more effort than should have been possible. Hephaestus's own frustration grew as we moved in a dance of fire and war, metals deadly as our limbs blurred in the melee. In any other world, I would have relished this fight, the worthiness of an opponent that could stand their ground against me, the beauty in the strong lines of his body as battle honed his skills and the world bent around his power.

The lapse in my attention cost me. The slice came quick. Just a nick, just barely there, across the skin of my neck, the blood a single drop.

Golden and wet, it slid down my neck as Hephaestus rushed forward with wide, apologetic eyes, weapon lowered, hands held aloft, but the damage was done. It was too much, the weight of it, the embarrassment and implication of it, and I unleashed with visions of his hands on her, his lips against her skin, their bodies moving together. Every drop of his sweat that could touch her skin, the smoky oak scent of him—it all bombarded me at once, clouding my sense and judgment. I unleashed, my mind warped, guts twisted up from weeks of silence from her. Weeks of them together, of agony and rejection and loss exploded from me as I lunged forward, slicing with everything I could.

He moved backward, body bending unnaturally, just barely escaping my wrath until I drove him down into the ground, the weight of my power pinning him to the dirt. His brown eyes, wide and still unafraid, reflected the orange and golds of the flames as I advanced, sword raised, both of our chests heaving, ready to kill him. To be done with all of this . . .

"Ares!"

I stopped.

Her voice, a soft plea I doubt anyone else heard, but her voice would wake me from Tartarus. Yes, I heard her, and when my eyes finally shifted, those beautiful pale blue irises were filled with fear and tears.

I lowered my sword as Aphrodite rushed to Hephaestus's side, checking over his face, concern etched into every stroke of her hands across his skin. I watched like a statue as he soothed her, assuring her he was unharmed, rose with grace as she wrapped around him.

The gathering was silent as the Pits when they took their leave, but Aphrodite shot a single glance over her shoulder as they retreated, the judgment enough to knock me to my knees. She looked at me now, like all the rest of them had always looked at me.

And I knew.

I had lost her.

Hephaestus

CHAPTER 6

Persephone led us through the long passages of the palace, toward a wing I'd never been to before. It wasn't all that shocking—the Underworld seemed to stretch on endlessly, so it made sense the palace felt that way too. She came to a descending stairway and stepped lightly through it. The darkness was thick, unnaturally so, and I felt the shift of a portal as we stepped farther down. The stone steps gave way to a cobbled pathway. I followed Persephone's footfalls, more than relying on my faltering sight.

Ares swore behind me, and I could feel the nervous energy roiling off him as we walked, the heat of his body, the whisper of his breaths. Each step from the room was farther from Aphrodite, and I doubted either of us could find our way back without a guide. The very pressure of his power rubbing against mine set my teeth on edge, and maybe it was just me feeling raw from what we'd just found out, what we were on our way to witness, but *fuck*, I needed some space. He filled the corridor, his body too big, aura pulsing against my skin, and a shiver worked down my spine as the air shifted and moved around him.

I cleared my throat and sped up to get closer to Persephone.

"Seph, what are we doing here?" I asked, but she held up a finger to her lips for quiet.

A slow thrumming was coming from just the other side of the dark veil, separating us from our destination, and on our abrupt stop, Ares's body halted too close behind mine. I could feel his breath on the back of my neck, the vibrations of his very cells charged. The hair on the back of my arms lifted in warning as the power welled up within the God of War, seeking out the pulsing magic from the middle of the room.

Persephone placed two hands against the dark wall of shadows in front of us and pushed, cracking open a door in the vortex of darkness.

Low light flooded the space we were in, and I stepped through after her into a large cavern. The air here felt charged, *electric*, an ancient power that seemed to be thriving and building. Low drums could be heard along with the haunting voices, the choir of the Damned. Each beat jolted through me, pulsing through my temples, my muscles, vibrating the metal in my cock. Energy licked up my exposed skin just as Ares shuddered behind me.

Too close.

The air tasted thick with magic and sweat and *him*, and it danced along my tongue as it propelled me forward.

In the middle of the circular cavern, on the floor covered in silver sigils within a circle of black-flame candles was Hecate, dressed in her traditional garb. Her usual braids were gone, her long silky hair instead wild and free as the tendrils swirled, electrified on the currents surrounding her. Hecate's black chiton splayed over her thighs like art as she knelt on the floor, writhing with her head thrown back to the ceiling. Her back and arms were exposed, covered in ancient runes painted in silvers that glowed against her brown skin while she writhed, her movements propelled forward with the music filling the room. Her body looked to be vibrating, seizing almost. I'd never seen Hecate during one of her rituals—they were private, deeply personal affairs—and I felt uneasy that we had insisted on seeing our blood used up, for fear of the violation to Aphrodite's privacy.

Persephone balked slightly before straightening and heading over to Hades, who stood vigil at the head of the circle. Persephone placed the vials of our blood in his palm, and when he kissed her temple, she let out a low moan that carried through the echo of the cavern, not quite drowned out by the music.

It sounded instantly wrong to my ears, and I shook my head out as Hades commanded the shadows to carry the vials filled with our blood over the threshold of candles and flames. The shadows settled them beside another—the vial closest to Hecate as she moved. *Aphrodite's blood.*

Once they were together, Hades grabbed Persephone and lifted her expertly, locking her legs around his large frame. She licked up the side of his face, grinding her body onto his, and he grimaced as he tore his face away.

"I have to get her out of here. It's not safe in her condition."

Confused, I opened my mouth to ask what was happening, but he didn't elaborate further, except to say, "Do not interrupt the circle."

With that, Hades swept past us in a flurry of shadows, kissing his wife with a nearly indecent level of intensity.

I turned to look at Ares, whose eyes were locked on Hecate, squinting. He unclipped his tactical vest and shimmied out of it, then undid his blouse before dropping it to the ground as well. The God of War stepped closer, and I followed, something warm coiling low in the pit of my stomach like a tether wrenching me behind. The air got thicker, *sweeter*, as we approached, but my feet wouldn't stop moving as the blood beneath my skin surged to the surface.

Hecate let out a moan that shot straight down my spine. From below her, Hermes blipped in and out of existence, and it hit me, what this feeling was, the call of it, the rush of adrenaline.

Ritual sex magic.

Fucking Fates.

Hermes sat beneath her, thrusting into Hecate with such speed that he literally blinked in and out of sight. The music swelled, another wave of desire crashed through me, and it didn't matter that a part of me was incredibly grossed out at witnessing this, at being so damned affected by it, because all rational thought leaked from my mind as the baser part of my carnal nature took control. It made sense that Persephone had lost control standing so close to the circle; the magic would draw from all sources it could, and right now, there were two Bonded gods in close proximity.

My cock lengthened in my jeans, and I knew if I glanced at Ares, he'd be just as hard. My mouth went dry just thinking about it, because I knew what he looked like naked, what he looked like when he fucked and *took*, the way his muscles in his back bunched, the way he sounded when he *fucking* came.

Hermes faded into view as he thrust into her, naked from what I could see, but his lower half was covered by Hecate and her silky chiton. Sweat slicked the planes of his chiseled chest as his abs twitched with each pump. They looked every bit as beautiful together as any rendition of two gods could have been, his pale skin against the darkness of hers, and if I could separate the sex from it, it was the most selfless offering. Hermes grabbed her face with such reverence, such worship, it felt intimate in a way that broke my heart.

I knew they had grown close, and after his admission when we'd almost died at the safehouse, I knew he loved her but this . . . This was the type of love Bonds were made of.

Hecate moved on top of him, his hand on her face and cupping her ass to him as he worked her higher. The mix of the music and their bodies slapping together thundered through the room and reverberated off the walls as Hecate's moans and Hermes's grunts grew deeper, more frequent.

They're close.

Persephone's words made sense now.

I chanced a look at Ares. His face was tight, hands opening and closing in fists by his side. I could feel the tug of the magic on my cock and knew for him, the self-control it was taking for him not to fuck or kill, was enough to break worlds. War used blood magic as well, and much like an addict having their own brand of heroine dangled in front of them, Ares was going through it, every moment he didn't succumb a miracle. His sharp jaw was set, beautiful, striking, and *Fates*, he looked poised to burn down the world around him.

My cock pulsed *again*, and I shook my head once to snap myself out of the lust-fueled energy taking over me, but over and over, the visions of him, of her, of their bodies moving together . . .

Hermes whispered to Hecate, soft and commanding, as they vibrated higher and higher, his words barely audible over the blood roaring in my ears.

"It's yours," he offered. "Take it."

Hecate reached down as she wound her hips on top of Hermes to grab the vials in a shaking hand. Hermes slowed slightly, blinking back into view in a low blur as she smashed the vials onto his chest with considerable force. The glass and blood embedded into Hermes's skin, and he bucked as he came, hard, spilling everything into his beloved. A blast of energy erupted around them in a shimmering iridescent sphere, crackling with power as they rose into the air together.

Hermes and Hecate were still pressed chest to chest, hands moving over the other, still thrusting and rocking as they reached the middle of the floating cage. Time inside the sphere slowed, stilled, putting every caress, every kiss and thrust into slow motion for us to see. Hecate flattened Hermes onto his back, laying her palms on his chest as she rode him, head thrown back in ecstasy. Blood and glass smeared his torso and hers, and with a final thrust, she broke apart on top of him. Hecate's head flew back, eyes completely blacked out as energy pooled around her before bursting from them in a pulse of power.

The shock wave sent Ares flying into me, knocking us both to the ground in a tangle of limbs and lust, and Fates, the weight of him, the *warmth* of him . . . Where his skin met mine lit up, fire burning through me, and for a moment, I forgot the person touching me was Ares. *Ares, my enemy*. Ares, who had me pinned beneath him, seemingly as shocked as I was at the electricity shooting through us. It felt good. Too fucking good.

I let out a breath, and he dropped his weight farther into me, just a touch.

How long had it been since I'd been touched like this? Decades.

Desire flooded through me, but my mind couldn't reconcile that I should be repulsed by the god pinning me to the ground with his hips, whose breath fanned over my face, the scent of him making my mouth water. Instead, I could feel him lengthening against my thigh, and my breathing quickened at the friction, at the cum that leaked from the tip of my cock and slipped down the piercings. Our chests rose and fell together as we stayed locked like that, both afraid to make a move. His weight felt insanely good against me, and while he was much broader, we were roughly the same height, which provided some delicious friction when we'd move even the slightest bit.

This is wrong.

A wave of need crashed over me again, and I was enveloped by the smell of him: gunshot residue and the tang of salty sweat mixed with something *more*, something spiced. He smelled like the burning fires of my forge, like home.

I rolled the thigh pressed up against him, lifting slightly to add some pressure against his cock. Ares's eyes zeroed in on mine, hooded with lust, glassy even. I watched his own internal battle play out behind his brown eyes, saw how undone he became as I rolled the muscles in my thigh again, harder this time, and his full lips parted, letting loose a breathy whine that nearly undid me. This was wrong on every level, but I couldn't stop, the urges that welled up inside of me too strong to ignore.

My hips jerked at the sound of him, the needy little moan that I couldn't fathom dropped from *his* lips, and Fates alive, I wanted *more* of that. More breaths. More whimpers. My hand came down between us, and I slowly, cautiously wrapped my fingers around the base of his throat. Another whine, needier this time. I squeezed, ever so gently but firmly in my hold. The guttural moan that left him resounded through his throat, and I felt the vibration in my hand, wrapped around him, and there was something in knowing this deity capable of great violence was under my command. The rational, functioning part of my mind shut off.

There was only pleasure.

Only feeling, as I worked my thigh under him, watching as he fought to resist, to defy. I wanted that submission, the God of War surrendering under my control. The thought had me painfully erect between us, desperate to see him strapped to my table, arms wide and manacled as I bent him over the bench and found out just where his limits were.

As if sensing my thoughts, Ares rocked his hips upward, sliding down my length. The air pulled around us, pulsing and shaking with the tremors of power emanating from the sphere above us.

Ares's lips were inches from mine, a centimeter, a breath, and I groaned when he sank his canine into his bottom lip, the tip sharp enough to break the skin. I wondered what that mouth would feel like wrapped around my cock, and without thinking, I applied pressure on my grip on his neck, pulling, coaxing him lower. I expected him to buck or fight for control, but Ares kept his eyes on mine as I slowly lowered him down my body, toward the crown of my cock peeking out from my waistband.

He flicked his eyes from mine to the glistening head, slick with desire, back and forth, as though waiting for permission. His tongue darted over his lips to wet them, and I smirked, satisfaction swelling in my chest at his act of supplication, at the power in it.

This isn't real, I reminded myself. This is magic, ritual magic.

I nodded once and watched him take the command, eager to obey, the harsh lines around his face relaxed in a way I'd never seen them, and I recognized it then, the surrender of control, the beauty and power in it. His face inched closer, the anticipation causing pre-cum to bead on my crown, and I thought of her, of Aphrodite, the visage of him and her flickering between my vision, as his hand came up to open my button, to slide down my zipper.

Close, so close.

I could feel his warm breath as it fanned over wet skin, as Ares opened his mouth to take me in.

Closer. Closer.

Without warning, the magic snapped.

Ares's eyes darted to mine, panicked, mortified, as a gust of air cleared the haze between us and a familiar hatred burned through my veins. Judging by the look on his face, it had done the same to him. He flung himself back in disgust, breathing hard, shaking his head hard to clear the lust and magic. The space between us stretched on, and I felt anger well up inside, and something else burned low like a sickening pit in my stomach. If I was able to be honest with myself, I might have been able to admit it was the sting of rejection that had me ready to vomit and not that my cock had almost been buried down *Ares's* throat.

"What the fuck was that?" he seethed, running his hand under his lower lip, eyes darting frantically around the room, like his greatest worry was anyone could have seen what happened. That burned, searing deep as I tucked myself back into my pants and zipped up with probably too much force.

"How the Hells am I supposed to know?" I shot back, embarrassment burning hot through me. He took a step toward me, fists clenched at his sides, and I bowed right up to him, refusing to show an inch of weakness.

"Can you two not kill each other for once? Meet me in the battle room in an hour, we'll have news," Hermes called to us from the center of the ritual circle.

I turned to see a passed-out Hecate held aloft in his arms. Hermes's sharp cheekbones, which made him way too handsome for his own good, were slightly flushed, as was his chest, as he walked past us unabashedly. He didn't seem to care that he was naked, cock swinging heavily between his legs, while he carried Hecate to rest.

Ares was still breathing hard but put his hands up and backed up a few paces, eyeing me warily before turning and tearing out of the room as well.

A million emotions ripped through me, not the least of them being guilt. I knew that we had been separated for decades, and I knew she didn't hold me to a broken Bond, but how in the Fates was I going to explain this to Aphrodite? It was an effect of the magic, right? Then why did I feel so wretched? Four thousand years, and I'd never broken my vow.

Until today.

What the fuck just happened?

Ares

CHAPTER 7

I tore from that room, hot on Hermes's heels as he commanded the portals to open, eager to put as much space between me and Hephaestus as possible. My brain felt glitchy, like a circuit had been tripped, and suddenly *everything* I'd ever known turned on its axis. I struggled to calm my breathing down as my chest constricted, pushed faster to get back to Aphrodite, my mind reeling with revelations I wasn't ready to confront. Blood magic affected me more profoundly than others, it was what fueled me for battle. That thin line between lust and fury was a razor's edge so sharp, yet I spent most of my time walking it.

Since Aphrodite had left me, I'd thrown myself completely into war and conflict, taking out my bloodlust there, the Bond in my chest not allowing me to even think about taking another lover, but that magic Hecate and Hermes evoked . . . I hadn't felt it before, and it scared me. It had been powerful enough to drive me to Hephaestus, and I couldn't shake that feeling of power he'd held in that moment. That *need*. I had always been dominant in bed, whether with Aphrodite or any of the other partners I'd been with. I'd had him pinned beneath me, the magic pressing on me and tearing at my skin to touch him, but it felt as though *he* were the one in control. That metallic warm scent of his skin overwhelmed all sense and reason, and I'd wanted to taste him, to *obey* him.

My cock twitched at the memory, and I fisted my hands as we rounded the corridor and up the stairs. On the landing, Hermes split left with a sleeping Hecate, ignoring me altogether. I turned the other way to Aphrodite, letting the Bond guide me through the maze that was the Underworld palace to get to her. I needed to see her, to taste her and know she was okay, that she was still *mine*.

I had questions, serious ones, but for now, the river of lust and rage flowed inside of me, and I needed release. My thoughts flitted back to Hephaestus and those deep brown eyes with golden flecks, the blond locks that fell haphazardly around his face as he'd looked up at me, the steel of his cock against my

No, what the fuck was wrong with me?

I thundered off toward the door of Aphrodite's room and pushed through, exhaling a deep breath at the sight before me.

She sat propped against the headboard, picking at her nails, looking much better than she had when we left her earlier. At least she was conscious now. Color had returned to her cheeks, her pale hair more vibrant, her lips rosy once more.

Deep blue eyes turned to me, Bond-driven hunger lashing across my skin, and I felt the inferno heat up inside me at the need of her. The ache to feel her come apart around me, to feel our bodies as they become one. Forty years since I'd kissed those lips, since I'd left her to fight a war she'd begged me not to, but it was as though no time had passed. I still craved her in that same bone-deep way, the hooks and talons of our Bond infecting every part of me, pulling me closer.

Her eyes went wide as she took in my disheveled appearance, the blood stains on my uniform. She knew me better than any other, and though she had spent the last forty years denying us, denying our Bond, I could feel how the tether called to us, demanding more.

I raked my eyes down her frame with such intensity, I could visibly see her body react to my stare, and I stalked forward, amping up the tension. She wanted this, wanted us. But after hearing she was trying to find a way out of the Bond, I needed to hear her say it. I needed to know the Spring Queen was mistaken, or if there was another explanation, because any other reason was blasphemy of the highest order.

I was at her bedside in three strides, and Aphrodite sat up to greet me as she hungrily reached for my belt to unfasten it, both of us driven by pure instinct. I captured her mouth in a kiss as our bodies molded together in our familiar way. Her nipples pulled taut as I palmed a hand roughly over them, giving her pain and pleasure in equal measure. Her fingernails scraped across my throat, sending unfamiliar flashes of memory bolting through my mind. Memories of dark eyes that stared at me while steady, calloused fingers gripped me tight, ordered me in movement and body to submit. Even thinking about it pulled a moan from my throat, a nearly needy whimper that had Aphrodite cocking her head questioningly.

I shook the memory loose and ran my thumb over her full, pink lips, pushing those errant thoughts to the deepest recesses of my mind. She sucked the pad of my finger inside her warm mouth, slicking it wet with her tongue, and at once, I was rooted in the present, in *her*. She moaned, and I needed her, wanted her permission for what I needed to do to erase any memory of what had nearly transpired in that fucking ritual space. To command. To dominate.

"*Please*," she moaned, reading my thoughts. The words didn't hit me the way they had for centuries, but I tightened my grip on her, nonetheless.

She expected dominance, expected my need for her compliance, and I wanted to give it to her. She liked to be handled, controlled. Something shifted in the darkest corners of my mind. *Maybe I did too.* The thought stopped me, and Aphrodite caught the hesitation in my posture.

She looked at me, concerned.

"Are you sure you want this?" she asked, and I wavered. I did want her, always, and I didn't know what was wrong with me. Maybe the remnants of sex magic still clung to me, driving my arousal?

Aphrodite brought her hand to my face, delicate and loving as she poured into the Bond, and that confused me too.

"I will always want you. I just want you to want it too," I conceded, and her eyes turned soft, understanding even, as she lifted her head to press a kiss to the inside of my throat. The tenderness of it shot straight through me.

"I want you, Ares, Hells help me, but I love you," she answered, grabbing my hand and guiding it down to her throat. My fingers wrapped around her reflexively, and Aphrodite shuddered with the same resigned surrender that had first given me hope someone so good could love something as wretched as me.

Her admission was a blessed gospel falling on damned ears, and after so long without her, even knowing what she was planning, I couldn't deny either of us. I grabbed her swiftly, slamming her to the bed, chest heaving as I crawled up her form. Aphrodite cried out in pleasure as I devoured her mouth with mine, ignoring the wave of wrongness filling up inside me, pushing down the intense confusion that threatened to knock me unsteady.

I wanted her. I *only* wanted her. I wanted to command her. I wanted to possess her, to own her in all the ways she demanded. I repeated the mantras as I kissed down her chest, ripping the shirt from her torso as my teeth scraped and nipped at her skin, over the planes of her stomach. She arched beneath me, and I watched the inflamed mark she bore from Hephaestus soothe.

I tore at her pants with my free hand while the other tightened my grip on her throat, pouring my power into her, healing her in a way he hadn't. Couldn't. She smelled like jasmine, sweet and warm, beneath my tongue as I slipped down her panties to spread her legs over my shoulders.

This was comfortable. *This* was the way it had always been. Me, taking my pleasure, and Aphrodite, getting off on it.

"Eyes on me," I commanded, pulling Aphrodite's head, angling it down to make her watch as I feasted. Her golden hair was tousled around her. My visage mirrored in her stare as she watched my tongue slowly, teasingly lick between her folds, the taste so exquisite I nearly combusted. Her arousal coated my chin as I dug in, rough and domineering as I sucked and licked over her clit, *savoring*, relishing the taste of her. She arched beneath me, but I kept a firm hold on her neck, arm locked as I watched her disappear in and out of view over ragged breaths. Her stomach tensed, rising and falling rapidly while she rode my face, chased her pleasure.

I straightened my tongue, delving deeper until I felt the ring of her pulsing cunt. A growl tore from my chest when I looked up to see her staring at me, eyes hooded and lower lip trapped between her teeth, biting back a moan. I slapped her clit lightly, eliciting a hiss. Sensations overwhelmed my body as I rolled my tongue over her heated flesh, as her fingernails dug into the back of my neck, my shoulders, marking and claiming in a primal display that had the beast inside me beating my chest in approval.

This was familiar, the way our bodies moved together with every kiss and nip. I drove thoughts of *him*, of what had just happened, away, losing myself in her. The Bond between us sang out, vibrating between her shade and mine, and I wondered if he was as dominant with her, if he knew all the ways to make her body catch fire.

Aphrodite's body started to shake, and I smirked against her heated flesh, proud of how she responded to me, how well I knew her from the inside out, even after all this time. Her thighs trembled, trapping my legs, and my hand wound down her body, needing to feel her from deep inside.

My fingers grazed the tattooed skin over the Bond she shared with Hephaestus, and a flash of memory burst across my vision, causing both of us to cry out. She arched, hands wild, clawing at my skin, threatening to tear the hair from my scalp. I knew I shouldn't, but I was too curious to look away, and she too lost to realize what she was projecting.

I touched it again, and she moaned, showing me, projecting memory straight into my mind. It was shattering the way I couldn't stop seeing. I recognized her hair, the metal band on her finger forged by her new husband, the bed he sat on in his ceremonial garb.

Their wedding night.

"Are you nervous?" she asked, looking down at Hephaestus, her hand cupping his cheek. He flushed and offered her a shy smile.

"I'm afraid I have very little experience in this realm, and I do not want to disappoint you," he admitted.

"And does it offend you? That I have had others before?" she pressed. His eyes were wide and sheepish as he searched her face, love and wine shining in the glassy orbs.

"I do not care who you were, only who you want to be, little love. Be patient with me, show me what you like, and I will learn to master it."

She leaned down to kiss him then, and his hands searched between her tresses to pull the pins holding her braids free. Aphrodite lifted the edge of her wedding chiton, slowing exposing her delicate calf, then knee. She raised it, resting her foot on the bed next to him, and I watched as Hephaestus leaned forward, placing a sweet kiss to the inside of her thigh.

Gently, she settled over him, straddling his lap, and I watched, transfixed as she unclasped his armor, pushed it from strong shoulders until his chest was exposed to her. I traced the movement of her hands as she reached between them, grabbed his cock, lifted her hips to line them up.

"Wait—" he whispered on broken breath, and she stilled, confused. "The wedding. I do not wish for you to do this if you do not want to, Aphrodite. We have fulfilled the marriage contract, but I do not own your body. I know I am not your first choice, but if you wish for it, I will be a good husband to you."

I saw the moment she fell in love with him.

It should have crushed me.

She smiled. Kissed him, lovingly deep, and offered herself to him with a rock of her hips, welcoming him into her body. Her shade. I watched as she rode him, his breaths falling in pants against her neck, the rhythm they created together . . . beautiful.

"Where can I touch you?" he asked, buried deep, and she nodded, wrapping her arms around his shoulders with a breathy "Everywhere . . ."

Her body tightened, back arching for him just as her muscles contracted under my lips. I released her Bondmark, and her eyes snapped open, glassy, drunk nearly from the memory and power my lust fed her.

I wanted her *here*, with me.

"Eyes on me," I reiterated before licking over her mound, soothing the stinging skin. A movement, almost imperceptible, caught my attention at the cracked door behind Aphrodite. My cock jumped, and I knew, without knowing how, that *he* was there. He was watching.

The thought should have filled me with rage or some sort of sadistic pleasure. To make him watch while I fucked her with my tongue, made her scream my name for him to hear. Instead, my cock ached for the command, to the quiet dominance I'd never let another being exert over me. My cock leaked, making a mess of me as my eyes adjusted to the darkness beyond the door. I saw them then—a set of umber eyes burning into mine from the shadows, watching raptly as I snaked my hand down from Aphrodite's throat, trailed over her breasts, and brought my fingers to rest on her ribs. Right over his Bondmark.

His eyes grew wide, glinting dangerously, and I felt my cock, already stiff, grow painfully harder still. I stayed there, unmoving. Waiting, without knowing *why*.

Slowly, tentatively, he nodded. *Once*, just once, but it sent a bolt of pleasure down my spine. *Do it*, his eyes commanded.

I delved in deeper, my tongue a cyclone against her hot cunt as she screamed and cried and begged for more above me. I lied to myself that this was some sort of fucked-up payback, to make him watch while I made her body come, to listen as she cried out my name, but my eyes never left his. I could smell him, that cinnamon fire that wafted from him, and I could barely acknowledge the shift in the air as their scents blended, or the way it made my fucking mouth water. Instead, I watched his eyes as he held mine.

When Aphrodite came, her arousal shot forth, soaking my face, and I grinned, lapping it up as the deluge washed over me. Proud, I pulled myself up carefully, ripping my cock free above her as I stroked it. The thick veins pulsed between my fingers, hot and heavy. Aphrodite spread wider for me, still shaking, wanting.

I waited, eyes flicking between the goddess before me and the god behind the door, held in place by a divine leash I hadn't freely offered and yet still seemed beholden to.

Another nod.

The tension snapped as I obeyed, thrusting inside of Aphrodite's soaking wet cunt, and *Fates*. The feeling was euphoric, *bliss*. Sheathed inside of her, the Goddess of Love pulsed around me as I thrust brutally deeper, desperate to reconnect, searching for my salvation in her body. She loved the pain and the pleasure, two things I could give her in tandem, and a few quick slaps to her breasts sent her over the edge again as I pounded into her, fingers working deftly over her clit to maximize her euphoria. I had missed this, craved it.

No other compared to her—my most beloved, most revered, my Aphrodite.

Reclamation spurned me on as I sank into her repeatedly, eyes now *only* on her. He was there, bearing witness, but this was her and me. Better than any battle I'd ever fought, more exacting than any sword cutting through my skin had ever been. Her body jolted with each thrust, but I held on, gripping around her ribs, brushing my thumb over that cursed mark as it shot electricity up my arm. How many times had I recoiled at the sight of it? How many times had I taken her from behind just to avoid it? It was a different feeling now, stroking it as I stroked into her. Knowing *he* was just out of sight, feeling all the same intensity I was.

Aphrodite moved her hand down her body and wrapped it around my wrist, over the Bond. A wave of arousal and need shook through me again, one that tasted like her. She liked when I touched it as I fucked her. In all these years, I'd never even asked.

I circled her clit slowly, a stark contrast to the quick snapping of my hips as I slid in and out of her channel, my own release screaming in my blood. She gripped me, rolling her body, owning me. Desire coiled low in my balls as it built and built, and I looked up, searching the darkness for those eyes.

Hephaestus

CHAPTER 8

By the fucking Hells, I shouldn't be here. The wet slaps coming from Aphrodite's room held me rooted to the spot, cock hard in my hands as I stroked myself through the crack in the door like a fucking pervert. I should have left the moment I realized what was happening, but hadn't I known, from the moment he'd left, this was what he'd do? It's what I wanted to do as well, bury myself inside of Aphrodite, wash away the memory of what just happened—or rather, hadn't happened.

I stood and watched as shame bloomed in my chest. The only other time I'd seen them together had been the worst day of my life, and just like this moment, instead of rage, I just felt insatiable hunger. They weren't blatant with their affair, and until Hermes came to me out of mercy, I hadn't even suspected. The moment I sprung the net to catch them as he took her, over and over again, remained imprinted in my mind's eye as memory and present became one once more.

Flames roared from the mouth of the forge, groaning with scorching heat, furious as it fed and choked on my own rage. Molten metal and smoke clung to me, the iron, the sweat of it all as I stood at the anvil, bare arms blackened with soot, my hammer clutched in a white-knuckled grip.

I hadn't struck in hours, and Hermes's words beat against the inside of my skull, echoing my darkest fears.

"Your bride looks too often to the west, Hephaestus, and war awaits there. Always waiting."

I'd cursed him for his cautions, thrown an axe at the Messenger God's head, told my oldest friend never to darken the steps of my forge again. But those words, those cursed words, had taken root, festered, and the rational part of my mind insisted that Hermes was a trickster, but he was no liar. Still, I wanted so badly to believe that this was true, that command had grown to something stronger between the goddess and me.

Aphrodite smiled when I brought her bangles and jewels, touched my shoulder lovingly as we passed, curled her body against me in her sleep, full and sated . . .

But there were moments. Fleeting, barely there. But they came with increasing frequency when her blue eyes stared past me, past Olympus . . . to the west. Moments when her jasmine scent shifted and changed, grew heavy with a sorrow I couldn't understand. Sometimes her laughter did not reach her eyes. Sometimes her kiss would land gently, but her hands would shake.

And I was a coward for it, for seeing the little things and letting her soothe them away with placations. For not striking deeper, for being so pathetic that the thought of her loving me and losing that kept my lips sealed. But Hermes's words tore at me and ate at my thoughts, maggots on flesh. I found myself doing the unthinkable: forging a net with a weave so fine, it could contain god power. Dipped in the Styx, threads spun with hands full of jealousy and a deep, resonating desperation to be wrong.

I hung it above our bed—the bed I'd built for us with the same treacherous hands—and swallowed my guilt when she never even noticed. I watched the metal melt, not because I had a weapon to forge or a project to complete, but because the tug of the spell, the ripple through the web, sang out to me tonight. I stood stone still, watching the molten liquid pool like the pain in my gut, that tiny flicker of magic more devastating than any moment of my life.

So far.

The shadows welcomed me when I arrived, but I kept to them, terrified to look up as the sounds hit my ears. I let my gaze fall on the bag by the door, half packed. Higher and higher I lifted, until I saw them.

Tangled bodies, hungry and tender, the God of War's hands tangled in Aphrodite's hair, lips pressed against the collar of her throat. I swallowed back the noise of my heartbreak, because when I traced up to her face, her hands, I saw the wedding ring I had forged for her, from fire and promises I was too naive to understand, cradling his jaw, eyes glistening with tears and so much love.

She whispered something against his hair, but I could not hear it over the rushing river of blood in my ears, could not bring myself to look away from her face as their bodies writhed together, his hold possessive, bruising, brutal with his thrusts. He was rough with her in a way I had never known or thought to be, dominant where I hesitated.

Ares pulled up, capturing her lips as the sweat-soaked muscles of his back tensed and rocked with each thrust. He turned them, then, twisting her legs until he laid slightly behind her. I watched, transfixed in horror and fascination as his cock thrust deep inside her, creamy thighs spread as he whispered against her flesh, kissed and bit and nipped and slapped over her breasts and jaw. It looked angry, as though he were punishing her, but she cried out for him, for more, sweet whimpers she had once shared with me.

The betrayal swirled in my chest, hot and tight, and I could not understand the arousal warring with the disgust, the anger. None of that shattered me. No, that killing blow came from the look in her eyes as they came together, his hands wrapped around a glowing mark, cum spilling from between the spaces created with every thrust, the color of golden honey.

A Bond.

I watched, rooted in place as he pulled his cock from her, breathing hard, pressing tender kisses to her temple. His fingers gathered up the mess seeping from her, brought it to her lips, and she parted for him obediently, expectantly. This was more than lust or rebellion. Their foreheads pressed together as she licked his fingers clean of them, and the look of home in her eyes broke me.

The fire inside my chest snuffed out, and for the first time in my existence, I felt numbing cold. The net fell at the thought of the command, and I watched from the dark at the only thing I ever made that I could not fix, a vow broken, slip through the weave of that net.

It became my greatest moniker. *Hephaestus, the Cuckold.* Something traveled across my skin, blooming from the Bondmark I shared with Aphrodite that chased that shame away. Desire.

His hand pressed over her mark as it shot into mine, forcing the lust and need forth. The need for release. The need for *permission.*

I stroked harder, hands gliding over my pierced length as his eyes found mine. He maintained his rhythm, holding Aphrodite with the reverence she deserved but his eyes . . . Those were on me. She had come twice, and he wanted instruction.

I shook my head once, and he turned back to her, thrusting. Aphrodite was moaning, shaking with pleasure as he flipped her over, still so deep inside of her. Watching his body move behind her propelled me forward. Desperate for what, I wasn't sure.

I gripped the doorframe tightly, so tight that, had it not been stone, it would have crumbled under the pressure. Ares's body was incredible, though I never would have allowed myself to admit it out loud. His broad chest was marred with scars and old wounds, a tapestry of war and ruin across his tanned skin. His torso flexed as he sank deeper inside Aphrodite, and my cock wept with want as the pre-cum slicked down my hands.

Ares's hands gripped her torso as he dragged her body to his, and Aphrodite's blonde hair fanned around her as he pressed her back against him. Her slender arm hooked over her head and around his neck while his hands roamed, one settling over her needy clit and the other still gripped on her Bondmark. Her tits bounced with fervor with every thrust, punctuated by the wet smack of his sweaty body on hers. He was riding her hard, too hard so soon after her episode, but neither of them cared.

Ares whispered to her, coaxing, as he took her from behind, and I watched as she shook apart for the third time. Sprays of her arousal shot from where their bodies were joined together, squirting as she came around his still-thrusting cock. I tore my eyes away from the poetry that was Aphrodite's naked body to see his brown eyes staring into mine, a plea clear.

Let me come, please.

The urge to deny him, to see how far he'd let me push him and if he'd obey was strong. The pettiest part of me wanted to edge him for eternity.

Ares grabbed Aphrodite's chin and pried it open as he held it apart with his fingers.

"Stick your tongue out, my love," he cooed, and she obeyed. He stared at me, presenting her mouth, the sight of it depraved and wicked and consuming all at once.

My hand flew over my shaft, stroking faster, the friction hot and slightly painful as the fire raging within me blazed to an inferno. I nodded my head frantically, giving him the permission he inexplicably craved, and he sighed with relief as he slammed into her with finality, shooting load after load inside of Aphrodite.

I came hard, great spurts splashing my chest and abs as I focused on her mouth, her tongue, the way his muscles rippled as he came inside my fucking wife.

My breaths fell harsh against the darkness as my rational mind tried to understand what had just happened, but the Dominant side of me had no problem keeping up. I had let Ares come, and a submissive side of him had surrendered his control. He had put on a show, one just for me. An offering.

The post-orgasm euphoria started a slow come down, and I watched as Ares held on to a shaking Aphrodite, kissing her neck and smoothing her hair while he lowered her onto the bed.

I tucked my cock back into my jeans as Ares climbed off the bed and started toward the door, but old insecurities flared up in my chest, shooting tendrils of panic through the haze of lust. Whatever happened in that moment had passed, and I wasn't keen on sticking around. Confusion and shame bubbled up once more, and I set off quickly down the corridor toward my quarters, in desperate need of a hot shower.

Aphrodite

CHAPTER 9

I slumped forward on the bed, breathing hard and exhausted as Ares seeped out of me onto the soaked sheets beneath my body. I grimaced, knowing this would be embarrassing to explain to Persephone, disappointed in myself for being so easily tempted.

Ares made his way over to the door, pulling his pants up to button over his cock as he went. His dark hair was slick with sweat, but he looked better, energized even. A good fuck always did that to him.

He swung the cracked door wide, peering out, and I realized how careless we had been. Hephaestus was here, in this palace, he could have walked in at any moment, and the memory of that kind of pain on his face ripped through me with crushing guilt. It was always like this, and I cursed myself, these damned Bonds, the two of them. Every time I slept with Ares, the weight of the implications for Hephaestus wrapped around my chest and threatened to squeeze the life from me.

Alternatively, Ares saw himself as this caustic, unlovable thing, and when the Bond demanded I go to Hephaestus, Ares threw himself into war, into chaos that could kill him. Sure, we as gods heal, but we weren't completely invulnerable. If a wound was bad enough, or we were blown to pieces by a bomb, we could slip out of the coil of our immortality. It was the same old song and dance, and I was tired of it. In the twenties, Hephaestus finally had enough and told me not to come back. In the forties, I said the same to Ares.

Anger and disappointment with myself flared in my chest. I'd lasted so long—*so long*—without caving, even though it had been a feat of Olympus. No one felt the same, could make love to me in a way that quenched the thirst I had for them, but I told myself this was better for them, better for all of us. Then, when Hephaestus got hurt, I felt the world break inside of me.

I'd never admit how close I felt he was to dying. It was the most terrifying moment of my existence, and if I never had to feel that again, it'd be too soon. The Bond had all but snapped, and I knew I had to get to him, had to help him. My golden flame. My gentle, kind man. I'd saved him, but now at what cost?

Ares cleared his throat from the other side of the room, and I looked up from my hands, avoiding his gaze as he shifted awkwardly, cleaning up his glistening abdomen of me. Lust coiled low in my belly, that pang of hunger intense as I ran my eyes over him, and I cursed myself for it. It was as though the last forty years meant nothing. Not the time, not the distance. My body was ready for him again without hesitation. I pressed my fingers into my eyes, frustrated and annoyingly horny again.

I'd come three times. Get it together.

"Ditey?" he whispered, and I groaned, turning to look at him. Heat flooded through me again as I pressed my thighs together, prayed to the Fates to get myself under control. The corner of Ares's mouth lifted into a small smirk, and I knew he could feel what I was feeling.

I hated that too.

"If you need more . . ." he offered, those skilled fingers dropping to unclasp his belt with one hand, but I held up my own to stop him before I lost all my resolve.

Shut this down.

"This doesn't change anything, Ares. You needed what you needed, and the Bond enslaved me to it. I needed your energy, and you gave it, and I'm grateful, but it doesn't change anything. It's over now. You got your release, and I'm feeling better. Let's just keep that as it is," I snapped, and he instantly recoiled, hurt flashing in his eyes, but as quickly as it'd come, he smoothed it over with a cold look.

"Happy to be of service," he bit out, turning to storm out of the room with a slam of the door.

I fell back into the sheets, fisting a pillow over my face, letting out a scream of rage and frustration. I hadn't meant to come off so harsh, but I was so fucking angry at myself, at him, at Hephaestus, and at the Bonds we all shared. I just wanted them *gone*. As long as they existed, none of us were free to make our own choices. They would always choose me over themselves, over self-preservation, over the fucking world. And I, no matter who I chose, would leave the other out in the cold.

I was fucking sick of it.

A heavy sigh dropped from my lips as I tossed the pillow to the side and looked myself over. In the haze of the lust, Ares had ripped my shirt and broken the zipper on my pants, and I grumbled in annoyance as I stood, wrapping the top sheet that was mostly dry around me in a chiton and tying it tightly with my belt. I fumbled around in my discarded purse, grabbing a hair tie to try and wrangle my mane before heading out to find Persephone. Hopefully, she'd have some clothes I could borrow, and with any luck, I'd find her before I ran into Hephaestus.

I stepped into the corridor, willing my terrible sense of direction to take me to Persephone's quarters. I padded down the hall, taking in the palace around me. I'd only been here a few times before, and none were for happy occasions. Now, the place was warm and inviting, a stark contrast to the cold and desolate halls we'd walked when she was taken. I shuddered at the thought of her missing time, of all she had endured. I was happy for Hades that Persephone had returned, and they were reunited, though I was saddened to have not been there for her recovery, but her proximity to Hephaestus, to Hermes and the rest of the others, had kept me on the outskirts.

Their happiness was hard-won, but Hades and Persephone had persisted and endured. More than once I had envied their Bond, their love. Whoever penned the phrase "Love does not envy, or boast, or beg" never spent eternity split between the love of two with no way to coexist.

My feet led me to an open space, filled with voices, and I stopped in my tracks, heart hammering in my chest. I heard Persephone's voice rise as she screamed with laughter, and when I poked my head through the door, I found her slung over Hades's shoulders, giggling and kicking her feet as Hecate and Hermes looked on, amused.

Hephaestus and Ares were nowhere to be seen, and I stepped inside to join the others, straightening myself as best I could.

Hermes turned those keen, judgmental eyes on me, taking in my makeshift chiton and tousled hair with a lifted eyebrow.

"I see Ares found you." He sneered, not kindly. There wasn't a single trace of the teasing humor he'd once used with me.

Hecate elbowed him in the ribs, hard enough that he yelped. He looked at her, resigned as he rubbed his side sheepishly. "Apologies, Aphrodite. I hope you're feeling better."

Hermes hadn't forgiven me for what I'd done to Hephaestus.

That made two of us.

I nodded my head to him, and he turned, hands grazing over Hecate as he pulled her into him, ignoring me. I gave her a small smile of appreciation. Hecate had always been understanding, had never judged, and perhaps she felt a little guilty that it was she who used witchcraft to apply the Bondmarks on Ares and me, against her better judgment. She had warned us they may not take, that she wasn't the Goddess of Marriage and couldn't lay the Bond properly, but we had been desperate, and she was my friend.

When I'd come back to New Orleans and asked for help breaking both Bonds, she had agreed to try. I could see the sessions she'd had with Hermes to unlock her visions had grown into something far more meaningful than ritualistic sex, and I grinned, because Hermes could hate me all he wanted, but he owed that to me, as I'd been the one to suggest she try it the old-fashioned way.

Hecate leaned her back into Hermes's chest and smiled up at him. Her hair was wild, free and haloing around her. The God of Thieves pressed a kiss to her temple, and she tightened her grip on him, possessive and tender all at once. Claiming.

The room was filled with so much love and joy that it pricked at my skin, feeding into my power. I wanted to reach out and touch the magic in the air, taste it, but I knew better. Love scorned couldn't receive the love presented properly, and it was better to abstain than risk corrupting it. My presence alone could cause fits of lust or lover's quarrels, entirely dependent on my mood.

Unfortunately, I wasn't feeling particularly affectionate. I took a step back and looked at Persephone, whom Hades had set down.

"Persephone, would you mind if I borrowed something to wear?" I asked quietly, eyes darting to make sure the boys weren't going to appear from the shadows.

She broke away from Hades and moved closer to me, hand extended. "Yeah, of course. Come with me?"

I took it, gratefully. The last thing I needed was to parade around here in sex-soaked linens.

Hades crowded her space, pressing a kiss to her temple.

"Do you want me to come?" he asked, hands on her face.

She smiled and shook her head.

"I think we're okay, you should stay," she assured him, but Hades remained unmoved. His eyes flicked to her abdomen once, quickly, but I caught it, the reticent look of him to let her pass. "Hades, I'm going to our bedroom. Nothing is going to attack me from the closet. You need to stay here and make sure the boys don't kill each other until we get back, yeah?"

Her words were calming, soothing, a balm on the cold fire that was Hades's demeanor. His face was tight with tension, but he let her pass, running his hand down her front just briefly.

I smiled wide.

Persephone led me through a portal of shadows that dropped us off in a wide closet, floor-to-ceiling and stuffed with all sorts of dresses and pants and accessories.

I let out a low whistle, and she giggled softly.

"I know, it's a bit ridiculous, isn't it? He bought me clothes the entire time I was missing. Said he didn't know when I would return, but when I did, he wanted me to fit in with the world. Believe it or not, this is just for *this* decade. The entire south wing second floor contains rooms through the ages. I told him we should donate some of the pieces to museums." She walked along, sifting through the hangers and pulling garments out at will.

"You're pregnant, huh?" I asked, and she turned to me, eyes wide.

"No way, how did you know?" she squeaked, coming forward to take my hands in hers excitedly. We sat together on the small bench in her walk-in, and she glowed, blossomed, a light radiant in the space around us.

"Well, for starters, you're literally glowing, Persephone. Like, this weird mixture of gold and black? I imagine it's the duality of your powers. But also? Hades touched your stomach twice and kept glancing at it. Doesn't take a rocket scientist to put together that you've probably been fucking like rabbits since you returned."

Persephone blushed just slightly but smiled.

"Goddess of Love and all."

She laughed, and I pulled her into a hug.

"I'm really happy that you're back. I don't know what all you remember, but we were actually friends before." My words were small, shy. I didn't want to press too hard or assume that I was still welcomed into her space. She and Hephaestus had grown incredibly close by what Hecate had told me, and I knew she probably had big feelings about me.

But Persephone only smiled wide, squeezing my hand reassuringly. "My memory returned. I remember it all, and please, call me Seph. I'm really happy to see you, too, girl. I'm sorry, someone should have told you. You were just so focused on getting to Hephaestus and healing him that there didn't really seem a good reason to interrupt all that, and when you went down from healing him, everything just happened so fast.

"And speaking of? Ares. Hephaestus. You with an incredible amount of sex hair, and them both having received a healthy dose of ritual sex magic? Spill," she demanded, standing again to sort through clothes.

I let out a breath and caught the bra and underwear she threw to me. "I don't know about them with any ritual sex magic, but it does explain the state Ares came to me in."

Persephone handed me a pair of green cargo pants and a black tank top. I shimmied out of the makeshift dress and slipped my undergarments on.

"Hermes said they had been . . . close . . . during the ritual. That can have some lingering effects, trust me." She ran her hand over her stomach absentmindedly as she leaned back against a shelf full of shoes.

"Are you scared?" I asked, gesturing to her hands where they rested.

Persephone looked down briefly before beaming at me. "Yes and no. I know that Hades is going to be an incredible father. It's not something we ever talked about before, but I like to think that we would have if I hadn't taken a dirt nap for two thousand years."

My face scrunched up at that, and I pulled the tank over my head before turning to face her.

"About that . . . I just wanted you to know, I'm sorry we didn't look longer. We shouldn't have given up," I admitted, biting my lip. She was my friend, and we had left Hades more or less to his own devices not long after she'd been taken.

Persephone waved a hand dismissively. "You did what you could, and I'm grateful you all kept him alive for as long as you did." Seph plopped down on the chair with a footrest and clasped her hands over her still smooth belly expectantly. "Though, I am curious as to why you weren't around during my reintegration. Hades explained that you and Hephaestus split up again. Care to fill me in on what I missed? Hades was a little tight-lipped about it earlier, when I asked."

I stepped into the pants, which were a size or two bigger than I usually wore, but comfy, nonetheless. I grabbed the belt from the floor and fastened it around my waist, cinching the fabric before turning to face her.

She was quiet, patient in that way of hers. I sat on the bench and rested my elbows on my knees, bent forward with my head in my hands. Where to even begin? "I left Heph in the twenties. Ares came back from World War I, and he promised it had been the war to end all wars, that he was done."

"You can't imagine the destruction," he'd said.

"I'd never seen him look so utterly satisfied or so devastated after a fight. The things mortals had the capacity to do to each other . . . I think, in the end, it even sickened him." I dropped my hands and lifted my chin to Persephone, who watched me curiously.

"I'm confused, doesn't Ares love war? It's kind of his entire personality?"

I felt my hackles rise. "It's not that he loves war. It's that he *is* war. He derives his power from it, but he doesn't start it or seek it out. He didn't get to choose his powers, any more than you or I did," I snapped defensively.

Seph raised an eyebrow, lifting her hands in mock surrender, and I deflated, apologetic.

"I'm sorry, it's just . . . Ares isn't just a blunt instrument. He's the God of War, yes. But he's also passionate and sweet. He cares, sometimes so deeply, I worry if it will consume him from the inside out. He worries constantly for his soldiers and those that die next to him; he ushers them to the gates of the Underworld personally. Just as Hades is misunderstood, so is Ares. He carries the weight of every death under his command on his shade and hates himself for his need for destruction."

Persephone nodded slowly. She knew something about loving that which no one else understood.

"He came home, and he begged for me back, and I tried. Fates, I tried to deny him, but he'd never done this before, never sought me out. He was truly convinced that his thirst was quenched, that he could finally hang up his sword. And it didn't help things at home were . . . tense. Hephaestus and I had been together for about two hundred years during that stretch, but he, too, came home different. He was withdrawn. Some days, I'd come home, and he wouldn't speak to me at all, like he wasn't even there. It was like living with a ghost of his former self, and no matter what I did, nothing brought him back. Hygieia and Hermes checked in, but nothing really helped. The screams . . . The nightmares . . . They called it shell shock then. PTSD now. I'm not proud of it, but in the end, I'd neglected the Bond with Ares for so long that it—I can't explain it—*demanded* retribution. I'll never forget the day I left."

I picked at my nails, uncomfortable in the memory, the sickening feeling that pushed bile up my throat.

"He just looked at me, Seph. He looked at me with eyes so far away, I couldn't be sure anything was left of him. He said, 'When you go, don't come back. I don't want this anymore.' And his words broke something in me. My kind Hephaestus, my warmth. He was gone and he hated me. *When you go*, not *if*. He had made up his mind to give up on me, on us, and it hurt me so deeply, even though I had no right to, because he had lived through it so many times. I had been fighting it so hard, wanting to do right by him. Knowing he didn't have faith in me and none of my sacrifice mattered ripped me apart. So I took the coward's way out and left him. It was winter, and it was cold."

I stared past Persephone, who, for her part, made no move to interrupt me. She just listened, green eyes glistening like she could feel my pain while I recounted the moments when my world crumbled.

A small tear broke past my own defenses, sliding down my cheek in a hot trail. I would carry the shame of giving up on us until I met my True Death.

"And Ares?" she asked quietly.

I swiped the tear away and let out a small laugh. "Ares and I lived in the honeymoon bliss stage for a few decades. He was a high school football coach, and I owned a beauty salon in a small town in Mississippi called Biloxi. He said football was close enough to the act of war that it kept his bloodlust at bay, but I never really believed him, even though I wanted to. Football was enough, he'd say, and burying himself in me. But it wasn't true. After a while, he grew bitter and distant, missed the action of battle, and by the time World War II kicked off, I was terrified that, any day, that trumpet would sound, and he wouldn't resist the call."

I let out a sharp breath as the pain cracked my ribs. "He held out, all the way to December 7, 1941. Pearl Harbor happened, and suddenly, he had to go. It wasn't just that he had to. He *wanted* to, and I was bitter about it, Persephone. Angrier than I'd ever been. I had given up Hephaestus for him, for *us*. And he was going back to the true love of his life, and there was nothing I could do. You gotta understand, our powers are so diminished. I realize it's different for you and Hades, but for those of us not fueled by the shades of the Underworld, we can be killed by more than just Poisoned Ambrosia now. The day he shipped off for command was the day I packed up our lives and left. He knew when he kissed me goodbye that morning that I wouldn't be there when he returned. And I wasn't. I couldn't crawl back to Hephaestus, even though I ached to. I left for Los Angeles, and I didn't look back.

"When you were found, I flew in, but Hades was keeping a lid on where you were and what you were allowed to know. I hadn't spoken to Heph since I left, and I knew he was near you. I didn't want to intrude. He felt me here though. Just like I felt him. Like Ares could feel me."

I swallowed, running my hand over the back of my neck. "A few weeks after I arrived, I had coffee with Hecate. I asked her if she knew how to break the Bonds, or maybe how to heal at least one of them in the hopes that maybe the other would fade."

I sat back and watched Persephone's eyes go wide.

"Who would you have chosen?" she breathed, leaning forward, and just hearing those words had me flinching involuntarily.

I shook my head. "I honestly don't know, Seph. I love them both, so much. They're both written in my bones, on the very marrow of who I am, but we can't live like this anymore. It's so fucking unfair to them. I suppose, if she succeeds, I'll let them decide. I couldn't possibly." I hadn't allowed myself to think about that, or acknowledge that I could be split from one of them, let alone that it would be me deciding. The thought cracked a chasm in my already injured chest.

Persephone nodded. "Well, Hecate and Hermes were . . . successful? Odd way to say they got off, but here we are. She was telling us a little about what she saw when you came in."

Persephone stood as my head snapped to her.

"What did she say? Is there anything to be done?" I asked, half fearful, half hopeful, my stomach twisted in knots.

"You'll have to ask her. I think she's got a lot more info, and I'd rather not risk saying the wrong thing and fucking this up even more. But Ditey, I have to ask . . . as someone who loves Hephaestus, who cares about you . . . is this what *you* really want?"

Fates, the way she looked right through me waivered my resolve. Persephone had a Bond. Had suffered for it in madness and chaos. I thought of how broken we all were, all these pawns of Olympus . . .

I offered her the only answer that felt honest.

"I want us to have a chance to be happy. Whatever that looks like, I know that what we have now isn't working. It's never worked, not really. I'm just fucking exhausted with it, Seph. I'm sick of hating myself for shit I can't control. Of hurting them, and them hating one another. None of us asked for this."

"Let's go find out what Cate knows, then," she replied. "You look great."

After slipping on the black boots she'd pulled for me, which looked like the standard issue boots Ares wore, I surveyed myself in her large mirror and frowned. "Seph, why do I look like a wilderness scout?"

"Because you're going on a quest, and as much as you look killer in a set of red bottoms, I'm afraid the Underworld would ruin them instantly," she teased before stepping from the hall into a waiting portal. I took a deep breath and followed after her, curious.

A quest sounded like progress.

Progress I could work with.

Hephaestus

CHAPTER 10

Heavy streams cascaded down my arms and back in scalding sheets, sweeping away the dirt and grime of the Underworld, but also the touch that still burned against my skin. The water ran tinged with red as I scrubbed away the dried blood caked to my sides and torso, taking special care to not disturb the Bondmark over my chest.

I felt a lot of things about what had transpired in the last few hours that I didn't have the emotional capacity to even begin to unpack, especially not when white-hot shame still sat coiled in the pit of my stomach.

As I ran my hands over my body much harsher than necessary, I let myself sink into the punishing friction.

Ritual magic was infectious, everyone knew, and what had transpired in that altar room had been the result of proximity. *Right*? It had affected Persephone and Hades as well, and for Ares, it called to his blood.

I exhaled, convincing myself I could explain it all away . . . up to that point. *But after*? I'd followed him. I knew where he was going before he took his first steps. His jacket and Kevlar served as little more than a weak justification as I'd scooped them up and marched off behind him, guided by the Bond back to Aphrodite.

Aphrodite.

I felt it when he touched her, and before I ever made it to the landing, a bolt of electricity shot straight down my spine, reverberated in my aching cock in a way that lengthened me before I ever even got close enough to hear her moans. It was so different than it had ever been, and I didn't understand why *now* I could feel them together. Ares and Aphrodite had been intimate countless times over the years, and I'd never *mercifully* been able to know when it happened.

I knew now. Fucking Hells, I knew. Just the thought of his hands on her, the way she melted for him . . . And earlier, when his body had bent like a mighty oak in the force of a storm for me. I wanted to command them both, to push them to their limits. Aphrodite was the Goddess of Love, and there wasn't much she couldn't take sexually, but my appetites were shaped and built around her, the pleasure she craved. She'd taught me much of how she liked to be handled, but it had been when I had discovered their affair that taught me the most.

I handled her carefully, so carefully. Firm but in control when I had her spread before me. The urge to swat her skin and then smooth away the sting with my hands swept through me constantly. Aphrodite was strong, so strong, but I didn't want her to feel used. Ares held no such compunction.

He was rough with her body. He toed that line between pain and pleasure a lot more liberally than I did, and she didn't just let it happen. She *wanted* it in a way I'd never let myself enjoy. The way he punished her with those powerful thrusts flashed across my mind, and my knees buckled as the swollen, heavy length that bobbed between my legs throbbed, begging for release.

I bit my lip, searching for any thoughts that would push the memory from my brain. My cock ached at the swell, and I grabbed it hard in frustration, squeezing the head. I stroked once, twice, the pads of my fingers caressing the studded metal adorning the underside of my shaft. I groaned, sensitive so soon after coming but needing *more*.

I hadn't had Aphrodite in a very, very long time, and she'd never wrapped her lips around my piercings. The thought sent another bolt down my spine, eliciting a deep grunt from my chest as I stroked now, harder, *wet*. Pre-cum beaded, a glistening, perfect pearl at my tip, and I smeared it with my thumb down my shaft, back over the head. My mind worked overtime to recall the image of Aphrodite on her knees, looking up at me as my cock disappeared deeper and deeper into her mouth. Faster, I stroked, pulling the frustration and anger and shame from the very inside of my bones as I glided and worked the head between my fingers.

I was close, so close, focusing on her golden hair, the way she would look up at me through those amazing fucking doe eyes as her lips, so plump, so perfect, *mine*, glided over my shaft rhythmically. The memory, burned into my retinas, as she hollowed out her cheeks and took me deeper inside her, choking slightly at the pressure at the back of her throat.

My Aphrodite worshipped me as she trailed that sweet tongue over my tip, down my piercings to the base of my balls, moaning louder and rougher as I fisted my cock.

My core temperature rose dramatically, evaporating the water to steam before it could reach my body. The sounds of wet skin bounced off the stone, punctuated by my pants as I buried my fist in my mouth to stave off the grunts.

I was angry now, so fucking angry that Ares got to her first. *My goddess*. He'd stolen her from her rest and then used her body to relieve his rage.

I was so close, my strokes erratic and unyielding as I pushed my hand harder, palming at my too hot flesh. Memory Aphrodite was putting her all into it, gliding me in and out her mouth with true fervor as she drove me higher. Just like I remembered. She had always been eager to please, eager to love, and apparently, a different kind of lover to each one of us. The way Ares had taken her . . .

My mind conjured the memory before I could even register what was happening, Ares fucking her hard from behind. Aphrodite standing tall against his chest with his hand around her throat and the other circling her clit as he commanded her mouth open, his powerful muscles jerking forward with the effort. The memory did me dirty, and I came with a shocking force, splashing cum all over my torso *again*. At least I was in an actual shower this time, not spying on my wife and her lover like some voyeur.

My chest heaved on the come down, and I wondered, not for the first time, what the hell was going on. I hated Ares. I wanted him to fuck off back to whatever war-torn hellhole he'd come from.

No matter what the cum being washed down the tiles said.

Ares

CHAPTER 11

I stormed through the doorway of Aphrodite's room, forcing as much distance between us as I could manage, fighting every cell in my body that pulled me back to her. One taste wasn't enough—wasn't nearly fucking enough—but she wanted space, and she did *not* want me, that much was obvious. I cursed as I looked around, annoyed that this place had me turned around.

I needed to change. Aphrodite had soaked me thoroughly each time she'd come, and as much as I'd love to walk around with the proof of her arousal covering me, I needed to clear my head. She had rejected me again. The wounds buried deep inside me, slashed by her words, bled out the scar tissue easier than a sword could have cut through me.

She loved me but against her will, and she thought us all stuck in some cosmic torture cycle. The truth was never that way for me though. I had loved her with everything, *fiercely*, from the moment I'd met her. When Persephone mentioned she was looking for a way to sever the Bonds, the panic in my stomach mirrored on

Hephaestus's face. He loved her, too, and like me, it wasn't just because of the corrupted Bonds we all shared.

I never expected to find an ally in him, the one slated to be my greatest of enemies.

I raked a hand through my hair, frustrated and pent-up again.

Hephaestus.

What in the Hells had that been about? Standing in the shadows, watching, getting off on the pleasure I drove into Aphrodite. My cock twitched, and I stopped, fisting my hands at my sides, taking deep breaths. Ritual magic lingered. That was the explanation. I blew out a long breath, centering my core, forcing my jaw to unclench, to relax. Next moves.

I needed clothes. Hades was about my size, surely his wing would be around here somewhere. So I walked on, my boots scraping along the stone floor, blue flame sconces dancing along the walls merrily. Merrily? Not a word I would have normally used to describe the Asphodels, but Persephone was in residence, and the whole Underworld lost its mind. I was happy to see her, happy Hades had her, even if we had never shared a kinship.

Hades and I had never been close, but he understood the weight of my position, and I his. He and Hephaestus, however, *were* close, and like Hermes, I expected the same amount of loyalty to place me firmly on the outside of their bubble. I had never been popular with their ilk.

No, the only friendly face I hoped to find amongst these people was Helios, and though it had been decades since I'd seen him last, I knew that he, at least, wouldn't be outright hostile. He didn't mind the temper or the rage that came from me, spurred on by the same fire within. He was charming where I was harsh and unyielding and unworthy of more than just a drunken bar night, which inevitably ended in a brawl.

I couldn't blame them, that they all preferred the company of the God of the Forge.

I was everything opposite of Hephaestus. He was kind, patient. Fuck, even after he had caught us together, there wasn't rage or anger. Just sadness. So much sadness. He had gone to Hera, demanded to be let loose of his marital contract. Hephaestus should have demanded blood. *I certainly would have.* I would have split him from neck to navel then dragged his body across the planes of battle for all to see. But not Hephaestus. He never disparaged Aphrodite, never cursed her.

I could still remember the look of pain etched in those eyes.

"*Why?*" was all he'd asked.

Aphrodite had fallen apart completely under his gaze, the kindness and pain that swam in his eyes, and it pulled her under like a great tidal wave. My heart shattered then, the first of many fissures, knowing that even with my Bond on her body, she loved him too. I was not Hephaestus. I did not have his grace. So, instead of understanding, she met rage in my eyes. I was a vengeful God, hated, *feared.*

All except Aphrodite. She held on, Fates bless her, and defended me, though she knew she shouldn't. It didn't make me grateful; it made me bitter. Every fight, argument, war that took me away, I saw it behind her eyes. She regretted our Bond. It had twisted all the good inside me, this forced sharing. Jealousy tore at me constantly, along the insecurities that came with it.

I wasn't him. I couldn't be gentle with her heart, with her feelings. If I were a better god, I would have thrown myself on my sword centuries ago. There were times, in the heat of battle, that I considered it.

During World War II, the Germans were hunkered in. They had the numbers, the high ground, and a battalion siege ready up the side of the hill. An infantryman ran toward me, young, full of fear. He was German, but he could have been anything. Ottoman. Greek. Moor. Thousands of young men had attempted to make me die for whatever country or empire I fought for at the time, and time and time again, I had dispatched them to the Underworld on behalf of theirs.

I hesitated to lift my M1. *It could all be over.* A fleeting thought, in the blood-soaked sands of Europe, knowing this war had taken her for good. She wouldn't be waiting at the end of this, I could feel it in my bones, so what was the point?

I stood, waiting for his blow to fall. It never came.

The young man, fair-haired and pale, hesitated at my surrender. *Mistake.* My hands, fast as lightning, squeezed the trigger. Two quick shots, and the young man blew backward, rifle still clutched in his hands. Blood bloomed red around the wound, and I approached him slowly, assuredly, as bullets whizzed past my head. He was on his back, gurgling, eyes wide and face flecked with crimson stains. I knelt down to him, taking his shaking hands in mine.

He was babbling, staring off somewhere above his head, just a boy with a head filled with the cruel lies and twisted propaganda of his homeland, but that marked his shade for death, fighting under that banner. He called for his mother, for his father. The harsh Germanic tongue soothed as it translated to me. He prayed.

I squeezed his hand as I had squeezed that trigger. He was young, so young, more boy than man as he shook loose his mortal coil.

I helped his shade to stand, grasping his incorporeal forearm in my palm, and nodded in the direction of Thanatos, urging the soldier to leave the field.

The God of Death stood sentry, drawing the dead to him. Thanatos would keep the shades of the fallen protected until they could be judged by the kings in the Asphodels, and if their cause was righteous, they would be brought great fortune in the afterlife. There would be no mercy for this young shade, no peace for the oppressive cruelty he had helped perpetuate.

I turned to see others from both sides, rising from their bodies, searching in confused desolation.

I wanted to give comfort, as Thanatos did. Healing, as Hygieia and Hermes did. Kindness, as I knew Hephaestus did.

But I was not that God. Forged in my father's image, I only knew how to be cruel.

Memory faded as my feet found purchase on the stone landing outside a set of double doors I didn't recognize. It seemed opulent enough to be a bedchamber, and I raised a hand, knocking lightly on the wood. I could hear the shuffling of soles against stone and fisted my hands in my pockets, hoping Hades was in a fair mood still.

The door swung wide, and every muscle in my body pulled taunt. Standing before me was Hephaestus, toweling off his shaggy sandy hair, completely naked save for the towel that slung low over his hips. The muscles in my abs constricted as I stared straight into equally shocked eyes.

I trained my gaze on his face, careful not to let my eyes roam, unsettled to find out how much discipline that took. Water dripped from his long strands of hair onto his shoulders and torso, and I wanted to taste, to li—

No. *Fates, no.*

I cleared my throat as he watched me, a curious caution lingering in his gaze. It was good diligence to know one's enemy, and I wanted to know what he was thinking, to map the cogs as they churned behind his eyes.

"Sorry, I was looking for Hades."

Hephaestus raised an eyebrow. "These are my quarters. You're looking for the East Wing."

I turned to retreat, but he opened his mouth to speak again, hesitating. "Is everything okay? With Aphrodite, I mean. I-is she okay?"

His voice was earnest, kind.

I turned back to him, worrying my fingers through my hair.

"She's fine. I left to find some clothes. All I have are the BDUs I had on, and they're, well, not in the best condition now," I grumbled, gesturing to my front.

Hephaestus's gaze raked over me, and I felt myself bristle. His eyes had gone colder, more predatory. I had pushed him in some way.

"That's quite a mess," he gritted out.

The silence stretched thin between us, heavy and tense, both of us knowing just *where* this mess had come from, but neither of us willing to admit it out loud. This was the most alone time we'd ever spent with each other, and without the buffer of Aphrodite, I wasn't sure how to behave.

Hephaestus broke from the entryway and shuffled into his room, leaving the heavy doors open behind him. He began sifting through piles of clothes stacked precariously on an overstuffed armchair in front of a massive fireplace. The flames crackled happily as they lapped at the wood, filling the room with the faint smell of cedar smoke.

Hephaestus turned his back to me, and I took the opportunity to survey the room.

It was . . . somehow different, and yet exactly how I'd imagined his dwelling would be. Not that I had honestly ever given it much thought, but as I stood there, taking in the simple furnishings, it made sense. The large bed, the four posts, and a simple blanket that looked jarringly familiar, save for the carvings in the headboard. It was part of a set, I realized. A matching wedding set, gifted to Aphrodite.

Memories of a golden net entwining us together surged through my mind, and I grimaced with something that felt a lot like . . . *shame*.

"These may not fit. I'm not as tall as Hades," he murmured as he tossed over a pair of jeans.

I caught them deftly, and as he returned to the pile to find a shirt, I continued my examination of the room. The large bookcases flanking the fireplace caught my attention, and I itched to step over toward them.

I loved to read. I loved to study strategy, delve into the journals and diaries of the most famous generals and commanders that had lived. It fascinated me, their take on war, and gave me a sense of twisted fatherly pride at how they excelled coming to the same conclusions: war was necessary but also Hells, and it should be avoided whenever possible.

Hephaestus turned back to me, a T-shirt clutched in his fist, and I watched as he hesitated before stepping closer a few paces, hand outstretched.

I took the soft cotton from his hands, well-worn threads caressing my fingers.

We lingered there, the air between us thick and charged as I nodded once. He gestured to the open door at the opposite end of his chamber, and I shuffled to what looked to be a bathroom.

There was no door to shut, so I began to strip swiftly, toeing off my boots. I pulled on the jeans, which fit fine in the waist, then tucked them into my boots before lacing them back up.

I should have left then, but I could hear him moving around out there, and I wasn't ready to face that awkwardness again, so I walked to the sink and turned on the tap, let the water pool in my cupped hands, overflowing with the cold bite of the Rivers of the Underworld. I splashed the water over my face, scrubbing the blood and grime of battle from my skin. I ignored the sting as I ran my hand over the stubble that ran up my jaw, careful to wash the scent of Aphrodite from my beard, needing it gone so I could think clearly. I'd never be able to focus, walking around coated in her scent after so long without.

I reached for a small hand towel hanging next to the sink, brought it to my face to soak up the excess water and stilled. It smelled like spices, like woodfire. It smelled like him.

I inhaled once, *briefly*, before catching myself and ripping the cloth from my face then made quick work pulling the shirt over my chest. The material was a bit tighter than I'd normally wear, but I was built stockier, heavier in the chest and torso than Hephaestus. I straightened the shirt and surveyed myself in the mirror. It would have to do.

I stepped out of the bathroom, ignoring the knowledge that in wearing his clothes, I was *enveloped* in Hephaestus's scent, and even more resolutely ignoring that I didn't hate it nearly as much as I should have.

"Should we head down? Hades just sent a shadow to let me know everyone is ready to talk." Hephaestus sat on the edge of his bed, buckling his bootstraps as he spoke.

I dipped my head in agreement, and he stood, giving me a once-over so lingering that goose bumps erupted over the back of my neck.

"Not bad, considering," he mumbled and moved past me, heading to the door. He slung a green fatigue jacket over his shoulders as he went, and I followed, unsure what bizarre magic had my back straightening, had my hands running through my hair to tame the wild, sweat-dampened locks, had me wearing the God of the Forge's clothes.

Ares

CHAPTER 12

The walk to the throne room was quiet, the silence stretched between us like a great chasm filling up with hurried footsteps and stolen, awkward glances, and enough tension to make my skin crawl.

I followed behind Hephaestus as he led us through the labyrinth that was this stupid palace. Hades lived by himself for centuries, who needed this much room, for Fate's sake?

He turned sharply through a stone archway, and I recognized this as the throne room, a space I *was* familiar with. The large chamber rose before us with intricate ore and stonework adorning the wide cavern. The thrones of Hades and Persephone sat dark and opulent, unoccupied as the two sat together at a raised war table I recognized from the old days of Demeter's Rebellion. Aphrodite had been with Hephaestus then, and they worked diligently with the Underworld to thwart the destruction Demeter was wreaking. Volatile and still fresh on our humiliation, I'd opted to work with Dionysus and Thanatos to secure the expansion of the Elysian Fields, venturing into the main palace as little as possible.

Seeing so many of these same faces gathered around that table felt like a time warp, and I bristled, lowering my stone mask of indifference, insulating myself from the bullshit I knew was coming.

Hecate had composed herself, back in her modern garb, though her hair was braided in a silky plait. She looked invigorated, *satiated*, next to Hermes, who sat relaxed, stretched out, feet casually propped atop the stone table. His arm slung wide over the back of Hecate's chair, bright red Converses bobbing as he jiggled his leg.

Medusa sat opposite to him, dark shades obscuring her stony gaze as she spoke with Hygieia, who looked . . . tired.

A pang of sympathy resonated through me as I took in the dark circles and tense muscles of the Goddess of Mental Health. We worked together many times over the centuries, and I'd seen her attend to many wounded soldiers on the battlefield. Though I wouldn't call us friends, it bothered me to see her run ragged. She always gave too much, stretched herself to the point of breaking. I didn't know the specifics of the ordeal that brought Persephone back, but whatever it was had almost killed Hephaestus and probably wounded others.

Artemis shot off a terse nod as we entered, jaw tense as she sat next to Persephone, who chatted happily beside to her.

Hades held his wife closely, practically pulling her into the chair with him. I didn't blame him, though, for wanting to keep her close. If Aphrodite were stolen for over two thousand years, and I got her back? I'd never let her out of my sight again.

His arms were wrapped protectively around Persephone's torso as he stroked his thumb over her abdomen, and something in the action gave me pause as his words from earlier replayed in my ears: *It's not safe for her, in her condition.*

She was pregnant.

Blood magic was potent and wild and could have indeed hurt the goddess if it got its claws into her. Persephone was already so powerful, I could feel how strongly it radiated off her, a pulse of dark growth and strength. She truly was the duality of life and death. The eminence of divine destruction. The despair. All entwined with her power, of the child that grew inside of her.

Dionysus sat near, cheeks red from laughter rather than the wine I'd heard he'd hung up after the abysmal affair of Sodom and Gomorrah. He lifted a cup, which he offered to a very grumpy-looking Helios, and I felt my chest heave a breath of relief that there would be at least one set of eyes that wouldn't shoot glares at me just for existing.

The titan looked annoyed, his usual smile replaced with a nervous pinch as though he would rather be anywhere else but here. Something was off with him. He looked . . . gray, muted. Lackluster. *Sick?*

An empty chair separated him from Aphrodite, who sat quietly, picking at her nails. Anyone else would assume disinterest, but I could see the anxiety lining the muscles in her neck, the tension in her posture. Her beautiful golden hair fell in soft curls, naturally gorgeous down her back and over her shoulders, but I knew she wore it now like a shield, a barrier to protect herself, because while she was also once beloved, there were those in company who had shunned her for the part she'd played in Hephaestus's pain too.

I stepped toward her instinctively, her stress pulling the protectiveness from my bones, eyes instinctually scanning the room for threats. Stuck in the safety of routine, with her body and shade calling to mine down the fed Bond, I reached the chair between Helios and Aphrodite, reflexively swooping in to plant a swift kiss on her head as I did. To my surprise, she didn't bristle at the contact, but instead, sucked in a deep, calming breath.

The chair slid out, and I settled in with a small nod at Helios, who wouldn't look directly at me.

Hephaestus pulled out the chair on the other side of the Goddess of Love, then leaned over to squeeze her arm. She smiled, and my jaw ticked, jealousy coursing through my veins, but it felt less heated, nearly shallow, as though I knew I *should* be upset that his hands were on her rather than *being* pissed about it . . .

Medusa hopped up and rounded the table in a blur, snakes whirling as she crashed into Hephaestus. The wily snakes atop her hair coiled around him as she squeezed, and he laughed, a deep, rich sound, I realized I hadn't heard it in a very, very long time.

"I'm alright," he cooed, reassuring a now sniffling Medusa, petting her snakes good-naturedly while they hissed and pecked at him.

"You ever do that again, I'll kill you myself. I'll stone you. I swear. Don't play with me, white boy," she chided, pulling back.

He rumbled again, an amused smirk on his face as he offered her apology for . . . *getting impaled on a fucking tree?*

I had zero time to unpack that as Aphrodite had gone still, sitting ramrod straight while she looked on at the interaction unfolding.

Pinpricks of jealousy hit me from somewhere deep and unfamiliar, not entirely just my own. He must have felt the spike of emotion too because Hephaestus's eyes cut sideways to Aphrodite before he cleared his throat and gently broke the hug.

Medusa walked back to her side of the table and sat, brushing small trails of tears from under her sunglasses as she went.

An unfamiliar lick of embarrassment surged through me, not mine, maybe Aphrodite's, but all I could see was the storm cloud that had settled over her.

Hygieia reached across to rub small circles on Medusa's back, and Aphrodite's gaze flicked back and forth between the Goddess of Mental Health and Hephaestus, her indignant jealousy barely contained.

I knew I should be upset that she was getting so riled up over him, but a much larger part enjoyed the golden boy, *Mister Impossible-to-Hold-Up-to-Himself*, had landed himself on

Aphrodite's shit list. It was a petty thought, but I clung to it, nonetheless. The alternative was showing how much this affected me. How the insane mix of emotions seemed to be leaking from her to me in a way they never had before.

Hermes snorted, rolling his eyes at the interaction, staring at Aphrodite with a look of disgust.

My blood roiled just below the surface at his disrespect, because while I knew there was a tension between the two of them over Hephaestus, Aphrodite was mine, and I'd take his fucking head if he pushed me.

"You can't be serious," he scoffed, ignoring the sharp look Hecate gave him, crossing his arms over his chest. Aphrodite turned to face him, chin held high, that cold stare in her eyes. "You can't truly be jealous considering your *many* infidelities."

It was a scathing indictment, and Aphrodite flinched, just barely, but it was enough.

"Hermes!" I growled at the same time Hephaestus, barked "Enough," warning mirrored in his tone. I moved to stand, reaching instinctively for the knife I kept in my boot, but Aphrodite raised a hand to stop me, knowing full well what I would do to anyone who disrespected her. Pink nail polish highlighted the sharp talons of her nails. Beautiful, but deadly. Just as she was.

Aphrodite brought her gaze to rest on Hermes, ice etched into her stunning features. Always graceful, those blue eyes shone pale gray as she surveyed him, sizing him up, unraveling men in that way of hers.

He shifted, slightly uncomfortable under her gaze, and I smirked as she rose in her power. When she spoke, her full lip flattened in a sneer.

"I've got this," she whispered to me, staying my movements. "I have listened to you slip barbs about my character and my situation every chance you've gotten for centuries, Hermes. I've let them tear me down, cut to the bone, but *no more*. I weathered the insults in silence because, deep down, I felt I deserved your judgment and your ire. No more. I'm done with that shame. I did not ask for what happened to me. I hate what it has made of my marriage and my relationships. None of us wanted this. We begged for it to be released.

"You're unBonded, and perhaps that's because you couldn't be bothered to stop judging others long enough for anyone to actually *want* to be tied to you for eternity. Until you are, you can never understand what the constant torture an unfulfilled Bond is. So, if you're not going to help, shut the fuck up, or I'm happy to leave. But I won't take your abuse any longer. Whatever you think of me, I promise, it doesn't come a fraction close to how much I hate myself over what Hephaestus has endured for loving me. *And* Ares. They're both victims in this."

Stunned silence rested over the table as she finished speaking. Hermes looked as though she had slapped him, and it may have been less embarrassing for him if she had.

Aphrodite was breathing hard, her hands shaking, and I knew what standing up for herself had meant. She'd taken their whispers and criticism, but none had been as venomous as Hermes. She'd said she'd understood, but seeing her defend her own honor filled me with pride, even as she trembled from the adrenaline.

Hephaestus and I each reached toward her lap to gather each of her hands, our fingers grazing as we entwined with hers. Both offering the comfort we could feel she needed. Aphrodite looked so beautiful but so fucking delicate. It was clear she hadn't fully recovered, and though we had fed into the Bond, it wasn't enough. She needed more, but I didn't know how to fix her.

Hecate shrugged Hermes's arm off her shoulders and glared at him. Persephone, too, looked ready to smack him.

Good.

"Oh, Hells no," Medusa chastised, just as Artemis glared at him from her seat and said, "This shit is why you don't get a pass."

I didn't understand the weight behind that one, and Hermes looked a little taken aback at the defense of the goddess. It was his own, though, that put him firmly in his place.

"We've talked about this; you're not going to embarrass me by showing your entire asshole. Apologize. *Now*," Hecate hissed, pissed by his behavior.

A part of me knew Hermes was just defending Hephaestus, but having never had anyone besides Aphrodite to defend me before, the concept of that kind of loyalty was foreign. She was the only one who truly cared for me, not for what I could kill or conquer.

The room filled with awkward silence, possibly more strained than the walk we'd taken to the throne room.

Hermes glanced at Hephaestus, who just glared back stonily.

"Now," Hecate repeated, and it was clear she wouldn't do so again.

Hermes raked a hand down his face, searching for words he probably didn't believe, but he cleared his throat to say them anyway.

"Listen . . . You're correct. That I don't know what it's like to have a Bond, but I know what it's like to watch my friend suffer, and I'm just . . . protective. I won't apologize for bloody caring about Hephaestus, but I will endeavor to keep any errant thoughts to myself, moving forward," he grumbled.

It was a non-apology at best, and I still would have preferred to crack open his insides to make them outsides, but Aphrodite sent him a curt nod before turning her attention back to Hecate, who still frowned up at her consort.

I rubbed my thumb across Aphrodite's knuckles soothingly, trying to show she wasn't alone here.

I would fight for her.

"Have you had any luck, Hecate?" Aphrodite's voice was strained but hopeful, and the reality of our situation crashed back down on me, suffocatingly oppressive. *Any luck in breaking our Bond?* she meant.

My stomach dropped out as I tightened the grip on her hand reflexively, fighting back the anger, the despair of it.

"I've got some news. We were able to trigger a vision." She shot an annoyed look at Hermes before continuing.

Aphrodite's breath hitched just slightly in her chest.

I chanced a sideways glance to Hephaestus, who had stilled also. A muscle in his jaw ticked, but other than that, he looked passive. *Damn it.* He even handled the possible dissolution of our Bonds with Aphrodite with grace, while I was fighting not to flip this damned table and bury my blade in Hermes's neck.

Fucker.

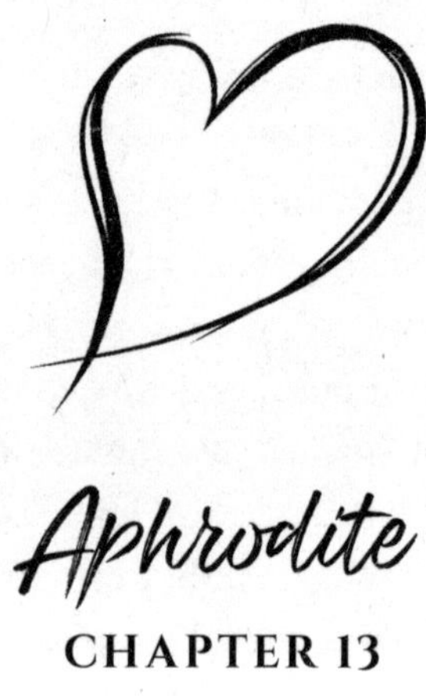

Aphrodite

CHAPTER 13

"Go on," I urged, leaning forward. Panic and turmoil assaulted my senses, anxiety flooding in from both Bonds, but I worked to tune them out, to focus on Hecate's voice and the salvation she could offer us. They didn't understand now, but they would, sooner or later. I just hoped that we'd eventually get there.

Having both of their hands in mine at the same time, *openly*, left me feeling a sense of contentedness I'd never dared to dream could be reality. The connection, the soothing warmth of it, lent me enough strength to fight the onslaught of their uncertainty.

"It didn't show us a cure, or a way to . . . get rid of the Bonds." Hecate's eyes flickered between Hephaestus and Ares quickly before landing back to me. "But it's a way to get some answers on how to try. Have you ever heard of the Cult of Dodona?" she asked.

I shook my head, not sure I'd ever come across such a community before.

Persephone's ears perked up, and she raised a small hand.

"You mean the Oracle of Zeus?" she asked.

Hecate nodded. "Yes, the same. One of the very first places of prophetic power. The first Oracles were born of their gifts there. The Priestesses—"

"Wait, but there were no priestesses at Dodona, only Selloí, only priests?" Persephone interrupted, confused.

Again, Hecate nodded. "The lore is that there were only priests, and that they slept on the floor and had unwashed feet. That was true, to an extent. The first priestess was an Oracle by the name of Melia. In the beginning, she was revered, worshipped even. Her gifts came from the Fates themselves, and all listened to her prophecies, including Zeus. He kept audience with her whenever he wished, but she thwarted any advances he made . . . Of which there were several."

Artemis let out a snort. "Shock and surprise."

Hecate gave her a knowing look and continued. "Yes, well, her loyalty to Hera and respect of their marriage and Bond, in spite of defying Zeus, garnered her much favor with the goddess. It's said that Melia eventually took a lover, which angered Zeus. Holding such favor with Hera, the Goddess of Marriage granted her and her lover the ability to Bond as the gods do. At the time, the Oracle power inside her made her akin to a demi-god.

"And so they were Bonded. Zeus raged. He coveted her, and her denial sent him into a fury. He killed her lover, struck him down on the night of their marriage when he left their bed to gather more wine. Zeus latched his body to his chariot and dragged him around the city for all to see. Melia begged a few of the gods to help, but none would, unwilling to incur his wrath. Zeus had made it clear: Any who defied the God of Gods would suffer the same fate."

The table sat in a heavy silence, enraptured by this untold history, but it was nothing new to me, the vicious cruelty of Zeus.

"The Bond was broken but still alive with rotting power. Melia plotted her revenge quietly. Zeus continued his advances, but her strength and resolve held him at bay. I suspect Hera did as well. What happened next is blurry at best. Wide speculation has alternate accounts, but it is *said* that Hera went to her with a plan to resurrect her lover, should she complete a task for the goddess. It's also said that Melia got close, but Zeus was made aware of the arrangement . . ." Her voice dropped low, and I didn't need to hear the next words to know what he'd done. Phantom hands ran the length of my body as memory choked me, stole my breath, put me right back in that tent.

"*Breathe*," Ares instructed, reading my body, knowing me.

I kept my eyes in my lap as Hecate continued, but her words burrowed against my skull, dug at wounds I'd long ago buried deep.

"He went to the sacred Oracle of Dodona and he . . . forced himself upon her. *Brutally*. She . . . didn't survive the assault. Partly from his savagery, partly because of the broken Bond that rotted her from within."

Medusa and I shared a look, one full of deep knowing, the shared pain inflicted by powerful men.

Artemis and Persephone were furious. Dark shadows swirled low on the ceiling, blotting out the ambient light from the blue flames dancing in the sconces.

Hades gave Persephone a gentle squeeze and gestured to the shadows she was subconsciously calling, casually dispelling the power that lapped at her in waves.

"When the priests found her, she lay broken and discarded on the small island in the middle of the walled temple, under the open sky. Legend says that Hera, in her grief, acted in the only way she could to defy Zeus: Where Melia's blood stained the earth, a mighty tree grew. Her name means 'ash tree.' It became a sigil of remembrance. Zeus decreed, from then on, all Oracles must remain pure. They were to never take lovers, or they'd risk losing their abilities. He willed it so, and so it was. He thought the ability to freely love another circumvented the power of the gods," Hecate finished, voice heavy.

"That's absolutely awful," Hygieia whispered, horror written across her features.

Hecate sucked in a breath as Hermes squeezed her hand in support.

Nausea tore through me, and I was tired and angry that we had dragged this woman's abuse out into the light.

"What does that mean for us?" I asked.

Hephaestus leaned over, pressed his lips to my shoulder blade, offering me comfort and strength as I started to wane.

"Well, I was actually going to ask Hades. I think he may be the only one who knows the next bit." Hecate gestured to Hades and sat back, rubbing her temples.

Hades brought his fingers to his chin in contemplation, and Persephone studied him.

"You're speaking of the trade?" he asked. "I was aware of the . . . general idea of what transpired at Dodona, but not until Hera came to me and pleaded with me to intercede after Melia was murdered. Her shade became entwined with the tree, not truly dead, but not really alive either. Her husband, Pentaculos, was very much dead. I couldn't do much, but the dead *are* my domain, so I went to Dodona. I couldn't just uproot her from her circumstance; there are rules in the Underworld, but I offered her a trade. A chance for them both to live. I couldn't resurrect him, but I could swap him.

"I offered her seven years in my service. She'd be safe here in the Underworld, and he could walk and live amongst the mortals. Then, after seven years, I would come and take him here, so she could walk amongst the living for her time. Eventually, they'd grow old and get a life here, together, in the Asphodels, but the crux of it all fell in the contract. Pentaculos had to come back willingly. She was so sure he'd come for her. He promised he would. I stood and watched them embrace as she settled into the Underworld, and he followed the golden path to the surface.

"Seven years, I watched her wait. And when it was time to collect on his debt, to set her free, he balked. Refused to come. He'd fallen in love with another mortal, forsaking her. She was devastated. I set her up in the Unknown Lands and released her from my service to live in peace. She was never the same after his betrayal."

Persephone let out a small sniff as Hades brushed a finger over the apple of her cheek.

"You're the kindest of us all, my love. The literal best of us," she cooed, and he smiled, shyly.

"Don't tell anyone else that, Little Flower. I have a reputation to uphold." He kissed her softly on the top of her hair and turned back to Hecate.

"Do you think she figured out how to break the Bonds?" Artemis asked.

Hephaestus and Ares both shifted, adjusting uncomfortably in their seats.

Hades nodded once. "I think Melia probably got close. Hera has only ever come to the Underworld on a few occasions. One of those was shortly after I released Melia from my service. She demanded an audience, but Melia wanted nothing to do with her. I think, in her way, she blamed Hera in the end. For not keeping Zeus accountable, for sending her on the quest that led to her desecration, for not protecting her when it happened.

"Hera left after I refused her, but she found other ways to try to get to her. A throng of mortals sought Melia out on her behalf, all from the Temples of Hera. Eventually, we had to develop a system to keep them at bay."

Hades shifted his attention to Hecate. "Are you suggesting they attempt the trials?"

Hecate turned to me. "The lore states that, if you complete the three trials, you'll be granted an audience with Melia herself, and you can ask her a single question. You have to make it good and airtight; apparently, she's very good at skirting answers with technicalities." Hecate then sat back, folding her hands neatly in her lap.

"I'll do it," I answered, without hesitation. A tiny sliver of hope burned through me, and I clung to it, even as Hecate's eyes darted to Ares and then Hephaestus.

"I'm worried but you won't be able to complete them alone, Ditey," she whispered gently. "They're extremely grueling and you are already weak." Her lips tightened into a grimace. "Many have perished in the quests, even those who were shades and essentially already dead. The dangers of the trials render even the most powerful of gods just barely stronger than mortals." She shot a look at Hades, who lifted his hands in defense.

"We had to make it a challenge, or she'd have been overrun." He turned that cold gaze of his on Ares. "She will need both of you. I can tell that she doesn't have much spark left. The Bonds inside are eating her divinity." He gestured toward me, nearly apologetically.

I pulled my hands free, missing the warmth, as I folded my arms across my chest protectively.

"I can't ask them to do that. I'll take my chances," I whispered, and before Ares or Hephaestus could protest, Persephone cut in.

"Absolutely not. You're barely standing," she chastised, and I could feel the onset of tension fill the air as I straightened my shoulders, prepared for a fight.

Ares

CHAPTER 14

"Let's just talk about this for a second," Hephaestus pleaded, turning the full weight of his attention on Aphrodite as I sat, rooted in place, paralyzed by fear.

I'd heard of these trials. I knew the dangers of tangling with the Fates, but if Aphrodite had made up her mind, I knew there would be no stopping her.

She and Hephaestus were locked in a tiff, exchanging words, but before I could open my mouth to argue my case, a small shuffling from the archway drew the attention of the room.

A mortal I didn't recognize limped inside, a bandage wrapped tightly around his torso. He smiled sheepishly as he leaned on a long walking stick, and Helios jumped up with a look of concern, nearly knocking over a chair in his haste.

Ungraceful in a way so unlike the Titan of the Sun.

The feeling that something was *off* with Helios gnawed at me, and I furrowed my brow. His movements were . . . sluggish and uncoordinated, lacking divine skill and grace. He was a pale shade, drained completely of his bronze sheen, and dark circles, even darker than the ones on Hygieia, gave him a sullen, hollow look.

A pressure pulsed, tension lapping over my skin, as I watched Helios attend to the mortal. I turned to see Hades's icy stare spearing through the mortal with fury etched in the outlines of his face. The temperature of the room dropped, rapid and pointedly, as the shadows at the end of the table skittered back and forth restlessly.

"What are you doing out of bed, baby boy?" Helios asked while running his hands gingerly over the man, as though inspecting for the possibility of more injuries.

The temperature dropped again by at least ten degrees as Hades continued his piercing stare.

The man shrugged, wincing as he did so, and Helios frowned as Hygieia jumped from the table and walked over to assess the mortal. He shooed them both with a casual wave of his hand, but the silence from the others was deafening.

Hephaestus looked over curiously as the rest of the gathering waited.

"I woke up, and you were gone, and . . . I don't know. You were gone for a while. I didn't mean to interrupt." The mortal cast his eyes downward, avoiding eye contact with the God of the Dead.

Another temperature drop, this one significant enough to let us see our breaths. Whoever this was had made an enemy of Hades, a feat that never boded well for anyone.

"Enough!" Persephone hissed. She stood to make her way to the group clustered near the archway, but Hades wrapped a long arm firmly around her with an indignant grunt. "Hades, you're acting insane. We talked about this. What's done is done. Nick is our *friend*."

Anger radiated from the Goddess of Spring, and I shifted slightly, putting myself directly in the open line of sight of Persephone and Aphrodite. Pregnancies of the goddesses could make emotions even more heightened, and I wasn't going to let Aphrodite be caught in some sort of crossfire.

"I told Helios to keep him out of my sight. He is not my friend, Persephone. He only still draws breath because of the courtesy I allow for the sake of Helios." Hades's words were calm and cold, menacing in a way that chilled even me to the bone. I'd heard it many times in our interactions, but I could tell by the look on Persephone's face, it wasn't something she'd ever been on the receiving end of.

She balked like she had been slapped, and Hades immediately softened his tone, looking stricken. "You have to understand, it's going to take time. I'm allowed that much, aren't I?"

His words were simple, but I could see a chord had been struck with Persephone.

She nodded her head once, and he reached to tuck a lock of hair behind her ear.

"For Helios, try a little harder, please? Now that he's mortal, we aren't going to be able to see him that much . . ." Persephone reasoned.

I whipped my head around to face Helios, one of my only friends and allies, as loss enveloped me. *That* was the reason for his changed demeanor. He was a titan no more. I had missed something, and somehow this mortal was involved with it.

I stood, nervous energy thrumming through my body. Gods didn't just *become* mortal. It was a process, and it was irreversible. Did he get tossed in the Styx?

"You're mortal?" I asked, more bark than question.

Hephaestus stood, too, confusion etched on his face.

Helios stepped slightly in front of the mortal . . . Nick? I think that was what Persephone called him. A curt nod.

I let out a quick breath.

"Was it an accident?" I demanded as a buzzing started in my ears, pitching higher with each second that passed.

Helios gave me a sympathetic look, like he understood the weight of this, the impact of his mortality.

"I chose it. It was the only way to save Nick, and for us to be together," he explained kindly. There was no waver to his voice, only fierce conviction. My brain short-circuited trying to put all the missing pieces together. Why the fuck hadn't I checked in more often?

I raked a hand through my hair, the buzzing too loud, and turned to look at the others, who seemed . . . uncomfortable with my outburst. The sympathy in Helios's eyes burned my blood.

"Who in the fuck is Nick, Helios? Why does Hades hate him? Why would *you* become mortal on purpose? Why the fuck are you staring at me like that? I just need some answers!" I grounded out, anger spiking inside me like a volcano getting close to its pressure point.

The silence persisted. No one answered, instead they looked at me like I had four heads, or stared at the ground as though I hadn't even spoken. Even Aphrodite looked at me with confused sympathy.

"I'm sorry" was all Helios managed, the weight of the bombshell dropped between us too heavy.

I had seen him at his worst. Lowest. Picked him up when he wanted nothing more than to drink himself into oblivion, and time again, he'd done the same to me. It was more than just drunken nights and raising Hells. Helios *knew* me. He cared about me. And when the world blew apart, and I was the villain in everyone's eyes, he had stood with me while I watched Aphrodite marry another. Had stopped me from walking into the Styx myself.

And now that was over.

Aphrodite wanted freedom from our Bond, and once she had it and Helios's mortal life was spent, that would be the end of it. I was standing in the middle of a room full of people who wouldn't care if I died, and I pondered if perhaps it would be a mercy on Aphrodite to walk right outside and do the same.

"Ares, I—" Helios began, but I shook my head, letting out a frustrated breath that sounded more like a warning.

No one tried to stop me as I turned on my heel and stormed out the door. Fuck them. I would never matter to them. I would never ever be *one* of them. That was fine. I'd be fine on my own.

Always was.

Hephaestus

CHAPTER 15

"What the Hells is his issue?" Hermes asked, perplexed.

Hecate elbowed him softly.

"What was that for? I'm not the one who lost my shit over someone else's drama," he said, rubbing his sternum where her elbow had connected.

"Maybe there are some unrequited feelings there, Helios. You ever had a thing with Ares?" Artemis smirked.

Something about that interaction felt intrinsically *wrong* to me, as did the ribbing at Ares's expense.

Helios turned to Nick, who looked a little concerned.

"Nothing has ever happened with Ares. It's not like that. I think he's just . . . upset that I'm mortal," he explained to Nick, who had gone paler and was leaning heavily on his walking stick.

"Why would he give a shit about you being a mortal? He doesn't care about anyone," Hermes quipped.

Beside me, Aphrodite shook with anger, and she stood to undoubtedly let Hermes have it again, but Helios beat her to it.

"Hermes, you haven't been this petulant in fucking decades. What in the Hells is your beef with this situation?" Helios asked, snapping the tension in the room.

Hermes stood as well, and I watched Hades subtly shift Persephone behind his hulking frame, much like Ares had with Aphrodite earlier.

"I just don't understand. I get their Bonds are fucked up. I know it's gotta be hard, but Ares is a straight-up dick all the time. This entire situation could have been avoided if he would have just minded his own business and kept his dick in his pants. I've watched this masochistic love triangle play out over the years, and every time, we have to pick Hephaestus up and watch him rebuild himself again. It's torture. I'm not trying to be an arsehole, but you can't deny how hard it is to witness each time the wheel turns," Hermes finished, throwing his hands high.

Helios yelled, "And who do you think picks up *Ares* every time she goes back to Heph? *He* does. *By his fucking self*. None of you ever cared to see his side, and none of you notice how heavy that kind of pain is. He doesn't have anyone to lean on, and the only person he's ever known that cares about him is actively trying to break her Bond to him. Then, the only one he ever let in to glimpse that pain occasionally, when he's so deep in his cups he can't keep me out, is going to *die*. I've got, what, maybe fifty years left?"

Silence. Revelation. An uncomfortable burning in my chest.

"You see one perspective, and I never felt the need to correct you because it's not my story to tell. Maybe come up off your high horse before that big ass head of yours floats you into the cosmos. Be upset for Heph, sure. But recognize that *none* of them asked for this. You don't have any idea what you're talking about. And the rest of you? Making jokes and shit? You should be ashamed." Shockingly mortal as Helios might have been, his righteous anger swelled through the room, more divine than I remembered as he dressed us all down.

"When Demeter rebelled, he showed up. He cleared out half of the Elysian Fields with Thanatos. Helped bring the soldiers dying of famine here *personally*. He sided with you on Olympus, even though *I* was his friend, because he believed in the right for Hades and Persephone to be together if that's what they wanted. Be better than this. You *have* to be better than this."

A red blush crept up over Helios's neck and cheeks, and I felt shameful for not seeing it all before. Helios's words bounced around in my rib cage like a bullet ricocheting, puncturing holes, blowing crags of my bubbled reality apart with every breath.

He was right.

I always had a solid foundation to pick me up again when Aphrodite inevitably went back to him.

She cried silent tears next to me, and I reached for her, but she flinched away, the shame heavy on her too.

"I'm going to find Ares. Cate, I'll find you later to get questing instructions. Thank you." Aphrodite started toward the door, but Helios reached for her elbow, stopping her.

"I'll go, Ditey. Let me go."

His eyes were sincere, but I swore I could hear the crack in Aphrodite's chest as Helios turned to Nick and brushed a kiss over his knuckles.

"Hermes, Hygieia—will you please get Nick back in bed and make sure he stays there this time? I'll be along soon, baby boy."

Nick nodded in submission, turning for the door with an uncomfortable Hermes and Hygieia on his heels.

The former titan pointed a finger at Hades, who looked like a scolded schoolboy.

"You and I will discuss this later."

Helios was firm, and Hades grimaced, clearly already regretting his tantrum.

I reached for Aphrodite, who let me touch her without recoiling this time. I felt her despair, her guilt, as it flooded our Bond. I pulled her close, running my hands over her shaking body. She was devastated, the wounds open and fresh and laid bare for all to see.

As for me . . . I found myself wanting to go and explain myself to Ares. I wanted to . . . I don't know what I wanted to do. Where would we even begin?

Instead, I focused on Aphrodite, on the demolished goddess in my arms, on the one I could fix and give comfort to.

"I can't ask him to be a part of this, Cate." Aphrodite picked at her nails nervously. If she kept on, she'd bend and bite them down to the quick and be miserable.

I placed my hand over hers and gave them a gentle squeeze.

"You're just not strong enough for the trials without them. You could die a True Death out there, Ditey. It isn't remotely safe in the best of conditions, but especially so when you're Bond sick."

Cate's assessment scared me.

"Okay, so how do I cure the Bond sickness? It just started, so maybe it's like a bad fever. Is there a cure?" Aphrodite asked, hopeful, the gears turning behind those dark eyes, shining with fresh determination.

"Well, there is something that could . . . keep the sickness at bay, but you aren't going to like it." Hecate seemed nervous now, her eyes traveling anywhere but to meet mine.

I had a sinking feeling I knew what this secret cure was, but I swallowed down the nerves and let her finish.

"Okay, great, tell me what to do." Aphrodite leaned in, intent to catch every word.

Hecate looked at me, finally, and mouthed a silent "I'm sorry" before turning back to Aphrodite. "You can feed it. The Bonds, I mean. They need connection, Aphrodite. They're rebelling because of neglect and then overuse, the same as Persephone and Hades had. Feed into it. Give them every chance to suck the corruption from your bones, disperse it in small doses."

Aphrodite looked skeptical, and Hecate stood, pointing a finger at her in warning. "Before you dismiss my words, hear this: That corruption is *going* to spread. Those Bonds aren't just corded around you; there's one that leads to Hephaestus, and one to Ares. Once you reach a point of no return, where a necrotic Bond is riddled with corruption, it'll feed itself off of them, and then you'll all be lost to it."

I watched the moment realization dawned in Aphrodite's eyes and a flicker of temptation passed over her face before she schooled her expression. She could martyr herself for her cause, but she was less likely to allow Ares and I to do the same.

"I'll consider what you've said. We all have a lot to talk about. Heph?" She held her hand out to me, and I noticed how low to the nail bed she'd chewed her nails in her intense anxiety. The tender pink flesh swelled angrily around her choppy cuticle, and I reached for her hand, without hesitation.

Warmth spread between us where our skin touched, starved for so long. I sucked in a breath and led her out into the hall, tracing the familiar path to my quarters. The silence grew thick between us as we walked quietly, as her melancholy leached through the Bond, and a ball of pressure took up residence in my chest. I needed to assure her, to command that pain away from her.

The desire to protect her was ingrained in the very marrow of my bones. I stopped short, tugging her into my arms, soaking in the feel of her body against mine. Her soft curves melted against the hard planes of my body, caged by my arms, her breasts pressing against my chest with every shallow breath that fell from her lips. My proximity made her nervous, and I craved that too.

Those eyes . . . The pale blue-gray irises that shifted every which way in the light. They were depths I used to love getting lost in, when I'd convinced myself they were only mine.

Aphrodite, as the Goddess of Love, was the personification of desire. That led to its own list of complications, but one of the minor inconveniences it caused was her appearance to others. If the person looking at her was attracted to brunettes, her hair would appear just a few shades darker to fit that preference. Same for her eyes. They shifted depending on who looked into them, and no two people gave the same description of her. She was an enigma of desire, of want, of cosmos-shattering beauty, evoking all the feelings of lust and need. Only I saw her as she was, *exactly* as she was.

Maybe Ares too, but I'd never asked, never wanted to know. I could pretend that those eyes were only for me. Now, they were glassy with unshed tears as Aphrodite stared up at me, cheeks flushed with self-hatred. She cast them downward, and I traced my fingers under her jaw and tilted her head to look at me properly.

"Tell me what it is you need," I demanded, and I watched her lips part a fraction, just a millimeter when my breath fanned over her. Something deep and ancient rumbled inside me. Something primal, familiar.

Aphrodite let out a small huff, a cynical sound that shot straight through my bones. "I want all of this to not be so fucked up, Hephaestus. I should have stayed away. All I do is mess your life up, and no matter how much of an asshole he is, Hermes is right. This is my fault. And now? You could die because of me. Ares could die because of me. All because I wasn't strong enough to do what needed to be done."

Her voice cracked, shaking a deep chasm across my chest. "Heph, I don't know what to do here."

She looked pale, shaky, and her pallor reminded me of someone who'd spent their life in the darkness. Aphrodite wasn't built for that. She was born of the sea, of the sun and foam and waves. She was life. She was an entire solar system within herself. She was *my* sun.

And I burned for her. I knew what she needed, and she knew that I could feel it, and yet she stood steadfast, unable to ask it of me. Even if it meant she withered into chaos and corruption. Even if it meant I did eventually too.

I smoothed a piece of hair back from her cheek and tucked it behind her ear. "I don't want you to apologize, Ditey. I want you to take what you need. There are things we need to discuss, and don't for one moment think that I'm going to let you wither away in front of me."

My words were soft, commanding. I could feel the sensation of power waking up within me. The need to command. The need to feel her pulse under my fingers.

The need to control.

Aphrodite opened her mouth to protest, ever the defiant little thing. The edge of my lips quirked up just a fraction, anticipating the way I knew she would fight me.

I backed her up until we were standing at the threshold of my door, twisting her as we walked forward so her back pressed against my chest. My elbow came to rest just over her breast, now rising and falling in rapt attention. My fingers snaked up the valley of her chest to wrap around her throat, not tightly as to obstruct, but enough that she understood.

And understood she did.

Aphrodite inched forward, pressing her delicate neck into my palm, and I lavished the feel of her, of the pleasure that spread in a consuming wave through my skin. She loved this, loved the passion, the possession, and fucking Hells, I wanted to show her everything we'd been missing out on these last years.

Urgency fueled me, warned me that, any moment, she could push me away, return us to the darkness. I backed her through my door, kicking it shut behind us as we ventured deeper into my chambers, eyes blazing into hers, my grip firmly in place as I rested my other hand on the hip of her low-slung pants.

Her blood called to mine, singing a siren song from just below the surface, and I was reminded of how hot we burned together, skin and breath and teeth, her tender flesh flushing, begging for me to knead it, to strike it, to watch the skin bloom deep crimson.

As if reading my mind, Aphrodite arched her ass into me, grinding against my lengthening cock. It didn't matter that I'd come twice already today, she hungered for my desire, and she would have it, always. Such was the might of her power.

She could pull from me as many times as she needed to be satisfied. No limit existed. I would always be willing to give her more.

I pushed my hand slowly down over her hip, sliding gently over the exposed skin there, tracing the path *he* took. When my hand disappeared behind the waistband of her pants, her breath hitched, chest rising in an arch, an offering. Painfully slowly, I slipped the pad of my finger between her folds, sliding around her clit without actually touching it, teasing her, torturing us both.

Aphrodite's succulent moans fed me, stoked the need I had for her, soothed the ache of missing her, and I was as desperate to feel her as she was to have my touch.

I inhaled her scent slowly, filling my lungs with her anticipation, her eagerness, with hints of the jasmine that swirled in the air, and other notes, new and spellbinding, as I ran my fingers through her hair and buried my nose in the crook of her neck. My lips followed the trail others had taken to the side of her throat, nestling in the long tendrils of her hair, tasting another essence on her flesh. Her pulse jumped under my lips, her temperature rising with every delay, every fucking moment as I edged us both.

"I want you to undress for me, Little Love. Slowly. Take your time. And if you do, if it pleases me, I'll give you what you crave," I whispered into the shell of her ear, the words unhurried as I steeled my resolve.

Aphrodite stiffened, just a fraction, just for a moment, but I felt the alarm and her hesitation as it seeped through our Bond.

"Do you object, Aphrodite? Words, Little Love." I loosened my grip on her chin, and air flooded past her lips on a gasp when my fingers passed gently over her clit, the touch no more than a tease.

"It's not that," she panted, breathless, driftless and needy.

I ramped up the speed, the pressure, delving deeper. She was soaked, warm and aching, and it was within my power to give her the relief she needed.

Or to deny it.

"Then, tell me, love. Why the hesitation? Is your mind elsewhere?" I asked, trailing my lips under the soft flesh of her ear, my breath dancing down the tender skin of her throat. Goose bumps erupted over her neck, traveled down her top, and though she writhed, she didn't give me what I wanted.

"*I need . . .*" she panted, breathless. "I need to shower first."

My body responded to her confession, violently opposed to moving her even an inch, to letting her put any space between us. She had been with Ares, just hours ago. I'd watched him fuck her, witnessed her riding him, and even now, I could see it so clearly, but instead of loathing, I felt only power. Power, at the knowledge I'd made him wait to have his pleasure, pushed him to give her satisfaction until I'd allowed him to come. *Inside her.*

I groaned, inhaling deep, scenting him on her, now that I had placed it. She still smelled of jasmine, yes, but there was more. A hint of the spiced edge, of fire and fury and, Fates, him. The knowledge slithered through forbidden parts of me, down my spine, straight to my already leaking cock. I felt my torso heat, felt my goddess melt into the warmth and comfort there. The thought of him being inside her should have repulsed me, should have made me blind with rage, but instead, I felt a rush and burning curiosity.

A challenge.

My limbs maneuvered us to the edge of my bed, of our bed. One we'd shared so many years ago as I kissed her, drinking deep the whimpers of protestation she offered, forbidden wine from tormented lips.

Aphrodite's knees brushed against the edge of the bed, and I spun her, releasing my hold on her cunt and her throat, my tone both gentle and mocking as she cried out at the loss. I soothed her as I sat her down on the edge of my bed, lifting her slightly to clear the footboard, and she stayed, knowing the reward would be divine pleasure.

I stood, reaching above to pull down the beam I'd built to swivel from any side of the large bed it was accessible for use. The steel came alive under my touch, releasing the chain that lay threaded through a metal rung. Aphrodite adjusted, body arranged obediently on the edge of my bed, back straight, head tilted toward me, soft palms open and facing up on her lap.

A thrum of electricity coursed through our Bond, and I knew that, under her shirt, her nipples would be puckered and ready for me to devour, that she was sliding into a space that only I could reach her, my goddess barely breathing in anticipation.

I pulled the chain lower, adjusting to her height as Aphrodite's eyes followed my every move.

Waiting patiently.

So fucking patiently.

Keeping the chain in one hand above me, I reached the other down and unbuckled my leather belt, flicking the end lazily, sliding it by the buckle out of the loops. The soft leather gripped naturally in my hands as I tested the edges to make sure there were safe for this. This belt had been with me for so long that the leather was well-worn and pliant, supple.

Just like my needy girl.

I gripped the belt firmly between my fingers, and Aphrodite inched a centimeter closer, rolling her hips, searching for friction on the silk sheets beneath her. I reached to trace those full, magnificent lips. Lips I very much wanted to taste, but not yet.

Not quite yet.

I smeared her soft pink lipstick with my fingers, painting the area around Aphrodite's mouth, making a mess of her before tracing a line down her jaw, over her chest, until my hands found her wrists. I brought them up together, higher to me, and pressed a kiss to the soft flesh of each, feeling her pulse flutter beneath the delicate skin.

"I should shower," she whispered, so tender, barely audible. A deep blush crept over her chest, and I groaned deep and low in my throat, wanting more of that beautiful color staining her skin.

"Ditey." I sighed as I wrapped the leather deftly around her wrists, binding them in a safe but secure fashion that would release when only the right pressure was applied. She knew how to get out of this knot if she wanted to; we'd used it countless times in our bedroom activities. Safe words, hard limits . . . we'd explored them thoroughly.

I lifted her up, eyes catching on the curves of her breathtaking body as I draped her bound wrists through the chain dangling from the rung. Her muscles pulled taunt, just barely comfortable on the floor, and I hummed in anticipation.

The skin of her stomach peeked out from her top, the urge to put my hands on her overwhelming. I splayed my fingers over her abdomen, relishing the way she leaned toward my body, how hers called for my touch. I turned her slowly until she was facing the headboard, bound standing still to the ceiling, and with one arm, I grabbed the hem of my shirt and ripped it over my head. I climbed onto the bed, using the beams to hold me steady, and all the while, Aphrodite watched, eyes hooded with desire as I approached.

Her pink tongue swiped over her bottom lip, hungry, starved as I flicked the button of my jeans free. The zipper came next, slowly, deliberately. I thought of how Ares had taken her, with wild abandon. She'd enjoyed it, wanted it, but she also loved this, loved what only I could feed her. She leaned forward as far as she could, chest high as she tried to close the distance. Keeping her so far away was torture to her.

Sweet, delicious denial.

I slid my hands into my jeans and fisted my cock, already red and swollen and heavy with want for her. I slipped it past the zipper, preened under Aphrodite's ravenous gaze, the jasmine that bloomed heavy in the air at the sight of my piercings.

"Those are new," she breathed, straining more. She bit her lip, and I reached for her mouth, which she opened obediently. The pads of my fingers slid inside, and her mouth closed around them, tongue tracing the heady tang of her arousal from my fingertips. So wet, so fucking warm.

Aphrodite moaned, and I pulled from her to cover my swollen head with her saliva. A bead of pearlescent pre-cum pooled in my slit, and I wanted her, needed her, to taste it, but I was patient.

Slowly stroking my shaft, fingers dancing along my piercings, I waited. Watching.

"You remember your safe word?" I asked, knowing full well that she did, that I would still have to watch her body, because she wouldn't heed her own limits in the pursuit of pleasure.

"Yes." She opened her mouth.

I slipped the tip of my head just inside, brushing past lips that could launch a thousand wars.

She moaned as she sucked me deep, pulling my body forward with the sheer force of her will and tongue, so divine I had to grab the beam to steady myself.

This was what true nirvana felt like.

Aphrodite took me deeper, hungrily devouring my thick shaft, but it wasn't rushed or hurried. She ran that wicked tongue over the studded metal, eliciting a moan from somewhere deep inside my chest, and she preened with satisfaction, so in tune with the slightest admission of praise. She pulled on the restraints as she took me faster, deeper in her hot, wet mouth, frustrated she couldn't do more to touch me.

I reached a hand down to wrap around her soft locks, pulled her tighter against me, obstructing the airflow.

The Goddess of Love relaxed her throat, encouraging me deeper, her lips pressed flush to my base as she sucked what little air she had inside her cheeks out, molding the flesh of her mouth around me in a vice.

My knees buckled, vision darkening in the corners as flashes of someone *else* forced themselves in my mind. *Memories not my own, of her, of Ares, of tender touches and whispered secrets, of a rage-filled moment in a dark tent, the fury of the God of War as she ran into his arms with a torn chiton and tears in her eyes, as the God of Gods straightened himself, as Ares drew his sword . . .*

I gripped both sides of her head and braced, pulling my shaft free of her protesting lips as she fought me for control. My entire body shook at the implications of that shared vision. That unintentional memory knocked the breath from my lungs.

"Flame." I wheezed, reaching up to undo the knot in the leather.

Confusion. Rejection. Emotions flashed in her pale eyes as I scrambled back off the bed, pacing away the rage flushing my spine, curling my hands into fists at my side.

"Hephaestus?" she asked. "What is it? What's wrong?"

I turned, mid-pace, to see her sitting there, hands clasped in front of her, eyebrows furrowed in worry.

"Did you mean to show me that?" I croaked, throat burning.

She shook her head, confused.

"Show you what?" The stricken look on my face must have really scared her, because she rose from the bed, crossed the space between us, and when her hand met my cheek, it was my body that shook hers.

"I saw something just now. Something you never told me about. A memory, I think, but it flashed by so fast, still—" I looked down at her wide, lovely eyes, the words dying on my lips. How could I ask her this?

How could I not?

"Heph, you're scaring me. What did you see?" she urged, petting my jaw, brushing the hair that had fallen into my face back.

"You can tell me anything." I responded, and she narrowed her eyes, tilting her head.

"I know that, Hephaestus, I—"

"Did he hurt you? Did that bastard— Did he— " I couldn't speak, for the inferno that ripped up my throat arrested my vocal cords.

"Ares? No, of course not. He would never hurt me, Hephaestus," she defended, but I shook my head.

"Not Ares, Aphrodite. Not him. *Zeus*." I spat his name with a deadly hatred, and the way the color drained from her face was as much damnation as I needed to see.

"H-how did you . . . ?" She searched my face, my eyes, the shake of my hands as my body vibrated with violence.

"I saw it. I saw the after. I saw Ares, you running to him. Crying. I saw him draw his sword against his father."

Her hands retreated from my body, wrapping around her torso as she stepped back, turning away from me, shielding herself. I hated the distance between us, but so much made sense now.

"I never wanted you to see that, Hephaestus. I didn't want you to have to know. I'm sorry, I'm so sorry," she pleaded with me, turning to face me once more, and the internalized shame and guilt tore a fresh wound inside my shade. How could this be her fault? Any person's fault, other than the monster who hurt her?

"You *never* have to apologize to me for anything, Aphrodite. I'll kill him, I swear to you. I'll find a way to rip his shade into nothingness for what he did to you," I vowed, taking a step closer, then hesitating.

Tears welled up in her eyes as she tilted her head, gave me a soft, sad smile. "He didn't. *Almost*. But I was lucky. Ares heard my screams and he . . . I called. He came."

She sniffed, and I felt my hands flex open at my sides, the want to hug her, to soothe her nearly overwhelming, but having been best friends with Medusa for over five centuries, I had some experience with trauma survivors. I knew I needed to wait for her to tell me what *she* wanted.

Fucking Fates.

"I'm so sorry, Little Love. I never knew."

She shook her head, swiping away tears from beneath her eyes. "I know. I didn't want you to know, and it wasn't like we could tell anyone."

"He married you to me to punish you, didn't he?" The words tasted like ash on my tongue, as we stood there and ripped it all open.

She nodded as she sank down onto the bed. "You asked me only once why, and I couldn't answer you. But it was because I was scared of what he would do if I told. Scared that no one would believe me. But you, Hephaestus, you looked at me like I was good, and I wanted to be that for you, but I already loved Ares too, and, Fates, I . . ."

Tears broke then, bursting like a dam, and I knelt down, lowering myself to her, crawling across the floor on my knees, stopping just short of where she sat.

"I loved him, but I loved you too. Ares was falling apart. He was falling apart in a way I couldn't watch, and you were so loved, Hephaestus. Maybe not by Zeus, but by everyone else, and he never had that. You were born of Hera, raised with her love and protection, but Ares was born of Zeus, from his rage and spite, and he never had a kind hand to touch him. Zeus honed him into a blunt instrument of rage and killing and pointed him at enemies with not a scrap of affection. But he came when I called. He always does."

I reached for her then, hesitated, but she only cried harder.

"Please, don't do that. Don't treat me like glass, like you're afraid to touch me!" She sobbed, and it was all the permission I needed.

My fingers laced through her hair as I lifted her body to mine, cradling her against my chest, her fingers a death grip on my bicep, my nape, anywhere she could reach. I rocked her, sat with her, cried with her, buried my face in the crown of her hair, and let my heart beat a metronome in time with hers.

It was a long time before the sobs quieted and the grip lessened; and though questions still burned inside me, I waited, stilling my tongue, because that was what she needed right now.

When she finally did speak, her voice was soft and raw, messy in all the ways this had always been.

"Everyone thinks he's just like Zeus, but he's not, Hephaestus. He's not." She seemed desperate for me to believe her, to see him for more than what he'd always been, and I wanted to give her whatever she needed.

"Show me, then. Show me the Ares you know."

She looked up at me, eyes rimmed red. Sniffled. "Are you sure?"

I nodded.

Aphrodite pressed a still trembling hand to my face, cupping my jaw as her eyes fell shut, and she made me *see*.

Aphrodite

CHAPTER 16

ANCIENT GREECE

I felt his presence before he melted out of the shadows. My body lit up as soon as Ares's chest pressed against my back, strong arms banded around me, pulling me into the privacy of a small room off the main Olympian Hall.

He was on me instantly, the heat of his touch staggering as his lips sealed to mine, desperate, aching as his fingers held me close.

I melted against him, needy and wanton, as he pressed my back to the cold stone, lifting my legs to wrap around his torso. The dance was automatic, so natural our bodies reacted on their own accord, the stubble of his beard scratching along the column of my throat.

I moaned against his lips, wincing as his hand skated over my breast, tender from Hephaestus's bite.

Hephaestus.

Cold water doused over me as my wits returned, and it took all my divine might to push my hands against Ares's chest, breaking his kiss. Anger and shame burned heaving and hard in my chest as I shoved, and though he could have easily stood his ground, Ares gently set me back on my own two feet and retreated a few steps, both of us gasping for air.

I looked at him then, and what I saw wrecked me. It had been months since Zeus and Hera had announced my betrothal, since I'd ended things with Ares, and every inch of that distance showed on his face.

"We c-cannot do this," I panted, pushing my hair back.

Ares let out a wounded noise, a strangled choke from deep in his throat, as his eyes raked over me, red-rimmed.

"Teaching him all the ways the Goddess of Love enjoys being fucked?" he asked, voice low. He nodded to the exposed skin revealed beneath the strap of my chiton as it fell down my shoulder, exposing the bruises Hephaestus had lovingly left, gentle hands turned rough at my request. Ares's eyes caught on the darkened spots before I could cover them.

I lifted my head at the venom in his tone, at the anger and ire and betrayal.

"He is my husband, Ares," I defended, gently though. None of this was his fault, but it wasn't Hephaestus's either, and the God of the Forge had . . . inspired something I hadn't expected, that I wasn't sure I could put into words yet.

"Does it mean nothing to you? What built between us?" The defeat in his words wounded me more deeply than if he would have shouted.

I shook my head as tears welled in my eyes, cursing Hera, cursing Zeus.

Hating them all for this pain.

I closed the distance between us, allowed his hands to circle my waist, offering us both comfort that wasn't mine to give.

"You know it was everything. Everything," I whispered, pressing our foreheads together.

"Then let us run. I love you, Aphrodite. I cannot do this. I cannot watch you give yourself to another. Choose me, little goddess," he urged, bringing both hands up to my face. Tears leaked from the corners of his eyes, and his hands, the ones that inflicted so much carnage, so much violence, were tender against my skin. "Am I yours? And are you mine?"

We both stilled as the words fell from his lips, neither of us drawing breath, both of us knowing the impact and covenant they conveyed.

"Ares, I—"

"Do not. Do not stand here and tell me placations. If you love me, choose me. Choose us." He dropped to both knees, reaching for my hands, eyes full of hope, and all the feelings and affections I'd felt for Hephaestus quieted. "If you want me to beg, I will. You are the only weakness I would ever bow to, Aphrodite. Please." His resolve shook as he searched my face, unsure.

Undone.

"You are. I am." The words left me on a rushed breath, but the smile that lit his face, Fates, it was everything. I had loved him for so long, Ares was woven into every part of me, except the way that would defy Olympus. I had thought of a thousand ways out of this, when we'd first been told of the edict, and Bonding had been something I'd considered before.

Before.

"How would we do it?" he asked, and I knew he was worried about Hera. The Goddess of Marriage was the only way to solidify a Bond, or so we had always been told.

"I think I know of a way."

We wasted no time in searching out Hecate, and though it was a risk even telling her of our intentions, I leaned on the love our friendship carried. I spent all the goodwill I had ever earned just for her to try.

I stood in front of the God of War and pledged myself to him, in heart, body, and shade, but the entire time, I ached for the loss of Hephaestus, the heart I knew would break, but he would survive. Surrounded by love and affections, he would heal and love again.

I feared that Ares wouldn't survive losing us, the only gentle touch he'd ever had.

When the Bond settled over my skin, there was a bittersweet comfort to it, a painful edge like the blade of a knife. But then, the pain had begun. Splitting. Blinding.

We tried everything to fix it, the Goddess of Witchcraft working overtime to heal the tether that should have never taken, but it was only Ares's touch that soothed it. We were reckless, him consumed with fixing me, and I out of my mind with pain. It was in my bed, with the God of War's hands on my body and Hephaestus's scent surrounding me, that the pain finally subsided enough for me to see him there, in the shadows.

Betrayal etched into brown eyes that had broken us all.

*

Hephaestus sat still, hardly breathing as he watched, and when I lowered my hand, I felt a weight—the burden, maybe—of carrying these secrets for so many lifetimes lift.

His eyes fluttered open, glassy and full of pain, but understanding, too, because now he knew. Not everything, but the most important of those things. The rest belonged to Ares, and only he could share those things with another, the way he'd shared with me.

"He must have been so lonely." The words left his lips on a low whisper, and I wondered what he was feeling, what he made of it all, now that he knew.

"He was raised to be an island, and I don't think he ever learned any other way to be. He wasn't gifted a chosen family, Hephaestus. I wasn't either. Hells, I doubt any of the other gods would have ever even spoken with me if I hadn't been your wife."

I watched as the God of the Forge scrubbed his hand down his face and let out a low, frustrated sigh, because he knew I spoke truth.

"I was the interloper here. All this time, it was *him* being branded a homewrecker, but it was actually *me*. No wonder he fucking hates me, I'd hate me too."

"I think he envies what you have, and I'm not saying you didn't face hardships. I know how rough it was growing up having to see Zeus, but it's different," I replied.

"Do you think my mother knew? When she helped arrange this, do you think she knew about the two of you?" he asked, and I could see it gnawing at him. His relationship with Hera had been strained since she'd refused to let us out of our marriage, had basically forced us to Bond. Sure, it would erase the one between Ares and me, but it hadn't. It had ruined us beyond repair.

"I don't know," I answered as honestly as I could. "Zeus forbade Ares from being with another divine deity, convinced it would be a conflict of loyalty and somehow have him compromised in his duty as Warden of Tartarus, but even after he pulled Ares up from the Pits, he never lifted the edict. By the time things escalated between us, he had already marked me as a threat to his power over his son, but we were careful. He never could prove it . . . until you caught us. The punishment Ares suffered was . . . severe."

I shuddered, thinking of the scars on his back, the thousand lashings Zeus had personally whipped across his flesh . . .

The screams he'd held inside as golden blood painted his skin.

Hephaestus's hands cradled my face, his thumb brushing softly across my cheek as he looked into my eyes.

"I'm so sorry for all the pain I caused, Aphrodite." Such bittersweet sadness. Such kindhearted, genuine care. It leaked from him, every pore, every muscle, on every breath that filled his lungs.

"I'm not sorry for you. I'm not sorry that I got to love you, and that might be my greatest sin of all," I admitted on a whisper, dusting kisses to the corner of his mouth, the soft pillow of his lips. He had a beard now, shorn short, but I loved the way it scraped against my skin, roughed up against my cheek.

He hesitated, pulling back, searching my eyes for signs of distress, but he would find none there.

I deepened the kiss, clawing at him, holding on for dear life as he returned the embrace, gave my body what I craved by divine mandate.

He didn't hesitate again when he re-bound my hands, lifted my body back to that beam. His fingers no longer shook as he brushed the hair back from my cheek. No, Hephaestus was calm, steady as an oak, back in the saddle of control, and I let him give us both what we needed, for the first time ever, with no more secrets between us.

Hephaestus

CHAPTER 17

Too much information had overloaded my mind, but this was methodical. *This* I could harness and sink into, something much simpler than just myself. The chaos that wrestled with my mind—the knowing meeting the revelation—was too much, too big, and because Aphrodite knew it, too, she'd led us back here, to the push and pull that settled my bones.

Bliss. It was bliss to be inside her mouth, soft lips wrapped around my cock, tongue swirling over the sides of my shaft, caressing the barbells of each rung of my ladder. Her eyes softened as she whimpered around me, pushing her head deeper, choking on my length, *starved* for it.

I marveled at her, at her strength and resilience, but I craved her surrender. Easing my hips back again, I retreated, the air too cold against the mess she'd made of me.

Aphrodite let out a cry of frustration, indignant at the loss of her prize, and I smirked at the defiance in her eyes, that wild, unbridled fury in her stare. The force I was required to use, prying my cock from her lips, pulled a few pieces of hair from her roots.

I hissed, massaging her scalp with gentle pressure.

Aphrodite moaned, leaned into my touch, before shaking her head out of the fog of lust and shooting daggers at me with her eyes.

"You pulled away." She sulked, bruised lips pulled up in a pout.

I smiled down at her, letting a hand trail her jaw and grip her chin until there was nearly nothing between us. Her breathing stuttered and stalled in anticipation as she sucked up the air that fell from my lips to hers, so close to where she wanted me to be.

"You wanted to suck me dry, Little Love?" I teased.

She nodded.

I moved closer, invading her space, but not touching, not yet. "You wanted to shower first before I touched you. Why? Answer me, and I'll let you finish what you started."

My words hit her like a slap, a mix of crimson shame and something hotter, more forbidden, wrestled behind her eyes. Somewhere deep inside, the idea of admitting what she had done with Ares to me was enough to deny her the pleasure she wanted, but it turned her on to imagine it. It was the clearest I'd ever felt her, through our Bond, and Fates, the thought of it, of her full of us, the power she'd wield . . .

Aphrodite wasn't solely submissive, and I loved that fire within her, that she would push the limits of my own patience, seeing how far she could take it before I snapped. Power exchange between us had always been one of careful control, with rules and safeguards. I exerted only as much flex as she allowed, and she enjoyed watching me fall apart after pushing her to her limits, riding the lines between pleasure and pain, the cruel blade of it seductive as it was biting. I wanted her to admit her desires to me, to crack them open wide and let me feed her.

Serve her.

But she wasn't ready yet to admit those hidden thoughts out loud.

I tucked my still hard cock inside my jeans, not bothering with the zipper.

Aphrodite whimpered. She flushed deep, the blush delicate on her skin, and I bit down on a closed fist, steadying my breath as I watched it spread across her chest, up the slope of her neck.

My mind warred with my body, one needing release, the other needing supplication. In the end, the mind won, and I waited, considering, her pants dropping unevenly between us. Would she tell me, or deny us both?

Aphrodite sucked her bottom lip under her teeth, averted her eyes. Hiding from me.

Something seemed to be . . . *shifting* . . . in the confines of our relationship. Not just with Aphrodite and me, but with Ares too. I opened up the Bond between us, accepting the onslaught, feeling past the corruption and shame. I wanted to feel what she felt. For years, Ares had been the elephant in the room, the third person in our marriage, the phantom in our bed, the wind that took her away when she couldn't deny her love for him. I did my best to hide my hate, and she, her desire. No more.

The decision was far too simple to make, the choice clear as I closed my eyes, offering her the truth, uttering words that could either break us apart or build a new bridge.

"If I want you cleaned of Ares's cum before I fuck you, I'll bathe you myself."

Aphrodite's eyes flashed to mine; lips parted on a gasp. She shuffled slightly away, as though her position exposed her even fully clothed.

I snaked my hand out, wrapping a possessive hold around the column of her throat, gently pulling her closer. "You wanted to shower because he's still here, still inside you"

Tears welled up in her eyes as shame, white-hot and debilitating, began to leak. I kissed over them, tasted the salty wetness that painted her cheeks.

"Shh, shh. No need for tears, love. But if he's inside of you now, I can't let one drop of my cum spill down your throat. Do you know why?" I savored the harsh, shallow pants falling from her lips. My fingers gripped her chin, applying just enough pressure to make her focus. "Because if he's inside you, Aphrodite, it's only fair that *I* get to be represented there too."

Lust so potent I nearly came washed over her, thrummed through me, delicious and divine as her body admitted what her lips couldn't.

My mouth collided with hers in a searing kiss, a tangle of tongues and teeth as we fought for dominance. She wanted to lose, but she wanted to feel she'd put up her fight first.

I grabbed the hem of her shirt, lifting it high up her arms until I reached her elbows. The fabric stretched, twisting a small knot that kept her forearms bound together. Leather rustled as I unbuckled her belt, her pants next, taking care to kiss long trails over her bra, tonguing her nipples through the lacey cups.

I hopped off the bed, positioning behind her, palming the globes of her ass, kneading the soft muscle, fingers slipping beneath the lace of her panties. They stayed in place, a little something to play with later as I drank her in, parched, refamiliarizing myself with her body on every caress.

"He got to fill that pretty cunt up, Little Love." I slipped my finger under the lace gusset, teasing the slick seam beneath the flimsy fabric. "Is that him leaking out of you now? Should I fuck it back into you before I fill you myself?"

Sweet moans rewarded me when a thick finger sank inside, as she pulsed around me, welcoming me home.

"Is that what you want?" I prompted.

She shook.

"Then be a good girl and tell me, Ditey. Tell me where you want your cock." I stroked slowly, stretching her tight warmth through whimpers. I withdrew my finger and slid it up, higher toward her ass, circling her tight ring with the pad of my finger coated in her.

"Yes, there, here, I want you everywhere, please," she begged, *begged*. My cock throbbed for her.

"Everywhere, Little Love? We can make everywhere happen. Shall I get the Master?" At my words, I thrust another finger inside her, pulled her body flush with mine, leaned her head back against my chest as I worked.

Aphrodite bucked her hips, pushing herself farther onto my fingers as she rocked, chasing her pleasure. She was close, so close, and I gripped her breast with my other hand as I pumped inside her, until she dripped down my wrist, coating my skin with her sweet essence. I couldn't resist running a finger up to her tight ring, pressing inside to my first knuckle.

"You want me to fuck both these pretty holes? To fill them both at the same time? Use your words, Ditey, or you don't get to come." I stilled my hands and pulled my finger back to the first joint.

Her thighs trembled, the weight of her body sagging against me and the beam. A quick slap to her breast had her bucking against me, mewling as I thrust back in.

"Please, both, yes, oh Fates, Hephaestus. I can't. P-please let me come." Delicious surrender, as I continued stimulating her most sensitive holes, alternating between massaging and pinching her breasts.

I smiled as she rode me.

"Such a good girl, stretching for me. See what happens when you do what you're told, Little Love? You get to come, Ditey. I'm so proud of you." The hand attending to her breast dropped lower, delving between her lips to circle her engorged clit, her pulse wild beneath my lips.

"Come, and I'll fill you up, every drop," I promised, peppering kisses under her jaw, on her neck.

The sensations from so much stimulation shook Aphrodite apart, and she came, doubling over as she coated us both with her arousal. The fingers over her clit slowed and, with it, the wet sounds filling the room as Aphrodite moaned and panted.

"Such a beautiful mess, so hungry for me. Dripping for me," I groaned, breathless and triumphant, as she slid her tongue over her lips and looked up at me through long, pale lashes.

"Fair is fair, Hephaestus. I'll take that cock now," she demanded.

The taste of her was delicious as I cleaned my fingers, savoring her as I walked to the large closet hidden behind a panel and pressed a stone under my palm. The door slid back to reveal my toy box.

Our toy box.

The metal chest had resided here, in the only true permanent residence I'd ever had, since the last time she'd left me. I slid a hand slowly over each device, keenly aware of Aphrodite's eyes on my every move. I took my time, picking up a few and turning them over in my hands before changing my mind and replacing them. Every replacement was met with a disappointed sigh. I turned to see Aphrodite, a vision tied to the balance beam, naked and bound except for those panties I was going to ruin, the inside of her thighs coated in her slick and the remnants of Ares's cum.

As if summoned, a knock sounded at the door.

I turned, knowing, without knowing how, that Ares had made his way to my chambers. I locked eyes with Aphrodite, who looked mortified and vulnerable. My legs ate up the distance between us swiftly as I brought her face to mine.

"For every word you say, I'll go down an inch in size." I kissed her once, zipped up my fly, leaving the button undone, before I grabbed the rod, infusing it with my power. It started to ripple in my hand, a low vibration, while my essence welded to the metal. Gently, I traced the blunt head across the backs of her thighs, slid the warm gold between her thighs, teasing as I slipped it into her slick channel.

"Not a word," I commanded as she let out a soft moan. I turned back to the door, a little high strung as a pang of anxiety bolted through my chest. If we were going to rip off the Band-Aid of whatever this was, this was as good a time as any.

With a calming exhale, I opened the door to find a very awkward-looking Ares facing me, hands shoved deep in the pockets of *my* jeans. Hair tousled, knuckles busted, a wave of concern washed over me as I took him in. I made sure to open the door just enough to conversate but not yet expose Aphrodite.

Ares ran his large hand over the back of his neck uncomfortably. His gaze fell over my torso, down my inked arms to the sculpted planes of my chest, and there was something in the way he traced over my skin, a validation in his perusal, that stoked my ego. He cleared his throat, swallowing thickly, as his eyes caught on my unbuttoned jeans, the exposed skin underneath.

"Hey. Hephaestus. Uhm, have you seen Aphrodite? We should all talk, I think." His tone was clipped, but I could tell he was attempting neutrality, the restraint lined every tense muscle in his body. He looked so different to my eyes, standing there, and it was as though seeing him through *her* memory, the most broken and vulnerable versions that he'd only ever allowed Aphrodite to see, overwrote many of the preconceived notions I'd had about the God of War.

I studied him for a beat, sizing up the likelihood this ended in a brawl, the death of one or both of us.

The chances were high.

"I have actually. I want to invite you to come in so we can talk, but I'm in the middle of something. If you can behave, you can stay. If you are going to cause a fight, I'd ask you to turn around and leave now."

A low current of dominance thrummed between us, lacing my words. I watched Ares viscerally react to it, forcing myself to remain calm as he did. Part of him bristled at the command in my voice, the flinch in his face unmistakable, but another part of him, one that I'd seen during that ritual . . . perked up at it.

They warred behind deep brown eyes and furrowed brows, and I wondered which would win out, with what came next.

"I don't understand. Where is she? Hecate said some pretty intense things, and we need to figure out how we're going to move forward. If she gets sicker, it won't matter if she wants to break the Bonds. That won't be anyone's choice." The severe urgency of his tone, threaded with forced civility, went against his very nature when it came to me.

"I absolutely agree. And there's more. After you left, Cate suggested Aphrodite could possibly heal, but the method is somewhat . . . unconventional," I cautioned, but Ares zeroed in on the only sentence that mattered to him.

"Anything. I'll do anything. What does she need?" he asked, breathless, a cautious hope shining in his eyes.

The tendons in my chest pulled tight. I could feel the affection Aphrodite felt at hearing his words, feel a rush of tenderness flood through our goddess at the sincerity in his voice.

I braced my arm on the side of the door leaning closer.

"Anything?" I raised an eyebrow in question.

No hesitation.

"*Anything.*"

An unfathomable conviction.

"For starters, you can be *real* calm with what I'm about to show you. As I said, if you can behave, you can stay. If not, well, you may be the God of War, but I carry a pretty large maul, and I'm adept at using it. What do you say, Ares?"

He studied me, wary.

"Where is Aphrodite, Hephaestus?" His tone lowered, and the magic of his call permeated the room.

Aphrodite let out a small whimper.

I tensed.

Ares's eyes ticked to the side, the tumblers falling into place, but before he could barge in, I side stepped, held the door open. He wasted no time storming inside, shoulders tense, murder in those dark eyes.

I had potentially just killed us all.

Ares

CHAPTER 18

Rage.

The feeling tore through me, ricocheting off my bones, boiling my blood. I had come to speak with Hephaestus so we could work together to *help* Aphrodite, at Helios's encouragement. It was a good thing that fucker was mortal, and his days were already numbered, otherwise I just may have killed him for preaching caution and mercy . . .

Once I killed Hephaestus.

My eyes swept the room, assessing exits, gathering locations of weapons. Hephaestus was shorter than me, but I knew he was a fierce warrior, and I had no doubt he had several caches of weapons stashed throughout his chambers. Fury clouded my vision as my eyes fell on Aphrodite, her bound form, writhing, mostly naked and tied to a chain. I could hear the blood rushing in my ears, feel my muscles tensing to spring.

It didn't matter that, technically, Aphrodite was *his* wife. Or that, just hours ago, I'd fucked her right in front of him, or that, before that, I'd almost sucked his—

"Ares, listen to me," Hephaestus ordered in that voice that toed the line of annoyance and command. He held his hands aloft, unassuming in front of his chest, but I knew, at any moment, he could strike, and if he did, he'd be as deadly as a javelin. His chest rippled with power, lean muscles corded over his shoulders, his abdomen.

Aphrodite whimpered, then moaned, and I shot my gaze to her, arousal and fear firing down our tether in jolts. Something was happening to her, but I couldn't tell what. She wasn't speaking, though no gag obstructed her mouth.

"Ares, you can calm down, or you can leave," he repeated, and the authority in his tone drew me up to my full height. Who the fuck was this god? I'd known him, hated him, for centuries, and now I was to believe that this calm, sweet, golden boy Hephaestus had a power kink? The phantom sensations of his fingers on my neck sent a forbidden bolt of electricity through my body, pooling pressure in my groin.

Aphrodite whimpered again.

"What the fuck are you doing to her?" I hissed.

Hephaestus continued to walk me in circles, firmly planted between Aphrodite and myself.

I felt the stone of his bedchamber wall connect with my back and cursed myself for getting herded like a wounded animal into a corner. He made no move to tear his eyes from me and instead continued his slow progression, each step deliberate and calculated. He could have crossed the distance in a few strides and lit this firecracker off, but instead, he waited, inching slowly.

"I've done nothing she doesn't enjoy, Ares. Look at her, feel her. She's not in pain, I swear to you. Quite the opposite actually. If I show you that she is unharmed, will you sit?" he asked, and my bones jerked hard at the last word, at his ability to infuse his words with an order the soldier in me wanted to obey. Only I wasn't just a soldier, I was a leader. A general. I did not follow.

And yet.

I watched, deadly still, as Hephaestus backed away from me, crossed to a trembling Aphrodite. I tensed when he reached her, but she straightened, pushed her body closer to his, seeking his touch, and when he ran a hand up her back, long, lithe fingers tracing her spine, her eyes rolled back as the tremors intensified. He fisted the golden hair at the nape of her neck, leaned forward, watching and observing as her muscles twitched, both of us inhaling deep as the scent of jasmine and smoke filled the room.

A soft kiss on her shoulder, and Aphrodite mewled as he reached between her legs, rubbing in smooth, practiced motions. Just watching her, watching him, her pale blue-gray eyes so wide and full of trust . . . the ache of longing nearly knocked me sideways as I witnessed the power of the Goddess of Love and God of the Forge.

How they burned for each other. Him, feeding her flame, he a steady, stable power source.

Hephaestus removed a long, golden object, slick with Aphrodite's arousal, from between her legs, dripping and soaked, and oh.

Fuck.

Her essence and mine mixed together over ridged metal.

I couldn't breathe, couldn't clear my head, for the sweet jasmine as it wafted around me, calling to me, urging me closer. The need to taste her hit me strong, suffocating, unyielding, the air rife with her, the heady scent lingering on my tongue as I gulped the air like a suffocating man.

Hephaestus spoke praises in her ear, stroking her face, kissing her neck as she slumped against him.

"You did so well, Little Love, so well. I'm sorry that it took longer than expected, but did you feel good? Speak, Aphrodite." His words firm and coddling had her turning to me, skin flushed.

"I'm—I'm sorry. It just felt so good, I couldn't, I couldn't," she said, her breath falling in shallow pants.

Hephaestus rolled his hands over her shoulders, kneading the muscles stretched taut above her from her bindings.

"Do you want Ares to watch?" he asked, turning them both to face me, tracing a path up her torso, over her breasts, until his hand circled her neck in a gentle collar.

My mind stopped processing rational thought as I waited on bated breath for her answer

"I do," she admitted in a low voice, flushing deeper. "I feel better, with you both here."

Her confession clawed at me, and my eyes danced between his and hers, to the hold he had on her, to the prayer she'd whispered into the darkness of his bedchamber, that he seemed to be offering to make reality. My skin itched and pricked, and I waited for the anger, for the jealousy that had driven me to cut lesser men down for even looking at Aphrodite to roar in my chest.

It never came.

"Is this what Cate suggested?" I managed, and he nodded, dragging his lips down the column of her neck again.

Aphrodite mewled as he bit and nipped, and Fates, I didn't know how to even begin to know how to act here. Hephaestus groaned at the taste of her. The sound did things to me I wasn't proud of.

"I believe I owe you a debt, Ares. And I'd like to pay that now, in full. So will you behave? Or will you leave?" he asked, letting the implication linger between us.

I froze, unsure. I should get the fuck out of here. I should find Hades and make him throw me in the Styx so I could pretend whatever I was starting to feel within me wasn't happening.

Aphrodite's eyes pleaded with me to stay, and after what I'd felt when I first arrived . . .

"Fuck it. Let's try it your way." The words left me on a rush as I carded my fingers through already unruly hair. I had no idea what I was actually agreeing to, but a part of me felt a small thrill at that.

Aphrodite beamed, her skin pulsing with a glow I hadn't seen on her in so long, and a hum resonated from my chest, low and strange, nearly imperceptible to my ears, but I could feel it.

Maybe Hecate was right. Maybe she needed both of us.

"Come to bed, Ares. Take off your boots," Hephaestus instructed.

A buzz settled over my body. An unfamiliar feeling seemed to awaken within me, coaxed to the surface by his tone that surgically sliced through all my experiences, upended all my control, and with deft precision, extracted the need to *obey* from my bones.

I crossed the room in a few strides, kicking my boots free as I went. A small smile played on his lips as I moved, but I hesitated when my knees hit the bed, unsure of the rules of this particular engagement. What exactly was I agreeing to? I looked to Hephaestus, who studied every move I made with extreme clarity, and though I searched his face for distress, I found none.

He ran a hand over Aphrodite's chest, fingernails scraping against her pebbled nipples gently, before holding her chin in my direction.

"Tell him what you want, Aphrodite," he commanded.

"No shirt," she breathed, and without hesitation, I ripped it from my body in some sort of lust-filled trance.

"Good. Now climb into bed, Ares," Hephaestus instructed.

I went, gingerly climbing on the bed, settling my back against the headboard.

"Spread your legs." Another command. "Wider. Perfect. Now, unbuckle your pants."

My cock jerked at his praise, and again, I did as I was fucking told. I reminded myself this was for Aphrodite, that there was nothing I wouldn't do for her, especially with that look on her face she had now, like I was about to give her everything she'd ever desired.

Like I was more than enough.

Hephaestus reached up and tugged the knot securing Aphrodite. Her arms dropped, but he caught them with ease before they could smack against her, then he loosened the leather belt binding her wrists. His fingers worked over her reddened flesh reverently, placing kisses along her skin.

She smiled at him, soft and tender and my chest constricted.

She fucking loved him.

She may have loved me, too, but she loved Hephaestus just as fiercely. A hollow feeling racked through my body, but I maintained my composure, because this was about her, not what I felt. She needed us both. And she'd get it, even though I wasn't sure what that was going to look like.

Hephaestus applied pressure to the back of Aphrodite's knees, causing her to kneel on the soft bed. This mattress was incredibly comfortable, and it made me hate him slightly less for whatever he was about to do to me. He reached below the frame, and when he righted himself, another chain with leather cuffs at each end was held aloft in his hands. He connected one cuff to Aphrodite's outstretched wrist and threaded the other end through a loop on the floor.

Slowly, he reached for my ankle.

I should have moved, flinched, protested, the very idea of being trapped against my nature, but I didn't want to give him the satisfaction.

His fingers ghosted over my skin, and the warmth that spread from his touch crept up my leg, blooming heat that prickled my flesh. He secured the cuff before moving silently to the other side, repeating the process with her other hand and my other ankle. None of us spoke when he moved to stand behind Aphrodite's kneeling form, hands resting on her shoulders.

"Are you sure you want both, Little Love?" He planted a kiss to the soft flesh at the crook of her neck.

She smiled, adoringly.

"Are you sure?" she whispered.

He pressed a kiss to her forehead, the tip of her nose, then looked up at me, pinning me beneath a stern gaze.

"Whatever you need, Aphrodite." Meant for me.

I dipped my chin in understanding and shifted against the soft covers, preparing myself.

"Lay forward, my love." His words were . . . honey. Whiskey. Intoxicating, as he pressed his palm against her spine, pushed her body toward me.

My heart hammered behind my ribs the closer she moved, her eyes on mine, a coy smile on her lips, soft hands trailing up my thighs as he lifted her by her hip, her nearly bare ass in the air for him. The view from where I sat was spectacular. I couldn't imagine how good Hephaestus had it now, but he took his time, savoring it.

His head tilted to the side, strands falling into his face as his teeth sunk into his bottom lip. He was taller than her, so much so that, even over her, I watched him shimmy out of his jeans, her ass cheek in one hand, the golden rod from earlier clutched in the other.

Hephaestus pulled his cock free, and I tried not to focus on it, which was admittedly difficult, especially when I'd been so close to it earlier. The golden rod seemed to be a direct replica of his cock, minus the row of piercings that lined his heavy shaft. Three golden rings sat under the metal cock, and I watched in fascination as he massaged and threaded his balls and shaft through them. He stroked.

I stared. Watching the muscles in his forearm flex on every stroke, the slow, lazy pulls that had him glistening from the tip.

Fuck, he had a nice cock.

"Are you ready?" he asked Aphrodite, whose eyes hadn't left my face, watching me check out her husband with a small smile on her lips. It wasn't like she didn't know my appetites, couldn't feel how fucking turned on I was by this, by *him*. It pleased her, clearly. I'd always been far too possessive to share her before, so this was far beyond the pale of what we were used to together, and insecurity started to eat away at me as I wondered if Hephaestus *had* shared her before, if this was a thing they did often . . . He seemed so collected.

Controlled.

Hephaestus hissed, the potent smell of fire mixed with the jasmine tinted the air, and I peered over the top of Aphrodite in time to see the golden cock he stroked methodically transform, the metal smoothing to pale skin. A perfect replica of his dick, which hung hard between his legs.

"I'm sorry, are you fucking telling me that you have two cocks?" Stunned disbelief, arousal and annoyance whirled inside me as I watched him work himself, saw them both harden and stand tall, ready to conquer. *Why the fuck had she ever left this god?* Self-loathing permeated my thoughts. Who could possibly compete with this?

Hephaestus smiled demurely, each hand wrapped around a different shaft as he stroked.

"It's temporary, but I have a way with metals." He wasn't bragging, and that made it even fucking hotter.

"Do they both work? Like—" I swallowed, the words stalling on my tongue because I was hot around my ears, my chest, unable to look away.

"Yeah," he responded, voice a husky rasp as he looked over her at me. "Maybe I can show you sometime."

The implications hung heavily in the air.

Unsettled and bothered, I turned my attention back to Aphrodite, who began swaying her hips in the air.

Hephaestus closed the distance between them, took his time moving her lace panties to the side, and I couldn't see what he was doing exactly, but it was obvious when he thrust deep, and her incredible fucking body jostled.

Mortification washed over me. Fates, had I signed up to be some kind of cuck? Was this some sort of long-coming revenge, to make me watch, up close, as he made love to her?

Aphrodite let out a strangled cry as she gripped my thighs, and I felt the pull of her Bond sucking me in, sensations overwhelming, even more than they had been earlier.

My cock stood embarrassingly hard as he lined up his second head to her ass. He opened his hand, and, from the shadows, liquid poured, clear but thicker than water, as it dropped over his shaft, over her tight hole. He slid in, slower this time, mouth agape, eyelashes fluttering as his head titled back and it was . . . Fates, it was hot, watching his throat work around a groan. There was a confidence in his strokes, stemming from a lifetime of fucking her. With two cocks.

She gasped, and he soothed her, stroking down her back, eyes on the holes he was buried in. He pulled back, gently, spreading her cheeks wider, bending to let a slow line of saliva drop from his lips. His fingers moved, smearing the lubrication over them, rocking his hips in shallow thrusts as she adjusted and shivered between us.

Hephaestus was a gentle and kind shade in every aspect I'd ever known him in. But here? In the bedroom? He fucked as good as any god. Like a demon. Like a monster. He gave only a few warning strokes before he snapped into Aphrodite, filling her impossibly full. The speed he used would have put Hermes to shame, and the power behind each thrust had my cock weeping.

I glanced down at my tented jeans as he took her, wet slaps echoed off stone, focused on the way her tits bounced in front of me, heavy and peaked with each thrust. And the way he talked to her, Fates, the way she moaned for him. I slid my hand slowly over my abdomen as he fucked her, listening to his words as my own desire ramped up unbearably.

"Fuck, yes, fuck," he whispered, canting his hips.

Aphrodite's body responded to his, throwing back to meet each thrust, her eyes on me.

"You like that? This what you wanted, Little Love? Don't be shy, tell Ares how good it feels."

Primal grunts, desperate pants, it was too much and not enough. I gripped the base of my cock, squeezing my balls as I moved. I stroked up the long shaft once, with incredible strength.

"*Mmhmm*, I missed it so much. P-please, don't stop," she begged, and I stroked harder, more aggressively, as I lifted my hips to fuck my hand.

The sexual energy rolling off us pressed all the air from the room, depriving us of oxygen, reason, *sanity*. There was only pleasure, only Aphrodite's hooded gaze and bouncing tits while she took every inch of his cocks inside her deepest holes, as he commanded us both with a domineering presence like no other.

"Look at that thick cock between his fingers, Aphrodite. Did that cock fuck you hard and fast earlier? How pretty is it? Isn't it beautiful?" he asked.

I blushed at his praised, my pace shifting slightly, adjusting my strokes to match his thrusts. I was close, so fucking close, and I could tell Aphrodite was, too, by the way she gripped my thighs, struggled to breathe.

"So pretty, feel s'good," she choked.

The sharp stings of his hand smacking her flesh cracked through the air, and my hand jerked hard at her moans of approval. Hephaestus locked eyes with me as he snapped into Aphrodite, his hips faltering the tiniest bit in their rhythm. So close to losing his release.

"If you want power, you take it from us. Both of us, Aphrodite. Open your mouth, breathe on his cock while your husband fills you the fuck up."

Lightning shot down my spine, nearly paralyzing me at the filth in his words, the anger behind them.

She licked her lips hungrily at the streams of slick slipping down my shaft.

"Spit on it, love," he commanded.

She obeyed immediately, coating my hand and shaft until we glistened with it.

"Good girl, make a fucking mess, just how I like it. You're both doing so well for me, so obedient. Good behavior is rewarded." His voice tightened, the veins in his neck strained as he worked Aphrodite to a place of frenzy, and Hells, I was right there, too, ready to fall apart, and she hadn't even touched me.

"Do you know what would please me? Hmm? If you wrapped those lips around his cock, Aphrodite. Suck him fucking dry while I give you everything."

A moan slipped from my mouth as she did as she was told, and Fates, the pressure, the suction . . . I felt the fire in my balls. With her lips on me, I had mere moments.

"*Don't you fucking dare, Ares*," Hephaestus snapped, pointing a finger at me over her back.

I groaned, slowed down my pace, pinching my balls with slightly too much pressure to bring me back down.

"You think after she walked around with your cum seeping out of her and mine nowhere to be found on her, I'm gonna let you come anywhere near her until I've thoroughly punished her?"

There it was. The anger. The ire. Fates, why was it so hot on him though? I had no idea how to respond. No one had ever spoken to me like that before, and I was so deep in my lust that forming a coherent thought felt like a Herculean task as she hollowed out her cheeks, took me as deep as she could go.

"I'm sorry," I choked out between thrusts.

Hephaestus trained that golden gaze on me, eyes darkening. "Never apologize for making her come. But if you fill her, so do I, or I'll do the fucking same to you."

A wounded noise broke past my lips, the muscles in my abdomen bunching as Aphrodite shook apart under the weight of his words, soaking the sheets with the torrent, and I couldn't hold it.

Hephaestus snapped her head up with his hands, her lips inches from my tip.

"Open for him, Little Love. Let him come inside that mouth, because *I* said he could," he whispered.

I felt my cock slip past her bruised, swollen lips and explode immediately.

Hephaestus came with a fury-filled cry that wrenched another orgasm from Aphrodite, still firmly locked around my shaft. I shot rope after rope inside her hot mouth, splashed down the back of her throat. I fucked in and out of her as she swallowed me down, drool and spit and cum bubbling around her lips, and it was euphoric, the torrent, the circuit of pleasure that wouldn't fucking quit until Aphrodite collapsed in a spent heap between us, hair wild, flushed skin peppered with small bruises.

She looked magnificent.

Chest heaving, Hephaestus pulled slowly out of her. Sweat soaked her face, her back, the tops of her arms as she twitched. He made quick work of detaching the bonus shaft, now returned to gold, and sat it gingerly on the bed while still holding onto Aphrodite. His chest rose and fell sharply as he tried to regain his own breath, winded as he gestured with his head to the restraints.

"Hit those release clips, would you?" he asked.

I scrambled forward, bending over to work the cuffs on Aphrodite's wrist. They loosened easily enough, but small red splotches from where she'd struggled against them marred her otherwise perfect skin.

Hephaestus lifted her easily against his chest, whispering words I couldn't hear against her temple, then disappeared into the bathroom. The splash of water hitting a basin reverberated off the walls, and then soft murmurs, intimate in a way the sex hadn't been, clawed at my insides.

I suddenly felt . . . extremely intrusive. Like I shouldn't be here for this part. In the post-orgasm clarity, panic riddled my chest, my mind. What had I done?

Was there any going back after that?

I couldn't stick around to find out, and I sure as fuck wasn't about to wait to get kicked out of their little love nest. My body ached, drained in a deep way as I swung my legs over the side of the bed and stood on shaking feet. Hastily, I tucked my still semi-hard dick away, scooped up my boots, and made my way to the door. I was almost there when a sharp voice cut through the air.

"Where do you think you're going?" Hephaestus asked, something low and dangerous in his tone. Like there was a wrong answer, and I found I very much did *not* want to fail this test.

I jerked my thumb over my shoulder and gave him what I hoped, was an unaffected shrug. "I figured whatever this was, is done, and I'd better move on. Aphrodite looks better."

My voice caught, but Hephaestus just studied me as he leaned against the bathroom door, still fucking naked. I worked to keep my eyes trained on his face, to not let them wander any farther south than what was proper. I'd fucked a lot of men in my life, enjoyed them, thought they were beautiful but . . . Fates, had he always been so good-looking?

"You need to shower. You need water and rest. Let's go." He turned on his heel, like he expected me to just follow after him.

I didn't. Couldn't.

Sensing my reluctance to move, he raised an eyebrow, half challenge, half warning. A stillness sat between us, an unexploded IED just waiting for a signal.

I padded across the floor of his bedchamber sheepishly, which seemed silly. I wasn't a high school boy who'd just had his first sexual experience. I'd fucked, a lot in my life. Men, women, the uncategorized. But in those encounters, I'd always been in control.

This felt . . . fundamentally different. And with who participated, the added complication had my chest tight.

I reached the door and went to move past Hephaestus, who scooped low to tug my boots from my hand. Too close. I could smell him, nearly taste the sweat that dripped from the ends of his hair. He waited until I stepped into the same bathroom I'd been in just this afternoon to move, and that felt like a power shift too. Aphrodite washed herself, humming in the large walk-in shower, and though she'd nearly died today then been fucked mercilessly by not one but two gods, she didn't seem exhausted.

I was.

Honestly, I felt satisfied, but also like I'd been hit by a truck, a look Hephaestus also shared while she seemed . . . invigorated. *Jovial.*

I shuffled out of my jeans and stepped into the water behind her. The spray was hot, nearly scalding, just the way I liked it.

Aphrodite held up a small bottle and emptied a glob of clear orange liquid onto my palm. It smelled like Hephaestus, like his chambers, like his bed.

Spicy and warm.

The scent didn't repulse me, and I tried not to let my mind roam too far down that rabbit hole, because there was a neon sign in my subconscious screaming "WHAT THE FUCK" in the boldest letters known to man.

Hephaestus slipped into the shower, and we shifted, making space, our bodies twisting naturally to accommodate him and me both in the small space. He grabbed a small bottle of shampoo that smelled like jasmine, like Aphrodite, and rubbed it through her wet hair. She relaxed against him as he washed her gently, careful when he got to the apex of her thighs and between her cheeks. Once she was clean, he stepped out long enough to grab a large towel, opening it for her. She moved without instruction, like this was a routine for them, a form of aftercare baked into their sex life. Tightly bundled, he instructed her, "Go lay down, we'll be out soon. I'll light a fire."

He kissed her temple, but she lifted an arm to me, accompanied by a smile, her touch light and playful as I took her hand in mine, stepping out of the spray to drop a kiss to her palm. Then she was gone, and there was nothing but the void of silence, broken only by falling water between the God of the Forge and me.

Hephaestus turned back to me, rolled his shoulders, jaw tense.

My heckles immediately rose in defense.

Here it comes, the other shoe.

We eyed each other warily as he stepped back into the shower, and I recoiled when he reached past me for another bottle. He moved in slow motion, unhurried, deep brown eyes locked on mine.

I finished rinsing the soap from myself as he plopped a dollop into his hands, rubbing them together until the suds dripped from his fingers down his forearms. I focused anywhere but his eyes, desperate to put some distance between us, and it took me more time than I cared to admit to realize my heart was beating loud enough to bounce the sound off the tile. There was no way to hope he couldn't hear it, with his divine hearing. His stilled, calming in a steady rhythm that unnerved me, and the knot in my chest whispered that there was *more* to this anxiety.

I needed out of here. Away from him.

One step, and his hand came up to grab my bicep. Instinct had my hand swatting him away, had my body on high alert as I turned to square up with him. I'd fight a man naked in a shower. It wouldn't even be the first time.

His lips thinned, eyes searching mine. He stilled again, let out an exasperated sigh as though trying to teach himself patience, and then, slowly, his fingers stretched wide, slid over my bicep again, halting me in place.

This time, I didn't stop him, utterly perplexed by his actions, by the betrayal of my own body as his hands roamed over my arm, squeezing the tight muscles, massaging the soap into my skin.

His fingers, strong, slightly calloused but capable, as he worked, radiating soothing heat.

I felt the anxiety ball in my chest loosen slightly at his touch, and for a second, I let myself melt into the connection. It felt fucking good. Tender.

He turned me with subtle pressure, until my back was on display for him. I heard him suck in a sharp breath, as he saw them up close.

The scars.

Battle wounds, sure, but underneath, deeper, were the remnants of punishment, of disobedience that I would have chosen in every lifetime. I felt his eyes as he tracked his gaze over my skin, the burn of them, then the soothing warmth from rough hands that moved too gently. Patiently. He didn't ask where they came from, but my station was enough for him to guess probably. Countless battles left their mark. The rest was none of his business.

Hephaestus was silent as his fingers worked out the knots in my back, the only sounds the water, steadied breaths. The hiss that escaped my lips when he dug too deep into muscle and scar tissue. I swayed, as he washed my back, my shoulders, up my neck. If I closed my eyes, I might have been able to pretend he was someone, *anyone*, else . . . but the scent of him, the inferno of his body at my back, was unmistakable.

He was here, pushing the tension from my bones, hands roaming, washing my thighs and even my feet. When his soapy hands traveled higher again, sliding on the inside of my thighs, he paused, waiting for permission.

I gave it to him with a grunt, all the acquiescence I could manage. There wasn't anything sexual in the way he washed me, even though the heat and languid stroking had my cock half-hard again. It was just a reaction to the touch. The comfort. It was . . . careful. *Kind?*

Something cracked in my chest at the tenderness. How long had it been since someone had truly touched me? Not to fight or fuck, but to . . . soothe?

Hephaestus washed the soap from me, and then, as he'd done with Aphrodite, wrapped me tight in a towel he'd warmed with his power.

"Go lay down with Aphrodite. I'll be in after I finish cleaning up."

I didn't argue. I wasn't sure I could have if I had wanted to. It scared me that I didn't want to.

"And Ares? Be in that bed when I get out of here. I'd hate to have to come find you." His words brooked no argument.

Aphrodite had already toweled off and crawled in bed, her blonde hair fanned over the pillow like spun silk.

I ran the towel over myself, clearing the tiny droplets that clung to my skin. My hands held the slightest tremble as I pulled the covers back and slipped beneath them, behind Aphrodite. Sleepily, she wiggled back into me, pressing her softness against my body.

I wrapped my arm across her torso, pulling her tight. Her face lifted with a sleepy smile.

"So that was . . ." I began, my mind racing, but Aphrodite shushed me softly.

"Not tonight. We can panic tomorrow, let's just have tonight, Ares."

I kissed her shoulder, relaxing into the sheets. My body was spent, and my shade . . .

When Hephaestus finally emerged from the bathroom, I was nearly asleep, but I cracked an eye open, watching him move silently through the room, stoking a fire in the grate that roared to life at his barest touch. He grabbed a few bottles of water and sat them on the end tables before crawling into the bed on the other side of Aphrodite. He shook her awake, smiling as she protested, but he was unrelenting.

He uncapped one and pressed it to her lips.

"Drink, Little Love. Then you can sleep. Two gulps."

She complied, snuggled closer to his chest.

He turned his gaze to me. "You as well. At least two."

He was treating me in a manner I would have never expected, as the god who ruined his marriage.

I popped the cap and drank half the water, wanting to do as he asked.

He buried his lips in her damp hair, blowing softly, commanding the power of fire and heat. I watched it lighten, drying as he hummed.

Safely between us, Aphrodite's body moved only slightly as he waved a hand, snuffing out the flames in the sconces.

"I love you," she whispered into the darkness.

"I love you too," we replied, and I knew, in that moment, we were fucked.

We were royally fucked.

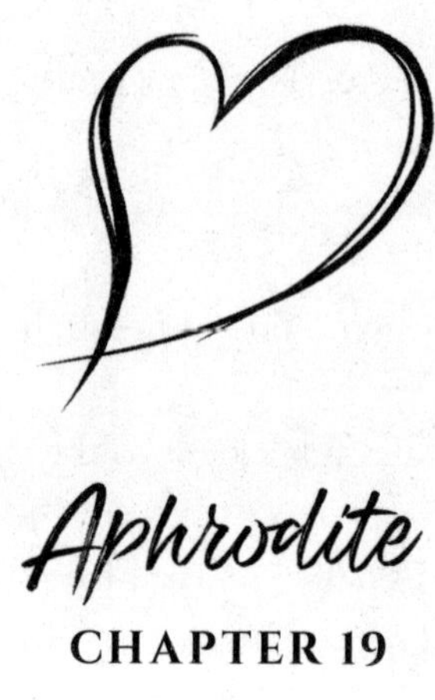

Aphrodite
CHAPTER 19

Consciousness came to me in the middle of blissful serenity, only I didn't fight against it like I normally would, because the warmth radiating all around, luring my body in a cocoon of safety and comfort, felt like kismet. My body felt better than it had in years. Centuries, if I was being honest. Strong arms cradled me to the hard chest at my back as another set wrapped around my hips, a large hand splayed on the curve of my thigh. My leg was draped unceremoniously over a chiseled thigh, heating my already radiating core.

Was last night real?

Visions flitted through my mind on a loop, salacious and delectable, but there was something sinister on the edges of the bliss, lying in wait to ruin this pocket of paradise I floated in. I tried to calm my racing heart, to lay out the facts as I could remember them.

Hephaestus and I had sex last night.

So had Ares and me.

And then, Hephaestus went full Dominant on us both, and Ares had let him. *Fates*. I had been totally drunk on the lust that filled the room, absorbing the power radiating off the two loves of my life, but last night was every repressed fantasy I'd never let myself indulge in, after a fashion. In those dark corners of my mind, I'd wished to have them both, imagined them putting their feud aside for my sake, for the sake of all our sanities . . . They'd ravished me together, which I suspect they'd claim as their reasoning, but last night, I had seen the breaking. The understanding. *The yearning.*

They had wanted it, wanted more, their desires had clouded my mind through their respective Bonds. I saw it in the way Ares, my possessive, hot-headed, stubborn god sat obediently as Hephaestus ravaged my body. The strain in his muscles as the god who once struck a sword through a mortal for simply looking at me with lust in his eyes, watched another devour me. Never in even my wildest fantasies did I ever see Ares submitting to anyone, even me, but to Hephaestus? Impossible.

But he had.

And Hephaestus. My sweet, gentle, kind Heph. Who lived with honor and discretion above all. The one more likely to fall on a sword for a stranger. The god who flipped like a switch once the door was closed and the world was tucked safely away. My blood rose to the surface at the mere thought of his hands, his voice, his presence. It was intoxicating knowing he held my breath, my comfort, and my pleasure at his whim. To trust so completely for him to catch me if I fell too far. He had never let me down. Our power mingled together, twinning and twining, charging the very air around us as a wave of need hit me so strongly, I nearly wept.

The fingers around me flexed.

I grinned, eyes still closed, body fully awake as Ares's cock grew steadily against my lower back. Hephaestus was still, the gentle pressures the pads of his fingers made as he rubbed subtle circles soothing. His cock was hard, velvety against the inside of my thigh, and I circled my hips just once, searching for relief, clenching around nothing, an empty ache only they could ease. Smoke and metal, rich and heady blended with the jasmine as the Bonds gnawed at me, starved for a potent combination they'd never received before last night.

Both.

I popped my eyes open to find Hephaestus's honey stare boring into mine, bottom lip tucked under his teeth.

"Good morning, Little Goddess," Ares's gravelly voice whispered in my ear, his large hand cradling my breast, fingers plucking my nipples, rolling them teasingly into pert peaks.

I moaned, winding my hips harder against Hephaestus's thigh.

I wanted him to touch me, too, but he made no other move to stroke the fire building inside me. Doubt crept in, seeping through our barely stitched together Bond, and I stilled, unsure if I was going too far, asking more than either of them were able to give.

He held my gaze, and I was lost in the deep browns and ambers when a wave of guilt washed over me, souring the haze of lust I crested.

Ares kept his movements slow, sensing the tension, but none of us spoke, too afraid to break the silence.

The moment snapped as rapid banging startled us, the spell holding us enthralled, broken from the interruption. Hephaestus was up in an instant, feet flat on the floor as he adjusted himself in his joggers and headed toward the door.

I wanted to call out to him, to tell him to come back to bed, to keep the outside world away from us, but I knew he wouldn't. That we couldn't.

Ares disentangled himself from me but still lay close.

More banging.

Hephaestus stopped as he reached the door, one unsure hand on the knob as he turned to look at us. The magic of what happened last night was fading, we could all feel it. A small, sad smile tugged up the corner of his lips. He understood too.

Once he opened that door, it would all change.

I wanted to cry.

Another round of banging. A collective breath between the three of us.

With a grimace, the God of the Forge cracked the door just as discreetly as he had last night with Ares, but this time, he slid his muscular body nearly out the doorway, obscuring the bed from view.

Hiding us.

"Hey, man. I wanted to come check on you." Hermes's voice rang clear through the cracked door, and I tensed. He was far from being my or Ares's biggest fan, especially of late, and no part of our interactions suggested he'd take this development with any sort of grace. The sting of rejection speared through me because there had once been a time when I considered Hermes one of my dearest friends, an ally against the political—and often dangerous—pantheon from which we all heralded. Now, he could barely stomach my presence, and though I couldn't blame him, it hurt, the barbs.

Ares hadn't moved at all, his mind probably surfing the same wavelength as mine. Maybe.

Uncertainty settled over me. We were in such uncharted waters; I couldn't be sure what either of them were thinking.

Hells, I didn't even know where my head was at.

"I'm okay, Herms. We're handling it in the best way we know how," Hephaestus answered in that easy, assuring voice of his.

Hermes seemed unconvinced.

"C'mon, Heph. You don't have to pretend with me. This situation is shit for you, and after what happened last time . . . you can't blame me for being worried. We came so close to losing y—"

Hermes's voice cracked slightly, but Hephaestus cut him off before he could finish his thought.

Every nerve in my body tensed at the implications of what he'd just said, at the genuine concern in the Messenger God's voice. *We came so close to losing you.*

What happened last time?

Hephaestus shuffled uncomfortably on his feet, casting his eyes briefly back around the room before turning back on Hermes. "I'm fine, Hermes. It isn't like last time. We have to be on the same team if we're going to find a way to move forward."

My heart constricted as hope sliced through my chest. He was saying this to Hermes, but he was speaking to me, to *us*.

Ares's hand slipped up to rest on my thigh and squeezed reassuringly.

I turned my gaze to see his own brown eyes locked on Hephaestus's back, jaw tense.

Hermes laughed.

"Same team, huh? That means you're considering what Cate suggested? Gonna play harem husband to Aphrodite and Ares?" he asked, and the muscles in Hephaestus's back rippled with tension. Hermes was pissing him off, and though it shouldn't be, it was incredibly attractive when Hephaestus got angry.

Blood rushed in my ears, flushed beneath the surface of my skin. He was so sculpted, carved from centuries in his forges, swinging hammers as he made the weapons of the gods, of the world's fabled heroes.

"I think there's a lot the three of us need to discuss, and until we do, it needs to stay between the *three* of us. And yes, if you're asking if I would rather see her die from Bond sickness or find a way to be civil with Ares, then you already know my answer."

"I can't believe you're considering this, really? He's his father's son—" Hermes argued, but Hephaestus crossed his arms over his chest, rising to his full height.

"Are you?" he retorted, defensively.

Silence.

"You know that I'm not," Hermes huffed.

"Then maybe he isn't either. I love you, I do, but if you continue to push this over your own grudge, we're going to have a problem. This is *my* marriage and *my* Bond, Hermes. Butt the fuck out, or take your ass back to New Orleans."

Quiet command thrummed in the timbre of his voice, shooting desire straight down to my core.

Ares's fingers slid closer to my center as he covered one of my nipples with his luscious mouth, and I ignored the confusion flowing from him at Hephaestus's defense. Eventually, I would have to tell him what I'd shared.

Eventually.

Ares slid the pad of his finger through my soaked lips, already slick with desire.

My eyes found Hephaestus, who'd turned just a fraction. I knew he could feel the arousal through the Bond. Ares kept an eye trained on him as he dragged his tongue over my sensitive nipples and plunged a finger into me, *deeper*, curling.

Hephaestus shook his head once.

Ares smirked. Kept going.

"If that's what you truly want—" Hermes mumbled while Ares bit down sharply and circled my clit, teasing out the sting.

I let out a sharp hiss, much too loud.

Hephaestus coughed to cover the sound.

Ares was three fingers deep as he laid soft kisses and bites down my chest and torso, lips grazing the Bondmark that lay over my ribs. Pleasure bloomed under his tongue.

Hephaestus slapped the door frame with considerable force.

"It's what I want. I get it, and I . . . *we* are going to be careful moving forward. If Aphrodite is Hells-bent on this quest, then we need to figure out some way to keep her safe." He was struggling to finish his sentences, our desire leaking into him. He could feel everything, but to his credit, he was doing a good job hiding it from Hermes. I had that man committed to memory, knew every muscle that spasmed, every hitch in his breath when he was turned on, and Hephaestus was barely hanging on.

Ares had me right on the peak, and I bit down on his shoulder as he worked me over. Fates, his hands were amazing. Where Hephaestus was controlled overstimulation, Ares was wild, unrelenting chaos.

"Hey, you okay? You're sweating, Heph. Do I need to come look at you?" Hermes asked.

Hephaestus shook his head and held a hand up. "I was up all night. Just gonna lie down and grab a nap. Thanks for checking in."

The door snapped shut along with a bolt to boot. Hephaestus turned to us just as Ares squeezed my clit, applying enough pressure to knock an orgasm through me.

I shook, convulsing, as I coated his hand, the bed, our thighs.

Starved, Hephaestus's eyes darkened as he stalked over, power rolling off him. The temperature spiked higher with every step. He stood at the foot of the bed, drinking the sight of our naked bodies. Ares had all but discarded the covers we'd been wrapped in, the God of War lying next to me, licking my taste from his fingers, looking extremely pleased with himself.

Hephaestus said nothing, but his hand darted out quick as lighting, latched around my ankle. He hauled me to him, and I squealed with laughter as he dragged me near the edge of the bed.

Ares was up and alert in an instant, but before he could fly off the handle, Hephaestus pinned him with a look. Never breaking eye contact with Ares, he spread my legs wide, exposing my bare cunt to him. He lowered his body to nestle between my thighs, and then his hot mouth closed over my still-sensitive clit, spiking my adrenaline.

I saw stars, my back arching as he grunted and ate me out like his last meal. His groans sent vibrations up my core as he devoured me, strong arms hooked under each of my thighs, those long fingers splayed wide over my flushed skin. Hephaestus's blond hair swept across his face, but those deep eyes bore straight into Ares's glare.

Ares looked frozen, chest heaving.

I lifted my hand to him, reaching for his muscular thigh, his stare faltering at my touch, and another wave of desire ripped through me as Hephaestus ran his hand, palm up, under my rib, caressing Ares's Bondmark.

Ares yelped, the sound nearly comical as he doubled over.

Hephaestus chuckled against me, shooting vibrations across my sensitive clit.

Ah, so this was payback.

Ares let out a deep primal growl that had me clenching around the fingers Hephaestus was working inside.

"Please," I begged, not entirely sure who I was beseeching.

Hephaestus peeled his lips away from my core as he casually stroked inside of me.

"You made her come. I told you both yesterday, I would not be unrepresented. Now sit the fuck down and let me enjoy my breakfast in peace."

I clawed for Ares as he deflated, scraped my fingers down his body. The bed dipped as he climbed back onto the mattress, settling behind me, situating my back flush to his chest, legs spread open in offering to Hephaestus.

Ares leaned us back onto the pillows, hands playing with my breasts, stimulating my nipples under rough fingers. Wordlessly, they lifted me higher, until there was nowhere to go, until my body was so tight with tension, the release cracked a sob from my lips.

I *shattered*.

Hands, there were hands everywhere. Caressing my body, squeezing softly, kisses peppering the inside of my thighs, the side of my neck. Warm and euphoric and blissed out, I opened my eyes to see Hephaestus rising back to his knees. He reached under his waistband and pulled out his thick cock, the sharp glint of metal catching the light as he stroked himself. He reached across me to bring his hand to my neck.

"Look at me, Little Love. I wanna see your eyes when I come." Watching him fist himself over me with Ares behind me had my head whirling.

Hephaestus was fucking beautiful, every blessed inch of him. Even the scar on his cheek, it only added to his handsome, rugged features. I watched in a daze as he brought himself to orgasm, splashing my still-exposed core and stomach and thighs with warm ropes of cum.

He braced on my bent knee, breathing as hard as I was, and when he crawled over my body to kiss my lips, smearing his release between us, I melted.

Hephaestus sat back on his heels and checked the clock on the wall.

"I'm going to get a shower," he said, before reaching down and swirling a bit of his spent cum between his fingers, pushing it inside me. "Feel free to clean the rest off, but that stays put."

Hephaestus

CHAPTER 20

Instead of clearing my head and getting a grip around the situation we were in while I was in the shower, the only thing I had a grip on was my painfully hard cock. I spent the entire time fucking my fist while Ares filled Aphrodite twenty feet away. Her moans, the sounds of their sweaty flesh smacking as he drove into her, had me rock hard instantly, and the bouts of desire ripping through the Bond were doing me no favors.

How the fuck were we supposed to function like this? Ares's voice filtered through the room, his deep timbre shooting down my spine and curling my toes.

"Fuck yes, Little Goddess, take it, take it all. You have no idea what it was like for me last night, watching this greedy cunt take two cocks, and neither of them mine," he growled, and I jerked hard, desperate for release.

"He got to fuck this ass last night, but I got to fuck your throat. Shall we even the score, Little Goddess?"

My cock swelled, squeezing the skin around my studs tight. I stroked under my shaft, felt the pleasure bloom from around my piercings.

Aphrodite made noises of ecstasy mixed with broken words of approval.

"He's all over your thighs, baby. Come here." The rustle of covers and subtle grunts meant he'd switched positions.

"Open for me, Little Goddess. Taste him, lick him off my fingers. Good fucking girl."

Slurping noises accompanied the rough smacks, and I could see him, swiping me from between her thighs, thrusting his fingers deep. Warmth bloomed in my chest as I realized he was honoring my command, keeping it fair.

"You like the taste of him in your mouth while I fuck you, Aphrodite? Yeah, it tastes good, doesn't it? He's been down your throat, now I'm gonna fuck this ass. You want that?"

She whimpered. The sounds of smacking paused, and I groaned. Ares grunted at the loss as he slid out of her cunt, quickly followed by a sharp hiss. My breath hitched as the sounds of her moaning reached me once more.

"Fuck, this is the most divine place in the cosmos." His breath was labored as he slid inside her tight hole. Sharp pants punctuated his deep strokes, and I braced myself on the stone wall as water pelted me like lava. "You take my cock so well, so beautiful, my goddess, devourer of my soul, master of my body. The greatest beauties in the universe pale in comparison to your divinity, your mind, this temple of power inside you. Let me worship you, Aphrodite." Reverent, holy words punctuated by small slaps and grunts as he worked her higher.

"How will you worship me, God of War?'" she demanded, and my chest almost imploded with the force of the pressure in her words.

"With my heart, my cock, my tongue, with the blade of my sword. I would worship your body on an altar of your enemies' corpses, should you wish for it. Reduce this world to ash at your whim, you need only ask my goddess." He panted.

"Fuck, yes, don't stop, don't ever stop!" she demanded, falling apart beneath him.

"Never," he whispered, and the sheer willpower behind his words undid me.

I felt myself jerk forward, releasing all over the wall and the floor and myself.

Ares roared a strangled sound as he filled her up, their breaths soft, competing with the beating of my own heart in my ears. The water cascaded to the floor as it washed my sins away.

I needed to get out of here. If we stayed holed up here alone, we'd never discuss this, we'd never *actually* figure anything out. And while wasting all our remaining years to this . . . insanity . . . sounded lovely, I knew that, once the lust cleared, nothing would have really changed.

Aphrodite had set out to dissolve our Bonds. Pain shot through me at the thought, but it was true. She had corrupted our already fragile Bond when she drew on it, and this madness, this intensity, was the pendulum swinging as far back as it could to balance momentum.

Ares and I were programmed to take care of her. Perhaps that's why, in all these centuries, I'd resented him. I hated his presence, but I didn't hate *him* for loving her.

I turned off the shower, slipped out of the walk-in, toweling off as I went and dressed quickly, sweeping up my wet hair in a messy bun on top of my head.

I caught a glimpse of myself in the mirror and had to do a double take. Stubble peppered my chin, and I looked tired. Exhausted, though I'd slept more soundly last night than I had in fifty years.

I stepped into the room and found Aphrodite and Ares stripping the bedsheets, oddly domestic as they gathered the soiled linens into a basket. Aphrodite had a sheet wrapped around her, and for a moment, the way she had it tied reminded me of the beginning, when we were new. Her pale eyes had color in them, her cheeks pink, and a subtle glow lapped at her skin.

Hells, she looked beautiful. Healthy. *Alive.*

She turned to me, and that smile stuttered my heart.

Ares busied himself with cleanup, turning his back to us when she stepped into my space.

I pushed a lock of wild curls from her face, and she kissed the inside of my wrist. I could feel the pull to go to her light within me, watch the hunger mirrored in her own eyes. Insatiable, my Little Love.

I sucked in a deep breath and stepped back from her.

"I'm gonna find Hades. We all need to talk, but I think, until we get some air, we won't have clear heads. How are you feeling, Ditey?" I asked, looking her over.

"Better," she admitted, reluctantly.

A small dagger twisted at her admission, and I wondered if she was regretting what we'd done. She wanted the Bonds gone.

I nodded once, lips thinned so I didn't say anything to make this worse.

"Please eat. The shades will bring you food from the Upper Realms," I said, voice soft. We weren't in that space of command any longer, and I made sure my tone reflected that.

I shot a look at Ares over her shoulder. "You too. It's been a long night, and we don't know what's yet to come."

Ares's expression was unreadable. Not exactly hostile, but not friendly either. He gave a terse nod as the energy shifted at the mention of the trials.

I brushed my knuckles over Aphrodite's cheek, checking to see if what we'd done had made her change her mind.

It hadn't.

*

Hades sat comfortably in his high-backed chair, a large tome open in front of him, body bent forward in rapt attention, still as a statue save for his eyes that flew over each page.

I cleared my throat as I approached, and still, he remained silent as I took my seat across from him.

Hades's blue eyes peered at me over the pages, studying me. After a moment, he spoke.

"Persephone is pregnant. You're going to be an uncle." His words were tight, but happiness burst from me for him.

I shot up out of the chair, circled the desk to grab his shoulders. He didn't protest when I pulled him to me in a tight embrace.

"Congratulations, brother." I clapped him on the back. "You're going to be an amazing father."

Something like uncertainty flashed in his eyes, and I knew *exactly* where his mind wandered to.

I gave him a stern look.

"Don't. Don't give him any of your power. He's gone, Hades. You can't turn into him; we would never allow it." I shook him slightly to make him look at me.

Hades's father was a monster of a titan, one who'd actually eaten him back in the time when the world was new. After the abuse he'd endured, it was a wonder Hades came out so compassionate. The others who called themselves his kin, including my mother, hadn't been so lucky.

"Look at me, I mean it. Don't let Cronos take this from you. How is Seph?" I asked, keen to steer the conversation to a happier place. We broke apart, and I made my way back to my chair.

"Insatiable," he mumbled, adoration clear in his tone.

I smirked.

"She's been wearing you out, old man? Do you need to call Dionysus and get him to find you an elixir so you can keep up?" I teased.

He rolled his eyes.

"I keep up more than enough, fuck you very much. And besides, it wouldn't be this bad if the entire palace wasn't full of horny gods fucking constantly." He shot me a pointed look, one that told me he knew exactly what had gone down last night. And this morning.

Fates, did I smell like sex? I felt my ears heat, suddenly regretting my decision to sit.

Hades steepled his fingers under his chin, pinning me with his eyes, a smirk tugging at his lips.

"How did you know?" I asked, shifting uncomfortably.

Hades scoffed and closed the book in front of him with a snap.

"Nothing happens in the Underworld that I don't know about," he mused, crossing his arms over his broad chest. He had forsaken the crisp black suits he normally wore in lieu of jeans and a dark V-neck, one that exposed his inked arms and just a bit of his branded torso. Happiness looked good on him.

"If that's true, then what are these trials, and how do we best them?" I asked, grabbing onto the segue like a lifeline. I wasn't prepared to get into whatever had happened last night with Hades. With anyone. I hadn't even processed it my damned self.

He bristled. "They're death, Hephaestus. I designed them myself to be damn near unbeatable. You three have to let this go."

There was no anger or mocking in his tone. Hades truly thought it a lost cause. I cursed.

"We have to try. She's not going to quit, and she can't do it alone." I let out a long huff that did little to ease the knot in my chest. I couldn't tell if the anxiety was mine or belonged to one of the others, but feeling shit that wasn't my own seemed to be part of the deal now.

"I can't tell you what the obstacles are, Heph. Everything in the Underworld is a contract, and I'm just as bound as anyone to them. But these aren't some minuscule Herculean Trials, that I can say with certainty. I set them, and I had to do it with

Otherworlders in mind. They're dangerous, absolutely lethal, and you're going to get yourselves killed." His voice hardened on the warning, stern and cold like the persona he presented to the rest of the cosmos. Only I recognized it for what it was: genuine fear.

"If I don't go with her, she'll just go by herself," I said, feeling defeated.

Hades nodded in understanding. If anyone understood a strong-willed woman, it was the God of the Dead.

"Do you know why I think you shouldn't break the Bonds? It's not because I believe they're the holiest of covenants between our people. It's because I think there's something to be built here, between the three of you." His words held no judgment, no superfluous emotion.

My chest tightened. "She wants out, Hades. No matter what had or hadn't happened, it was just the Bonds trying to feed. I just want her to be happy, Hades, even if that isn't with me."

I cast my eyes to the ground and let out a tired sigh. I was tired, in more than a physical way of the hurt and pain, the push and pull of it. Maybe I wanted it over too.

Maybe.

"Aphrodite presented as such a . . . vain and vapid thing, to all that knew her. Zeus groomed her to use her charm and wiles as a blade to collect conquests for him. But she was smart, too, Hephaestus. When she went to Ares on Zeus's behalf, she saw a way out. They were two objects —one of lust and one of fury. Weapons in Zeus's arsenal to be sold and bartered at his discretion. There was a kinship in that. They found each other."

Hearing this was like ice in my veins shattering any grand notions that may have started to form in the recesses of my mind, reminding me she'd chosen him long before I ever came along.

"Hades, I didn't chase after Aphrodite. We were betrothed without my input at all, and of course, I wasn't going to complain, and I fell in love. She did too . . ." I pinched the bridge of my nose, sucked in a deep breath. "Listen, I've had a weird few days, and if you're trying to make me feel like shit, it's working, bud." My words burned my throat.

Hades sat back. "Calm down, Heph. Let me finish. I was going to say, do you remember the time leading up to your Bonding?"

I nodded. I remembered every moment I'd ever had with her.

"And what did you ask of Hera?"

I shot him a puzzled look, unsure of where this was going.

"Humor me," he barked, impatiently.

"I asked for time to get to know each other, before we would marry," I replied, and he smiled.

"And at your Bonding, which I attended, when your mother asked Aphrodite if she wanted the union, what did she reply?" Hades leaned forward, arching his eyebrows.

"She said yes," I admitted.

Hades smacked his hands together and gestured them toward me.

"What does this have to do with anything?" I asked, still confused.

"At the time of your wedding, Aphrodite and Ares were already Bonded, though botched. Hera has confirmed herself that the Bond ceremony forces a bubble of honesty. If Aphrodite didn't want to be Bonded with you, she *couldn't* have lied. It's impossibility. It meant she loved you then, before you had a Bond to '*force*' anything. She loved you both then, just as she does now. The only thing you need to consider is if you love her enough to share."

I had never put that timeline together, never considered the implications. I looked at Hades like a dumbstruck idiot.

"I don't know if I can share, Hades. Long-term. I don't think Ares could either." I sighed.

Hades let out a small gruff of laughter.

"From what I hear, you both share just fine," he mused as a blush crept over my cheeks and neck.

I ran my palms over my thighs a few times nervously.

"Does everyone know?" I asked, as that old feeling of shame sunk deep into the pit of my stomach.

Hades gave a slight smile and shook his head.

"Only me and the shades, and they have been ordered not to speak of it," he assured me. This was bad enough without having to entertain everyone else's opinions.

"Thanks, Hades. I just . . . I need some time to get my head on straight. I know we don't really have it, but there's a lot to consider." I made to stand, and he followed suit. "I'm going to need you to tell me how to start this quest though. For real this time."

I leveled him a look to show I was serious, and he sighed.

"Even if I wanted to tell you, which I don't, I couldn't. Call it a preliminary trial. I think it's for the best. This is too dangerous to embark on," he quipped, and I frowned at him, crossing my arms over my chest.

"If you don't tell me, I'll put real fire on your kid's crib," I threatened, and he laughed.

"Listen, the rules are rules. Why don't you take some time, stretch your legs in the Underworld. It's been a while since any of us have been here for long. Maybe see if Ares wants to check in with some of his people? He hasn't been to New Asphodel in a long while. Might do him some good to see some of his favored. Fair warning, you may have to drag him out by his heels."

Hades clapped me on the back, and I pulled him into another tight but brief hug. He looked at me incredulously, and I laughed, knowing almost anyone else would be dead.

I set out the door to find Ares, trying not to let my brain panic over spending more time with him, unchaperoned.

On the bright side, Hades had given me our first clue.

Ares

CHAPTER 21

I sat on the edge of Hephaestus's bed and studied the room around me. Aphrodite had showered, and I'd promised I'd follow behind her, but I was in no rush. She hadn't stuck around to talk about this . . . thing between us, and I wasn't sure I would have had anything worthy to say. I needed some space from the fog in my head when she was around.

This room looked different twenty-four hours ago, and as I looked now, I could pick out the parts that were intrinsically *his*. The smokey tendrils smoldering from the remnants of the fire filled the room with his smell. Books were stacked haphazardly on the bookshelves, and I stood, curious. I ran my fingers along the spines of the well-worn tomes. He seemed to favor the classics, philosophy too. I pulled *The Art of War* from the shelves and skimmed through it. He'd made notes in the margins, his handwriting small, deliberate, and neat—the opposite of my messy scrawl.

I slid the book back into its place and turned to look at the exposed panel in the wall. Hanging inside in neat rows were all manner of toys, and I reached up and touched the leather of a set of cuffs hanging there. The material was smooth, well-oiled, and soft, and I wondered what it would feel like on *my* skin.

I thought back to what I'd walked in on, the way Aphrodite had been bound by her wrists and hanging from the contraption Hephaestus had built. Seeing her like that and him half-naked . . . My bloodlust had coursed through me, but underneath was something more than the need to kill, and even now, my brain struggled to wrap around it. Aphrodite consumed me, every cell in my body, and that devotion demanded I consume her completely. Over the years, when we'd been apart, I'd taken lovers, quick flings in the heat of battle, and some repeats when I knew no attachment could be formed.

In the moment with her, I'd never been able to temper my jealousy enough. Watching the way Hephaestus devoured her, commanded her, had brought my blood to the surface, but I wanted to see more. This Dominant side of him wasn't something I ever expected, and no other lover I'd ever been with had commanded me the way his words had. There was an undercurrent of need when he told me what to do. He needed me to obey, and I needed direction. I'd never been truly topped before, not by a man or woman, but as I flexed my fingers over the metal clamps set neatly on a shelf, I wondered what it might be like.

To submit completely.

To give him that control he obviously craved.

I shook the thought from my head. The lines between us were becoming blurred because of our need to be with Aphrodite. I'd seen it before—her ability to unite those around her in service of her pleasure. In times of war, Zeus would send her to use her ability to inspire love to manipulate. She didn't even really have to do much of anything, just to be in her presence was to love her. Part of me wondered how Hermes managed his vitriol. Another part of me wondered if she allowed his verbal barbs because, deep down, she thought she deserved it. Like she was the wicked one in this situation. Like I wasn't the real one to blame for everything we went through.

It was my fault we had Bonded. I had asked her because I couldn't let her go, even though I'd known then Hephaestus was the better match for her.

I let out a breath and closed the panel. I doubted Hephaestus would want it just out here. I suspected that, had he not been in a desperate hurry to put as much distance between the three of us this morning, he'd have closed it himself.

I heard him jacking off to me fucking Aphrodite. It made me ramp up my dirty talk, made me desperate to serve it back to him, hear him fall apart at the way I worshipped her.

I needed air.

I headed for the door, snatching a clean shirt from the pile on the chair. He really needed to organize this shit. I pulled the shirt over my torso, not bothering to see what asinine graphic was on the front, and headed for the door.

Aphrodite's Bond drew me to the throne room where the goddess was found with Artemis, Hecate, and Persephone. They were huddled together, laughing as they ate. Aphrodite was glowing, and the tightness in my chest loosened just seeing how much better she looked than she had yesterday. I'd never seen her that sick before, not even when our Bond corrupted, and it scared the fuck out of me to think it could happen again.

Bond sickness.

It would happen again then. At least she was eating, as Hephaestus had instructed her, and I instinctively reached for a waffle teetering precariously on a large platter. *You too*, he'd said.

I shoved half of it in my mouth, and Aphrodite smiled, clearly pleased I'd obeyed his command. She plopped a grape between those soft lips and desire flooded me. Her breasts heaved, her body feeling the spike too. The others carried on, oblivious to the building tension, but I was drowning in us. It had to be the corruption of the Bonds. The pull had been strong in the past, but never *this* constant, this unrelenting.

Artemis carried on speaking with Aphrodite, who nodded politely as she worked to keep herself controlled.

It was fucking difficult.

". . . but yeah, I'm so glad that you're okay. You're looking so much better. Maybe when you come to New Orleans, I can show you the sanctuary? It's a wildlife preserve, and there are all kinds of creatures there." Artemis was clearly trying to make up for lost time, and I smiled at her. She looked bewildered but cautiously smiled back.

I knew how much the rift with Hephaestus had cost Aphrodite. Their friends had naturally sided with Hephaestus, and only Hecate had ever bothered to bridge the divide. I was glad she was starting to feel like part of a community again. Hephaestus must have told them all to behave.

Gratitude filled me as I grabbed a plate and loaded it up before taking a seat at the end of the table. I didn't want to sully their conversation.

Hephaestus walked in minutes later, looking fucking amazing. A small spike of jealousy lit my core when I watched Aphrodite's hungry eyes rake over him. He stopped behind her chair and made to bend down and kiss her but opted to squeeze her shoulder instead.

Aphrodite's face fell.

He looked troubled.

Understandable, considering.

Aphrodite shook her head once, plastering on a smile before she dove back into her breakfast.

Hephaestus sent me an appraising look down the table, eyeing my half-empty plate with a small smile on those smug lips.

Emotions warred inside me. A confusing, swirling vortex as I stuffed my face with more waffles and syrup. On the one hand, I was pissed he'd made Aphrodite upset. On the other, his quiet look of praise that I'd eaten when he asked me to warmed me from the inside out.

Shut it down.

"Ares, have you been to New Asphodel lately?" Hephaestus asked through sips of coffee. He lowered his mug and studied me as I chewed.

"A few weeks ago, I dropped over a few dispatched shades. Why?" I asked, curious at the line of questioning.

Aphrodite turned to me with a similar look.

"What is New Asphodel?" she asked, looking between the two of us.

I swallowed my last bite of food and took a swig of the coffee a shade had dropped in front of me.

"The Elysian Fields were overrun during Demeter's Rebellion. Thanatos and Dionysus came to me and asked me to help them expand. They'd done all they could with the shades under their command, but their hands were tied when it came to the ones under mine," I answered, sipping again.

Artemis leaned forward, curious.

"You have shades under your command? In the Underworld?" she asked.

I sipped my coffee, dipped my chin.

"The dead belong to Hades, and they are under his rule. Some fall under the purview of others, but he has final say. During that time, Hades was stretched pretty thin, so those of us with subjects here helped out. In my case, some devoted their lives and deaths to me as soldiers. And between the famine and the wars, the part of Elysian Fields dedicated to warriors was on the brink of collapse. Thanatos and Dionysus asked for a bit of my essence to help build them a separate space. I gave them the power that was required. We called the location New Asphodel, and from that, carved a place called Elysium. All the greatest warriors reside there together," I finished with a shrug.

"It's actually quite impressive," Hephaestus chimed in.

Heat crept along my spine as Artemis raised an eyebrow.

"It's the only place in the Underworld where the sun shines," he added.

"How is that possible?" Hecate asked, curious.

"Helios, actually. I asked if there was a way for them to experience the warmth of the sun, and he made it happen. Speaking of"—I frowned, thinking—"now that he's mortal, I wonder if the sun will still shine on them. I should go check," I mumbled, mostly to myself.

"I'll go with you," Hephaestus offered.

I nearly choked on my coffee, but I recovered quickly, eying him suspiciously.

"I don't need a supervisor," I quipped defensively before I could stop myself, the urge to be shitty with him too much of a passive reflex. Elysium was my domain, and they were my soldiers.

Hephaestus set his jaw.

"Hades dropped a hint about the first Trial. Said he couldn't help, per the rules, but then he mentioned you possibly wanting to visit New Asphodel. And he mentioned you may want to check on some of your favored warriors. I was wondering if you knew of anyone who he may be referring to?"

He sat his coffee down, and I chewed sheepishly.

"I have more than a few favored on that island," I admitted. "Did he mention anything else?"

He shook his head.

"Just said I'd probably have to drag you away by the heels." He shrugged.

I ran my tongue across my teeth, contemplating. That wording seemed specific, and Hades was known for skirting the rules by using creative language. In the mortal world, he would have been an excellent lawyer . . . heel. *Ah*. The tumblers clicked into place.

I looked up at him. "Achilles is on that island."

Aphrodite looked between us, her beautiful face filled with excitement.

My heart fell through my fucking stomach, and suddenly, I hated myself for saying anything. She just wanted to get out of this, and I was helping her. How masochistic.

"Okay, when can we go? Can we go now?" she asked.

I cast my eyes downward.

Hephaestus cleared his throat.

"I'm sorry, love, you can't go," he said, and she turned to him, hackles raised, sitting at her full height in the high-backed chair.

"And why the fuck can't I?" she challenged, a dangerous glint in her eyes.

I knew I should jump in and help, but he shifted nervously in his seat, and a small sadistic part of me wanted to watch him squirm. Telling Aphrodite to not do anything resulted in a death wish to the layman, and though I'd seen a different side of him last night, it seemed that dominance was contained to the bedroom.

He knocked back the last of his coffee and studied her. "Not because we don't want you to, Aphrodite. Admittance to the island is only permitted to soldiers and warriors. It's not personal, Little Goddess, you just won't be able to cross the barrier."

Damn it. I could see how his calm and logical voice wrapped around her, cooling her fire from within. Annoying.

"I've fought plenty in my time," she retorted, and he shook his head.

"No one is challenging your skills or abilities. The crux of the stipulation is that you've taken or given a mortal life in battle, in service," I chimed in, unable to see her upset, or think we doubted her. "It wasn't a rule meant to exclude those who participate. It's just that this island is specific."

Aphrodite crossed her arms, still pissed, and Persephone reached for her arm.

"Why don't you stay and help me pick out some things for the nursery? I could really use you on my team. Hecate will insist there are sigils and dried plants everywhere, and Artemis will demand she has a bow before she can walk. I need a softer touch, so we don't end up with a deathtrap in there," Persephone begged, and I saw the corner of Aphrodite's mouth quirk up just a little.

"How do you know it's a girl? You're barely showing," Hephaestus asked.

Persephone shrugged.

"Cate said so. Hard to argue with a goddess who sees the future." She looked back at Aphrodite. "Please, come with us. I've had over a year to catch up with everyone else. I want some Aphrodite time too." Persephone batted her eyelashes dramatically, clasping her hands together in prayer.

Aphrodite's smile cracked wide.

"Alright, fine. But only because I don't want my niece's entire nursery aesthetic to be dark and creepy and stabby."

She laughed as they stood, backing away from the table. Aphrodite shot me and then Hephaestus a wary look. "Try to have a good day. And try not to kill one another, or I'll be very upset," she chided.

I offered her an innocent grin, hands held aloft in surrender.

Just as Hephaestus had, she, too, looked torn between coming to me for a kiss and walking away. Unwilling to let her leave my sight without my mark, I stood and closed the distance between us by taking her by the hips and pulling her tight against me. The kiss was deep, intimate, a radiating heat that flowed between us. A deep voice cleared their throat, and I turned with some satisfaction to see Hephaestus had absconded from his seat to wait his turn.

To mark her lips. To be represented.

I half expected him to command her to his arms, but gone was the Dominant from the night before. He simply opened his arms, and she peeled herself from me to reach for his outstretched hand. Hephaestus pulled her close, kissed her softly, sweetly. She melted into his touch, threading her delicate fingers through his messy bun. When he broke the kiss apart, the room had gone stone still, but there were no jabs or barbs. Only Persephone, who clapped her hands together and grabbed for Aphrodite.

The goddess allowed Persephone to lead her away, moving as though she were in a daze as her fingers lingered over her lips, where he'd kissed her.

Gentle fucker.

Persephone opened a portal of shadows, and they tumbled through it in a mess of laughs and giggles, no doubt dissecting every moment of that interaction. *Good*. Maybe they would figure out some answers as to why this was happening and what it all meant, then report back to us.

The mass of shadows swirled shut, and I turned to look at Hephaestus, who'd clammed up again.

"Should we go?" I asked, ready to get this over with, but also a little excited to see my people.

"Sure, just one problem. Persephone just left, Hades is out in the field now, and neither of us can summon shadows here. Guess we're walking." He frowned, worrying his fingers through his already tousled hair as he let out a breath.

I considered. New Asphodel was probably an hour's walk from here, which meant a lot of awkward silences in our future . . . I cocked my head, an idea forming.

"Do you think the stables are still in working order?" I asked.

"Probably," he replied, studying me curiously.

"Well then, I may have an idea to get us there faster." I shot him a mischievous grin, and despite what I'm sure was his better judgement, Hephaestus smiled, lifting an eyebrow at my grin.

Maybe this wouldn't be so terrible after all.

Ares

CHAPTER 22

Hephaestus led us through the palace, since I still could barely navigate the corridors without getting lost. Not that I'd ever admit that to him. We moved in silence—not quite comfortable, but perhaps neutral. He moved with confident strides, the hard muscles in his shoulders and back highlighted by the fitted T-shirt he had stretched over them. It was distracting in a way that made me nervous. There seemed to be a bleed between us all; Aphrodite's feelings leaking down our Bonds. That was the only reason I was struggling with this, because I could feel how *she* felt about him, and that twisted me up.

"I just wanted to say thank you for earlier and how you honored my request that we be fair," Hephaestus called over his shoulder, so soft and timid that I almost missed it.

I picked up stride, closing the distance between us until we were nearly shoulder to shoulder. He eyed me nervously, like he hadn't just casually thanked me for stuffing his cum in his wife's mouth while he was in the shower and I was dick deep inside of her.

Bold admission.

"I'm a big believer in fairness, Hephaestus," I replied, and a smile curled my lips. "Besides, she seemed totally into it."

The corner of his mouth lifted just a little as we entered the foyer of the palace. With a heave, he pulled open the large iron doors and waited for me to pass before following me down the precarious steps toward the back of the palace grounds. And because I'd never learned how to shut the fuck up while I was ahead, I kept talking, filling the quiet space between us.

"That being said, one may say it's unfair to create a second cock. How's a god supposed to compete with that?"

Hephaestus raised an eyebrow at my brash questioning, but that smile was back, shy and humble just as it had been when he'd first put on the mechanism last night.

"She fucking loves it. I can forge you one, if you'd like," he offered.

I let that bounce around in my head for a moment.

"Will it become a part of me like yours does? And can you feel it the way you feel your true cock?" I asked, curiosity getting the better of me.

We crossed the back lawn, making our way to the stables that loomed ominously in front of us. I could hear braying and excitement pumped through me.

"I don't know, actually," Hephaestus replied thoughtfully, shoving his hands in his pockets as we walked. "I've never made anything like that for anyone else. Metals kind of . . . meld to me effortlessly. I wanted it to be a part of me, and so when I wear it, it becomes so. It feels just as sensitive as mine, and I can come with it just fine."

Something white-hot pulled down my spine, the memory of his parted lips, the flex of his fingers digging into her skin as he'd come smacking into my mind. I flexed my fist to calm my heartbeat, swallowed.

"I think it'd be cool to try, if it's not too much trouble. Maybe you could make it ribbed for her pleasure," I joked, but he shot me a smoldering look.

"It's *all* for her pleasure, Ares." His tone shifted, and Fates, why was that so hot? I was going to have to get this shit under control. Lines were already blurring, and the last thing I needed was to confuse what any of this was.

Hephaestus reached for the stable door and pulled it wide for us, ushering me through.

I scanned the room as wild snarls and whines ripped through the air. My eyes fell on the back stall, pure joy shifting through me. I jogged forward as four large heads poked through the stall grates. My war steeds greeted me, nuzzling into my neck and nipping at my shoulders.

"Phobos, my boy," I whispered as my black stallion pushed to the front and demanded my hand. I ran the flat of my palm over the ridge of his long muzzle. "Aithon, Phlogios." The girls whipped their manes back and forth, preening as I stroked their soft hair. They had been gifts from Aphrodite, given to me so I'd have a piece of her to take into battle.

I looked around for their brother, and from the far side, Konabos let out a disgruntled *harumpft*. I barked a laugh at my firstborn, my beating heart. Molded by my hands out of clay, he'd always been the most headstrong of his siblings. So defiant, so willful.

The most like me.

"Konabos, come." I tsked as he turned away from me, stamping his hooves. "Konabos, come *here*."

My words were laced with command, and he balked, whinnying.

"I'm sorry I've been gone for so long, son. I promise to stretch your legs, if you'll forgive me?"

Konabos ripped his head around, dark eyes shining.

I smiled, unlocking the gate. They wasted no time bolting out, running up a whirlwind of chaos with each stomp of their hooves. I laughed at Hephaestus's startled expression as he flattened himself against the wall in alarm. The shades that were milling around, cleaning the stalls and completing other mundane tasks, watched on with amusement.

I motioned for the shade nearest me to come forward.

"Lord Ares." He bowed.

"Is my chariot here still?" I asked, and he nodded. "Could you fetch it for me, so I may ride?"

He was off in a flash.

I turned to Hephaestus, who was gingerly making his way across the stable.

"They looked happy to see you," he noted, shoving his hands back in his pockets as he approached. He did that a lot, when he was uneasy.

"I shouldn't have kept away for so long. I'm sure they'll make me pay for it," I grumbled just as Aithon barreled up, skidding to a stop between us. She shoved her head toward Hephaestus, who jumped back, uncertain. I chuckled as he eyed her nervously.

"She likes you, but I guess I shouldn't be surprised . . ." I said, reaching for her neck to pat.

Hephaestus looked at me bewildered. "Why would she like me . . . ?" The implication of "if she belongs to you" remained unsaid.

I shrugged. "She's Aphrodite's. Gifted to me with her sister, Phlogios."

I beckoned him forward, and he approached, cautiously.

"Do horses make you nervous?" I asked.

"They're magnificent, but also their reputation precedes them." He raised a hand to gently pet Aithon, who would have none of that. She pushed forward into his hand, pressing her large head up against him and letting out a low whinny.

"It's alright," I assured, and was surprised when he believed me, trusted my words enough to wrap both hands around her, stroking along the underside of her jaw.

I walked out of the stable, pushing past the open door and laid eyes upon my chariot. Black and sleek, with spiked wheels and red hardware all around. Shades busied themselves around it, attaching buckles and reins and harnesses as they led my steeds to take their places.

Aithon trotted right next to Hephaestus, who seemed to have warmed up to her. Not like she'd give him much choice.

The shades fitted her with her bridle then and attached the chariot to it with the yoke. I dismissed the help with a thank-you, turning back to Hephaestus who lingered toward the back, tucked out of the way.

"Have you ever flown in a chariot before?" I asked.

He grimaced. "A few times, with Helios. I'm not a huge fan," he admitted, eyeing the small area that would be the bucket. The sloping arches of the sides barely came past his hips.

I gestured toward it. "Climb up. It's safe, I promise."

He stepped forward, and there was something in his nervous hesitation that soothed me. This was my domain, and I was in control. Hephaestus climbed the single step and positioned himself closest to the rail. He wasn't as large as me, but his frame still filled up most of the free space.

I hauled up behind him, pinning his body between the front of the chariot and me, knowing this fit was far too intimate, but what choice did we have? He stiffened as I wrapped the reins around my hands and pulled them tight.

"Hold on," I cautioned, and he replied, but whatever his words were became lost in the rush of wind as my horses let out a cry and thrust forward.

The chariot rocked and the force knocked him flat against me, his back to my chest. Instinctively, my arms wrapped around his waist to steady us both. Hephaestus's knuckles were bone white as he gripped the edge of my chariot. I squeezed my forearms against his sides and leaned closer to his ear to speak above the roar of the wind.

"Relax. They can sense your distress, and it will drive them bat-shit. I've got you," I reassured him, ignoring the way Hephaestus shuddered when my breath fanned over his ear. But he did at least try to relax. His body sank deeper against me, warmth bleeding from where our bodies connected.

The hooves of my horses galloped heavily, churning up the black earth of the Underworld as they gathered speed, racing toward the sky.

"Brace yourself, we're about to fly," I warned, shifting my reins into one hand to wrap my other around his torso tightly, telling myself it was so he didn't throw off our balance and cause us to both fall to our deaths.

He released one of his hands and laid it across my arm, entwining our fingers as the chariot left the ground, and the shake of them showed how truly scared he was.

I softened, controlling my breathing, acutely aware that the rise and fall of his chest slowed to match mine as we climbed. We soared higher and higher, the cold biting into our skin as the air thinned. Hephaestus trembled, and I curled my body around his, shielding what I could of the brutal bite from him.

"I'm sorry about the cold."

He turned his head slightly, raised his voice above the wind. "I'm not cold. Are you cold?" he asked.

A burst of warmth radiated from his back and arms, sinking through the fabric of our clothes, lighting me up. It felt as though the sun itself shone upon us in the Underworld as we flew across the Elysian Fields to New Asphodel.

Still, he shuddered.

"Are you . . . Is this nerves?" I asked gently, gesturing my hand over his tense body.

He nodded once, just once, curt and tense.

"I'm sorry, it's almost over," I whispered into his ear.

He squeezed my wrist. "It's okay, it's beautiful. I'm just not the best with heights," he admitted as the horizon crested, and we angled down, circling Elysium.

"Bend your knees when I say, it'll help with the impact," I instructed as the horses galloped. Lower, we circled, spiraling down to a soft patch of grass.

"Now, bend!" I hollered, and he did as told, his body sinking, moving in tandem with mine. The chariot crashed down, bouncing back and forth as we knocked against each other. I pulled the reins back, slowing our momentum.

"Whoa, whoa, there. Nice and easy," I cooed, and the horses slowed to barely a trot before coming to a stop.

Back on the ground, I became hyperaware that Hephaestus was still wrapped in my arms, still radiating heat against my body.

He looked over his shoulder, a question in his eyes, and I panicked, flinging the reins over the side as I hastily disembarked, stepping away from him. The air instantly cooled, and goose bumps rushed along my skin as he clamored down after me.

I walked to Konabos and gave him a few head rubs. "You did so well, thank you. Rest now, we won't be long."

Konabos nudged his muzzle against my pocket, where he knew the ambrosia and honey sugar cubes the shades had given me sat, tucked away.

I smirked, rolling my eyes as I dug deep into the denim, grabbing enough for each of them.

Satisfied they would stay put, I turned to find Hephaestus watching me.

"You're very good with them," he noted, sounding nearly shocked that any being could stand to be in my presence.

Something ugly writhed in my gut, twisting and turning at the thought. Wordlessly, I pushed past him and began the long trek up the grassy knoll.

Soft grass soon gave way to sand, and as we approached the gates of Elysium, two sentries stood facing us, swords crossed. The massive walls that encircled the warriors' resting grounds rose up imposingly behind them.

I felt the breath release from my lungs, and with it, my tension. This was comfortable. These were my people.

Hephaestus
CHAPTER 23

I hadn't been to Elysium for a very long time. Almost seventy years, if my recollection was to be trusted. Tightness spread through my chest, but I employed the techniques Gia and Hermes had helped instill in me, when I was at my worst, and I'd sought treatment here.

"You good?" Ares asked, startling me. I looked over to see him frowning slightly, eyebrows pinched together.

"Good," I quipped, pushing past him.

We approached the gates, guarded by two Greek warriors, sunlight glinting off tarnished metal as it shone down like a crack in the sky. I was grateful that a small aspect of his contribution remained intact, despite Helios's newly minted mortality.

"Lord Ares, Lord Hephaestus," they greeted.

Ares walked slightly ahead of me, and even now, I could see him subtly angled to keep me behind him. Almost . . . *protective*. He extended his arm out as another guard passed through the gates—this one taller, broader, wearing a blinding smile as we approached. He clasped forearms with Ares then stepped back, looking me over.

"Veraclese, this is Hephaestus, God of the Forge," Ares introduced us.

Veraclese fisted his hand over his heart and bowed slowly.

"Forgive me, Lord Hephaestus, I need to confirm your entry." Veraclese looked uneasy, but I shoved the collar of my shirt down to allow him access to my chest, the same as the first time I'd entered these gates.

He nodded appreciatively as he placed his hand over my sternum, searching. His brows creased as he settled over my credentials—the pain of war, the cost and sacrifice. *The blood of it*. He stepped back, and I let my hem go, straightening my shirt, fidgeting.

"No need to verify your credentials then?" I raised an eyebrow to Ares, and Veraclese sent me a look of disbelief before schooling his features as he led us through the iron arches.

Ares let out a real laugh before leaning back, crowding my space.

"Maybe you can check them later." His words were playful, something I never thought of him as being able to be.

I stared back into his dark eyes, and thoughts of what it could mean took off like a shot in my head.

He winked and turned back around to follow Veraclese, as though he hadn't just set my insides on fire.

"What brings you to Elysium, Lord Ares?" the warrior asked as we made our way through the large square. These buildings were more modern, simple barracks that housed many of the fallen from the last century.

"We're here to see Achilles. Is he still in the old guard?" Ares asked, and Veraclese nodded, gesturing to the northwest corner.

"You have excellent timing; it's Challenge Day. I'm sure any of the men would be honored to have you preside, or even participate."

The electricity in the air crackled around Ares, excited anticipation rolling from him, and as we delved deeper into the city, the God of War visibly relaxed. He held himself with an inherent power, divine grace amongst his people, and it was intriguing, getting to see this side of him. Ares always presented with such arrogance, such short-fused anger. A blunt instrument of destruction. I was beginning to think that, underneath all that bravado and shrouds of blood, were the makings of a decent god.

We traced familiar steps, each part of the city built to represent a different point in human history, and it was like walking through an immersive museum of time. Many took to the streets, eager for a glimpse of the God of War, but more rushed forward to greet him. Some bore his mark upon their wrists; others offered him a round of wrestling or wine.

Ares stopped and spoke to almost everyone, or at least acknowledged them with a handshake, remembered their names, every one. It made our crawl through the city slow-moving, but I didn't mind.

We crossed into an area that saw brick and stone structures making way for the ancient war tents, to linens and silk banners from the height of our creation. Sand crunched between our boots as wild yelling and screaming echoed from a distance.

A large crowd gathered around in a circle, watching two mostly naked men fight with swords. I could hardly see them clearly through the throng, but the reverberating clash of steel on steel punctuated by the cheers and groans of the crowd was enough to let me know they were giving it their all.

Ares was abuzz as the thrill of the fight pricked at his skin. It was obvious how badly he itched to enter that ring, but there were important things to get to first.

We crossed the sand to enter a great tent, one fit for a general. It was sturdy material, vast and regal, opulent and practical all at once. The entrance was tied back with two leather tassels, and Veraclese stopped just short of the threshold.

"This is where I leave you, my lords. General Achilles is just inside." Veraclese clasped his fist over his chest and dipped his head before turning to head off toward the fighting ring.

Ares strolled right in, with me following close behind. The tent brought me back to an ancient time: the smells, the decor. Large silks adorned the walls, inviting pops of color through the space. A massive bed lay against the far tent wall piled high with thick furs and pillows. Giant rugs crisscrossed over the bare sandstone floor and jugs of wine rested on a large dining table. This setup reminded me of Troy, and I had the feeling I had been in this very tent before . . .

During the Trojan War, a bitter feud had broken out, with gods on both sides of the conflict. Zeus ordered me to forge armor for Achilles, to protect him from the fall of any sword, and I did. He never mentioned anything about an arrow or a weak heel, though I had born the blunt of his fury for that particular mishap, nonetheless.

Achilles sat on a long bench wearing that exact armor, battle-worn but still in excellent shape. It glinted in the torchlight that flickered off the lanterns. He was tall and broad, long dirty-blond hair braided back and muscles bulging and straining against the clasps holding his armor intact.

"Ares, my Lord, you are most welcome in the home of the Warriors," he greeted, voice much softer than I expected from a man with his reputation for carnage.

"Lord Hephaestus, I never had the chance to thank you for the armor," he noted, following my eyeline as I inspected the metal from afar. Achilles then turned back to Ares and asked, "What brings you out, and on Challenge Day no less?"

"Cut the shit, Achilles. Let's not pretend Hades hasn't already stopped by to warn you of our arrival." Ares leveled him a knowing look.

Achilles pressed his lips together and cracked his neck. "Fair. If you wish to gain access to the Trials, you must learn to light the path from one who has already attempted those trials. And lucky for you, one such person stands before you." Achilles grabbed his sword from the wall and fitted it into his sheath at his hip.

"Let me guess, you can't just tell us," Ares observed, voice flat.

Achilles crossed his massive arms over his chest and shrugged his shoulders. "Afraid not, my lord. If you want it, you're gonna have to fight for it." A maniac gleam lit up Achilles's features, and I saw it then. The bloodlust. The *need* to fight.

The flap at the other end of the tent opened, and another man entered, this one smaller, leaner cut. Patroclus. He was smaller than I expected, maybe a few inches shorter than me, and held himself with such a quiet grace. He was lithe, corded with lean muscle and dark hair. His face held a delicate beauty, so different than the warrior next to Ares, and I wondered how anyone in Troy could have confused him with Achilles.

"Ares, I know you've been wanting to take a swing at him for years, but I implore you to not destroy his shade," Patroclus said as he entered the room in a low-cut himation.

Achilles placed his hands over his heart in mock pain. "You wound me, my love. Do you doubt my ability?" Achilles admonished before pulling Patroclus back into him.

Patroclus laughed and kissed Achilles softly on the cheek. "Of course not, but when you square off with the God of War, I fear expectations must be managed," he turned in his partner's embrace to speak to Ares directly. "I just need him in one piece when it's done."

Achilles grabbed Patroclus, kissing him until he was breathless. When they finally broke apart, he let out a laugh that was warm like honey.

"What say you, Ares?" Achilles lifted an eyebrow, holding Patroclus in his arms.

Ares shot me a quick glance. "This is the only way to begin the Trials?"

Achilles dipped his chin, eyes sparkling in anticipation. "Correct. It's the first step."

I wondered if Ares would go through with it, and if he didn't, if I could. It would be so easy for us to return empty-handed, and I would be a liar if I didn't admit the thought appealed to me. The look in his eyes gave me the feeling the same weights were being measured in Ares's mind. We could go back to the palace, try to figure things out with Aphrodite . . . But that would take her choices, and I couldn't do that to her. Couldn't keep her shackled against her will.

I saw that same conclusion mirrored on Ares's face. "I accept."

"Excellent. My love, would you send for a set of Lord Ares's armor?" Achilles asked Patroclus, who nodded and pulled from his embrace to carry out the request.

"What? Afraid I'll kick your ass dressed like this?" Ares laughed, gesturing to himself, and next to Achilles in his traditional armor, he looked comically out of place. Ares was wearing a pair of my dark wash jeans tucked into his boots and my white tee that read "FRANKIE SAYS RELAX" in bold, red letters.

Achilles snorted and rolled his eyes. "It's Challenge Day. Let's give these folks a show."

Patroclus returned, carrying heavy golden armor, sandals, and several swords that he set down reverently on the bed. Achilles crossed the room and kissed him deeply, roughly.

"Be ready for me after, yeah?" he demanded hungrily, and Patroclus nodded with kiss-swollen lips. Achilles paused, glancing over at Ares and me. "It will be an honor to beat your ass, Lord Ares," he goaded, cocky smile on his handsome face, before waltzing out toward the screams of the fighting ring.

"I'll give you some privacy, my lords." Patroclus waved before he, too, disappeared out of sight.

Ares started to pull my clothes off him, taking time to fold them neatly as he went.

I looked away, but in no time at all, he stood before me, naked, the scars on his back pale white against his tanned skin. He reached for the jug of oil Patroclus had carried in, then dumped a liberal amount of the slick liquid it held out. It coated the fingers he brought to his wrist, coated his skin as he rubbed methodically over his neck and arms, down his torso, as was tradition to stop the armor from chaffing. He covered as much of his back as he could reach, but there were large patches he'd missed, and while I was sure they wouldn't matter to him in the long run, I stepped in anyway, hand outstretched.

He hesitated, gaze meeting mine for only a moment before handing the jug over.

"I thought, for a moment, you weren't going to do it," I said as I slathered the oil in my own hands, warming it between my palms before placing them on his shoulders. Ares's muscles rippled under my touch just like they had in the shower, bunching and tightening.

I pressed deeper, my fingers finding all the knots of tensions he kept coiled there, on shoulders that carried the burdens of secrets and shame. I pushed warmth through my fingers, and Ares groaned, rocking forward to brace his hand on the bedpost.

"I thought about it, truth be told," he admitted on a low breath.

I leaned closer, seeing the tapestry on his shoulders, his back, feeling the edges of long-healed, through-and-through bullet wounds near his spine.

"Why didn't you?" Curiosity gnawed at me over him, over the layers that I was peeling back.

He groaned as I slid my thumb up the side of his neck, spending far more time than necessary with my hands on his body.

"Because I don't need to give her a reason to hate me or the connection we share, and if I didn't, you would have, and when I brought your body back, I would have lost her anyway."

I pulled back, shocked by the honesty of his words as I stepped away, wiping my oiled hands on my jeans.

Ares scooped up his armor, covering his bare ass with the leather pleats, fastening the tie with a tug.

"I don't know if I should be offended that you think I wouldn't survive in a fight or not," I said.

His massive breastplate came next, engraved with gold filigree, the crest of Aphrodite next to his own, right over his heart.

"It isn't about thinking you weak—I know enough to sense you're not. But being here, it's affecting you. You've been jumpy since we passed through those gates, fidgeting, and a few times, you had to remind yourself to breathe." He buckled his bracers and reached for his greaves, casually dissecting my behavior like it was nothing to him. "You're haunted by things you've seen, and done, in war."

I bent low, scooping the greaves off the bed and opening a clasp for him to slip his calf into. He watched as my trembling fingers worked the ties, fixing them tightly to his shin as a low current of embarrassment heated through me.

"She told you?" I nearly choked on the words as I moved over, securing his other greave.

"She didn't have to. It's written all over you, Hephaestus, and your shame of it. But you shouldn't feel it. Compassion isn't something to regret. It makes you kind. That destruction affects you; war is hell."

I slipped on his sandals, looked up at him to find dark eyes crinkled at the corners, understanding in his gaze. I shivered and straightened, feeling raw and exposed as I grabbed his sword to hand to him, but he shook his head, waving me off.

"I don't need it to beat him. Patroclus would be upset if, after all they went through to be together, I ruined it by destroying his shade."

Hephaestus

CHAPTER 24

We stepped into the sun to find the crowd had tripled in size.

"News travels fast," I mumbled.

Ares bumped into my shoulder and joked, "Not every day the God of War fights the greatest Warrior of All Time."

We drew nearer to the fighting pit, the sound of cheers thunderous and overwhelming. Spears and swords clanged together, bracers smacking against chest plates. Energy pulsed, heavy and electric, as Ares soaked up the glorious tribute beside me. The crowd parted for us to walk to the edge of a ring in the sand.

Ares turned to me, and it felt wrong to stay silent. "Try not to die."

"Worried about me, Forge God?" he responded, eyebrows arched.

"Shut up," I growled.

He chuckled, then flashed me the most devastatingly devious smile as he crouched low to step into the roped-off circle.

The crowd surged as close as the barrier would allow, cheering and egging Achilles and Ares on, feeding off the infectious energy.

The two circled each other, the blond warrior twirling his sword once as they danced around the edge. They were patient, nearly lazy with each step while awaiting the other to make a move. Ares cocked his head with a patronizing smirk on his face, fists barely raised in front of his body. Achilles struck, quick and precise, and the sheer force of it would have been a killing blow to anyone else.

Anyone except Ares.

The blade went straight for his chest, and my pulse quickened with worry until Ares slipped sideways at the very last minute, stopping the blade between his hands. He pulled the blade toward himself, knocking Achilles off balance before letting go of the blade and spinning to land an elbow to Achilles's nose.

A sickening crack was punctuated by cheers and groans alike as blood burst in a river from Achilles's face, splattering them both, running like a red stream down his face and neck.

Achilles kicked Ares hard, his sandal connecting over the War God's torso, separating them, fury etched into his features. They resumed circling one another, and Achilles lunged once more, causing Ares to arch his body at an impossible angle to avoid the blade.

The way they moved was a dance, graceful and yet so damned deadly. Sand kicked up around their feet as they lunged and punched and landed blows that shook the earth beneath us. Achilles hit Ares at a run, slicing through the air like a javelin, scraping the tip of his sword across an exposed area of his chest.

I could hear nothing over the excited roars around us, but as I watched a thin line of red bloom across the slice in Ares's flesh, my own blood ran cold. It was close to the wound I'd delivered accidentally, the only time I'd ever harmed the God of War.

I lunged forward on instinct to stop this, but a strong arm gripped me tightly. Patroclus had made it to my side. He shook his head once then lifted his chin toward the two warriors fighting in bloodsport.

"He's fine. It's the bloodlust," he reassured me.

I turned back to see Ares trading punch after punch with Achilles, a deranged smile on his bloodied face. My skin itched with an undercurrent of electricity that wound down deep.

Ares had Achilles pinned, their massive bodies pressed into the sand as the God of War wrapped his limbs around him. His eyes found mine.

A tribute.

Ares kept his eyes on mine as he cinched Achilles in a blood choke. I was rooted to the sand, watching in rapt fascination and horror as his fist found that sweet spot in Achilles's neck, knuckles pressing deep. To the sound of thunderous applause and mournful boos, we watched the consciousness leave Achilles's eyes.

The crowd erupted.

Patroclus tugged at my arm, moving me in the opposite direction as I tried to get to Ares.

"They're coming straight to us, trust me," he shouted over the roar.

We had only been back in the tent mere moments, when Achilles and Ares burst through the curtains, beaten and bloodied but looking elated. They parted ways, and the warrior headed straight to the couch, where Patroclus awaited him, himation halfway off his body. Achilles slid his armor off as he moved, then his bloodied fingers pulled Patroclus into a punishing kiss, desperate and charged.

Ares tugged on the back of my shirt, guiding me to another room. The curtain between us fell just as Achilles pushed Patroclus's head into his now-naked crotch, head dropped back in a sigh.

"Wrap those lips around me and suck me enough to take the edge off. Then I'll fuck you raw like you like, lover." Achilles's rough voice, and the sound of Patroclus choking and sputtering, wasn't the least bit dulled by the fabric hanging between us.

Ares turned, still vibrating with power and barely controlled bloodlust as he unbuckled his armor. Moans and the unmistakable grunts of ecstasy filled all the space between us, and I searched for an exit, some way to get us out of this before my body betrayed my better judgment.

The side of the tent split open, and in walked a warrior, handsome and strong with short dark hair and striking green eyes. He was naked, except for leathers that draped his waist.

Armor clanged to the ground with a metallic screech as I turned to see Ares stiffen in recognition. The warrior sauntered right up to Ares, too comfortable, way too fucking familiar being so close to the God of War.

"Excellent win, Lord Ares," he smiled coyly, kneeling slowly, ignoring me completely.

"Andreas," Ares clipped, voice tight as the man waited, too close to the unbuttoned jeans and unclothed torso for my liking. "What are you doing here?"

He stepped back, nearly to the wall, as the warrior brazenly licked his lips and batted his eyelashes.

"I thought you may require release, after that display," he purred, and the rage that flooded through me was a welling tsunami at this shade's fucking audacity.

He reached a hand up, to touch, but before Ares could move, I snapped. I was between them in a breath; my hand wrapped around his throat while Ares's breath tickled the back of my neck. A shocked cry left his lips as I lifted him, ripping his body from the ground until he was eye level.

"*He is Bonded.* Have some fucking respect," I spat, flinging the shade across the room, the crashing sound of metal trinkets and vases falling to the floor nearly deafening.

The curtain swung wide, and Achilles rushed in, still naked, sword raised.

"What in the Pits is happening here?" he demanded, but he took one look at me, poised protectively in front of a shirtless Ares, and one at the shade on the floor still grasping for air, then lowered his sword.

"Aphrodite is waiting for us," I snapped as the man looked me over, outraged and indignant as he scrambled up from the floor and fled the tent, but I didn't give a damn. The anger was slow to recede, and it wasn't until Ares placed a hand on my shoulder, almost willing me to calm down, that I loosened my jaw.

"Your quest has been presented to the Oracle," Achilles said, eyeing me warily, but I could swear there was a knowing glint in his eye, one that made me squirm. "I'll be in touch with her answer soon . . ."

The grip on my shoulder tightened before Ares gathered his clothing under an arm and grabbed my wrist, pulling me behind him as he went.

My skin was on fire. Every nerve flayed except for the part of my wrist nestled in Ares's grip as he led us back out the city. This time, he made no stops, everything in our aura repulsing a warning not to touch.

I was pissed, and frustratingly horny, thanks to the cross connection of the Bonds, and I just . . . *I needed Aphrodite.*

Ares put two fingers between his lips and let out a whistle that pierced through the air. Mighty hooves echoed on the sand as his chariot descended, skidding to the side as it landed before us. Neither of us had said a word, and that didn't change when Ares grabbed the reins and flung me forward into the bucket with some force.

My hips bit into the front rail, and I hissed at the sting.

His body pressed into me, the hard planes of his blood-soaked chest settling against my back as he snapped the reins, urging his mounts to ride harder, faster. I expected him to fly us back, but through my muddled fog, I was able to recognize that he was keeping the chariot grounded. For me.

We tore away from Elysium, wheels peeling through the rest of New Asphodel like lightning. White-hot fire surged through every cell of my body, and with every jostle, every jolt, Ares's scruff of a beard scratched and marked up the skin of my cheek as he concentrated on steering. It was driving me crazy, because there was a clarity that outburst had provided, one I knew we had to discuss, one that absolutely terrified me.

One of his arms pressed across my torso, and I leaned back, groaning at his touch. Power lapped over his skin, paired with a burning hunger that made me want to sink to my knees, to make him sink to his, to *Fates* . . .

Ares let out a string of profanities as he wrenched the reins to the side of the Asphodel countryside, stopping our momentum. He was out from behind me in a blink, and I turned to see him storming away.

"Ares!" I barked after him, and he turned, rage and need mixing over his expression.

"Where are you going?" I asked as he paced, wearing a path into the dirt.

"What the fuck was that about?" he asked, turning to face me, breathing hard.

I flinched back. "Did you expect me to sit back and watch you be unfaithful to Aphrodite in front of me?" I fired back, the barely simmering anger roaring to life again.

His eyes bulged, a vein in his neck pulsing as he fisted his hands at his sides.

"*I would never*. When we're apart, sure. But not now. And certainly not in front of *you*." He spat, pissed off, but there was a wounded edge to his voice.

"He had no right to touch you!" I growled back.

He stalked back toward me, crowding up into my space. My throat burned with the scent of him, that spice blended with the violence painting his chin, his chest, those hands.

"Why do you care who touches me, Hephaestus? Hmm?"

I opened my mouth to respond as his eyes shifted between mine, spearing me as panic and uncertainty crept up my throat, constricting my tongue.

"Because it would hurt her, Ares."

Fates, he was so close to me, the pull beneath my ribs sharp and visceral, but I fought to stand my ground, even as he raged like a bull.

"Why are you looking at me like this?" he asked, and I wanted to lie to him. It would have been better if I just lied.

"Because the Bonds have their wires crossed, and the attraction she feels for you keeps wrapping me up in a vice. And the thought of that fucking shade touching you, putting any part of you in their mouth, it—" I looked away briefly, then lifted my chin back to him. "I couldn't let it happen. So I stopped it. And as long as we're tied together like this, as long as I'm still feeling you through her, I'll keep stopping it."

He stumbled back, eyes wild, running the back of his hand across his mouth.

"You feel it too?" he asked, skeptically.

I nodded.

"Oh, thank the Fates. I thought I was going crazy." There was a pained relief in his expression, as he rubbed over his chest, over the Bondmark he shared with Aphrodite. "I thought, for a second anyway, that I—" He clamped his mouth shut, but my eyes snapped to him. I wanted very badly to know what he had been about to say, but he just shook his head, and turned, heading away from me.

"Wait, where are you going?" I called, jogging after him. He didn't stop until I grabbed for his elbow, and when I turned him, the imprint of his cock was straining against the front of my jeans.

"I'm not going to make it back to Aphrodite. I can't be this close to you, touching you, not right now. Go back to the chariot. I need to take care of this," he snapped in frustration.

I didn't decide to reach for him, but my hand moved. He jerked back, out of my reach. Hurt bloomed in my chest and spread up my cheeks in a flush as I started to recoil, but a regret flickered across his face.

Ares stepped closer, invading my space, and I thought of Aphrodite, of what she would have wanted in this moment, knowing she would do anything to ease his aches. Ares reached for my hand, breathing hard as he placed it over his bloodstained torso. Fire exploded through our touch, and I let go, leaning into him. Allowing myself to experience. I was shaking slightly from the adrenaline, but his hands were steady, so sure.

I'd never been with a man before.

I'd never been with *anyone* other than Aphrodite.

But I knew I wanted to satiate his hunger, to feed into my own pleasure. I wasn't sure I could do that without her here, but I knew I had to try. Maybe I wanted to try.

"Take out your cock." A demand. A question.

One he answered with deft fingers over the snick of a zipper. I put my hands on his shoulders, backing us up against a stone mountainside. Ares's back slammed into the cold shale, and he shuddered, fisting his thick length roughly.

"Now mine." I shut off my mind. I just let myself feel. *Let go*. Calloused fingers danced over my abdomen as he lowered my zipper and reached a hand inside. I groaned at the roughness of him wrapping around my cock, a foreign, firm grip—not mine, not hers. I slid my hand over his shaft as the Underworld around us silenced.

"Stroke," I whispered. Thick fingers moved over my piercings, the warmth of his saliva as he leaned down, the sound of his lips as he spit on my cock, stroking with slick, wet pulls that had my toes curling.

I leaned in closer, pushing and pulling as I flexed my fingers over him. Chests heaved. Panted breaths. Gazes locked.

"I'm so close," he grunted. "Please don't stop, Hephaestus."

My hips faltered, knees going weak at hearing my name fall from his lips. I pushed his head back against the stone and ghosted my lips along his collarbone as I ramped up my ministrations.

"Come then, Ares. Come *for* me."

I fought to hold off my own pleasure, but Ares was very talented.

"Come with me," he whined, the needy beg a vibrato that flipped a switch inside of me.

He jerked hard in my hands, eyes rolling back in his head as I brought his lips to mine in a searing kiss. Soft, tentative lips that turned demanding as our tongues battled for dominance. His release coated my hands first, and I was proud, as I shot all over his torso, mixing with the sweat and dirt and blood. His dark hair fell into his eyes as his chin dropped to his chest, looking at the mess of us, his panting breaths colliding with mine.

There were no witnesses here, just Ares and me and our cum dripping to the ground between us.

I pushed slightly to disentangle our limbs, but Ares pulled me back to him, so close his breath fanned over my nose and cheeks when he spoke.

"I want that. With Aphrodite. I've never . . . *shared* her before. But I want that," he confessed.

I nipped at his chin, his candor inspiring some of my own. I wanted that too. I'd never been with anyone other than Aphrodite. "I've never . . . been with anyone else."

"*Anyone?*" he asked, brushing a hand over my cheek. Fates, he looked good like this, dripping with us.

I blushed. He looked at me with such intensity, brown eyes almost black. It sent a rush through me, stealing my breath. Things were shifting, and I worried that what we were feeling wasn't just Aphrodite leaking over, and if it wasn't, how would we even know?

Ares let me go and jogged over to the chariot, returning with the shirt he never was able to put back on to clean off my hands and cock before tidying himself up. I let him work, his touch delicate as my thoughts raced. We needed to talk to Aphrodite about this, absolutely, but I had no fear that she would be upset. I'd felt her desires, known what she craved now that the Bonds between us were cracked open. That didn't scare me.

What if the Bonds were broken, and nothing changed? What if what I felt for him now was more than just collateral damage.

What then?

We remounted the chariot and set off for the palace, him with the reins and me leaned back into his chest. The silence that stretched between us was easy, but as Ares's arms held me tightly against him, I couldn't help but think the only thing missing was Aphrodite here with us.

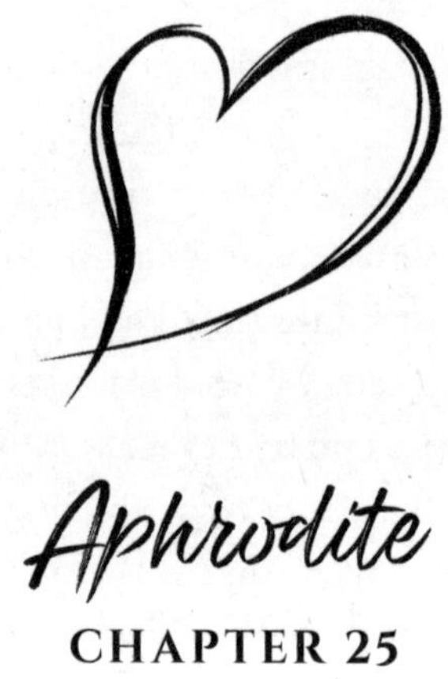

Aphrodite

CHAPTER 25

"Don't you think a macabre-themed nursery in the Underworld is a little on the nose?" Artemis asked, face scrunched in distaste at the skull mirror Hecate held.

We were in a small antique shop in the Quarter that Persephone had grown fond of during her residency in New Orleans. Persephone and I had been fairly close in the past, and Hecate and I had been as well, but Artemis and I had always just been two ships passing. I'd never formed a connection with them as a group before, and insecurity crept into the edge of my psyche, cold and unforgiving at how easily the three of them interacted and moved. I was an interloper, awkward and on the outside. My chest pinched just a bit at the casual way they joked and laughed together. I'd never had that before—Hera had seen to it. Her jealousy ran deep, and all the attention I'd received, *that I'd never wanted*, she'd punished me for.

I missed Ares and Hephaestus. I wondered what trouble they'd gotten into and if I'd come back to find them still in one piece. A blush crept up my cheeks as memories of this morning played on a loop for the millionth time since I'd stepped through that portal. I shook the thoughts away as my body flushed and glanced around to find Persephone staring at me with keen eyes and a slight smirk, like she could read my thoughts.

"What?" I asked, flustered.

Persephone cocked her eyebrows curiously and shook her head with a smile. She turned over the vintage record in her hands and studied the back of it.

"You just looked . . . deep in thought, Ditey. I was wondering if you'd want to share?" she offered.

I softened at the way she was trying to remind me that she was my friend. That she cared about what happened, far outside of the gossip. I chewed on my fingernails as she waited patiently.

"We slept together. All of us. Last night," I blurted.

Persephone's eyes went wide with shock.

"Aphrodite, what the fuck?!" she shouted, and I quickly looked around before stepping closer to her, lowering my voice as I eyed Hecate and Artemis near jewelry cases.

Persephone leaned in, and I closed my eyes, sucking in a deep breath. I had to talk to someone, right?

"I don't even know how it happened, honestly. After . . . you know, that meeting and hearing that my Bond sickness could hurt them, I was overwhelmed and still feeling like shit, physically and mentally. Heph, he could tell. He can always tell when I'm not okay. We ended up back at his room, and I'll spare you the details, but—" Persephone cut me off with a wave of her hand.

"Oh girl, do *not* spare me the details, I wanna know." She wiggled her eyebrows suggestively with a giggle, and I shot her a look. "What? You don't think I know you're into some kinky shit? Hades says Hephaestus has a sex dungeon in his room," she quipped, and my jaw went slack, cheeks flaming.

"It is not a *sex dungeon*," I defended, chancing a glance back to the girls. "He's just built some things that make it . . . Okay, it's a sex dungeon. But I have no complaints."

A smirk stretched across Persephone's face, and I felt the tension break away from the coil in the pit of my stomach.

"Think he'd mind if Hades and I gave it a whirl?" She laughed, and I doubled over from the effort of keeping our voices down. My breathing struggled to regulate through the fits of laughter.

"Seriously, though, both of them? How was it? I would have bet on bloodshed at the mere thought . . . Was that why they both kissed you this morning? Fucking spill!" She rapidly fired questions at me, and I grabbed her wrist to sit us down in an alcove of milk crates and a vintage couch.

"Hephaestus and I were . . . indisposed, and just when it was about to happen, Ares showed up at the door. He was looking for me, and because Heph had lost his entire mind, he let Ares in." I chewed on a fingernail too close to the bed, and a sliver of blood bloomed in the crease as Persephone sat back, shocked.

"How did Ares react?" She leaned back in, invested.

"Well, at first, I could tell he *wanted* to commit murder, whether mine or Hephaestus or both of us, I couldn't honestly say. But Heph, like . . . corralled him? I'm not even sure that's the word, but it's all I've got. He kind of calmed him down."

Persephone crossed her arms, cocking her head to me curiously. "*Hephaestus?* We're talking about the god that married you, and in Ares's mind, stole his lover? Ares calmed down. For him," she clarified, and I nodded. She let out a low whistle. "I've seen Ares out of control. It's terrifying."

"It can be, but Heph has an . . . authoritative manner when he wants to. I know I like it, but I've never seen him use it with anyone else. It was . . . kind of hot . . . He told—no—*commanded* Ares to calm his anger, and he did." My eyes darted around the room as I struggled to say more. I wasn't sure what part of this was a private confidence, and I didn't want to overstep any lines the boys may have had.

As though she could tell why I was hesitant, Persephone dropped her hand to my knee.

"Listen, I know that this is a hard situation. Whatever you say to me will stay with me. Even from Hades. He won't pry if I tell him not to. Though I think you'd find him far more intuitive than anyone suspects, and he loves Hephaestus. He would never judge him, or you. Or Ares." She looked so sincere that the dam in my chest broke, and I word-vomited all over her.

"I think they're starting to develop something." The words rushed out, and I clamped my hand over my mouth as her eyes went wide as saucers.

"Fucking Fates," she whispered.

I dropped my head into my hands, groaning. "I'm not sure if the Bonds being broken have ignited it, or if it's because I triggered this doomsday switch within me, but I can feel it. They used to be completely separate in my life, both equal but individual. Now? It all feels so fucking muddy. There is an attraction between them, and I know they're fighting it, but the more they struggle, the more I see, and I want it, Fates help me. It's shameful, after all they've been through, to ask this of them, but I don't want to choose, and I swear I can fucking see it, Seph."

I gritted my teeth, as though it could stop the next words from tumbling from my lips, but to no avail. "I know they're feeling something, and a part of me knows it's my feelings bleeding into the Bonds on either side too. How could we ever trust what we're feeling when the emotions may not solely be our own? And what's worse is that part of me doesn't care. I'm the most selfish person I've ever known, and they should both break these Bonds and find someone who will make them happy."

Heat rose up my chest as embarrassment sunk into the pit of my stomach, but Persephone gave me a small smile.

"Hey, it's okay. You love them both, and it would be easier if they were into each other too. What if you're not being selfish? What if it isn't the Bonds bleeding over that's causing this, and it wasn't you at all that is the root of all this?" she asked, thoughtfully.

I sniffed as a traitorous tear seeped out of the corner of my eye. "I don't understand what you mean?" I whispered, wiping my hand over my eyes in frustration.

"Maybe the reason it never showed up before was because you all spent so much time staying away from each other? Maybe they would have connected before, but their pride and anger and just general judgment stopped it. What if it was always meant to be this way?"

Her words struck a chord inside me, but I quickly stamped it out, terrified to give myself hope. I was desperate for an excuse for this to be real, anything that absolved me from the guilt of what I'd put them through over the centuries.

"Would you be angry if they developed something without you?" she asked, and I snapped my attention back to Persephone, shaking my head.

"I don't think I'd be upset that it was happening. I think if they loved each other, too, it would take some of the pressure off me, and even thinking that wracks me with guilt," I pondered, and she nodded her head. "If they did develop feelings for each other, I'd just want it to be real. For them. Not because it was what they thought I wanted. Or needed, like now. They're sharing me, and I'm terrified that's killing them."

"Hades and I haven't ever shared with anyone else. Just us and the shadows. I don't think either of us want to be with anyone else, and I know that, sexually, he's all I want. I used to think something was wrong with me until we met, but something in him called to me. I can see it with you and Heph *and* you and Ares. Maybe now they're just giving themselves permission to explore some feelings," she finished, and I chewed on her words.

"They hated each other for so long, Seph. I just don't know how they could put millennia of anger and aggression on the backburner," I whispered.

"There's a fine line between love and hate, Ditey. Maybe they'll build a bridge for you and themselves. Either way, you're going to have to feed the Bonds. When it snapped back into place for Hades and me—it was like we were possessed. I was in so much pain unless he touched me, and at the same time, I craved him the more he did. All that to say, if yours is as hungry as mine was, you may as well let yourselves indulge while you can?" Persephone stood, nodding her head toward the approaching Hecate and Artemis.

We paid for the albums and a small lava lamp that Persephone insisted on, but all I could think about were her words. Even before Hephaestus and I were officially Bonded, how had I fallen in love with him while I bore Ares's mark? Could that have meant something? Would they have been able to form a friendship if they hadn't been cast on opposite sides of this? Everyone threw them apart, drawing a line in the sand, and most of them stood on the side of Hephaestus, the one who they'd seen as wronged.

I saw the way Hephaestus took care of Ares. I felt the way Ares complied obediently with a subtle look or a direct command. I bit my lip, unsure if I should press them to talk about the issue, or if I should let it develop as it will. My thoughts swirled through my mind as we ventured out into the city.

We had walked around New Orleans a bit when we arrived, and I was slowly falling in love. It was so alive: People milled around, an eclectic mix of tourists and locals, and I found myself transfixed by the art in Jackson Square, propped up on the fences, on display for purchase by local talents. I heard all about the band they were in with Hephaestus, and I couldn't help the pang of sadness that I'd never seen them play. He had always been a skilled musician, so free when he let himself get lost in the music.

I'd never spent much time in this part of Louisiana. When Hephaestus and I were together, we'd been in New York, far from the city and the rest of the gods. My stint in Mississippi with Ares had us visiting occasionally, but neither of us were exactly welcome amongst the others, and it seemed easier to just stay on the coast.

There was a magic here, a deep wealth that thrummed beneath the streets, the modern mixed with historical architecture. Many other deities called this place home, sectioning off the city and surrounding lands into domains. The First Nations people had their own gods and spirits on these shores for centuries, when this land was known as Bulbancha. Mass genocide and colonization had all but eradicated these beautiful cultures from the collective consciousness of America, but against all odds, small pockets of resistance could still be found throughout this land. Displaced and ravaged people who clutched the spirit of their communities and ancestors close to their chests like armor, the songs of their mythos flowing from their mouths in hushed tones. They were huddled together in a fraction of the land they still had autonomy over, but they were a proud and resilient people.

The Afro-Caribbean influence was also incredibly strong here, a result of the slave trade. The LOA ruled this land, and effigies and sigils could be found all over the city on doors and in shops, a nod in tribute to the powerful gods that came to the aid of the enslaved humans who faced atrocities on these shores. I could feel the warring magics as they mixed through the fabric of the city, embedded through history and blood and joyous rebellion.

I could have loved living here, if things were different. Walking these streets, I saw glimpses of an alternate reality, of a world where Hephaestus and I rummaged through the vintage music shops we passed on South Rampart. A world where we watched Ares fight at the local boxing club on Poydras, bought trinkets from street artists at Jackson Square, huddled together drinking coffee and eating beignets in a café the city built itself around, hands roaming softly under the table as we teased each other before heading home to make love all night. I wished for that life. Mourned it.

When we reached another store, Persephone dipped inside, looping her arm with mine. I gave her a smile as the Southern heat permeated through my bones.

The shop was a beautiful secondhand place filled with golden trinkets and plush couches. Persephone let out a small whoosh of breath at a deep purple tufted settee, and I knew instantly it would find its way to the Underworld. She would look like a dream settled into it, holding whatever little shade was growing inside her.

The humid air choked me, slicking my skin as hair clung to the sides of my neck, as Artemis sat next to Persephone on the settee, flinging her toned arm over the back while they spoke about color options. They were so close—I swallowed the pang of jealousy down. I was truly happy they had all found their way back to each other, all taken up easy strides within their friendships.

Hecate tugged at my arm, guiding me through the shop, fingers ghosting lightly over the delicate lamps and knickknacks that adorned the deeply stained shelves. This place was pricey, but it screamed class and elegance without being inauthentic. She picked up a small hourglass filled with black sand and intricate gold spindles.

I wiped a few sweat-soaked strands off the side of my neck, desperately needing some AC.

"Do you have a hair tie?" I asked, and she nodded as she slipped a thin black loop from her wrist. I smiled gratefully, sweeping my hair into a messy high bun. "Thanks, I forgot how muggy this heat could be."

She laughed. "You've been gone too long. You'll reacclimate soon enough." She moved farther along the shelves and readjusted the two long sticks she had holding her wild mane in place, with expert precision. "So . . . how are you doing? Truly? I know you're probably sick of people asking."

I thinned my lips and cast my eyes down, shrugging. "Actually, besides you, Persephone is the only one who'd thought to ask."

Her jaw tensed, like she was clamping her mouth shut. She looked pained. "They just don't know how to take you, Ditey," she soothed.

"No, it's really okay. They hate me for Heph, and I get that too. I hate myself. Hermes has made it pretty clear how much pain I'm responsible for, and even if they don't say it out loud, the rest have a right to feel how they do. I can take it, Cate," I lied. Uncomfortable pricks stung behind my eyes, and I quickly looked away from her intelligent stare, the dark irises that bore straight through me to my very core.

She reached her hands high to rest on my biceps, gripping me firmly as she demanded my full attention.

"*I* don't hate you. None of us do. Hermes doesn't even hate you. He just doesn't understand it, and I think, when it all happened the way it did, he felt a small betrayal too. You two used to be as thick as thieves. Why won't you let us tell them about the Bonding before you married Heph? If they knew you were already Bonded to Ares, they wouldn't have thought anything less of you. The public blame would lie on Hera for her cruelty."

I shook my head. "Because I don't want to bring any further shame or pity on Hephaestus. I'll bear that burden. It's fine. I'm fine," I repeated the lie, centering myself. It had taken three thousand years before I'd come clean to Hephaestus about why we never spoke up, and I don't know that I ever would have if he hadn't *seen*.

The heat in the shop ramped up, causing sweat to trickle down my spine and between the valley of my breasts.

"It doesn't have to be this way. No one else ever got your side, and Heph won't talk about it at all. They all were left to draw their own conclusions . . ." Cate's words trailed off, her voice lost in the buzz ringing in my ears.

Another wave of heat washed over me, the oppressive warmth nearly suffocating me in the too tiny shop. My breath hitched. Eyes rolled. Something deep curled low in my belly and a wave of desire ripped through my core, so powerful I wanted to throw up.

Hecate was shaking me, her hands roaming, too cold, over my burning skin. She was saying something, but I couldn't hear her through the haze and sound of my own heartbeat in my ears.

"Aphrodite!" she cried in alarm.

A sharp sting on my cheek brought me back to consciousness, my body pressed into an overstuffed chair. Hecate, Persephone, and Artemis hovered above me as the heat continued to sizzle over my skin, wrenching my breaths. I needed air. Needed space.

"What's happening to her?" Artemis whispered, concerned. *Concerned?* That didn't make sense—she didn't care about me. "Is it their Bond? Is she having an episode?" She brushed a hand over my sweaty brow. "Cate, she's burning up. We need to get her out of here."

Another bolt of lightning struck down to my core, and my back arched as I writhed. I was soaked, thighs sticking together as my body burned, and I realized, with horror, this wasn't just humidity. *This was lust.*

Something spiked my arousal so high that it bloomed and permeated the small shop.

Persephone shifted and stood, making a line toward the small woman behind the counter. I was unsure about what she said, but moments later, the little old lady was heading toward the door and flipping the sign to "Closed" before she, herself, exited.

I clutched at my neck, my collar, trying to scratch the sensation away.

Pain and pleasure were old friends, and I knew, if I could push hard enough, I may be able to bring this to a stop.

Artemis had backed up, clutching a clammy-looking Persephone.

What was happening?

Lust rolled off my skin in a tidal wave, all-consuming, and I felt my body convulse with the force of release. My head snapped back painfully as I let out a small cry. The vice grip that held me coiled loosened, and I blinked the confusion from my eyes. I was a mess on this chair, in a room full of people who looked at me with concern and, in Persephone's case, a little sickness. I straightened, still breathing hard, embarrassment pressing on my chest like a two-ton boulder.

"Are you okay, Ditey?" Hecate asked, leaning in.

I nodded frantically, though I was still unsure myself.

Persephone let out a small whimper, and my head snapped to her. She looked . . . pale. Her own chest heaved as panic ripped through me.

I moved quickly to get to her, but Hecate tugged me back before I could get any closer.

"She's reacting to whatever just affected you. That's blood magic, and if you go near her now, it could get worse."

Horror washed over me at her words, but Hecate squeezed the hand that was holding mine still.

"It's not your fault. She's pregnant, out of the Underworld for the first time since becoming so, and had been doused with a few doses already. It's volatile." She flicked her eyes back to Artemis. "I'll portal Seph home. Will you take Aphrodite to Heph's? I'll come back for you after I talk to Hades."

Artemis looked on the verge to argue, but Persephone doubled over and let out a small cry that shot straight to my heart. Guilt beat a welt in my chest, just knowing that *I* had hurt her. If something happened to her or that child, I'd throw myself in the Styx.

"I'm so sorry, I don't know what happened," I cried, tears staining my face. Everything had been going so well, and then I'd ruined it all by being here. *Daughter of Chaos and Spite.* That's what Hera used to call me.

Artemis and Hecate moved quickly, ushering Persephone to stand in front of a closet door. The frame was large and the door a deep shade of maroon, and Persephone leaned on Artemis while Hecate shifted her weight and arched her arms wide, incanting. The door shuddered and popped wide, revealing dark stone and the unmistakable dark blue glow of the Underworld.

Artemis reluctantly handed Persephone back to Hecate, and with a nod of silent understanding, she turned to me as Hecate stepped through the doorway. It shut with a soft click, returning once more to its mundane state. The silence left behind was brutal.

I shuffled on my feet and straightened my shirt before running a few fingers through my hair to tame it. The bun I had put it in had deflated in the heat of things.

"You don't have to take me to Hephaestus's place, I can just grab a cab," I said, throwing more confidence into my tone than I felt.

Artemis's silver eyes raked over me as she sized me up. They softened in the corners while she took in my posture, my flippant tone. I hated that. I preferred indifference.

"No, we are going together. Whatever just happened could happen again, and we need to make sure you're safe." Her tone wasn't unkind, but she eyed me warily as though waiting for my protest.

I considered my options. I was drenched in more than one place, in a city I didn't know extremely well. Sure, I could get Hephaestus's address and find a taxi to it, but if something like this happened again in public, I could be in trouble.

Artemis let out a grateful sigh when I nodded. She threw a hundred-dollar bill on the counter before ushering me out the front door into the cloudy street. The sun had been shining hard before, but the Gulf storms came on quickly.

"Let's get out of here before all Hells break loose, yeah?"

I followed behind her brisk pace, but I could tell she was slowing down for me to keep up. The walk to Hephaestus's home wasn't a far one, and it passed mostly in silence. She led me down to a building recessed into the street with giant roll-down garage doors set on opposite sides of a normal door.

Artemis drew a copper key off her keyring bundle and pressed it into the lock with ease. She walked inside, leaving the door cracked just enough to allow me entry. The Goddess of the Hunt moved through the halls like she was comfortable here, and a prick of jealousy speared through me. Not in an amorous way, but in that she got to spend time with him, got to hear his laugh.

Hells, I'd missed his laugh.

The doorway led straight up a small staircase that landed us squarely on the second floor. Twenty-foot-high ceilings rose around us on metal beams with cherry wood flooring and brick walls. It looked to be a perfect amalgamation of the industrial home renovations and workspace I knew Hephaestus was fond of. The garage below must belong to him too.

This space was open—a studio of sorts. The living area was neat and well-kept, with a fireplace that lay centered against the side brick wall. Large, worn, leather couches were piled around the living area. An open-concept kitchen with stainless steel appliances sat to the side, a large butcher block table stretched wide in the space. Floor-to-ceiling bookshelves lined most of the other wall and a drum set perched itself in a far corner, with pages of sheet music and compositions scattered around. The sparse décor somehow felt warm, and I inhaled his scent. This was his home.

Artemis didn't speak as she studied me, allowing me the time to explore this space with all my senses. I appreciated that of her, even if it was born of awkward silence.

I walked slowly down a hallway that bisected the area where the kitchen and living room met, running my fingers along the beautiful wallpaper there. A door with a shiny brass knob caught my attention, and I turned to it, grasping the handle and shoving. The door was heavy, solid, but it gave way to another large room, this one bright and airy in contrast to the warm, moody essence of the front of the house. I stepped through, heart falling through my stomach.

It was a dance studio.

Long mirrors ran along the entire interior wall and one short side wall, from the white crown molding to the beautifully buffed wood flooring. A matching wooden bar ran along the short side wall as well. Four arched windows with long, sheer, white curtains ran along the exterior wall. The brick was soft, almost white in this room, and it reflected the natural light, soaking it up and radiating it through the space.

I took a few steps inside, struck by both the beauty and the weight of it.

"Aphrodite," Artemis croaked, and I turned to see her gesture to the last remaining wall behind me.

My eyes grew wide as I spun, taking it in, an uncomfortable buzzing settling over my bones. The last wall held *everything*. Our memories. Hephaestus had taken up photography in the early 1900s, and he used to take photos of anything he could. The technology was bulky and cumbersome then, but he'd take his time, ever patient, to set up a shot.

A canvas took up a massive chunk of the wall. The person on it was smiling, head turned high in a pose that was slightly blurred. My own face stared back at me in black and white, dressed in a full tutu. The shot was from the twenties, when I became a prima ballerina from the Hazard School. I'd studied in Philadelphia, before the war.

Things were so fucking good between us then. I'd always loved to dance and spent many centuries touring with different companies in Europe before we settled in America. Hephaestus supported me, learned to dance with me.

Other portraits of me dancing through the years in different companies hung in the room. I recognized the different costumes, the different poses. I hadn't seen Hephaestus in seventy years, but he had come to see me.

These were his works.

I could feel it; I knew it in the way he saw the world through a lens. *When you leave to go back to him, don't come back . . .* His words sliced through me. He gave up on us . . . practically screamed at me to go. And then he followed me around for the next few decades but never said anything?

I grabbed the waist-high bar next to me, willing my chest and lungs to work as Artemis approached and wrapped her strong arms around my shoulders.

He gave up on us, but he built this room for me. Just in case I ever came home.

I sobbed.

Artemis pulled me tighter against her, unfazed by the fat droplets staining her top as she held me. Sorrow and loss at the life we could have had crushed me. The knowledge that we were on a collision course and the only way to save them was to sever our ties pressed into me like a stone.

"Why?" I choked, to no one in particular. This wasn't fair. It wasn't right that we should be made to suffer so dearly for eternity.

My knees buckled, and Artemis lowered me to the ground, settling me in her lap while great rivers of grief burst from my chest. I'd never gotten to cry over them. Not over Hephaestus when I left him, nor over Ares when he left me for the war. I didn't allow myself to feel the loss.

I fucking felt it now.

Artemis caged me close to her while my body shook and heaved, running small circles on my back. There was no awkward hesitation. Artemis was the protector of women, and regardless of her personal feelings, there was no doubt I was in distress. I tried to pull away, but she shushed me and kept me close. I had no idea how long we stayed like that.

"I'm . . . so-sorry," I hiccupped, and Artemis did pull back to look me in the eye this time. Her long black hair was pulled into two French braids, and I stared horrified at the wet spots on the bottom of her hair where I'd laid my head.

"Aphrodite, listen. I didn't know this room was *this*. He doesn't let any of us in here. Even Hecate couldn't get in, and she's the Goddess of Pathways. I wouldn't have let you in if I'd have known. I'm shocked the lock even opened for you." She studied me, face serious. Artemis really was as fair as she was deadly.

"I know you hate me for everything, and you should. I just . . . whatever you may think of me, I never wanted to hurt him. Either of them," I sobbed, choking slightly on air.

She looked at me, perplexed, like I had just struck her. "I don't hate you, Aphrodite. Why do you think that?"

I shrugged and wiped my nose on my sleeve. "Because you're so close to Hephaestus, and it seemed pretty clear what side you're all on. And when we were younger, back in Olympus, we never really had any sort of friendship. I thought that was changing when the Rebellion happened, but then I left Heph, and it seemed like that spent any good faith I'd built up." I shrugged, embarrassed to be snotting myself on her lap.

Artemis still looked slightly confused.

"I don't hate you. I feel bad for you and the situation you're all in. Heph hasn't ever said anything to disparage you or have you seen as less. Quite the opposite in fact. He and Hermes have almost come to blows a few times. And as for Olympus, you seemed to be the 'favorite' of Zeus, and that alone had me keep my distance. He isn't to be trusted," she finished, and I scoffed.

"Oh, I'm aware. I wasn't his favorite; I was just the tool he used to manipulate and get what he wanted. I had no control, and some of the things he had me do to garner more power?" I shivered over that darkest time in my life then finished, "I prayed for his death."

"He's a fucking pig." Venom laced her tone.

My head was pounding, and every part of my body ached. Artemis helped me to my feet and brushed the stray tears from under my eyes.

"Come on, I'll get you to bed," she offered, and it felt really fucking good to have someone here.

My limbs felt heavy, both with exhaustion and the weight of the emotional beating I'd taken over the last few days. I stepped forward on unsteady legs, but my head began to spin, churning my stomach. Pain shot out from my Bondmarks, and I opened my mouth to scream, or to let Artemis know something was very wrong, but the sound died in my throat as my vision blurred, and the world went black.

Ares

CHAPTER 26

Nothing in life made any sense. We were living in a bizarro timeline—one where Hephaestus and I weren't enemies. One where we shared Aphrodite, wrapped our hands around each other. One where he was a complete Pleasure Dom that commanded every part of me in that space.

His hard body pressed into mine with the force of the chariot as it raced back to the palace, through the dark roads of the Asphodels. The nearly constant blueish hue of twilight kept the Underworld casted in an eerie glow, the crags and ridges of obsidian mountains rising up against cavernous sky. The wheels of my chariot sent sparks skittering over the ashen ground in our wake, the uneven terrain jostling, but every jolt sent his warm body against mine, and when he didn't pull forward to keep the distance, I smiled, even as panic of this unknown path we'd started to walk attempted to claw its way up my throat.

I was drunk off the power that bloodsport brought on, high from the release of his hands on my cock, and dare I say, *hopeful* that this meant something more for us and Aphrodite. Maybe if we learned to share, she wouldn't want to go through with this breaking.

Hephaestus's warmth soaked through his back and into my skin, settling somewhere below my rib cage, pooling low in my bones. He didn't say much when we pulled up to the stables, even less when we disembarked to make our way to the palace steps, and that had doubt chipping away at the little spark of hope I'd fostered on the chariot ride back from New Elysium.

I wanted to stop him so we could speak. Maybe to get an idea of what was going through his mind. I always prided myself on my ability to read people—it served me well in times of war, and even more in times of peace. Hephaestus, however, was a steel trap, unyielding now, and that ate me up. I had confessed that I wanted *more*. But more of *what* I didn't elaborate, and he hadn't asked.

This attraction between us felt more than physical—I knew what carnal pleasure felt like. It was an urge, fleeting and satiable, so unlike this burning inside my chest. No, this was deeper, a reckoning that scared me, because Aphrodite had been the only being to ever see something worthy under all the destruction and ruin I brought.

And Hephaestus . . . He was good. Kind. *Beloved.*

I fisted my hands at my sides, opening and closing them reflexively and counting the number of repetitions. Allowing myself to feel out of control was dangerous. I lived my life with regimented schedules and routines for good reason. I maintained order so that I could maintain my sanity. If left to my own devices, I was prone to destruction—self included.

Something monumental had just happened between us, and yet he acted unfazed, like it didn't matter to him? Had I made an ass of myself in speaking on it? He'd said he had only ever been with Aphrodite—was this just some sort of sexual awakening for him? It felt wrong to cheapen this, and it out of character for everything I'd ever heard of him, but I clung to it because it was easier to be defensive than vulnerable.

Embarrassment from the unknown mixed with the anger that welled up in me, and I stalked forward, eager to put some space between us. I didn't have to wait around for his rejection to come.

The entryway was lit with dancing flames, which meant the Spring Queen had returned. *Good.* Aphrodite would be back. I needed to see her and felt her calling to me.

A portal of shadows opened just to my right, and Hades stepped out, looking moody and brooding.

I stopped short.

Something was very wrong.

"What happened?" I demanded as Hephaestus caught up to us, standing closer than he normally would. I pushed the intrusive thoughts from my brain and focused on Hades. The temperature was dropping by the second, and my flesh broke out in goose bumps.

"There was an incident today. Aphrodite had an episode, and Persephone was standing too close," he gritted out, like it was costing him effort to not waste us both. Fear—real fear—spiked through me that she may be hurt while we were circle jerking in the Asphodels.

"Is Aphrodite alright? Where is she?" My voice broke, and Hephaestus brought a hand to the middle of my back, but I shook it off in annoyance. I wasn't ready to be coddled.

Hades gave a curt nod.

"What happened?" I repeated.

"Something set off her bloodlust. Hecate said it could have provoked the Bonds, but either way, I'm here to let you know that none of you can stay here right now. It's not that we don't want to help, or that we don't care about what's going on. I told you before, keeping Aphrodite here was draining her. Now Persephone has been hit twice in twenty-four hours due to this mess, and this time, she fell ill. I'm sympathetic, but I have to think about my wife and child," he finished, tone curt.

"Is Seph okay, Hades?" Hephaestus asked. The concern in his voice ran deep.

Hades gave him a soft nod, and I saw the vulnerability in his eyes flash for just a moment before cold clarity took back over.

"She is . . . She's resting now, thank Hells." He brought his hand up and pinched the top of his nose. "I don't know how to do this, Heph. She's furious I'm making you all leave, but she knows it's the right thing. Until you get this"—he gestured between Hephaestus and I with a tired look—"under control, we just can't chance her or the baby. I'm so out of my depth here. All the offspring of Zeus and Poseidon were unpredictable. But this? The child of Persephone and me? It could be an atom bomb."

Hephaestus reached forward and clapped Hades on the back. "I know. We understand. Keep me updated, please? We need to get to Aphrodite and check on her."

Hades nodded, flicking his wrist behind him to conjure a portal that swirled black and inky in its own shadows.

"Thank you, Hades. For everything."

Hades dipped his head again as Hephaestus stepped forward, only hesitating a moment to look back at me before he stepped all the way through. I moved to follow, but a pale hand struck out to push slightly against my shoulder, blocking my progress.

"Don't hurt him, Ares." Hades's words a cold warning.

I lifted an eyebrow. *How much did he know?*

Hades let out a small smirk. "The shades talk. He doesn't do casual. If he lets you in, it's serious."

"I don't want to hurt him," I confessed, throwing all caution to the wind. Hades and I had always had a decent respect and understanding for the burdens we carried, but we'd never been friends. I wanted to lie and say there was nothing to worry about, that there was no chance that Hephaestus would let me matter enough to hurt him, but having Hades threaten me over the God of the Forge had my stomach doing somersaults, my flare of anger ebbing away at the validation.

"See to it that you don't, or I'll come to call." The threat was crystal clear. He stepped back to let me pass.

The portal closed with a soft gasp behind me, and I looked around at the unfamiliar room. The ceiling was high, crossed with exposed beams, and the room a vast space, sparsely decorated with wide planked floors stained a deep cherry red. A weathered leather armchair sat near a fireplace, a drum kit near the far window. My eyes caught on the chrome hardware; the bass drum splattered with graffiti that spelled out *The GorgonKnots* in pink letters with a green Medusa head dripping behind. It smelled like cedar smoke.

This must be his home.

Hephaestus was nowhere in sight, but the room only held one other exit, so I walked toward it. My chest itched, right over the Bondmark I shared with Aphrodite, and I sped up, suddenly anxious to find her.

"Aries!" Hephaestus's voice broke through the silence, panicked.

I practically ran down the long hallway to the door that stood ajar at the very end.

Aphrodite lay in the middle of a massive bed, larger than the one in Hephaestus's chambers in the Underworld. Hephaestus was half sitting, half hunched over the side, both his hands wrapped around Aphrodite's small fingers.

My blood stopped pumping, my heart seizing in my chest. For the second time this week, I found her unconscious and withering with him holding on to her. She looked pale, fragile, and I balked. I didn't know how to push forward or handle this.

Artemis was talking, but I couldn't comprehend what she was saying. Hephaestus brushed Aphrodite's hair back as he answered, but all I could hear was the high-pitched whistle throbbing through my ears. I willed my legs to move, my hands to reach for her but I. Couldn't. *Move.* I was stuck, frozen to the spot like roots had grown from the ground and ensnared me through the hardwood.

My chest tightened, and I vaguely could make out Hephaestus. He was suddenly in front of me, filling my vision, his warm hands on my face.

"Ares, come back to me, we need you. *She needs you.* Ares, can you hear me?" he asked, but he sounded so far away, despite his breath fanning over me. He sounded like he was underwater. Hephaestus's mouth kept speaking, but I just couldn't anchor back down. My breathing instead ramped up painfully.

Hephaestus turned around to look at Artemis, who lifted her hands confused, and then gripped my face tightly before he crashed his lips to mine.

That jolted me back to reality. His lips were gentle, coaxing, as he slid his tongue around mine, pressing our bodies together. All I could feel was *him*, and the world quieted, the ringing in my ears quelling to nothing. Hephaestus pulled back slightly, carefully. We were so close, the golden flecks in his eyes stuck out against the rich brown so starkly, I could count them.

"You're okay. *We're here*," he whispered, low enough for just me to hear. He grabbed my hand and pulled me over to the bed, and I complied.

Aphrodite looked so fucking frail. Hephaestus sat next to her, and I folded in next to him. I took her hand in mine and looked at Artemis; she hadn't said so much as a word about what she'd just witnessed.

"What do we do?" I asked, and she crossed her arms worriedly.

"I don't know," she replied, chewing her lip. "We wait. I'd suggest you two stay close to her. The proximity may help bring her back from whatever this is. Hecate warned you she would deteriorate."

The reminder broke me even further.

"I'll be in the living room. Call me if she moves or something changes? I'll need to let Hecate and Hermes know," she said, and Hephaestus muttered something, eyes on Aphrodite. The door then closed with a soft click.

Hephaestus moved farther up the headboard, and I moved to the other side in the same position. He hauled Aphrodite across his chest, and she lay there for hours sweating, *whimpering*.

Hours turned into days.

We changed positions. Sometimes I'd read next to the bed. We'd carry her to the tub and wash her. Hephaestus would hum gently as he cleaned her while she rested in my arms. She whispered in her sleep, sometimes tossing and turning.

They'd all been here: Hygieia, Hermes, Hecate. The Goddess of Witchcraft practically lived in a guest bedroom now, but Hermes came and went, thankfully.

The days passed, and we did not speak about what had happened between us, both sick and racked with guilt that smothered any thoughts I dared let myself think about him. It wrapped me in a vice, consuming any extra space that wasn't filled with care of Aphrodite. We had triggered this; Hecate had all but confirmed as much when Hephaestus confessed to her everything.

If Aphrodite had been conscious, she'd have been overwhelmed with all the concern and love. Artemis and Medusa checked in, and Dionysus brought elixirs. Hades sent daily shadow messages from him and Persephone.

Aphrodite wasn't getting any better, but it didn't seem like she was getting worse, either, and we clung to that.

Hephaestus and I communicated in guilty glances and one-word sentences, locked in purgatory for almost a week. Aphrodite rested in between the covers Hades had sent from the Underworld, linens dipped in the River of Sorrows that remained cool to the touch no matter how feverish she became. Otherwise, she sweated through the sheets in minutes. She didn't eat, so I didn't eat. We slept in shifts—Hephaestus and me—both too fucking terrified to not have an eye on her.

One night, Artemis poked her head in, and I looked up from my book. "We're gonna head out for the night. Cate said to call us if you need us. We're staying topside, just wanted to give you all some peace."

Hephaestus smiled graciously as he crawled into bed with Aphrodite. Artemis didn't wait for my response—she knew it wouldn't come from me—and closed the door, the sounds of her boots retreating on the hardwood outside somehow comforting.

I felt the moment it was just the three of us and took my first full breath in days.

Hephaestus pulled the covers back and settled against Aphrodite's body. A soft moan escaped her lips when he pressed up against her, and I stiffened. Hephaestus's eyes went wide and brought his hands to cradle her face.

"Aphrodite, baby? Can you hear me?" he pleaded.

She moaned a little deeper and nuzzled into his palm. I threw *The Art of War* across the fucking room, bolting from my seat to hover just near the side of the bed. She didn't answer him as he continued to gently try to wake her, but her body moved. Aphrodite lifted her leg to straddle Hephaestus's thigh, and for the first time since she'd gone down, an ember of lust and need sparked to life inside of me.

Hephaestus gasped, clutching at his ribs, feeling it too. We both froze.

". . . You don't think?" I asked, rearing back while he blinked several times.

She whimpered when he didn't touch her.

"I don't know," he whispered, torn and uncertain. "It . . . it helped last time, didn't it?" He was looking at me for input, but I had nothing of value to offer. I didn't know how to fix this, all I ever did was break shit. But . . . this was the most movement she'd shown in a week.

"Do it."

He swallowed.

"We don't have anything else to lose, and she isn't getting better," I said, then repeated, "Do it."

"Is that . . . Do you think that'd be okay? She's not conscious, Ares," he said, tension warring within him.

I climbed onto the bed, just barely close enough to not touch her. "I think it is. She loves being woken up with me inside her. We used to do it all the time." I could understand his hesitation, but I had explicit permission. I wondered if he did too. "Did you guys . . . ?" I asked, and he nodded.

"Yeah, she was pretty into it, but with everything so up in the air, I don't know if those same rules apply, and I could never, not after . . ." He closed his mouth sharply, looked away, refusing to meet my gaze.

It hit me then, the realization, the pieces falling into place. The change in his behavior toward me, the lack of animosity . . .

He knew.

"She told you."

He cradled her head against his chest, stroking her hair, shook his head. "Not tell."

When he finally looked up at me, there was so much apology in his brown eyes, and pity. It felt wretched.

"The Bonds. When we were . . . when we were together, before you came in that night and found us, she accidentally showed me some things."

I swallowed. "What things?"

He shook his head. "Don't be angry with her, Ares. She didn't know it was happening, until I had already seen."

I was numb, knowing that he finally knew that the missing vitriol from how he regarded me was because he'd finally learned that I wasn't the one without honor. It felt different than I thought it would.

Being seen.

Aphrodite pressed into him, a cry falling from her lips. He placed a kiss on her temple, holding her tight as she brought her arms up to clutch at his chest. The room bloomed with her scent, the jasmine spreading all around us.

He looked at her. Then back to me.

"Whatever she needs," I said.

"What if this makes it worse?" he added, and I shook my head, because I understood the fear.

"We have to try something. Just . . . let her pull from the Bond. You won't hurt her. It should be you."

He turned back to her. The space closed in around us, and Hephaestus stripped his shirt from over his head and shimmied out of his sleep pants. He slid down her body and swiped his head between her lips. She was wet and wanton, and she let out a hoarse moan when he pressed inside her, opening for him. I watched his cock sink into her, disappearing to the hilt through sweet moans and soft grunts as he rolled his hips slowly. Strong body, taut, graceful, as he fed her, poured all of himself into her, lips whispering against her flesh.

"Come back to us, Little Love. Open those beautiful eyes, see what you do to us." It was a special kind of torture being so close and not being able to touch. He made love to her for almost an hour before the first spasms of his orgasm began to overtake him, hips faltering, her body convulsing.

He peeled away from her body, and she whimpered, his cock heavy still between his legs. Aphrodite was a beautiful mess, coated in her own slick and sweat and him.

I pushed inside the warmth he'd left, and she sighed into my chest as she writhed. She was magnificent, divinity, the light of a thousand suns as I stroked into her while Hephaestus watched, eyes transfixed on our movements.

This wasn't sex. It was covenant.

Words between us were too often heavy things, sharpened by pride, weighted with past wounds from a tongue too sharp, an ego too bruised. But in this, between us, we were stripped down. Our bodies spoke a universal language, older than broken vows and torn oaths, older than the fucking cosmos. Every touch of Hephaestus over my wrist, every sigh from Aphrodite's lips, every shiver that worked through my body was a reckoning of truth that no fear or pride could misrepresent.

I held her close, wrapping my arms around her chest and circling her neck with my fingers. There was no real pressure there, only enough to let her know I had her. *I loved her*. We loved her.

With every slow thrust, I called her back to me, to us, willing her to open her eyes. My lips ran a trail over her shoulder as she shook apart once, then twice. Her body bowed and bent to my will, and Hephaestus let out a strangled noise as I came inside her, nurturing our connection through my power. I then traced a calloused finger down the inside of Hephaestus's forearm, my body reaching for connection my mouth couldn't ask for. His eyes, honeyed browns. Pale strands of his hair fell from a messy bun. But this touch he returned, an understanding clear in his gaze.

We could, and had, misinterpreted words, but we couldn't unhear the way our hearts beat together, the way our bodies spoke the same ancient tongue, a truce written in sweat and warmth and flesh.

"Her eyes fluttered," he said quietly, reaching to grab her face while I came down. At his touch, her body spasmed, stealing my breath.

"Touch her again, Hephaestus," I pleaded, lost in my own ecstasy. She flexed around me as he roamed his hands over her, and when his fingers brushed my too hot skin, my cock pulsed hard inside Aphrodite.

"More," she panted, voice hoarse and cracked from days of disuse.

Hephaestus looked at me, eyes searching for something. Maybe confirmation? Possibly permission? I didn't care. I'd give it to him. She needed us both, and this was the only thing that had produced any results.

He maneuvered to press his body close to her front, then hiked a leg over his hip. Barely there touches, then pressure against my base as he slid down, pressing against her stretched entrance, the rough hitch of air as he thrust slowly deeper and farther, every rung of his ladder massaging against me, inside of her.

He cradled her face, trailing soft nips over her jaw and neck, the pressure exquisite, divine, fucking cosmos shattering.

I pulled out slowly, deliberately, could feel the combination of her and me and him seeping down our legs, into the sheets.

Hephaestus spoke prayers into her flesh, peppering her skin with kisses. Aphrodite's lips parted in a breathy sigh as he slid home again, and I cried out at the fit.

"That's it, Little Love, have it all." Hephaestus's words floated over me, stilling my racing mind.

Our bodies were covered in a thin layer of sweat as we moved, as sparks danced along my spine. Time ceased to exist as we rocked Aphrodite between us, my hands on her hips controlling the movements and Hephaestus's calloused palms clasped firmly over mine.

The stimulation was overwhelming, the vice of her, each pass of his studded cock rutting against me too.

"Look at me, Ares," he whispered, and it took all the strength I had left to force my eyes open. I didn't remember closing them.

"Hephaestus?"

"*Hmm?*" he moaned, fucking long, deep strokes. I was nothing more than a body, a vessel for her pleasure. For his.

"Touch me. *Please.*"

Gentle fingers released their hold on her throat, crept over my skin, cupped my jaw. His forearm rested on the side of her neck, his grip on me, tethering us together.

We could die here, just like this. It wouldn't be the worst way I'd imagined I'd go.

Aphrodite

CHAPTER 27

A cold calm settled over my bones as I got to my feet and willed my eyes to adjust to the pitch black. Goose bumps ran along my arms and neck, prickling my skin. I rubbed my hands over my crossed arms for friction, stumbling around in the darkness, relying on nothing more than the instinct in my chest that pulled me forward like an invisible tether. I put one foot in front of the other, forcing my body to propel forward.

Toward that feeling.

I walked and walked for ages, still in darkness, still alone. Silent tears streamed down my cheeks. Had I died? Is this what awaited our kind? I thought of Hephaestus, sweet Hephaestus. And Ares. Would he raze the world in his grief? What happened to me? I couldn't remember.

Hells, I couldn't remember.

A soft orange light flickered up ahead, and my pulse quickened. I pushed my feet forward, urging my body faster, a surge of energy passing through me, propelling my feet onward. With each step, my footfalls echoed louder, more confident. The light pulsed in the distance, a faltering flicker that had a relieved laugh tearing from my lips.

Light was safety. If I could get to it, wrap it around me, I would be able to find my way out of here. It burned more steadily with each step, no longer blinking in and out of existence, and I pushed faster. Another surge of energy rocked through me, and this time another light pulsed, red and deep.

Ares.

It was them. I didn't know how, but I knew they were sending me a beacon, guiding me back to them. The world was silent except for the slapping of my bare feet on the stone and the heartbeat rushing in my ears. The lights grew larger, brighter, more defined as I approached.

Two chords, braided with strands of iridescent light—one in almost orange-gold, one in deep red—pulsed and writhed. They looked like ropes, long since frayed and neglected, suspended in midair. The closer I got, the brighter they pulsed, calling to me, empowered by my presence. The frayed edges floated over, stretching out to touch, reaching hungrily into the darkness. I grabbed red thread, glowing brightest, and in the touch, I felt Ares, desperation in his pull. I wrapped my fingers gingerly around the frayed threads and felt a jolt of pleasure, a bolt of power seeping into my skin. It settled under my bones and sinew, a raging inferno desperate to swallow me whole.

It wasn't enough.

I looked to the orangish, golden thread, still illuminated but diminished from its earlier grandeur. It had shone bright enough to guide me here, to cut through the inky darkness, and I wrapped it in my other hand, curling the strands around my pal. The golden threads blared to life, shining as brightly as the crimson, the rush of power electrifying as it sizzled across my skin.

"More," I demanded.

The threads tightened, twisting and coiling around my arms, wrapping me tight. Divine energy seeped into my skin, mixing the gold and crimson, and I relished it, let it deliver me from the abyss. Desire coiled low, the darkness fading as the chords enveloped me, as small flyaway strands reached toward . . . each other? I was transfixed as they braided together with some hesitation, but the ties that *did* form, Fates, how they shone, a lux so beautiful, I nearly wept as it chased away the darkness completely.

I felt them moving inside me as I slid back into consciousness, full to the brim, no room left inside as I clung to sweat-dampened skin and hard muscle. Hephaestus had me pinned to his chest, Ares hot on my back while they moved in tandem, talking to each other, sweet and loving. Nothing I'd ever expected from the two of them.

"Are you okay?" Hephaestus asked beyond me, and I shivered as I floated just on the edge of waking, not wanting to break their moment.

"I can feel your piercings. It's intoxicating," Ares groaned.

"Imagine how good they'd feel inside you. Maybe one day, when this is all over, I'll strap you to my table, and we can see," Hephaestus answered, desire heavy in his tone.

"I've never let anyone top me before," Ares admitted, his hips rocking at that excruciatingly slow speed. "I don't know if I could."

"You will be able to. You'll obey and open for me, and I'll fuck the submission into you." Hephaestus's words were a hot iron straight to my core, and my eyes flew open, inches from his honey browns

The relief in his eyes stopped my heart.

"Baby," he choked, barely able to restrain the emotion in his voice.

Ares let out a small grunt behind me and slid his hand from my chest to my chin, turning it to face him. I saw his dark eyes glisten, felt the wet droplets that landed on my shoulder and rolled down my chest as he leaned his forehead against my skin and sobbed gently. His body moved, thrusting harder, taking out his emotion on my body.

"Don't stop," I sighed as Hephaestus joined him, our bodies tangled together, me so full of them I could barely cry out as they talked me through it.

"*Look at you, you're a fucking mess, baby.*"

"*So beautiful, so powerful, Little Goddess.*"

I couldn't tell where my pleasure began and theirs ended, and it didn't matter. We climbed together, breaths in pants and sweat-slicked bodies writhing in this huge bed. I felt the thunder build low and steady, watched them stoke the fire until it reached an inferno.

"Your cock feels so good moving against me while she milks me. I might not survive this," Ares panted, racing toward his own release.

"Careful what you beg for, Ares," Hephaestus warned, gripping us both so tight.

I shook apart. The scream that tore from my throat would have shattered windows, set off alarms. I spasmed, unable to control myself, and Ares followed behind me, a gush of warmth that had nowhere to go. Hephaestus came last, snarling out his release as he stilled inside me.

We lay locked together and spent.

"Tell me this is real," I mumbled.

Hephaestus gave a small smile, running his fingers over my face then reaching past me to rest on Ares's jaw.

"It's real. You're back with us," Ares whispered as he pressed a kiss to my shoulder. He was still shaking, and it was unnerving to feel his breath fall unevenly against my back, knowing it was distress and not lust that stole his air.

"I felt you both in the darkness. Heard you calling me home," I said softly. I felt so powerful, so vibrant, so . . . *sated*.

Hephaestus shifted my shoulders, pressing us in a roll until he was on top of both of us, gazing down with warm eyes that danced between mine and Ares's.

At my back, I could feel the beating of Ares's heart as it slowed, his breaths evening out in time with mine. We didn't speak, only existed, only drank each other in as Hephaestus hovered over our sweat-slickened bodies.

The weight of him left me as he pushed himself up and rested on his knees. His eyes . . . they drifted between my parted legs, to where he and Ares were both still stuffed inside me, the look on his face pure rapture.

Ares's cock twitched with a grunt before Hephaestus lifted my hip gingerly, slowly pulling himself out. Rung by rung of his piercings dragged across my entrance, and I writhed even as Ares held me in place. The delicious sensation, the knowledge they were both inside me, coating each other, decadent.

"Don't stop," I pleaded.

With a dark chuckle, my tender god thrust back in and out, shallow plunges that plucked against my opening, massaged against Ares. Not enough. Not nearly fucking enough. We both cried out as he smirked and withdrew completely.

"Fucking tease," Ares grumbled, and I laughed, a full-bellied sound that cracked up my scorched throat.

Hephaestus shot him a sly look, and I lost it again.

"Don't be a brat, or I'll punish you for it," he warned, but his gaze was back on my exposed core, fixated on the deluge that dripped from my body. "Up you get, Little Love," he commanded, voice soft, barely a whisper as he lifted my hips again, this time enough that Ares slipped out.

I could still feel the warmth of him, the length hard against my bare cunt, but then Hephaestus moved, fingers and pressure and *ahhh*—

My back arched as I cried out, his fingers moving in deliberate strokes to push their essence back in. I was plastered to Ares's chest as we both watched him eye his fill.

He plunged deep, the sounds wet and depraved as he crooked those skilled, rough fingers until the sensation became too much, an edge of pain on the pleasure.

"We need to have a talk about things," he said casually, as though he wasn't wearing me like a hand puppet while Ares's hands rubbed under my breasts, fingernails grazing in teasing scrapes with every pass over my hardened nipples.

I struggled to breathe.

"You're so stunning like this," he praised.

I flushed deep, heat blooming up the side of my neck as he tapped that spot. I came on a soft, broken cry, against Ares's lips, and he swallowed every whimper that Hephaestus wrenched out of me.

Breathless, we turned to look at the God of the Forge, both of us riveted as he pulled his fingers free, then lifted them to his lips, tasting.

Savoring.

His eyes fluttered shut on a moan as he licked them clean of us, of the proof of what had happened here.

My vision faded in and out as I came down, but there were words and movements and then the scent of Hephaestus, the pressure of my head falling gently against his chest. I let myself sink into the warmth of him as he walked us into the bathroom and carried me down the steps of the large bathing area.

Ares followed close behind.

The tile was a deep blue; the rectangular pool recessed in the floor with a small border wall surrounding it. A statue of, well, *me* sat sculpted at the back edge, and the oil portrait painted by my good friend Henri Gervex filled the back wall. We had spent time in the same circles in France, and I had modeled for him many times before his death. Hephaestus commissioned this portrait in 1907, just a few years before he'd left for the war. Henri got my hair right, thanks to Hephaestus's coaching. The artist had seen me as a pure blonde, and though I was a bit slenderer in the portrait than in reality, he captured the other parts of me well.

Giant pearls and seashells were stacked artfully around my sculpture, the ceiling painted to remember the sky over the sea. I was written into the fabric of every room of Hephaestus's home, in the flooring and tiles and paint. Soft colors and portraits, tiny altars.

I was quiet as he turned on the four golden taps. The water rose steadily around us as Hephaestus emptied an apothecary jar with jasmine-scented crystals into the pool.

"Ares," he called over his shoulder, and in moments, my vengeful god appeared. His body was a tapestry of violence, every muscle in his bulked frame trained for destruction.

Hephaestus walked up the steps and whispered something to him. An easy smile cracked across Ares's lips as he dipped his chin. The two of them stood together, so alike but so starkly different, an understanding passing between them.

It was clear I had missed a lot during my illness.

Hephaestus had tightly corded muscles and fine blond hair that dusted his shoulders, a few inches shorter than Ares, but his muscles were sculpted by years in his forge. Ares was wider, broad at the shoulder and more narrow at the hip. His thighs were trunks of pure muscle, his dark hair cropped shorter at the sides and longer on top. They were beautiful in their own ways.

And mine.

They were mine. As though sensing my gaze on them, they turned to look at me. Ares's eyes darkened as he stepped down the top step, raking over my body hungrily. Hephaestus braced an arm across him before he could get too far and shook his head in warning.

"Wash. Rest. She needs to eat, and you need sleep. Keep your dick down. I'll be back in a moment." His words were firm.

A muscle in Ares's jaw ticked, but he said nothing as he continued down the steps.

The warm water was bubbly, lathered by whatever Hephaestus had dropped into it, churned up by the jets. I sank deep, scraping my back gently down the steps, letting it wash over my face and hair until I was fully submerged. The water was a comfort to me, my very divinity was born of it, and I let myself get lost in the push and pull of the current the jets were making.

A shadow cast over me, tall and proud, and when I resurfaced, Ares towered above me. I reached for him, but he shook his head, dropping to his knees gently in the water.

I frowned, and the corners of his lips perked up in an amused smile.

"You can't possibly still be hungry, Little Goddess," he teased, but I saw the desire in my eyes mirrored in his own. He was level with my face now, and he crowded my space, pushing me back against the tiled wall of the bath. Ares was warm to my touch, an open flame that made the water feel cold by comparison as I ran my hands up the sides of his face, dripping water down his cheeks and neck.

He closed his eyes and leaned into my touch.

"I thought we lost you," he whispered, so low I could have missed it if I breathed too hard. He'd shut the taps off while I was under, and the water sat just below my shoulders.

"Ares, I'm here, I'm right here." I grabbed his hand and pressed it over my heart so he could feel it beating. "I'm sorry I scared you. I don't know what happened, but it's over, and I'm okay."

An agonized look crossed his face. "*I* know what happened, Ditey." He looked so ashamed, his voice small.

I squeezed his fingers and looked up at him while he wrestled with something internally. Moments slipped into minutes, and worry started to eat at me, but I tried to be patient as he wrestled with himself.

"You can tell me anything," I soothed, and I knew it was true. I had a feeling the waves of desire that had driven me under had come from him and Hephaestus, but it was their story to tell, and I wouldn't demand it from them.

"If you want to," I added for good measure.

"We . . . We didn't . . . Something happened. I don't know how to explain it. I don't know what it means. But we touched, and then it was overwhelming. I don't want to hurt you ever, Aphrodite. I don't know what I'm doing." His words were broken, his grip on my hand and hip crushing as he stammered and choked on his words.

"Do you like it when Hephaestus touches you?" I asked, keeping my voice as even as I could. Ares had been with others before, that wasn't new. But this vulnerability I saw with him, with how he looked at Hephaestus, was different. He'd fucked others. He'd never let them *see* him the way Hephaestus had earlier. He'd never listened to them or entertained their demands.

Ares looked up, searching for some salvation in the vaulted ceiling.

"Yes," he confessed on a rasp. "Logic says it's the corruption of the Bonds making your feelings for him leak over into ours, but this feels . . ." He trailed off, and I waited, giving him whatever space I could to work it out. "The sex, I could see. But the rest of it? I'm noticing things about him I've never even stopped to consider before. I don't know how to feel like this with someone else. It's only ever been you, Ditey. And now I'm mixed up, and we're supposed to hate each other. How could he ever not hate me?" His words fell flat, full of self-inflicted venom, repetitions of words spat at a young boy by a father he only wanted to love him.

I held Ares tighter to me and pressed my lips to the soft flesh under his jaw, over his pulse. "He could love you, because you're worthy of it. Because I do. Because you deserve happiness, and so does he, and so do I. If you feel something for him, I encourage it. He's easy to adore, Ares." I kept my voice soft, a mumble against his skin.

"You wouldn't be angry?" he asked.

I shook my head. My jealousy regarding him or Hephaestus was legendary while we were together, but then again, so was his, and I understood his uncertainty. But something about Hephaestus quelled that fire in both of us, it seemed.

"I want you to be happy. I love you both. How could I be upset if you found that in each other?"

He looked at me with such agonizing adoration, and I slipped my hands down to wrap around his waist. Ares groaned at the contact, closing the millimeter of distance to press his forehead against mine.

"Would this make you happy?" he asked.

I sucked in a deep breath, arching my neck back to look up into his eyes, searched his face as my arms lifted to rest around the back of his neck, dripping water down our bodies.

"I don't want to answer that, Ares, because it isn't fair," I replied carefully. "Whatever happens here needs to be because you and Hephaestus both want it. Not because you think it'll Band-Aid what's wrong with us. We're too far past that point now. The Bond sickness isn't going away, Cate said so. This has to be about the two of you first, then we will find a way to make it fit. If it's what you both want."

Ares broke my gaze, chewing on his bottom lip as his hands roamed over my back. "I'm not sure I'm the type of person Mr. Perfect would be into, if there wasn't a connection between us."

I made a face. "Hephaestus isn't perfect, Ares. He has his own flaws, just like I do, but one of the best things about him is his empathy. His compassion. He gives freely, with his whole self.

Besides, I could be biased, but I'm not blind. He's got a fascination with watching you fuck me, it seems."

Ares barked a laugh at that, loud enough to echo off the walls as he squeezed me tight.

"And you've got a great cock. I've never even seen him glance at another man's cock, but he was up close and personal with yours."

Ares arched an eyebrow as a shiver ran down my spine, the memory of their words, whispered in the dark, as they shared my body doing unspeakable things to me.

Ares kissed me, coaxed my mouth open with teasing licks, but once he was in, he dominated me, angling my head up so he could devour my lips.

"We're going to get into trouble," I gasped, breathless as his large hands palmed at me.

A dark chuckle shook through him, and he pulled back ever so slightly, that mischievous glint in his eye. He dragged his lips up the column of my neck, barely touching, teasing—

A throat cleared.

We both looked up to find Hephaestus, arms folded and jaw set. He had a towel slung low on his hips.

Busted.

"Hades sent a shadow. We're being requested to the Underworld. It's time for the first trial."

The air left my lungs. Hells, it seemed to leave the room. Those words sobered me up immediately, and I clung tighter to Ares.

"When do we need to be there?" he asked, and Hephaestus sighed, running his hands through his hair.

"Now. Well, as close to now as we can get. Aphrodite, there are clothes for you in the walk-in closet. Medusa and Cate went shopping for you while you were . . . convalescing. Ares, you can pick something from mine. Let's go."

Ares lifted me, walking us both out of the pool with ease. He put me down next to Hephaestus, who grabbed a towel from the shelf and wrapped me tight, before doing the same to Ares.

I stopped to plant a kiss on Hephaestus's lips, soft, sweet. He smiled reluctantly, holding on to that semblance of authority, but his eyes gave him away. They sparkled with the anticipation of what he would get to do now that we had disobeyed.

I sauntered toward the door, and Ares went to follow but was stopped with a hand that slid deftly around his neck and pulled his face up to Hephaestus's.

"You disobeyed me," Hephaestus growled, stopping me in my tracks. Panic sluiced down my spine at the words, the danger in them. Was this the end to the peace? Was it so fragile that, now that I was awake, they had slipped into their old roles?

I swung around, ready to break them apart if need be, but was stopped by their expressions. There was tension there, sure, but it felt more like restrained desire than anger.

Ares smirked at Hephaestus, unfazed by the hand possessively collaring him.

"I didn't. You said to keep my dick down, and I *did*, at great personal cost I might add. You didn't say I couldn't taste her. My dick wasn't involved."

Hephaestus jerked him closer, colliding their bodies with a smack. His jaw was tight but the glimmer in his eye was hungry.

"You think that technicality will stop me from wearing that ass out later?" Hephaestus asked.

I balked, and Ares let out a small whine.

"*Holy Hells*," I breathed, sinking onto the golden sink. This was the hottest thing I'd ever seen. They were both breathing hard, and the power struggle between them had me amped up to a million.

"Why wait?" Ares challenged, and as quick as a cobra, Hephaestus's lips were on him, swallowing down each of Ares's moans. There was no battle for dominance, the God of War bent to him, like metal tempered in Hephaestus's forge.

I watched, stunned, as he bit down on Ares's bottom lip, feral sounds tearing from his chest.

Hephaestus leaned back, blood dripping down each of their mouths. "Because we have things to do. *And because I fucking said so.*"

He swiped his thumb across Ares's lip gently. "You taste like her, it's lovely," he said, then turned toward the huge walk-in shower to rinse off.

Ares watched the muscles in his back as Hephaestus walked away with fierce longing.

"Come on, we need to get dressed. It's going to be a long day." I reached for his hand.

Ares took mine, and I tried not to think too hard about what we were about to face, what could make or break us.

Hephaestus

CHAPTER 28

The kitchen was mercifully empty when we finally emerged from our bedroom fully clothed. There was a slight ache in my bones I wasn't accustomed to, but the activity we'd exerted had been strenuous. Still, it settled uneasily in my bones that we weren't all at peak strength, even for our diminished forms. Aphrodite would never admit it, but she was only partially invigorated. Last time, it lasted less than fourteen hours, and the recoil had been a week of agony for all of us.

Mostly.

"Are they sending a portal?" Aphrodite asked as she sat at the dining room table and stretched back. She was wearing tights that hugged every inch of her curves and a matching sports bra under a little athletic jacket, all black. It made her look deadly. She had her long tresses piled into a high ponytail and the combat boots she'd borrowed from Persephone on her feet. How we were supposed to focus on anything other than her in that outfit was beyond my realm of understanding.

I glanced at Ares, who wasn't doing much better. He eye-fucked her from over the cereal I'd made him, and she let him, matching his gaze, feeding off his worship. I felt my own cock stir but clamped it down. *Cursed Hells*, we'd never make it out of the house.

"Yeah, it's ready to call upon when we get ready. We can't be too much longer," I answered, feeling wound up.

"Where's the gaggle of geese that are normally here?" Ares inquired, and I shot him stern a look. There was no malice on his face, but I did catch how still he was. Like he was overcompensating for nerves, willing himself to appear as calm as possible.

I bristled at his unease. "They're meeting us in the Underworld, somewhere outside of the palace. Hades insisted."

"I'm sure Persephone is psyched about that one," Aphrodite replied.

I grimaced then mused, "I would hate to be the God of the Underworld right about now."

She let out a low laugh.

"Is this really necessary now? Even with the Bond sickness, we know how to get you back to good. Hades said this was deadly, and I'm concerned about you going into battle in the Underworld. Where you're not a full strength." Ares murmured.

The air in the room stilled, and I didn't think any of us were breathing.

Aphrodite swirled her finger around the edge of her cup nervously. "I still want to go through with the trials. I want to break the Bonds."

The words sank like a stone between us, my heart tied to that rock bound for the depths of Tartarus. I forced myself to look at her, to hear all that she had to say, a pathetic part of me desperate for her to clarify that she still loved me. *Loved us.*

Ares's lip curled in a sneer, and my stomach sank as hurt bloomed across his features. Before he even opened his mouth, I knew it would be venom, and it wasn't my place to try and stop it, but Fates, I wish I could have.

"That's odd, considering you were screaming how much you loved us an hour ago. Or do you only love me when you're on my cock?" he spat, and she flinched. I didn't miss the way he'd left me out of that last question, like he was certain of her feelings for me but not for him.

Aphrodite took a deep breath and leveled him with a look, unshed tears shining in her eyes. "You're *not* going to talk to me like that, Ares. If you're going to throw a tantrum like a child, you'll stay here, and I will compete in the trials alone."

Her voice was calm and clear. She had experience in dealing with his particular brand of asshole.

Ares sat back, deflated but scowling. He shot her a sideways glance. "I'm sorry," he huffed. His fingers trembled, the spoon shaking in his hand.

"I understand that you don't get why I want to do this—why I *need* to do this. But before we go down there and put our lives at risk, you need to know." She paused, looking between the two of us.

A large lump had taken residence in my throat, and though I felt the need to handle this, to manage the situation, I was unable to speak. Instead, I waited for her to continue, tongue-tied and useless.

"These Bonds . . . They're sick. Corrupted. Hecate warned that if they were allowed to carry on of their own volition, they could kill you both in the process, after they kill me. You both know this. It's not speculation; this is happening. How many times do you think fucking me back from the brink of death is going to work?"

Ares opened his mouth to protest, but she held up a hand to silence him.

"No. *Don't.* It's a fact, and I don't care if *you* don't care if you live or die. I do. To me, that's reason enough to try, but there is more. I want you to choose me. And I want the chance to choose you."

I cleared my throat before Ares could wedge his entire foot down his throat. "I do choose you, Aphrodite. We choose you," I clarified, and gestured to Ares, who nodded. It was bold, speaking for him, speaking on us as a unit, but it felt like the right thing to do. Like the most natural thing in the cosmos after this last week.

"I know things have been really fucking hard, but things are changing. They're different from before, Ditey. I just—" Ares's voice broke. "I just got you back. *We both did*. Please, don't do this. We can ask for her to heal the Bonds," he begged her, the plea visceral in his voice.

The proudest man I'd ever known reduced to a pleading mess.

"Ares." She whispered his name with so much emotion, it cracked at my already weakening defenses. Aphrodite reached over and grabbed his hand. Then mine.

"I don't want to break the Bonds and leave you. I want to break them so we can be together. Truly together. We never got to choose what happened to us. We were forced into a hellish cycle of heartbreak and pain, and I don't want that anymore. I want to know that you're here because you want to be, without doubts, from the depths of your heart, and I want to know the same of you." She nodded her head to me.

I opened my mouth to speak, but she pushed on before I could.

"I want the chance to prove to you that I do love you. Both of you. I said as much at our Bonding, Ares. I chose you then. And you, Hephaestus. I wouldn't have been able to lie under the Bond oath. Even Bonded to Ares, I loved you, too, then. I chose you then, and that's how I know I'll choose you both now. What we have now is forced. It's impossible to know what *you* would do if you weren't bound. Without freedom of choice, there can be no truth. No trust. I deserve that. And so do you," she finished, tears staining her cheeks.

Ares pulled her hand to his lips, kissing her knuckles as he shook. "I'll choose you. I don't know that you'll choose me. Not when you'll be free to be with each other." His eyes glanced at me once, and I could hear the pain in his words constricting around me. He still didn't see himself worthy. "And I couldn't blame either of you for it, but it's terrifying to think this is ending." He looked over at me then, showing me the softest parts of him he kept buried under rage and anger. "And this, whatever it is, before it's even begun."

A protective urge welled up in my chest, domineering and roaring like a train between my ears.

"I'll choose you, Ares." The words left my lips before I'd fully formed the thought, but they were right, even as they fell between us. Even as his jaw went slack, the God of War speechless at my declaration. I was, too, and if I had more time to overthink it all, I would have probably done so, but we were out of time.

No more secrets. No more lies.

I walked around the table until I stood in front of him. He had Aphrodite's hand gripped tightly in his own, and I knelt until we were face-to-face, squatting next to him. "I'm not holding you to anything, but the 'whatever' you're referring to is real to me. As real as what I feel for Aphrodite, and I know that's true because I see how scared you are of it. Of me. I feel you in here." I placed my hand over my heart.

His nose went red, his eyes glistening. But he didn't look away, or fly off in a rage, so I pressed my luck.

"I'll choose you. I'm not Bonded to you now. I have no reason to lie, nothing forcing me to stay. But I will. I'll stay for you. Even if she goes. I'll stay." I grabbed his face between my fingers, and beneath them, I could feel the centuries of pain there. He'd picked himself up, Helios had scolded us. Ares had borne his pain silently, solitarily, for as long as we could remember.

"Choose me," I pleaded, and he lifted his red-rimmed eyes to mine.

Ares was stunning in his pain. He wore it like armor, but now he was raw, flayed, and I knew down to my shade this was *right*. Something like disbelief etched into his features, and I leaned forward, dropping a kiss to his forehead, slowly, gently.

"Choose me."

One of his hands loosened around Aphrodite to cling to my shirt, and we both watched in stunned silence as the God of War lowered his defenses for someone other than the Goddess of Love.

Aphrodite slipped out of her chair, kneeling next to me. "Choose me, too, Ares. Let's cut the infection out at the root and start fresh. We have to burn it down and rebuild it on our terms. I want to do that work with you. Please," she begged.

He sniffled hard, shying away from us.

I gripped him tighter to me, Aphrodite following my lead. Our hands moved and tears flowed, but we didn't let go. Never once let him go. We were a tangled, broken mess of fractured hearts and twisted desires. I understood what she wanted. I was as scared as Ares that she'd walk away once the tether was gone.

But I knew she was right. We had to try.

We stayed, huddled together, holding on to each other like a lifeline. Whatever the future may bring, I wanted them with me. No matter what manner that meant—Bonds broken or messy. I wouldn't give either of them up, now that I'd had a taste of what it could be like. Aphrodite was joy and love and tenderness, but Ares needed *me*. Needed what I could give him, someone to peel back the depths of his rage and not flinch. The irony of this fucked-up situation being the catalyst for me finally seeing the God of War for the person he is wasn't lost on me, but I felt an ownership, a responsibility for him that rivaled my commitment to Aphrodite. I could feel down to my shade that it was meant to be this way.

Perhaps it always had been, but we were too blinded by hubris and pride and everyone else's expectations to see it. I saw it now, even as Ares tried to convince me all the ways I shouldn't. It only made me want to prove to him how fucking good we could be together more.

"You don't know what you're asking for, Hephaestus. I'm *vicious*. Cruel. I destroy. These hands"—he pulled back, lifting them to his face, staring at his palms as though he could see the blood they'd spilled stained there still—"destroy. They ruin. *I ruin.*"

I felt cold then, from the inside out, enough to send a shiver down my spine.

Next to me, Aphrodite whispered to him, crowding his space, jaw cupped in her delicate hands with the chipped pink polish on her nails as she breathed into him, poured into him.

"Those are not your words, Ares. You look at me, and you remember who you are. Remember the poppy fields. Remember the sacred grove." She listed things, moments I was sure of tenderness, of love and vulnerability between them.

His eyes glazed over as he sank further inside himself, the damage inflicted on his shade a behemoth on his chest.

I squeezed his hand, brought his knuckles up to my lips. "Remember the chariot."

His head tilted as his gaze found mine, his lips tipped down in a frown.

"You hated flying," he grumbled, and I laughed, despite myself.

"Yes, but you were so confident, and it was the first time we touched each other outside of a spell, outside of Aphrodite. That moment was *ours*, Ares. Remember that. I always will."

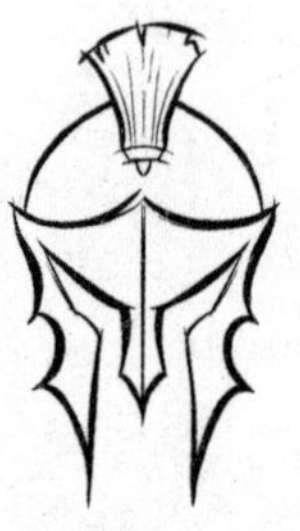

Ares
CHAPTER 29

I was a hollow shell, walking through the swirling shadow portal. Deep down, I'd known Aphrodite wouldn't have changed her mind, but she sure as fuck picked a time to pop the bubble we lived in.

My boots crunched loudly over the dark ground, Hephaestus leading the way to the arena floor. I'd only been to this part of the Asphodels a few times.

I didn't make it a habit to frequent halls of broken honor.

This coliseum was razed to the ground by Marcus Aurelius when he'd tried to unite Rome into a time of peace, outlawing barbaric practices like gladiator games. I respected him for his foresight, but it hadn't lasted long past his rule. The empire declined steadily without his strength and leadership, breaking the peace he'd settled for so long.

Aphrodite walked between the two of us, not quite touching but leaving very little space.

Hades was standing in the middle of the coliseum, which rose high around us. It wrapped around the edge of a mountainside and had a spiral path that led up to the top. In the distance, I could see Artemis, Hecate, Hermes, Dionysus, Hygieia, Thanatos, and Medusa sitting and standing in the first spectator row. Piles of broken armor and bones littered the ground around us, swords jutted up from the dirt haphazardly, chariots upturned and busted along the sides. This place was where honor went to die.

I bristled.

Achilles stood near Hades, head bent low with a frown on his face. I tensed at his posture and at the way Hades had withdrawn the emotion from his features as he so often did when he was worried.

A large board marked with sigils stood propped up, nails driven in long spikes peppering it in no particular order. We reached them in little time.

I stepped forward, a buffer between Achilles, Hephaestus, and Aphrodite.

"Achilles," I greeted, clasping his forearm as he reached for me.

"Good morning to you, Lord Ares. Are you ready to begin?" he asked, face searching each of us.

Before I could think too hard, or throw Aphrodite over my shoulder and drag her ass kicking and screaming out of the Underworld, I nodded.

Once.

Achilles clapped his hands together. "It is unusual to have three questers together for this. Due to the nature of your rank and status, Melia has agreed to alter the parameters of the trials. You shall be allowed to compete together, but there are rules."

He paused to make sure we understood. "First, not all of you will be competing in every Trial. Some will allow one, others two. The questers will be chosen by the Fates in a coin pull. Second, you may use any and all items and weapons present in the arena to complete your quest, but you cannot bring anything with you. And finally, you may not accept aid from any of the gods. Is that clear? I would like to remind your graces that the Trials cannot be stopped once they begin. Consider carefully before you accept."

His warning was ice down my spine, but Aphrodite moved forward just a fraction to separate herself from our flanking. In a clear voice, she answered, "We understand. We accept."

Achilles spared me one worried glance before a bag appeared in his hand. He opened it and presented it to us, ensuring we were all within arm's reach of the leather pouch, but it was Hades who reached into the bag. The clinks of small chits of wood could be heard.

The God of the Dead quietly withdrew a small token and held it aloft in his hand. He turned with it, placing the small wooden disc about the size of a coaster on top of the board behind us. One last look at Aphrodite for confirmation, which she gave with a stiff nod.

Hades sighed. Let the disc fall. Gravity pulled the medallion down, and we watched as it bounced between the raised metal nails, making its way to the bottom. The puck settled into a small slot that held a sigil rune for "one" on it, stamped on a black square.

"The first trial will be the Golden Fleece," Achilles announced. "There will be one quester. Please, step forward to procure your positions."

He opened the bag once more, and I plunged my hand in, impatient, Hephaestus right on my heels with Aphrodite bringing up the last.

"Reveal."

I lifted the medallion in my hand. It lay flat across my palm, marked with a red circle in the dead center. Hephaestus held up a matching one. Both of our eyes fell to Aphrodite, who held hers aloft, a blue blob of paint in the dead center.

"I'll swap," I began, but Achilles cut me off.

"Apologies, my lord, but you cannot. Lady Aphrodite must carry this task alone." Achilles bowed his head low.

"And what exactly am I to do with the Golden Fleece?" Aphrodite asked, head high and shoulders back. If she felt any fear, she certainly didn't show it.

"The Golden Fleece is set high upon that mountain. You only have to take it and bring it back down." He finished his explanation, but there was more. I could tell.

"And?" I pushed, but Achilles just lifted his hands in mock surrender.

"She must retrieve the fleece from the summit of the mountain and bring it down to the base. There is a banner pole to hang it from."

I looked up at the mountain, and at the very top, I could see the glint of something shimmering in the pale Asphodel light.

Hephaestus studied the landscape warily. He, too, knew something wasn't being said.

Achilles cleared his throat. "There is something more. I'm afraid both yourself and Lord Hephaestus will have to be bound here. There can be no physical assistance. The only way this ends is if she secures the fleece and completes the trial. At any time, my lady may give up and leave the trial, but there will be a price to be owed to Melia. She has quite a collection of boons."

Achilles bent down and pulled a rusty chain from the hard earth. He opened the wrist clasps and offered them to us expectantly.

I took one last look at Aphrodite. Her jaw set, back straight, and chin lifted with an air of confidence and authority. She gave me an encouraging smile. That was the confirmation I needed.

I stepped forward, allowing Achilles to bind me to these chains. He pulled the edges together, and with a click, my back bowed. A heavy weight pulled on me, rooting me to the spot.

"They're drenched in the Styx. It won't kill you, but it'll drain your powers," Achilles said, before turning to Hephaestus with the other set.

Hephaestus walked next to me and set his arms out, allowing the clasps to close. He stood tall still, but I could see the discipline written in the way his muscles shook.

Aphrodite approached us both, a hand on either of our cheeks. "I love you. I've got this," she said to one or both of us.

Hephaestus dipped his chin stoically, but I pushed forward, straining against my chains.

"Take a good sword and put another knife in your boot. Two, if you can. Find a good shield. Use your training. Follow through on your thrusts, just like we've done a thousand times. Something will be coming to stop you from making it down that slope. Make it die for its cause, Little Goddess," I growled.

Aphrodite leaned in and kissed me hard before turning to Hephaestus and doing the same. He pulled her close, manacled hands holding her tightly against him.

"Take this," I offered, reaching into my boot for my dagger.

She smiled when she realized it was the one she had given me centuries ago. Her small fingers clutched the hilt and settled it inside the side part of her boot.

"You've got this," Hephaestus encouraged, his voice sure and clear.

She stepped away and I moved closer to him, willing my own body to betray no signs of trepidation. We were close enough to touch, and the warmth that radiated off him soothed my nerves.

"Choose your weapons, Lady Aphrodite." Achilles bowed, sweeping his hand over the broken battlefield.

She nodded and walked around, kicking up pieces of broken and jagged metal before her eyes fell on a long sword. She hefted it and a dented shield to her body.

"I'm ready," she announced.

Achilles snapped his fingers, and we watched as shades appeared in the once-empty coliseum seats. Excited low murmurs could be heard zipping through the throngs of them, ghostly pale and some incorporeal.

Hades cleared his throat. "The portal will take you to the top. Once you're there, you're on your own. Good luck, Aphrodite. Persephone wished for me to tell you, and I quote, 'Kick its ass and do the damn thing, girl.' And I would like to tell you to do the same."

A small ghost of a smile played on his lips as she let out a small laugh.

"Hells, I love her," she joked, and Hades nodded in agreement.

"She loves you too. She wanted badly to be here," he said apologetically. He pulled open a mass of swirling shadows that Aphrodite stepped through without a backward glance.

I rounded on Achilles as soon as she was gone.

"What's she facing?" I demanded, voice tight.

He looked at me uncertainly, then glanced down at my chains as though assessing if they could hold me, lips pulled into a thin line.

"The Undead," he admitted uneasily.

Hephaestus's face went pale, and a strangled sound worked its way out of my mouth, but I clamped it down.

Hades remained cool and collected, which meant he had known. Fear prickled at the nape of my neck and sweat beaded at my brow.

"This is too dangerous. She isn't prepared," Hephaestus hissed, struggling against the long chains binding him in place, thundering mad.

I instead looked to the sky and found her small silhouette as she stepped through the portal and landed in a crouching position.

Her eyes scanned the area, assessing for threats.

"Good girl," I praised.

Aphrodite straightened and gingerly made her way to the banner pole that held the Golden Fleece. Nothing seemed to be activated yet. She walked around the pole a few times, no doubt checking for traps. When she was confident there were none to be found, she pulled her sword, and with a mighty heave, sliced the thin straps affixing it to the pole. The fleece loosened and floated down to her waiting hands. We watched as she used the remaining straps to tie it to her waist before turning to start her descent.

Anxiety knotted in my stomach through the Bond. This was too easy, and she knew it.

Fates help her.

Aphrodite kept her sword in position, her shield up and defensive, as she moved over uneven terrain.

We felt it first here, the slow rumble pulling from the earth. Aphrodite's head swiveled as the ground shook slightly around her. Panic shot through me straight from her, and I saw the way her body tensed.

The first of the Undead burst through the ground then, gnarled skeletons blooming from the cracked ground violently. These were from the depths of Tartarus, inmates on a pass in the yard to stretch their vile legs. They were humans, but often the worst of them, and their touch was necrotic.

In my peripheral, I saw Hephaestus reach for me, but glancing around, he must have thought better of it and brought his hand down.

Fuck that.

If I was going to sit and watch this, I needed him. I reached over and wrapped my fingers around his, caring little that we were in the open and exposed for all to see.

He let out a sigh of relief and pulled closer.

In the distance, I supposed the others couldn't see our hands, but it didn't matter right now if they could. Not when all I could feel was panic from Aphrodite and the anxiety rolling off Hephaestus in waves.

I spoke to Hephaestus out of the side of my mouth, but I never took my eyes off Aphrodite, who was readying her stance. "She's a fierce fighter. She can do this. She just has to focus. We have to send her calm through the Bonds. Push it through," I ordered, and he gulped a deep breath, exhaling slowly. I could feel him willing her to temper the ever-rising fear and panic as the first wave of Undead reached her, and I did the same.

Aphrodite's posture relaxed as she policed her breathing, tasting the air. She looked calm, more relaxed now.

Achilles squinted up at the scene, slightly uncomfortable, and I could read the tension there. The Undead were a formidable enemy, especially to take on alone.

"Don't worry, Achilles. Aphrodite is a goddess. Terrifying in her beauty, you'll see," I said the words to soothe him, but also myself and Hephaestus. To remind us all that her beauty was a gift but also a sharp blade, and that goddess had been born and forged in the crucible of Olympus. Raised with Amazons, blooded to them.

Bonded to the War-Bringer.

A pack of the Undead were steps from her, closing in a flanking manner. She kept her sword relaxed as they encroached on her space. Then, all at once, she sprung.

Aphrodite lunged, form precise as she slashed through the first Undead to reach her. Her sword found purchase again in quick succession with the one next to it and another to her right. Their swords, jagged and rotted with the pock marks of the pit, slashed at her in a frenzy, but she moved with skill and grace. Her blonde hair twirled around her as she danced her way through the horde, slashing and ripping at their heads and cores.

Two hulking masses barreled toward her, and Aphrodite hunkered behind her shield and charged, bashing into them with considerable force.

Spiking adrenaline raced down our Bond from her, raising my own. I willed for calm, willed for precision.

"That's it, baby, steady and precise. Save your strength," I mumbled, more for myself.

Hephaestus's hand squeezed tightly. I could feel his anxiety.

"Calm. We have to give her focus," I chided. I knew this was hard for him, the metal of the rusty chains bit into his skin from the pressure of his straining forward.

Aphrodite was fighting three-on-one now, sweeping low to take out their knees with a sickening crunch as she sliced through the rotted flesh.

The crowd roared, egging the fight on, the energy flowing around us in a frenzy.

A large formation headed straight for her, and Aphrodite let out a wild war cry before charging forward. Unafraid. Fucking stunning, the lines of her body, the power in her strikes. She used the shield on the fetid bodies she'd just laid to waste for a boost, planting her foot on the propped metal and using her momentum to spring forward. She flew through the air with such controlled fury, I couldn't help but admire how incredibly sexy she looked. Blood and sinew flew around her in great arcs; bodies left to ruin in her wake.

She was fucking magnificent.

Bloodlust ignited in my bones, pulling at my baser instincts. Hephaestus tightened his strangling grip, and the slight pain brought me back.

Aphrodite slashed and struck out, separating heads and arms as she went. She thrust her sword, pushing the strength of her entire body into it, at an approaching aggressor. The metal sank straight through the rotted flesh, and it grabbed the blade, dragging itself up to her. She cried out as it wrapped a diseased hand around her arm, the other cracking a fist over her jaw.

Pain shot through Hephaestus and me at once.

Aphrodite recovered, sweeping out of its cursed hold and backing up, creating more space, just like I taught her. With her good hand only on the hilt, she kicked out, planting her boot directly against desecrated bones, loosening them from the sword. With no hesitation, she swung forward, severing its head.

Agony radiated from my forearm and jaw, and I knew she was in tremendous pain, but she was still only a quarter of the way down the mountain. Aphrodite backed up slightly to give herself some recovery room, but the horde pushed on, determined to end her.

I made a mental note to kill Achilles after this was over.

"She's gotta get down that mountain faster. The poison will have set in, and she'll deteriorate," Hephaestus worried, and I grimaced because he was right. She had all of fifteen minutes before the spread reached up her arm. She'd need treatment as it was.

I glanced over, grateful that Hermes and Hygieia were in attendance. Hermes was clutching the stone wall, eyes wide as he watched Aphrodite's every move. Something close to fear peppered his posture. He knew what was happening too.

"Come on baby, move," Hephaestus encouraged beside me, and I looked back at Aphrodite. She had retreated up about forty yards, and the Undead were pulling themselves from the ground at an alarming rate.

I realized with a jolt that this would never end. She could not outlast them. She'd have to run.

"Run, Ditey. Get down the fucking slope." I willed the wind to take my voice to her, manipulating the Thrum of Battle to my advantage. My orders could be heard by any under my command on a battlefield. This was close enough, and I supposed the Fates agreed, because I watched her head perk up, searching for me.

"I'm still at the bottom. Tighten up," I barked, low and deliberately. "You can't kill them all. They're crawling from the Pits too quickly. You can't stay, Aphrodite. Find a way to slide your fine ass down that mountain before I break these chains and kill everyone in this arena."

She bit her lip and nodded a few times, hoisting her sword in her off hand. It was a bit awkward for her, throwing her off balance.

"Toss the sword. Pull your dagger. It's using up too much strength to wield with your off hand. Your form looks incredible; you're doing so well. Toss the sword, Little Goddess. Use the shield."

Aphrodite nodded and hurled her sword at the closest Undead approaching. With a loud crack, it impaled him through the chest and into the side of the mountain.

"Good fucking girl," I whispered again, this time sending on the Thrum, and she shot me a bloodied smile, her blonde hair coming out of her braids in wispy tendrils. She looked terrifying.

I'd never been harder in my life.

Aphrodite reached into her boot and clasped her fingers around the dagger. She hoisted her shield off and bolted like a bullet, her strong thighs carrying her quickly toward the horde.

Panic rose from Hephaestus, and I squeezed his hand.

"Trust her. *Calm*," I commanded again, and he swallowed.

She was going to try and use brute strength to bulldoze into the onslaught, a useful tactic if she had been built like a titan, or even me, but she was much smaller, with waning divinity and Bond sickness.

My chest constricted. It was a bold move, but she had to try something. My jaw clenched tight, Hephaestus's hand practically crushing the bones in my own as Aphrodite closed the distance, moving so quickly I knew she had pushed her remaining god power into the speed, building up force for the impact. I forced myself to not look away, to show her unwavering support.

The impact never came.

At the very last moment, she leapt up, using the shoulders and helms of the oncoming horde to propel herself high into the air. She flew, almost in slow motion, and I watched in awe as she positioned her shield under her boots and bent her knees for impact. She hit the hard ground on the shield and slid forward on the sharp slope, slashing and stabbing as she deftly maneuvered herself through the throng.

Clever Little Goddess.

She was using gravity to pull her downward, the shield's momentum to save her legs and strength so she could focus on defense. She was surfing down a cursed mountain in the Asphodels, leaving dropped bodies in her wake, a maniacal smile on her blood-stained lips. Her fury-filled cries echoed above the din.

The crowd in the stands were losing it, yelling and jumping and cheering her on. The power fueled her, feeding her ferociously savage appetite. The war cry of Aphrodite.

She was almost there, just a few more feet.

An undead burst from the ground abruptly, giving her no time to correct the momentum or direction of the shield. With a sickening crunch, shield bit into bone and halted, throwing her small body through the air. Aphrodite flipped twice before landing in a crouch on her feet.

The crowds were insatiable at this point, pushing over themselves in excitement.

Aphrodite took off running toward the flagpole without so much as a glance back at the horde that had started to come for her. She took the stairs up the dais two at a time and slung the fleece over the metal bar. With a mighty groan, the remaining members of the horde returned to dust immediately, and the crowd went wilder still.

The manacles holding Hephaestus and I fell heavily to the ground, and without a word, we were both running to her.

She had collapsed into a heap on the wooden steps, and all I could think of was the rotting flesh spreading up her arm.

Hephaestus sped up, his lithe form a spear through the air, but it was Hermes who beat us all. He blurred past us, whipping the air like a train in his wake. The God of Thieves skidded to a halt in front of her, leaving long grooves in the ground as he kicked dirt up everywhere. When we reached them, he had her in his arms, his hands moving so fast over her rotting forearm that they blurred in and out of sight, pushing his power into her.

Aphrodite's lids were heavy, but when we came into view, she smiled, wicked and bloody and feral.

I reached her first, pulled the top of her body from Hermes. Luckily for him, he gave no protest and instead continued his work on her arm. He was incanting under his breath, and then, suddenly, his hands were covering hers. They both let out a loud hiss, and I could smell burning flesh.

Hephaestus was on us seconds later, pushing Aphrodite's sweaty hair back and checking her jaw. It was bruised purple under the blood, and I knew it was likely broken, but the rot hadn't settled in. Probably from the closed fist and not the palm.

I hoisted Aphrodite up, cradling her body to mine with Hephaestus's arms supporting her head and holding her uninjured hand.

Hermes stepped back with a grimace. "I've stopped the spread, but she's fading. You need to get her out of the Underworld so she can heal." His words were different, softer. *Guilty*.

Achilles and Hades walked up, the rest of our party hot on their heels. The shouts of the shades were still deafening, and Achilles smiled, but my expression went cold.

I shifted Aphrodite to Hephaestus, cradled her against him gracefully. I pushed the sweaty hair off her forehead and planted a kiss at her temple. She was still breathing hard, but she gave me a small smile as she blinked through the daze.

Then, without warning or fanfare, I turned on my heel and hit Achilles with enough force to level a city block. It sent him flying backward against the side of the mountain, the stone cracking with the impact of his body.

He stood up, spitting teeth and blood onto the cold ground.

Hades stepped forward to put a hand on my bicep, but there was no need. I was done.

Achilles approached and stretched out his hand, which I took. He understood why I'd rocked his shit. He'd sent the love of my life to face the Undead with no warning, and he was lucky I settled for the hit and not flaying his flesh from his bones.

And he knew it.

He cleared his throat. "The first trial has been completed with distinction. Melia invites you to rest and regain your strength. Instructions for the second trial will be delivered soon."

He bowed once at me, and then Hephaestus. When his eyes came to rest on Aphrodite, he bowed lowest. "That was one of the most impressive displays I've ever seen, Lady Aphrodite. You are truly a force."

He straightened. Achilles cared not that she was a goddess, or a female. He knew warriors' hearts, knew they came in many vessels, and he had been impressed with her fight and spirit of conviction.

She gave him a weak smile before closing her eyes with an appreciative nod.

I turned to Hades.

"Portal," I spat out, and he moved immediately, producing one for us to step through.

Hermes and Hygieia made to follow, but I held up a hand to stop them. "She's out of the woods. We need some time to ourselves. Come by tomorrow." I wasn't asking.

I turned to Hermes, who looked fidgety, on the verge of arguing with me. "Thank you for getting to her so quickly," I ground out. It was against the nature of our relationship to be cordial, but I truly was grateful.

He tucked his tongue behind his teeth and lent me a terse nod. "Call me if anything changes."

Baby steps.

Hephaestus carried her through the portal without a backward glance, and I followed him, eager to put as much distance between this coliseum and the crowd as possible.

The first trial was done. We were in it now.

Hephaestus

CHAPTER 30

Aphrodite was sluggish in my arms. I carried her straight to the bathroom, eager to get the mud and guts and ichor off her. Hermes had acted quickly, and the wound on her arm was already starting to heal. It surprised me how fast he'd gotten there, and *why*. It went beyond his oath—he'd actually cared that she was hurt. Whether that was for my benefit or hers remained to be seen, but I felt the guilt roll off him while he worked over her. The worry he usually reserved for us.

I sat Aphrodite on the bench in the walk-in shower and laid her head back to the tiled wall.

"I feel like I've been hit by a truck," she groaned.

I reached to turn on the tap as she moved slowly, wincing anytime she had to tweak her arm. I crossed through the spray and helped her lift her bloodstained shirt over her head before dipping down and pulling off her boots.

"I did it, Hephaestus." Her words were small, but I could feel the relief and pride radiating from them.

I smiled encouragingly and leaned in to brush my lips across hers.

"Of course you did, Little Love. You were magnificent."

Aphrodite reached up to tangle her fingers in my hair, pulling me down to her. My chest and neck flamed with heat as she clawed at me, dragging me close, but I forced my muscles to restrain her arms and bring them to her chest.

"You're hurt, Ditey. You need a shower and rest."

She pouted up at me with those long eyelashes, and I almost buckled. *Almost.*

"If you eat and rest, I promise to make it up to you. Any way you want," I offered, and her eyes lit up.

"Anything?"

I nodded. "Can you stand to wash? I need to go grab your toothbrush and some clothes."

She stood, wincing slightly, pressing her fingers gingerly to her side.

"Broken ribs," she confirmed with another grimace.

"I really am so proud of you, baby. Don't take too long. I want you in bed." I stepped away, deflated by the loss of contact, but I gave her a few moments to herself, confident she was okay enough to stand. I needed to change my pants, now soaked from the water.

I'd almost made it to the door when I heard her suck in a shaky breath.

"H-Hephaestus?" she said.

I turned, giving her my full attention. I cocked an eyebrow as she padded forward a step, worrying her hands together.

"You—you understand, right? You understand that I don't want to leave you or Ares? I just want us to have a chance at something real, something normal." She looked so uncertain, so desperate for me to believe her.

And I did.

"I do. Ares will come to understand it, too, in time. He's had a lot of upheavals in a short time span, and he just needs time to adjust. But I'm not leaving him or you. Get a shower, Ditey. I'll leave your stuff on the sink."

"You're falling for him."

I stopped in my tracks, tensing as I slowly turned to face her. There wasn't an ounce of judgment or jealousy that I could see or feel, her face and Bond open and earnest as she waited for me to speak.

I dipped my chin in confirmation.

"I think I am. I don't really have anything to compare it to; it's different than it was with you. When we first spent time together, I knew you were going to be my wife. It was exciting, and I was just . . . awestruck by you and my luck. With Ares . . ." I trailed off, running my hand over my lip for a second as I thought of how to word it, if there even *were* words that fit this.

I continued in a rush. "He needs me. I don't know if that's good or bad, but he needs a place to feel safe in, and for some reason, he submits to me. I feel protective of him, with the damage of what he did to him, what I helped contribute to. I don't know if it's forever, but I'm not going to ignore what I'm feeling."

She beamed at me and turned back to the spray, shedding the last of her clothing before stepping under the water.

I headed to the closet and grabbed a pair of sweats for her and the toothbrush Hecate had gotten for her earlier this week. I set it and a hairbrush on the counter with her clothes before reaching for a towel. I ran my hands over the soft material, pushing my power through it until the threads began to heat. Unless she stayed in the shower for an extended period of time, when she pulled the towel to her, it would be extra warm on her skin.

Satisfied, I shed my own jeans and tossed them into the hamper before reaching up and losing my shirt as well. Everything smelled like death. It was a subtle, cold smell that saturated the Underworld. Not unpleasant, but I was eager to get rid of it. I grabbed a change of clothes and threw them on before making my way down the hall.

A delicious smell invaded my nostrils, and I heard the unmistakable sound of sizzling bacon in a pan. I rounded the corner to see Ares shirtless and cooking over a hot flame. He had bacon crisping up, eggs sizzling, and was in the process of flipping pancakes into neat little stacks.

I leaned against the doorframe to watch him work, mesmerized.

Watching him do something so domesticated fascinated me. I'd known him for my entire existence, and for most of that time, we'd been enemies. I only ever thought of him as being flung into war—killing, maiming, or destroying. I never considered he may also be kind, loving. We didn't need to eat, but most of us still enjoyed the taste of food. I suspected this was more of a way for Ares to steady himself as his adrenaline waned, and I took the time to study him. Thousands of years together meant there wasn't much about Aphrodite or myself that we didn't know, but Ares was still opening himself up, and I knew I wanted to know him. To see the parts of him he kept locked away.

He hadn't shaved in a little over a week, and his beard was coming in nicely, streaks of deep red mingling in with the dark brown. His hair was also longer on top, definitely out of regs. The muscles in his back flexed slightly as a pop of grease landed on his chest.

"*Fuck!*" he hissed, rubbing the spot tenderly.

I chuckled, and Ares whipped around, eyes guarded at first, but they softened when he realized it was just me.

I loved that. The automatic release of tension, that I was able to invoke that instinct within him.

I walked to the island and pulled out one of the barstools tucked underneath it. "I think that's why you're supposed to wear a shirt, or even an apron, while cooking," I teased, and he scowled.

"I don't want to get grease on any of my shirts. I don't have a lot of them here," he grumbled, turning back to the task at hand.

He pulled the bacon from the grease and piled it high on a plate laden with paper towels, then spooned the scrambled eggs onto their own dish. I watched as he turned off the burners and walked the food to the table, before heading back over to grab the pancakes as well. He'd put out syrup and orange juice, and I frowned, confused.

"Where'd all this food come from?" I asked, and he shrugged.

"I assumed it was you, but it could have been that they stocked the fridge while they were practically living here," he offered, moving back to start cleanup. Tufts of steam rose off the food on the table.

I shrugged. "I can't cook to save my life, so it definitely wasn't me."

He lifted an eyebrow. "Well, regardless, I'm glad it was here. She needs to eat. That was . . . a hard task," he said, wiping down the stove and counter around it.

I nodded and leaned over my stool to rest on the island counter. "Speaking of, how did she learn how to fight like that? I've never seen her on a battlefield,"

"I taught her," he replied nonchalantly. "Zeus kept her working in the shadows, preferring she use her . . . *wiles* to gain access to information or sway opinions. But I didn't ever want her to be undefended, especially after that day. So I taught her how to fight, how to assess a battlefield, and later, she went to live with the Amazons. It was actually Hera who sent her there. For what, I'm not sure, but Zeus was livid. I was proud. She did so fucking well today," he praised, voice laced with it.

"She did. I never thought seeing her plunge a sword into a corpse would do it for me but . . ." I trailed off, and Ares let out a small groan in agreement.

"I know. I was both scared for her and rock hard at how incredible she was doing, committing that much unfiltered violence." He adjusted himself, still scrubbing the counter. "Plus, the bloodlust and frenzy of all those shades didn't help. I was wound up the entire time," he admitted.

I stood silently then made my way over to him. Nerves fluttered in my belly with every step, every inch of space that closed between us, until I was pressed against his back, barely an inch between us.

"Is the pressure still bad?" I asked, running my fingers over the lines in his shoulders.

Ares let out a low growl and tightened his grip on the counter. The way he shivered with unleashed energy radiated through me, and I had my answer.

"She's tired, and she'll need rest. I can make it subside and take care of it later."

He brushed off his need but still leaned into my touch as I dug deeply, kneading my fingers into his tense muscles. His traps were so stiff I could have cracked my fingers with the effort to loosen them. Ares slapped a hand down on the counter when my fingers trailed down his shoulder blades, around his torso, under his waistband. I closed my fingers around the monster he kept sheathed there, giving him a tug.

"*Don't*. Don't tease me now," he choked, looking over his shoulder.

My heart was beating out of my fucking chest as I pressed my lips to his shoulder blade. I gave him another languid stroke, and he buckled, groaning against me. It made me bold.

"I don't want to tease; I want to help. Let me help," I pleaded gently, kissing along his back and neck. I flipped him around and slammed him back against the counter.

He dropped the towel he'd been holding and looked at me through hooded eyes.

"Last time we touched, it sent Aphrodite over the edge," he reasoned.

I paused for only a second before resuming my ministrations.

"Yes, but she was in another realm." I leaned in and kissed along his collarbone, up the column of his neck as I spoke. "She's fifty feet away now. I want to take care of you, Ares. *Let me take care of you.*"

He was crumbling. All the self-restraint he had balked against him as I kissed his chest and stroked his length. An excited energy pulsed through me.

"This thing is so heavy, Ares. I want to taste it, but I don't know how. I've never . . . done this before."

Ares let out a loud groan at my words, and I slipped a finger over the head of his cock, the slick he leaked smearing over the tip and down his shaft.

"Are you sure you want this?" He raised an eyebrow in surprise, but nothing could hide the *want* there.

I pulled hard, twisting my hand. Another moan. Another grunt. Another needy little whimper, each more salacious than the last, and I wanted this to fucking happen. "Yes. I'd like to learn all the ways to coax those sounds from your lips, and you've got such a pretty cock, Ares. If you want me to. But I don't know how."

My neck flushed with slight embarrassment, and all at once, I was back with Aphrodite on our wedding night, begging her to teach me how she liked to be pleasured. I knew what I liked and what the basic tenets were, but I'd never had a cock in my mouth. Hells, I didn't want just *any* dick in my mouth—I wanted *his*.

Ares reached his rough hand up to swipe across my lips. I parted them slightly, and he pushed one thick digit, the pad of his finger, against my tongue.

He leaned in closer. "Suck, Heph. Wrap your lips around my finger and show me how good you'll be with the real thing."

I did as I was told.

Ares grunted, thrusting into my hand as his fingers explored my mouth. I squeezed tighter, gripping him in a vice as he pressed deeper, demanding more, causing me to spread wider until his fingers almost touched the back of my throat. My eyes watered with the intrusion, but otherwise I was fine, and the lust that darkened his eyes was plenty of reward.

"Hmmm," he breathed. "No gag reflex."

He placed his hand on the side of my face, smearing my saliva along my jaw. We locked eyes, questions and doubts swimming in his, but I was in. I was ready to play and explore, to let him take the lead until I felt ready to top him from the bottom. I wanted the God of War reduced to a wanton puddle under my mouth, and I would make it happen, but Ares had never freely given up control.

Pressure, gentle and soft on my head and shoulders as he guided me down, until I was on my knees, looking at him towering above me.

"I don't want to do it wrong," I confessed, letting some of my real vulnerability coax his to the surface.

His dark eyes softened.

"I'll talk you through it," he promised, leaning down. He kissed me softly on my lips, and it was different than the others, without panic or fear or the haze of blood magic between us. This was just Ares. Just me, on my knees, eager to find out all the ways to make him fall apart.

I kissed him harder, stealing his breath, nipping at his lips before he straightened.

"Unbuckle my pants and slip down the zipper so you have better access," he ordered, and I complied immediately, careful not to snag any skin. I pulled his cock out from the top of his jeans, and he sprung forward unobstructed. I felt my pulse throbbing in my cock.

"Grip my balls tightly, Hephaestus." I obeyed. "Tighter," he groaned, and I increased my grip. "Flatten your tongue and slide me in. Mold your lips around my cock. Go on, you can do it," he encouraged, still holding on to that semblance of control, but his flustered cheeks and stuttered breath had me smirking. It was cute, the way he thought he was still in charge here.

I took him in my mouth, slid my tongue under his shaft as he threw his head back, hips pushing against me.

"Fuck, oh fuck. That's good, that's so good. Wait, don't move. Let me look at you like this."

I glanced up at him, mouth stretched impossibly wide around him, watching his chest heave and abs twitch as he rested on my tongue.

"Fates, you're fucking beautiful, aren't you."

I blushed, smiling as best I could around the mouthful, shivering as his fingers ghosted over the scar on my cheek, brushing a few tendrils of my hair that normally hid it back. The praise falling from him on gruff breaths warmed me down to my toes.

"Yeah, you know you are. So easy on the eyes. Okay, bring yourself down, relax your throat," he instructed as his hands applied a tiny bit of pressure to the back of my head to ease me to him. He tasted like desire, his cock hard and unyielding as he filled all the space in my mouth, pressed my tongue flat against his shaft, noting every hiss, every throb of his cock.

Ares let out a series of moans and pants when I bobbed my head rhythmically around him, but I just needed to move, needed to do *something*. I twisted my head slightly, catching him at several different angles, exploring and committing every moan and hitch of his breath to memory until I figured out the strokes he liked, the pressure he preferred.

"*Hells*, I could fuck this mouth for centuries." He licked his lips, head cocked as he guided me over his length, and with every flex of his muscles, every catch in his words, I grew bolder, more confident.

"Fucking Fates, you know how to suck a cock, Heph," he grunted, and hearing his praise, coupled with my nickname, *did* something to me. "Am I truly the first you've tasted?" he breathed, and I nodded vigorously, loving the way his shaft swelled at my confirmation. I moaned, the sound reverberating from my chest to my lips.

Ares faltered in his slow thrusts.

"P-please—" he whimpered, his grip on command slipping, and I complied, vibrating his cock as I sucked. I could tell he was holding back, being gentle. I didn't want gentle.

I ripped my lips free of him, and his eyes widened.

"Are you okay? Was that too much?" he asked.

I glared. "Stop holding back," I growled.

He cradled my face and said, "It's your first time. We should take it easy."

My eyes narrowed. "Does it feel good?" I asked, noting his glassy eyes, his slackened jaw, the twitch of his muscles.

"It feels fucking incredible," he deadpanned.

I preened at the praise. "Fantastic. Now, fuck my throat, or I'll stop, and you can jack off in the shower," I spat in a challenge, and he arched his eyebrows in surprise. We regarded each other for a moment and then Ares shook out his head once as he guided his cock back to my lips. I opened for him, sucking him deep.

"Remember that you *demanded* this," he warned, and with incredible force, Ares impaled my throat on his dick. He kissed the back of my throat with his tip as he held my head between his hands and fucked me mercilessly.

"Remember. I. Wanted. To. Be. Gentle," he snarled as the onslaught continued. "Breath out of your mouth." Every few words were punctuated by a sharp grunt or pant, and I was so fucking turned on at being used like this that it drove him crazy. I loved a good rough fuck, and it was interesting being on this side of it, but I liked it. The power dynamic. *The exchange*. Even now, with the God of War using my throat like a fucking cock sleeve, he was the one barely holding on, and I couldn't get enough.

"Wait, wait, wait," he commanded, but I swallowed, willing my throat to relax. "That's it, oh Hells, that's it."

His pace was punishing, and I tilted my head up as far as it would go to give him better access, watching his chest heave. His chin rested on his chest as he watched me own him, mark him with my spit and the streaks of pearly cum that painted his cock, coaxed by the work I was putting in. One hand gripped my head firmly as he slammed into me, but I could tell it was him holding on for dear life as I unleashed. I reached for the hand at his side, pressed it around my throat and squeezed with every thrust inside.

"Fuck, Hells, *fuck*. I can feel my cock through your throat with my hand, Heph. I'm not gonna last. Tap if you need to stop."

I shook my head and leaned into his thrusts, my nose brushing the beginning of the thin line of trimmed hair at the top of his base. My own cock strained painfully against my pants, and I wanted to relieve it, but I was afraid to break the spell we were under, too focused on draining him dry to stop.

"I can't wait to fuck you," Ares grunted, and my nipples pulled taut at his words, my balls drawing up. It was the strangest sensation, to be so turned on with no friction or stimulation, but I was *aching*.

"Fucking Hells, you're going to destroy me aren't you?" he whimpered, eyes fluttering shut.

I groaned, the vibrations wrapping him in a vice. Pleasure overwhelmed him, and it was holy, divine.

"Where do you want to wear my cum, Hephaestus?"

My eyes jerked up to his, nostrils flaring in what I hoped would be warning because, if he took this cock out of my mouth before he came down my throat, there would be Hells to pay.

His hips faltered once, then twice as he came with force, a cry expelling from his lips as I sucked him dry. He tried to pull away as I gulped him down, his legs and thighs trembling, his abdomen rippling as he doubled over panting. A spittle of cum squeezed from the seam of his cock and my lips.

"Fuck. Fuck," he chanted, pulling himself completely free of my mouth, but I shook my head and dove back in, licking over his head, pressing my tongue against the seam, sucking with all my might every last drop straight from the source.

Ares reached to wipe the tears that had escaped during his face fucking before he hauled me up and kissed me, deep and sloppy as his release dripped from the corner of my lips. I knew I tasted like cum, like him, but he didn't seem to give a single fuck. He held me tight to his chest as our breathing slowed, both sticky with sweat.

"You took it so well. You did so good. Are you okay?" he asked, and I nodded as he struggled to take back that control. I gave it to him, knowing that, soon, we wouldn't have to play games.

"I'm good. I hope it felt good," I whispered.

Ares let out a small laugh. "You're a fucking mess from what I did to you, and you're worried that it wasn't good for me?" He shook his head in disbelief. "That was incredible."

He kissed the top of my hair tenderly. I was plastered to his bare chest, smirking as his heart rate thumped against my skull, but I heard a soft crunch from somewhere behind us.

I turned, and Ares jerked his head up in time to see Aphrodite, fully clothed in the sweatshirt I'd picked out for her. It hit her mid-calf, and the way she sat in that chair with her legs folded gave me a slight peek at the soft skin of her thighs. Her hair was wild, freshly dried, and she was crunching on a piece of bacon.

I froze, as did Ares. We hadn't really discussed this yet.

The . . . *us* of it all.

"That was fucking hot," she commented and bit off another piece of bacon.

Ares relaxed a fraction behind me.

"I'm sorry, we should have talked to you first," I began, but she waved me off.

"Stop. You're going to be together, sometimes without me. It's all gotta be okay, or none of it's okay. That was beautiful to watch. I understand it's your private moment, but when the time comes for you to fuck for the first time, can I be there? If it works out. Don't ruin a moment waiting on me."

"*Yes*," we both practically shouted. I knew it was true for him as it was for me. I wanted her there. Hells, I wanted her between us.

"How are you feeling?" Ares asked, still holding me to him.

Aphrodite shrugged and picked up a pancake, biting it in half.

I grinned.

"I'm tired but okay. Horny as fuck now. Seriously, you two are amazing to watch," she answered honestly, and my cock jerked, swollen and stiff. The slight smell of jasmine and wood fire clung in the air, our scents swirling and mixing with the sex.

Ares chuckled behind me and bent down so his lips ghosted my ear.

"Go take care of the both of you. I'll be right here," he whispered, and I immediately broke rank.

I crossed the room where Aphrodite sat and lifted her firmly but gently from her chair.

"Hi." She smiled, seduction oozing from her voice.

I kissed her deeply, the taste of bacon grease and butter mixing with the taste of Ares.

"Hi," I answered, tone low. I turned her abruptly, and she fell forward on her hands, gripping the table. I gently, if not somewhat impatiently, nudged her legs apart and shimmied down my jeans. My cock was slick with pre-cum, and I fell forward, resting my head on the middle of her upper back. I flipped up the sweatshirt she was wearing to find her completely bare and sopping wet.

"You weren't kidding, Little Love. You're dripping right now," I breathed, and she nodded, a needy wanton sound.

Ares tucked himself into his pants and walked over to the head of the table across from us. He pulled the chair and sat, pouring himself a cup of coffee and grabbing a slice of bacon. He watched me push Aphrodite forward and slide my cock between her slick lips, groaning from the slide.

Aphrodite sighed, and I thrust in, hard, bucking the table. She flew forward, but I grabbed her hips, yanking her back and forth as I plowed into her, fucking her hot cunt over my cock.

"I'm not gonna be able to hold it, Little Love," I choked out, and she rolled her hips to suck me deep.

"Me either. Do you know how close I was just watching? Fuck me hard and fast. I want to come on your cock," she whined, and who was I to tell her no?

I obliged. There was no lovemaking to this, nothing gentle. This was raw aggression and power, a transfer of energy that she lapped up and converted into her own strength. She shook apart around me not a moment too soon, crying out my name as Ares drank his coffee and ate his breakfast, eyes never leaving us.

I bit down on the soft flesh between her neck and shoulder as I came, trembling from the adrenaline and release and ecstasy of the three of us. I slid back out of Aphrodite's spent body and helped her sit before collapsing into my own chair.

We sat together, eating and talking and joking, until it was time to retire for bed. We sent Aphrodite first, and I cleaned while Ares showered.

I fell asleep between the two of them, the most content I'd ever been.

Hephaestus

CHAPTER 31

A thousand times I walked these streets, but the air of the city felt different today, with *them*. The weekends were bustling and busy down in the Quarter, but Monday mornings down on Esplanade rolled slow and easy.

Ares walked a few steps ahead of us, broad-shouldered and restless, head on a swivel, ever vigilant. My fingers twitched in my pocket as I watched him, Aphrodite's arm wrapped around mine.

Sunlight filtered in through the canopy of old live oaks that arched overhead as we turned off the main drag, streetcars rattling past slow and loud. The heat was lazy, not yet stifling, and I couldn't believe this was where we were in our lives.

I tried not to let my mind wander to the Trials, none of us knowing when they'd send for us again. Instead, I rooted myself in the here, in the now, watching Aphrodite's white sundress twirl around her with every sway of those hips, my black button-down knotted at her waist. The wind lifted tufts of Ares's dark hair from under my battered Saints' cap he'd pulled low over his eyes, hands shoved into the pocket of faded blue jeans.

We made our way to the little café on the corner, the sweet scent of beignets frying growing heavier with each step.

"You're good with him, you know?" Aphrodite said, leaning her head on my shoulder. It was quiet enough I didn't think Ares could hear, but I glanced down to see her eyes on me, blue and dazzling in the morning light.

"He's guarded."

Her lips thinned as she looked up ahead. His pace quickened every few blocks, pulling away from us in a way that set my teeth on edge.

"He doesn't trust himself enough to deserve this yet. It's going to be hard to convince him, Heph. What if we can't? What if we lose him?"

I swallowed at the low fear in her voice, that ebb of panic flaring between our Bond. The last few days had felt nice, a low and slow routine of learning one another. But Ares . . . His skittishness made my palms itch.

"I'm the outsider here. He trusts you; it's me he has to make his way to."

Aphrodite was quiet for a beat before she let out a soft sigh. "He's not open with me either. It's taken years. Centuries, even. But I'm afraid we might not have that kind of time. That first Trial was hard, and the others will be just as heavy. I don't want to wait until the end to start living. And—"

She came to a stop, pulling me back as she hesitated, pale eyes searching mine. "I don't want either of you to be alone. If I don't make it. I want you to have each other." Her voice faltered as I tilted my head, my pained grimace reflecting in her watery eyes.

"That's not gonna happen, baby. We're gonna get through this." I pressed a kiss to her forehead as she quickly swiped under her eyes.

"Promise me you won't let him lose it. That you'll take care of him, like you do me."

I nodded, and she let out a tight breath, relief etched on her face. I didn't have to say the words, and she knew it. Knew that I'd hold him together not just because she'd asked me to but because she could see how my affections had morphed and altered toward the God of War.

Ares.

Our pace sped to match his, and Aphrodite reached out with a gentle hand that she looped around his bicep. He startled, then turned, the smile on his face wide and blinding as she reeled him back to us. Together, we moved like mismatched notes, ones that shouldn't have made chords but had quickly become my favorite song, sharing the shade of the leaves above us.

Under the same sun.

We stopped beneath the low green awning of Fury's, a little joint with mismatched tables set out on the sidewalk. Ares pulled out a chair for Aphrodite, and when I reached for his as he tucked her in, a small, endearing blush crept across his cheeks. He let me scoot his chair in, with a shy smile I was growing addicted to playing on his lips.

"Hey, Heph, how y'all doin', *bebe*?" Chelcie the owner slid out the door carrying menus I wouldn't need and a tray of waters, a bright grin on her face.

"Chelc, this is my wife, Aphrodite. And *our* Bondmate, Ares."

Ares nearly choked on the water he'd been taking a sip on at my words, dropped as casually from my lips as I could make them. I loved the way they sounded, but there was a prick of anxiety at how he would take a public declaration like that.

Too fast too soon?

Or . . .

I glanced up to see his cheeks flamed, sucking on his bottom lip with an eyebrow raised at me, but I couldn't see any anger there.

"It's so good to meet you." Aphrodite reached out a hand, shaking Chelcie's. The dryad, tall and stunning with dark brown skin and tightly wound curls, returned her greeting warmly, then turned to Ares.

"'Bout time we get to see you out here happy. Cora's gonna be pissed she missed meetin' y'all." She frowned, referring to her wife. They did a lot of work down at the center with Medusa, and they also happened to serve some of the best seafood in town.

I decided to press my luck and reach a hand out to take Aphrodite's on the table, resting the other on the top of Ares's thigh. With a squeeze, I smiled, pretending I didn't hear his sharp intake of breath.

Pretending I didn't love the way I affected him.

"That's alright. We'll be around more."

We ordered a few rounds of Abita, a couple of pounds of crawfish for Ares and me to share, and a plate piled high with powdery beignets for Aphrodite. The conversation flowed slow and easy, more laughter and smiles between us than I'd ever known. Every so often, Aphrodite would lean across the table to point out a balcony and the flowers that dripped from it. Ares would nod like he was looking, but the only attention he paid was to her, and it kept a smile on my lips, watching them together.

"I can see why you love it here," she mused. Her eyes bounced all around, taking in the wide breadth of trees, the spray of Spanish moss as it swayed in the breeze. "It's different than any of the other places I've been . . ." She trailed off, staring down at her plate, lost in thought. "I don't think I've ever felt this at ease in a city. Not even on Olympus. That felt like a fucking spectacle, polished and perfect to cover the ugly of its bones, but New Orleans"—she sighed, glancing at the cracked sidewalk—"it feels beautiful because it's lived in."

Ares tilted his head.

"You're saying Olympus felt fake?" There was a slight edge to his voice, one that wasn't hard to piece together. Olympus was where they'd found one another.

"I'm saying Olympus was for looking at. This place is for being in. It's charming but gritty, and the magic here. The *power.*" She shuddered, chewing on her nail as she looked between us.

Ares reached over, stealing a bite of her beignet. White powdered sugar rained down over his chest as he gave her a wolfish smile, seemingly satisfied at her clarification.

"It might charm you out of that armor of yours," she cautioned.

Ares scoffed, but she just picked up another fluffy pillow of fried dough and sank her teeth into it, speaking around bites.

"Look at you. It's already happening. No armor, no sword. Just you with your messy shirt, stealing my damned food." She laughed, and the thoughtful chuckle that broke past his lips turned gentler.

"Yeah. Maybe I could get used to this," he whispered, looking down the street before clearing his throat, and clarifying. "A place like this, I mean." His walls went back up, but they were a little shorter than they had been this morning. I counted that as progress.

Over the top of my lowered sunglasses, I watched Aphrodite make a mess of her plate and fingers, the table around her dusted with enough powdered sugar to kill a man. She caught me staring and gave me a devilish little grin as she licked her lips.

"Easy," I warned.

Her lips trailed over her knuckle. "Why? This is perfect. Warm, messy, *delicious* . . ." Her eyes blazed against me then drifted in a sidelong glance to Ares, who'd gone still. "Just my type."

"Messy, huh? Careful, Little Goddess. I might take that as a compliment." He leaned back, flipping my hat backward on his head, and I felt my cock wake up.

"I'm not the only one who enjoys a mess, am I, baby?" Her gaze locked mine.

Ares's eyes followed hers, and the intensity in my stare had him squirming in his seat.

"Mm-hmm," I responded, feeling the air pressure drop around us. "I fucking *love* messes. Love finding out what makes a mess explode, pressing those buttons, bringing them right to the edge and deciding if they've earned to have me clean them up."

Ares swallowed, and I tracked the movement of his throat hungrily. He was so close to accepting this, to accepting us, he just needed a firm hand to guide him.

That was exactly how, thirty minutes later, I had him showered and naked, arms stretched and strapped across my table. I stood in front of him, shirt off, barefoot with crossed arms as he strained to look up at me.

"Do you trust me?" I asked, keeping my voice even as possible.

Ares stared into my eyes, every muscle in his body fighting against the feel of the restraints that kept him confined. He could shred them if he wanted to, the leather would give easily under his strength, but they remained unbroken as he tried to surrender.

"*I want to.*"

His honesty pleased me, and I rewarded him with a smile as I approached, close enough to feel his breath against my abdomen. Harsh, hot pants, his adrenaline so loud as it coursed through his veins, reverberating off the walls. I waited, and the longer the silence stretched, the more anxious he became. His muscles flexed, testing the hold of the leather.

"If you want out, you only need to say your safe word. Or rip yourself free. You aren't trapped here, Ares. I don't want you trapped," I said softly.

Sweat broke out over his brow, the warmth of the room warring with the goose bumps pebbling his flesh.

"What do you want?" he asked, and it was nearly a plea, almost broken as he struggled to calm himself.

I raised a hand to stroke his cheek, and instantly, his body relaxed.

Touch.

He needed touch to feel grounded. Needed to feel tethered, not adrift in the cosmos. Not alone.

"Can I touch you, Ares?"

He sucked in a sharp breath. Nodded.

"Words," I demanded.

"Yes. *Please.*"

So pretty, when he begged. But I kept my thoughts to myself, giving him dignity as he fought against his surrender.

I walked in slow, deliberate steps around the table, keeping my fingertips connected to his heated flesh. His muscles bunched under my touch, rippling and spasming as I trailed over his jaw, down the column of his throat. Rough fingers on the scarred skin of his biceps, of his shoulders, the broad expanse of his back.

I traced the ridges of old sword cuts across his ribs, the puckered mark of a spear through his shoulder, the faint white lines of an incalculable number of battles.

Hundreds of them. *Thousands.*

"You've survived so much more than anyone could ever fathom. Than I ever did." My fingertips traced a long scar from hip to rib, applying enough pressure to reassure, but not enough to dig into the tissue as I mapped his wounds. Committed them to memory. "Every line tells me that you don't break."

The God of War barked a short, restless laugh. "That's the point, isn't it?"

I frowned. "No." I leaned closer, dragging my lips across his shoulder as my hand ran over the rise and fall of his chest. "The point is that you don't have to always be at war. You're safe here. With us. With me."

My thumb brushed over the faint hollow at the center of Ares's sternum. I could feel the strong, steady beat of his heart through his skin. I moved slowly, every pass of palm over muscle deliberate, not to test the strength of the god strapped to the table of my own making but to reassure him.

You are here. I am here. Nothing will harm you between my hands.

It was slow work, but I took my time, kneading flesh until my fingers ached, taking painstaking care to push as much warmth into his body as he could take.

He was slicked in sweat, trembling from my touch, his cock hard and leaking in fat droplets onto the floor between his spread legs, begging for attention that I would not give.

I stood behind him, slipping my palms down his lower back, palming at his cheeks, spreading him. His knees shook at the vulnerability, but he sucked in steady breaths, forced his body to relax as I ran a finger in a feather light touch over the tight knot.

He moaned, panting against the table, the sweetest little whimpers that tested my own resolve.

"You can't command surrender," I said after a while, still stroking around his rim, soft skin under rough fingertips. "It has to be given. *Completely*."

I pressed my lips to his spine, pinning him against the table with my hips, letting the weight of my body cradle his. He cried out as my fingers trailed higher, up his back, over his hip, against the tight muscle of his thighs.

Everywhere but where he silently begged for me to touch him.

My hands kept their unhurried rhythm, palm to scar, knuckle to ridge of bone, fingertips to the wet skin on the inside of his thighs. I nearly groaned at the mess he'd made of himself.

"This isn't a battlefield. You don't have to brace for the next blow."

The leather cuffs creaked softly as Ares's wrists shifted, not to test strength, but to sink in deeper. *Settling*. I preened, proud as he let go of just a little bit of that rope.

"It's n-not . . . It's not easy for me."

I smiled against his skin, kissing the tender flesh on the side of his throat as I lifted my body from his. He cried out at the loss of it, of the weightlessness, but I didn't leave him floating alone. I crossed in front of him, knelt to take his face in my hands. "I know. That's why it means something when you try."

Ares's eyes fell shut, his body sinking deeper. Not quite limp, but the tension in his shoulders melted. Surrender for him would never be soft, but the fight seemed to drain from his bones, heat tempered in the forge.

By my hands.

"That's good, baby," I praised, dusting kisses over his brow, his closed eyes. "That's you trusting me."

He didn't answer right away, but when his eyes—those golden, rich eyes—opened, the guarded edge had been dulled, replaced instead by a sharper, more dangerous thing. A rare vulnerability I wondered if Aphrodite had even seen. In the stillness, in the hum of the electrons in the space between us, I felt him. Ares, God of War.

But also more.

Mine.

"Tell me what you need."

His lower lip trembled, a shiver working its way over his flushed skin as he sucked in a deep breath. "It aches."

A plea. I nodded my understanding.

"Ditey," I called over my shoulder, knowing she was close but not watching. It took only a few seconds before she came through the door.

"Eyes on me," I commanded as he bristled, the compromising position too raw to be witnessed, but I shushed his worries, kissed his lips.

"Eyes on me. We're here. Little Love, show your God of War what rewards he gets when he's good."

I stood and lifted his body, using levers to adjust the mechanical slabs to keep him bound, but flipped around so he was on his back, supported by metal and soft wood. Slowly, I reached up on a shelf with one hand and tossed a pillow down between his spread legs to keep Aphrodite comfortable.

With a smile, Aphrodite knelt, so beautiful, running her fingers over his thighs as I took my place near his head, bracketing his cheeks with steady hands.

"I knew you'd find your way here," she whispered, licking up his shaft. He cried out, and I brushed his hair back, kissed him deeply from above as his tongue lapped into my mouth, breathless and wound too tight. The sounds of her swallowing him down, obscene, *mesmerizing*, coupled with his pleas and desperate breaths.

"You're not going to f-fuck me?" he panted as she continued to suck him off, that skilled tongue lapping up every drop.

I shook my head. "You're not ready. But I'm holding space for you until you are. That's all I can do."

His gaze shifted down, chest heaving, to watch her move over him. He sounded nearly delirious, driven to precipice of madness from the edging, from the overwhelming pleasure of her mouth. His cuffed fingers reached for her, and she gripped them with her own, anchoring him down as time slowed to the pace of our collective breaths, his pleasure, and trust.

Both given and received.

Aphrodite

CHAPTER 32

The room flew around me as I spun and twirled around the dance studio Hephaestus had built for me. My feet were bound in pointe shoes, my tights hugging every inch of my thighs and ass as I hurtled through the air in leaps. I had never had what anyone considered to be a "dancer's" body. Mortals had such horrendous body standards now, bordering on delusion in expectation, sometimes downright unhealthy.

When I first began to dance, women had *just* been allowed to participate in ballet. It had been completely male until that point, and I was anxious to try. What started out as something pure and beautiful quickly turned sour when the unrealistic expectations of body proportions and weight took over. By the late 1800s, ballerinas were expected to be fully grown women with the body of prepubescent boys. Flat-chested. No curves. Malnourished in the name of "easy to carry."

As the Goddess of Beauty, I was granted a small reprieve from the terrible comments other women received, but my body was often bigger than theirs. My divinity offered me a privilege, but the culture of pressure and expectation was toxic.

Over the last fifty years, I'd opened several studios on the West Coast that taught all sizes and shapes to dance. Then current beauty standards became some of the most horrendous we'd ever lived through. People were starving themselves of nutrients, surviving on a diet of cigarettes and heroin to achieve a gaunt, skeletal look. It was all over the fashion runways, and my heart wept at the oppressive regime settling over this world and the unending need for people to comment and pick apart people's bodies. Big or small, or whatever in between, as long as they were happy and healthy, they should be valued and celebrated.

There were thousands of depictions of me—in art, in statues—and not a single fucking one showed my true shape. I had curves and a tummy, and there had never been a moment in my existence since I crawled my way out of the seafoam that my thighs hadn't touched. Even I wouldn't hold up to modern standards. As the Goddess of Beauty, watching my name be thrown around as a metric to oppress pissed me right the fuck off. So we built a place for all to go. The classes were free to the public—ballet, tap, hip-hop, and ballroom, plus a few others peppered in. We offered nutrition classes that stressed the necessity of eating enough, and that everybody was worthy and different.

It was a drop in the bucket against a tidal wave, but it was what I could do. With modern technology, we couldn't risk being too heavily involved in the public eye. We didn't age, and in an industry that noted every laugh line, they certainly would catch on. So we set up a trust that would accrue interest to keep it going, and I stepped away. Muses and Sprites ran the brick and mortars, all of us in agreement at the damage we were trying to help heal. This new world was sometimes a wretched place, under the guise of civilized society.

". . . that's the third call since yesterday. We can't avoid them forever, Ares." Hephaestus's voice echoed.

Ares let out a groan.

"Can't we just tell them to fuck off?" he asked hopefully as they walked through the studio door, drenched in sweat in low-slung sweatpants.

I nearly fell out of arabesque. Why were they suddenly so much hotter than they ever had been? Which was saying something, because they were already the most beautiful creatures to exist.

Before I could drop my stance, Hephaestus ran up and lifted me into the air in perfect form, parading me around with his head held high. We promenaded around the room before he set me down gently, his hands firmly on my waist. We stayed together, letting the music swell around us.

Then Hephaestus took my hand, and we danced.

He had studied with me for a decent amount of time and was one of the most graceful creatures I'd ever known. His lithe body found the heart of the music and painted a portrait with his limbs as he moved. It was exhilarating, the feeling of being one, together on the dance floor. The music washed over us, ebbing out in a decrescendo, and we slowed our movements with it, breathing hard. The moment stretched between us, heavy and saturated with emotion. Hephaestus kissed me softly on my forehead and folded his arms around me, bringing my back to his chest.

"Well, that was actually quite nice," Ares appraised, and I laughed.

"I'm glad you think so. What have you two been up to?" I asked, and Ares closed the gap between us to sandwich me between their chests.

My core flared, and I had to focus on tempering it down.

"Working out," Ares said at the same time that Hephaestus replied, "Fighting."

I arched my eyebrows and laughed.

"So which is it?" I asked, glancing between them.

A dark bite rested just under Ares's jaw, and I smirked. I lifted my hand to his chin and turned it to expose the love mark.

"Working out, huh?" I chuckled, and Hephaestus snorted.

"Listen, I could feel the tension while you two were dancing. Fighting is a workout. And it also turns me on." He shrugged.

"I get that. Dancing turns me on too," I assured. "I know it's not really your thing, but it can be quite rewarding." I wiggled my eyebrows at him suggestively, and he pulled me forward to kiss him.

"Hey now, I dance," he muttered defensively, and I laughed.

"You absolutely do not dance, Ares," I chided, and he threw his hands over his heart in mock indignation.

"I *could* dance. I just never did the kind of dancing you liked to do." He pointed between Hephaestus and me.

I crossed my arms in challenge. "Well, I've never seen it."

He quirked up his lips. "Maybe that means, after all this time, I can still surprise you?" he mumbled, tracing my lips with his fingers.

My breath caught at the overwhelming sensation, the chemicals between us as desire pooled around our bodies. I shook my head to keep focused; I wanted to know what he was talking about.

"What call did you mean when you came in?" I asked, working hard to uncross my eyes as they followed trails of sweat down Ares's torso.

"Hermes. Medusa. Hades. They've been calling and demanding to see us for the last week. Three times since yesterday alone. We can't avoid them forever," Hephaestus said, and I groaned.

"Oh, yes, the fuck we can," Ares echoed my sentiment.

It wasn't that we didn't *want* to see them, per se, but the last week had been an actual dream. The boys had convinced them all that we needed space so I could "heal" after the first Trial, and we'd spent that time learning each other. Ares cooked our meals, and Hephaestus cleaned and did the mundane tasks that brought him order and control. I checked in on the studios and danced. In the evenings, we ate dinner together and found ourselves as a tangle of limbs in one combination or another.

I had some anxiety that we would have moments of jealousy, or even swing the other way and suffocate each other, but it wasn't working out like that. The time we spent flowed organically, and more than once, a bolt of fear shot through me that I might be dreaming. That I'd actually died in that Trial, and this was just a long fever dream of an afterlife.

They had gone off to the back room to "train," and that seemed to mean "take-turns-pinning-each-other-and-making-out," which I fully supported. That was their time, and though I knew I was welcome, I'd come to stretch my legs and dance.

Hephaestus nuzzled into my neck, kissing the soft flesh there. "They're just worried about you—all of us really. We are going to have to face them sooner or later. Persephone has threatened to come topside if someone doesn't lay eyes on you soon," he teased.

I grimaced. I didn't want her to come up and get hurt like last time.

"We could go out. If they're so worried, they can meet us. That way, when it's time for me to dick you both down, we can just leave." Ares's eyes lit up as he spoke, raking over both Hephaestus and me.

My core clenched under his intense stare, and I rolled my hips between them.

"Needy girl," Hephaestus whispered, sucking the flesh of my neck between his lips.

Ares crowded in, sliding his large thigh between my legs until it rested up against my rapidly heating core.

"Do you like the idea of me taking you both? Wanna be there for our first time, Little Goddess?" Ares teased and pressed up until he was working his thigh against my clit.

I panted, catching my lip between my teeth to bite back a moan.

As far as I'd known, they hadn't had full-on sex. The first time I walked in on Hephaestus going down on Ares, I'd almost spontaneously combusted from the sheer eroticism of it. He'd coached Hephaestus how to take him, and then, after he'd come, Hephaestus found his own release by impaling me on his cock at the dinner table while Ares watched. Watching Ares swallowing Hephaestus down the next night had been no less explosive. The group sex had been unholy in its carnality, but they hadn't taken each other yet. I thought it was good they were exploring and taking their time with it.

No rush, right?

"About that . . ." Hephaestus hesitated, still holding me close. "They're going to ask. Are we ready to tell them about us?" He gestured between the two of them.

Ares stopped moving his leg and straightened slightly, suddenly anxious. It crept up through the Bond, and I could feel it pulling him under. I reached for him, and Hephaestus did, too, bringing him back to us by some instinct. Ares looked between us, uncertainty burning in his eyes.

Fuck.

"Whatever you want to do is okay with me. It's your relationship. They're your boundaries. If you want to be public, I'll support it. If you want to keep it between you, though I don't think you have any reason to, I'll respect it," I said, bringing his hand to my lips, brushing a kiss along his open palm.

"I'm not ashamed of what's happened here," Hephaestus declared before clearing his throat.

Ares jerked his head to look at him.

"I don't think you should be either, but if you are, then we can work on that. You belong to me, Ares, and I to you, the same as we belong to Aphrodite, and she to us. I chose you, remember. If you want to be private, that's okay too. And you can decide now or later. It doesn't have to be discussed; we can shut that down." He cocked his head in my direction. "Ditey fucking adores telling Hermes to fuck right off."

"I . . . I don't know. I don't know what the right move is here. Part of me wants to lock us up here and never leave. The other part wants to just be fucking normal. I think I'm worried because we're in a good place. What happens when we let the world in? They're going to have opinions, and while I don't give two shits about what any of them have to say, I know you both do. What if they convince you this is a terrible idea?" Ares finished, biting his lip with eyes cast down. "That I'm a terrible idea?"

I grabbed his face with both hands and brought his too tall body down to meet mine. "Ares. That is *never* going to happen. Nothing anyone can say will ever change what you mean to me. I can't speak for Hephaestus. Wait. Actually, I can. He doesn't let what anyone says affect him either. I know because his friends have been calling me the Whore of Babylon for centuries."

He let out a growl, and while it was a hyperbolic generalization because they probably hadn't slut-shamed me to him, it didn't mean they hadn't thought it. Hells, I had.

"Let's keep it between us until you're ready, Ares. But just know that I am *always* ready. I don't care about their comfortability. Yours and Aphrodite's are all that matters to me," Hephaestus fiercely declared.

Ares sniffed. Too many emotions for him to process at once.

I released him and backed out of their space. Their eyes followed me, predators tracking the thing they desired most.

"I'm gonna go change into something slinky. Call Hermes. Let's go to Electric Delphi. I miss Dionysus," I said, and Hephaestus smirked.

"I like what you're wearing." His words held a tempting tenor to them as he eye-fucked me, walking forward.

"*Seconded*," Ares added, as he, too, approached. Too many emotions, too quickly, but this was our comfort. A language between us, to soothe the hurt and amplify the pleasure. They'd caught me during a session a few days ago and ripped my outfit to do unspeakable things to my body, and while I'd enjoyed every fucking moment, the loss of the costume hurt.

"Hey now, no, *no*!" I shrieked, backing up quickly, an awkward feat in pointe shoes. "You literally ripped my tights and leotard the other day, do not!" I demanded, picking up the pace.

"They were in the way, but I liked the way they looked hanging off you, ballerina." Ares shrugged, crouching low before he charged, lifting me over his shoulder.

I shrieked as my ponytail slung around us with wild abandon. A stinging slap jolted through my body from my ass to my core, and I flooded.

"They were my favorite set," I pouted as Hephaestus chuckled, pulling out his phone behind us.

"I'll buy you more," he promised with a wink as he brought the phone to his ear, dialing Hermes.

"Ah, I'm sorry, Little Goddess," Ares offered with another smack. "Here, come ride my face to make up for it."

I beat my fists on his back, but desire rushed through me at his words.

"I'm going to fucking drown you in it," I grumbled.

He met my threats with a sharp smack, harder this time, and I clamped my hand over my mouth to stifle the moan trying to escape.

"Can't fucking wait," Ares chuckled, turning the corner to our room.

Ares

CHAPTER 33

"Give them back, Ares," Aphrodite demanded, face red.

I reclined back onto the wall and crossed my arms lazily.

"No," I answered simply.

She seethed, mirroring my stance and stomping her foot. Her strappy heel thudded against the hardwood with some force.

I raised an eyebrow.

The long red dress she wore clung to her body, the spaghetti thin silk straps crossed over her shoulders, exposing her bare back. The fabric was expensive but delicate, and I could make out the outlines of her nipples budding under the sweetheart neckline. It tapered tight at her waist and fell in long sheets over her hips and legs, with two long slits up each thigh.

"They're the only pair that goes with this dress. *Give them back*." She looked exasperated. Her beautiful face was scrunched in anger, cheeks and neck flushed red. Her long hair was swept to one side, slightly messy from the activities we'd just been engaged in.

I loved it, seeing her flustered and undone, knowing my touch did that. I twirled the scrap of fabric between my fingers, the black lace slip of a thing, and tucked it neatly into my jacket pocket.

She rolled her eyes. "Mature," she bit out, and at that moment, Hephaestus walked in, stealing all the oxygen from the room as he did.

Aphrodite's mouth hung slack, and it did me a little bit of good to know she was just as affected. He looked good. No, that wasn't the word. He looked *devastating*. Had he always looked like this? Had I really hated him into not being attractive? He was fiddling with a long box between his fingers, and I swallowed.

"What are you two yelling about?" he asked, a smile playing on his lips. He knew better than to get involved in our antics, but I found I very much wanted to be under his scrutinizing eye tonight. Maybe under much more than that.

"He stole my fucking underwear," Aphrodite seethed, arms still folded.

I stared at her with a shocked expression. "Stole? No fucking way, I *earned* these. Fair and square," I argued, making a show of licking my lips.

Hephaestus tried to keep his expression neutral, but I could see the amusement there.

"And how did you do that exactly?" he asked, voice serious.

My cocky grin faded quickly, and Aphrodite propped her hands on her hips triumphantly. *Shit*.

"Well, I was in the kitchen, grabbing a drink. I was already dressed as you can see." I gestured to myself, and Hephaestus's gaze flicked over me appraisingly. The dark dress pants and fitted jacket tapered at my waist, with a deep crimson dress shirt with cufflinks. *His cufflinks*. His eyes caught on them briefly before traveling back to mine.

"And then?" he asked, and I loudly cleared my throat.

Aphrodite was shaking her head behind his shoulder, eyes wide.

I shot her a look.

If I'm going down, so are you.

"And then Aphrodite came in, and she was also dressed. In that dress, and those panties." I swallowed as he stepped forward. He cut an impressive figure, the deep red suit and jacket framing his silhouette, a dark gray shirt fitted underneath. Our outfits were inverted, and we didn't coordinate. I wondered if Aphrodite had?

"And then what happened?" he goaded me, and I felt like a fly caught in a spider's web, only I wanted him to catch me and devour me.

"And then I had a little snack to tide me over?" My eyes flicked to Aphrodite, who looked like she was going to kill me.

"And was it good?" he asked, closing the distance between us.

"Fucking decadent," I admitted.

He inhaled deeply. Hephaestus closed his eyes, and slowly, deliberately, opened them, his long hair pulled back in a bun, just a few stray hairs framing his face.

"Didn't I say you'd have enough *snacks* today? That I wanted you to have dinner and drinks before you partook? Didn't you spend the afternoon having a 'snack,' and didn't I tell you both not to ruin your appetite for tonight?" His hand crept up slowly, and I itched at the proximity, needing to be closer.

His hand pinned around my throat as he closed in, looking at me sternly. "That's the second time you've disobeyed me, brat. You have a tab now, and the bill has come due."

Anticipation poured through me as he gripped my throat and pulled me from the wall. Hephaestus marched me to the island in the kitchen, forcing me to face it and grip the top. His hand slid over my belt buckle and flicked it loose before his fingers released my top button and zipper. He pulled my slacks down carefully, underwear with it, and I trembled at the cool air.

"And you . . ." He turned to a smirking Aphrodite, who looked equally scared and excited. "You know better. Then again, you like this, so it's possible she's turned you into an unwitting accomplice, Ares. Get over here," he commanded, and she rushed forward, blushing on the top of her ears. She settled next to me, hands splayed on the counter, waiting.

Hephaestus stepped away from us.

"Don't move," he ordered before turning on his heel and heading toward the bedroom.

I glanced at Aphrodite, who winked but remained silent. I shook my head. She'd played me. I pursed my lips and sent her a kiss as I decided I was okay with it. Footsteps signaled Hephaestus's return, but I dared not look back. He'd instructed us not to move, and the parameters of that were slightly unclear. We were already in enough hot water.

He stepped behind Aphrodite and flipped the bottom of her dress over her hips. From the corner of my eye, I could see him biting his lip as he ran his hands over the swells of her hips, the globes of her perfect ass. His hand delved between her thighs, and she moaned, sinking down until her tits grazed the countertop of the island.

"Ares, hand me the underwear," he instructed, and I pulled them from my breast pocket with some sadness and handed them over. He crouched low, tapping her heel on each foot respectively before shimmying the thin lace back into place. He straightened himself, her dress, smoothing it back down over her hips and legs. It fell gracefully to the floor.

Deliberate footsteps brought him behind me and my tension ramped up, excitement plummeting through me. Hephaestus's hands ran along my glutes with soft pressure. His fingers splayed wide on each cheek as he pulled me apart before crouching down and running his tongue from my balls up my seam. My knees buckled at the attention, the teasing. I moaned as his tongue speared into me, pushing past the ring of muscle there, delivering a few soft strokes that weren't nearly enough.

He pulled away, and I grunted with disdain, the mere thought of what he could do to me like this warring with the need to top him. I heard a squirting sound and cool liquid plopped onto my crack. Hephaestus's fingers moved, pushing what I assumed was lube in and out, stretching me wide.

I hissed, body jerking at the intrusion, muscles bunched.

"Relax," he commanded.

I did my best to let the tightness drain from my body, but it was hard to do with him pushing in on that button, thick fingers pressing obscenely against my channel.

He withdrew his fingers this time, and I let out a shaky breath. Something warm and metal nestled against my hole. I tensed as he pushed.

"Just a little more. Relax, it's going to hurt so good," he promised. And it *did*.

The burn was extreme. Anal play was something I enjoyed, and being balls deep in an ass, I adored. Only ever as the giver, not the receiver. Sure, a finger or three milking my prostate during head was fantastic. It produced earth-shattering orgasms. But I'd never let anyone top me before, and I didn't know how to relinquish that control. I knew that, with Hephaestus, I *wanted* to. Still, this thing felt massive as he slid it home. I cried out as he whispered encouraging praises against my skin, pressed his lips to my hip until I adjusted to the intrusion. I felt full, overly sensitive, but there was a rush behind the sting, one that jolted through me even as I tensed around it. Hephaestus grabbed a towel off the counter and cleared up the smeared lube before pulling up my clothes and turning me around.

Every move felt electric. I'd never had something this far inside of me before. Methodical fingers tucked my shirt back in and buckled my pants before sliding my belt home.

"I have something for you both," he said, and we side-eyed each other nervously.

Aphrodite's gaze shone with love and adoration as she watched Hephaestus fish out the long velvet box he'd been carrying when he came in the first time. He opened it up, and I saw two thin rods made of gold and a signet ring.

"I know the situation we're in feels like, sometimes, we just aren't in control. But I wanted to do something to show you both that I'm really in this. So I made you these. They're bracelets, infused with my essence in a bloodlock. They will stay locked around your wrists until you take them off. The only time they would unlock for me is if I stopped loving you. This is my word that I will love you both. And I do. *I love you*," he whispered, eyes on me this time. He was offering me the most tangible proof he could, and it left a power imbalance, one he gave freely. Offering his heart to me, to this thing we were navigating.

To us.

Aphrodite sniffed, eyes shining.

He smiled and pulled out the first rod, stamped with seashells at the end. The metal bent in a perfect circle under his blacksmith's hands and sealed together with the heat of his power. A few stray tears dropped down Aphrodite's cheeks, but he kissed them away before turning to me.

I backed up, running from the weight of it. Skittish as a coward. He didn't chase me, simply stayed in place, waiting for me to come to him.

"You don't have to accept until you're ready, Ares. If you ever are, it'll be here for you." He moved closer, but only just so.

A knot in my stomach started to rise, restricting the air in my lungs. Aphrodite reached for my wrist, steadying me. I was scared of loving someone else I could lose.

Terrified.

He was offering me security, had only ever shown me kindness. Time and time again, Hephaestus proved to me who he was. But what if he wasn't the problem?

What if I was?

"What if I'm the one that fucks this up? Then you're tied to me, just like Aphrodite has been?"

Hephaestus walked closer, hands up. "I'm willing to take the risk. I don't want you to wear it unless you want to, but I want you to want to. And you can take it off whenever."

His words sliced me up from the inside out, and before I could register what I'd decided, I was extending my wrist.

The smile that broke across Hephaestus's face shattered me. He reached for the rod, molding it into a bracelet, and I saw the horses stamped on either end of the clasps. He pressed his hands over them, melding the metal together in a seemingly unbroken ring.

"You take them off by deciding you don't love me anymore. Other than that, they are unbreakable." He gathered us both to him, and we spent a few moments kissing and holding on to one another, every word soft. Comforting. Assuring in a way I'd never known.

After we'd settled, he opened the velvet box once more and grabbed the signet ring from inside. With a sly smile, he slipped it on his pinky.

"Now, as for your punishments. I made those plugs myself. They're . . . *special*." He smirked, and a dark feeling coiled low in my belly.

"How so?" I asked, swallowing nervously as I tried to keep my tone neutral.

His eyes locked on me as he raised the hand wearing his signet and swiped his thumb over it in a clockwise motion. Instantly, the plug went from dormant to a livewire, buzzing to life inside of me.

I bucked forward, grabbing onto him. Aphrodite's must have activated as well because she was bent, knees locked together. This thing was jackhammering inside of me. I was going to come any damn second.

With little warning, Hephaestus swiped again, and the fucking menaces inside us quieted to a bearable purr.

"Are you fucking kidding me?" I panted, and he smiled.

"I told you I'd wear your ass out." He chuckled. He kissed us both and turned on his heels to open the door, ushering us into the night.

Aphrodite straightened and fixed her dress before grabbing my hand and leading me outside.

We hailed a taxi to Dionysus's club, thank Fates. Walking across the city with this monstrosity inside me, on edge because I never knew when it would detonate, would have been a special kind of torture. And I knew torture. *Well.*

I glanced at Hephaestus, his angelic face catching the dancing city lights as the taxi trucked along, and wondered if maybe he was a demon. He looked at me and smiled before increasing the speed and intensity of the plug inside of me.

My core constricted, all the way through my abs. I tilted my head back and forth slowly, cresting the wave of my climax. I considered little of the kind of mess I'd make in this too nice suit. My toes curled with the expectation but, before I could fall over the edge, the terrorist fell silent, stopping almost completely. I huffed out a frustrated breath just in time to see Aphrodite do the same.

The car came to a stop, and we piled out. Aphrodite, poor thing, so flushed and flustered, blushed a deep crimson with every step over the pavement. At least I had a suit covering most of me, she was mostly exposed in all the places she flushed. Well, not *all*, but certainly the most noticeable.

The bouncers ushered us inside, and we were immediately enveloped in the pulse-bumping music blaring from the sound system. Strobe lights in bright green and purple hues cut through the darkness that blanketed the dance floor as we made our way to the private nook at the back of Electric Delphi.

Aphrodite looked incredible, like sin incarnate. She walked deeper into the club, her hips swaying in that tempting dress, and I flexed my fingers not holding her hand into a fist to stop myself from getting into any more trouble.

The usual suspects were already seated, or huddled near the back booth, when we arrived, and I tucked into Aphrodite just a bit closer.

Hephaestus caught Hermes first, who barely spared him a glance. He floated past Hephaestus and made a break for Aphrodite, who tensed slightly. He grabbed for her arm, gently but with extreme speed. Startled, she pulled back in surprise.

"I just wanted to check it and make sure it's healing," he shouted above the noise.

We were still on the outside of the booth, and the music was loud. She offered her arm back to him, bewildered. We'd told her he'd patched her up, but I don't think we mentioned the urgency in which he had done so, or how little pressure had been required to get him there.

I glanced over at Hecate, who sat with her smoking cocktail, a green liquid in a martini glass lifted to her lips. She wore a bemused expression as she, too, studied the interaction between Hermes and Aphrodite.

Hermes pulled Aphrodite forward slightly, bringing her into the fold and settling her into the chair Hephaestus had pulled out for her. He tucked her in tight to the table and planted a kiss on her crown before pulling the chair next to him for me.

I strode forward and sat next to him gingerly, and mercifully, the sound ramped way down. I could hear the chatter around us and sat back.

Hephaestus had his arm slung over Aphrodite's chair, and in the darkness, his other hand on my leg. We were all sitting close, and I was grateful for the comfort, even more so for the darkness. These gods had never been particularly kind to me, and in fairness, I understood. Now that I'd had the chance to really get to know Hephaestus, I'd probably impale someone who even spoke to him the wrong way, much less caused decades- and centuries-long bouts of depression. Guilt swirled in my gut, and as though he sensed my anxiety, he squeezed my thigh in comfort. His hand was a warm, radiating light that I clung to.

Medusa leaned across the table to hand me a drink, her dark eyes obscured by her sunglasses. I reached to take the swirling liquid, and she flashed me a bright smile, her snakes dancing and weaving to the music.

Hecate leaned into Hermes while he and Hephaestus laughed, and Dionysus came in to clap me on the back and popped down in the chair next to me. Artemis leaned across to ask Aphrodite to dance, then Medusa who, then, reached for Hecate, and suddenly, they left us all for the dance floor.

I took a long draw of the deep brown liquor. It burned going down the back of my throat as Dionysus leaned in.

"How are you? I wanted to check in, but Heph said you needed some space."

I leaned back slightly, letting out a sigh. Dionysus and I had decent rapport. We spent a lot of time together rebuilding the Asphodels and creating the Elysian Fields with Thanatos.

"I'm doing probably the best I've ever been," I answered honestly.

Hephaestus was still drilling slow, light circles on my leg, and I felt the intensity of the toy inside me ramp up, taking me off guard. It had been so calm, moving at barely a frequency I could register. It jolted deep inside me, and I choked on the gulp of alcohol I'd taken.

A small smile played at the corner of Hephaestus's lips, and my sideways glance narrowed. He continued on, talking to Hermes as though he wasn't electrocuting me with pleasure.

"That's so good, Ares. You and Aphrodite and Heph finding a balance, huh?"

Dionysus's words were casual, but I stiffened. He had a knack for sussing out things. He knew about Aphrodite and me, and even during Demeter's Rebellion, he was one of the only ones that never treated me like a pariah and never judged.

I nodded.

"So what's good with you? Club business seems to be booming." I gestured at the packed room, and my eyes fell on the group of goddesses in the middle of the dark floor. They commanded the attention of everyone in the room, probably in the cosmos too. None of them shined brighter than Aphrodite.

My cock twitched as Hephaestus ramped up the toy again. I watched Aphrodite suck her bottom lip between her teeth, stifling her own pleasure as she moved. I wanted to go to her. I wanted to hold on to her and never let go.

Dionysus was talking, answering my question, but I could barely register what he was saying. The pleasure radiating from the plug pushed me past my point.

Artemis and Medusa crashed back to the table, weaving in between us all to retake their seats, while Hecate and Aphrodite were out on the floor still.

Hephaestus laid a gentle hand on Hermes's back before standing and peeling off his jacket. *All the Hells in the Underworld be damned*, if there was any justice, I'd die right on the spot. I was half drunk from the constant edging I'd been subjected to for the last hour, and now Hephaestus was undressing. He loosened his top three buttons, his tattoos peeking out of his collar, and my mouth watered as he set his jacket on the back of the chair.

"Excuse me, I think I'll go dance with my wife."

The hold on my glass nearly crushed it into sand.

Hephaestus sauntered toward Aphrodite, who was winding and grinding with Hecate in a siren song. He uncuffed his left wrist and rolled it up his forearm slowly, then repeated the gesture, ramping up the bullet inside me with each pass. Sweat beaded at my brow, and I squirmed just a bit, sliding down my chair to relieve some of the pressure.

It did absolutely fuck all to quell the ache.

He reached Aphrodite as Hecate slipped into the shadows. All eyes in the room were on them as he moved behind her, wrapping his body over her back and pressing her close. They swayed together, two perfect puzzle pieces, their bodies as one. Aphrodite wound her hips down into him, and Hephaestus pressed his long fingers over her abdomen, creeping ever lower. His head was bent into her neck, and his lips were moving. Aphrodite had her head tilted back into him; eyes closed as she chased the high I knew he was giving her.

Hecate reappeared at our table and took her seat, eyes on me. I wrenched my gaze away from Hephaestus and Aphrodite to find the rest of the table staring at them as well.

"Holy Hells, that is bloody *hot*," Thanatos quipped, sliding forward.

"Have you ever seen them like that? Ever?" Hermes asked, bewildered.

Medusa's jaw went slack as she stared, and Artemis's eyes never left me, and I felt exposed, seen. It was like she was waiting for me to explode, to flip the table and make a run for Hephaestus.

I stifled a bitter snort, because there had been a time when I would have. I would have burned this place to the ground before letting him touch her like that, but Artemis had been there that day when Aphrodite had collapsed in the Upper Realm. Had seen me phase out, watched as Hephaestus brought me back by kissing the shit out of me.

"Something's changed, with them. They seem happier than I've ever seen them," Artemis offered kindly, her gaze still locked on me.

My chest heaved, from the pressure and pleasure as Hephaestus slowly tortured me to death.

Hermes noticed.

"Shit. Ares, listen. I know you and Aphrodite have your own thing, too. We just . . . We've never seen you together, so we can't compare," he offered, *trying*. He was trying, but I couldn't focus on the olive branch with my world shaking apart inside me.

Thanatos leaned over the table to look me in the eye. He asked, alarmed, "Ares, bruv, you good? You're shaking. You're not gonna rage out, are you?"

I shook my head and let out a small laugh. "No, I'm fine, not"—I panted—"in pain. *Not angry.*"

Dionysus sat back, eyes flicking from me to Hephaestus, who ran his hand absentmindedly over his signet ring as they swayed, his honey eyes on me while he continued to whisper to Aphrodite. He was playing with us like a yo-yo, and I needed him to stop. It felt like he was pushing me, taunting me, daring me to sit on the sidelines of this, of us.

I was almost at my limit, hot everywhere, and I slammed Dionysus's still mostly full glass, only to realize there was no alcohol in it.

Hells.

"Ares, we're sorry about how we acted. Truly. It is clear there are things we don't understand, and it wasn't right for us to ostracize you," Medusa said.

I blinked away the blurred vision, and I couldn't think, couldn't breathe.

Hephaestus watched. He was playing a dangerous game, pushing limits. I loved it. I hated it. I loved him.

I loved him.

The thought shocked me forward, sobering me, mostly. Why was I so scared of this? Of him? He had shown me over the past few weeks what it could be like, to be his. Theirs. I caught it in the glances between them, both he and Aphrodite handling me delicately. Like any wrong step would send me running for the hills. Hells, he had shown me over centuries through the way he loved Aphrodite what it was like to be in his affections. And watching them together, without me, hurt. But not because I felt left out or tossed aside, but because I had *chosen* to keep myself away.

Now, I wanted to choose us.

I mustered up my power, willing it to work as well here as it did in the fields of war.

"*I'm yours. Claim me. I love you.*"

My whisper carried across the floor, unheard by all, other than the intended. I saw the moment it flitted into Hephaestus's ear, watched his eyes lock to mine. He spoke a few words to Aphrodite, who smiled wide. She reached her arms high into the air and flowed on with the music as he untangled from our goddess. The intensity inside me eased, painfully still. but I shook, desperate now for release.

For them.

Hephaestus sauntered back to the table, oozing a quiet confidence I'd never picked up on before, the long lines of him, the strong shoulders and gentle power. Deft fingers picked up his glass. He brought his free hand to rest on the back of my neck, in the dip of my shoulder. The table quieted as each of the gathered noted the contact, and his smile grew even more stunning, his white teeth sinking into his plush bottom lip as he looked around.

"Ares and I are together. Aphrodite and I are together. Ares and Aphrodite are together. We are in love; it is our choice, and we will not be elaborating further at this time." His hand pulled me against him, fingers curled around my throat in a possessive grip.

I arched against him, my jaw falling open as he made me look up at him.

"Mine," he growled. Hephaestus took a long draught of his whiskey, but instead of swallowing it, leaned over the top of my open mouth and siphoned it to me, his lips to mine, the taste of him overriding the oaky notes.

My dick almost exploded. The liquor, hot from his mouth, raced down my throat, and he leaned in to kiss me hard before releasing me to stare down his friends, his *family*.

Daring them silently to challenge him. Or us.

"Gods be damned," Medusa whispered, fanning herself.

Artemis and Hecate looked smug as Dionysus leaned back comfortably. He raised his fresh glass to us, taking a huge swig.

"We'll need a key, Dio. Hermes, did you get what I asked for?" Hephaestus looked at him, and Dionysus obliged, opening his palm to reveal an intricate skeleton key of some sort. Hephaestus took it and twirled it between his fingers.

Hermes handed over a brown bag, still dumbstruck with the latest revelation.

"Are you ready to go?" he asked me, voice soft.

I stood, collecting myself.

"It was, uh, good to see you all," I offered, and they nodded, still shellshocked.

"We'll catch up soon." Hephaestus motioned to Hermes, who looked like he'd been smacked upside the head.

Still a little hazy, I let him pull me onto the dance floor to scoop up Aphrodite. She leaned in to kiss me, trembling herself, both of us buzzing from the pleasure and *him*. We followed Hephaestus in a daze of kisses and pleasure-drunk touches to an arched doorway. He inserted the old key into the lock and turned, pulling us in with him. A quiet room was revealed, and when the door snicked shut behind the God of the Forge, all sounds of the club disappeared.

He sat the key on a small table with the bag and turned. Slowly, he started to undress, stopping when he was only in his slacks.

The room was dark, illuminated by floating orbs of iridescent light. A large bed covered in silks and overstuffed pillows sat suspended in the air in the middle of the room. Slow, deliberate steps, bare feet over black hardwood brought him to stand in front of me. We regarded each other, both knowing that this would be the point of no return.

He tilted his head to look at me, the tiny lights reflected in golden brown eyes. Practiced hands undressed me, pushing my jacket from my shoulders. The toy inside me hummed on a low vibration.

"This is torture," I whined.

He clicked his tongue.

"You can say your safe word at any time, Ares," he reminded, eyes serious. "Do we need to stop?"

I shook my head.

Safe words and gestures were the first things we talked about, post-oral in the kitchen. It had come as a revelation to see just how fucking kinky Hephaestus was, what he craved. He'd been teachable with Aphrodite; they had grown together into a powerhouse of desire, and he'd thrown himself into research, wanting to be everything he could be for her. He liked it rough, liked to dominate, and that came with certain expectations and safety precautions, ones he'd been extremely serious about.

We'd chosen "peace" to signify I was approaching a hard limit. I'd liked when he'd had me strapped to his table, peeling back the parts of me I never wanted to see the light of day as Aphrodite sucked me off. He'd been rough, but also so loving in his actions, and the way my mind had quieted . . . I'd never experienced that kind of numbing bliss before. Still, this was the first time I'd come close to calling for sanctuary, but I desperately wanted to hold out.

"You've done so well for me, Ares. Can you undress Aphrodite?" he asked.

My knees buckled as the crest of an orgasm reared its head again. With a gentle kiss, he pulled it back, wrenching me from the edge.

Aphrodite's legs faltered as she approached, the Goddess of Love going crazy from the denial too. I slipped the straps of her dress off her shoulders and the silk fabric fell from her frame, snagging briefly on her hips as it went. She shimmied slightly until she stood, exposed and quivering like me.

"Up on the bed," he ordered.

I scooped Aphrodite up and jumped, using my power for the extra distance. We landed softly, and the bed stayed steady. Hephaestus lowered his hand, and the bed began to wind down, until we were waist level with him.

"Impatient?" he chuckled, and we both nodded.

Aphrodite was still in my arms, naked and on fire. The room filled with her scent, and his and mine. I was going to drown in it and the river of cum that would release once he stopped denying us.

He unbuckled his pants, slid them down, exposing his long, stiff cock.

Aphrodite bit and nipped her way down my torso until her lips were close, so close, to the tip of my shaft. I rocked, desperate to touch her. Hephaestus clicked his tongue, and she rolled off with a groan, panting beside me. He ramped up the intensity with a swipe of his finger, and we both cried out, writhing. Climbing into the bed, he attached the golden cock he must have pulled from the bag against his skin.

The Master.

I groaned.

He slipped it over his sack and shaft, and I watched as he palmed Aphrodite's tits, roaming his hand down to deliver a slap to her exposed cunt while the flesh of him enveloped the gold. He moved from her to wrap around my length, and a small spurt of pre-cum shot out at him, slipping down his hand, pearly against his tanned skin. He grinned, settling between my legs and angling my hips so I'd be off the bed, the backs of my thighs resting on the tops of his. He reached his hand between my cheeks, tenderly sliding the vibrating demon from inside me.

I cried out, spasming around nothing, my hole pulsing with tension. My back arched, knees bent as he leaned over me, kissing my lips, palming my cock.

"Do you want me inside you?"

I answered with a broken sigh.

He smiled, hungry and wanting, as lubed-up fingers pressed against me, slipped inside, making me ready to take him.

"You are in control here. With one word, it stops. The power is *yours*," he whispered along my jaw, positioning his crown at my stretched hole. The adoration in his gaze as he stared down at me flayed me raw, stripped me past my skin and bones until we were nothing more than particles of the cosmos, remnants of stardust from creation.

Then, he pressed inside me. I convulsed when the first stud of his piercing dragged against my too sensitive flesh, groaned at the exquisite stretch of him. Hephaestus gripped my hip with one hand, inching me deeper, fucking me on top of him while he stroked my weeping cock.

"I love you," he said, over and over. "You are perfect."

The praises fell against me as I sucked deep breaths, the stretch nearly breaking me even with all the lube he'd applied, until he was fully seated, until there was nowhere else for him to go. It could have taken minutes; it could have taken days. There was no time for me, beyond the moment he'd not been inside me and the moment he pushed flush to his base. I laughed at my assumptions that the plug had been big.

Hephaestus was a monstrosity, splitting me in half.

"Aphrodite, baby," he called, and she shuddered as she crawled over.

I had a clear view of her perfect ass and cunt and saw the moment his fingers pulled her toy free. My breathing came out shallow, harsh and broken, as Hephaestus rocked his hips with the lightest of pressure, testing my body.

"I dreamt of this, you know?" he whispered as his hand left my cock to grab her hips, lowering her down. "I thought of that night I saw you together so many times. So many times, I fucked my fist to the shame of it, of how good you looked together. How perfect. Nearly buried myself in the guilt of it, but now . . ."

His hand guided my strained cock to her tight ring of muscle, and I shuddered as he pushed her down an inch or so over my crown. Her ass flexed and constricted around me, and I let out a garbled moan.

"Now I get to watch anytime I want. No shame. Just desire. Relax, Little Love, let him in."

"I'm about to come," I wheezed, but he only smiled, brushing the hair back from my face.

"No, you're not. You want to, but you'll wait for me, won't you? Because you know I'll make it worthwhile." Hephaestus sent a savage snap of his hips into me, his cock kissing too deep, and I cried out as Aphrodite swallowed every inch of my cock.

"So precious," he praised, lining his once golden cock up with her cunt, slicking himself with more lube and a drizzle of spit for good measure before sinking in. Aphrodite's moans filled the room, mingling with mine as he gripped her ass and hips, lowering and raising her agonizingly slowly along us both.

It was a tight fucking fit.

Sensations were everywhere. I was full and filling Aphrodite. She collapsed back against my chest, and Hephaestus crowded over us both, kissing each of our lips while he destroyed our bodies. I didn't even attempt to hold on, just let my body become a vessel for them both. Let myself *feel*.

"Gods, this is so much more than I could have ever imagined. Nothing fucking compares," he moaned, barely hanging on. He lost himself, groaning and snarling, talking us through. It was bliss.

"I'm gonna—I'm right—" Aphrodite warned, but it was too late. She arched back, chest lifted completely off me, fluid drenching me while her ass sucked me in, convulsing through her pleasure.

Hephaestus held her face as he rutted into me, her beautiful tits bouncing between us with each thrust. He rested his forehead on mine, locking eyes.

I knew he was close. Fates, I was hanging on by a thread. But I wanted to wait, needed to. Aphrodite was a warmth between us, whispering how much she loved me, how much she loved him, while we moved in tandem inside her. I needed him to come first. It was primal, instinctual.

I reigned it in.

Fire exploded along my shaft, pulling from the very depths of my desire as my cock pulsed, spilling inside her while he hammered down on the sweetest spot inside of me. I saw stars. The Pits of Tartarus. The depth of every ocean. My body shivered and shook as I pushed against him, too sensitive, but his cock never relented, nor did his grip as he held us in place. Pleasure bound in pain, soothed with more pleasure.

"Mine," he grunted, his thrusts punishing as Aphrodite fingers clawed at my neck, my cheek, seeking purchase. She came again. "That's it, keep crying on our cocks, Little Love, *beautiful*."

Hephaestus pulled back, resting on his knees, his hands pushing Aphrodite's thighs back, pinning us open for him. His warm eyes had gone a little black, irises overtaking the brown, and in them, I saw the obscene reflection of us both, impaled on the God of the Forge, taking everything as he fed those cocks deeper inside us.

His fingers moved between Aphrodite's legs, rubbing against her clit, ripping a strangled cry from her lips as she squeezed the life out of me. His eyes narrowed as he slowed his hips, watching her, ever vigilant as she trembled in our holds.

"That's enough baby, shh," he cooed, pulling her against his chest. The angle pulled her free of us, and I watched as he gently set her next to me. Aphrodite curled against my side, eyelashes fluttering as exhaustion overwhelmed her, though she hadn't said her safe word. I knew she'd take that cock as long as he could go, but he'd made the choice to listen to her body when she wouldn't.

Such fucking care.

He took his time, chest heaving as he caught his breath. His hand fell to my shaft, delivering gentle touches that had my tip swollen and red.

"Come here," he commanded, pulling me up, and I let him, lending my weight until I straddled his lap. His cock sank deeper, caressing over that sensitive spot, every piercing massaging against my walls. Strong arms circled me, pulled my head back down until our foreheads were pressed together, the grip on the back of my neck an anchor.

Grounding.

"Be here with me," he whispered.

My body jolted when his hips rolled. He pressed open-mouthed kisses over my sternum, the corner of my mouth, as the God of the Forge made love to me. My cock and the Master brushed against one another, causing my eyes to roll back.

Hephaestus chuckled against my lips, the vibrations echoing in our bodies as he gripped our cocks with his big hand, rubbing them together with slow, torturous strokes while he fucked me.

My arms hung limply around his neck as he worked our bodies together, quivering, squeezing. Words fell like gospel from my lips, unlocked from the deepest parts of my shade. "You're our line."

He looked up at me curiously, hands still moving, body still rocking.

"There's a fine line between love and war. You're our line, Hephaestus."

A beautiful, brilliant smile lit his face as we continued to move, the admission a surrender more powerful than any sexual act. Smaller, delicate hands brushed his away, and we turned to see a smiling Aphrodite beside us, a silent command on her lips. Without hesitation, we opened to her, our fingers tangling together in the light strands of her hair as she bent between us, the tip of her tongue magic as she sucked and soothed along us both.

My release hit me like a freight train, embarrassingly fast, and I came so hard I almost blacked out, our foreheads pressed together as we watched the love of our lives lap up every drop. Warmth flooded me, deep, binding, and feeling Hephaestus tremble inside me healed a broken bit of my shade. Darkness peppered my vision as I collapsed against his chest.

Dizzy with unfocused vision in the low light, I somehow ended up sandwiched between Hephaestus and Aphrodite on the bed, a mess of tangled limbs and sweaty skin. A peace settled over me, one so calm and real that when I closed my eyes, I didn't see visions of battles or wars. I saw his eyes, and hers, smiling across the room at me, and not once did I ache for being on the outside, because I wasn't.

I belonged to them. And they to me.

Hephaestus

CHAPTER 34

The silence of twilight settled over us, the windows blowing in a quiet breeze, and I lay awake, restless, knowing that, tomorrow, we were again risking everything. Even with Aphrodite's body sprawled out over mine, and Ares gripped tightly to my side, I couldn't quell the thoughts threatening to overwhelm me.

I stroked my hand absentmindedly through Ares's hair, just watching him sleep.

"I don't know that you'll choose me. Not when you'll be free to be with each other."

Those words had haunted me since the moment he'd uttered them weeks ago, and even after all we'd gone through, worked through, they still kept me awake with paralyzing anxiety. Aphrodite was so steady and sure that we would all come out of this alive, stronger, but Ares . . . Was he still feeling that fear? Was he getting loved enough? I wanted him here, with us. We were reforging our own paths by the sacrifices we were all willing to make, but he kept so much of himself held back from us, from *me*. I wanted him to know he was one half of my heart. Needed him to trust in us.

"You're staring," he whispered, soft lips pressing against my chest. His eyes were closed, his lashes dark and long as they kissed his high cheekbones. He was beautiful. Fates, he was beautiful.

"You're stunning, you know?" I said, the corner of his lips tipped up just a little at the praise.

"What's wrong?" he asked, cracking an eyelid. The dusky brown of his eyes edged to slivers in the dim light, and I watched his gaze fall to check on Aphrodite, muscles tensed, assessing her safety. Once he was satisfied there was no imminent danger, he returned his attention to me.

I just stared down at him like a fool, my eyes catching on the bangle glinting softly in the pale moonlight.

"I love you, Ares. You understand that?"

His eyebrows knitted together, eyes scrunching. The look that passed between us felt weighted, as if his hurt was my own.

"You are mine, for now and forever. Tell me, baby, are you getting loved enough?"

I watched as a myriad of emotions played out in his eyes. Surprise to confusion, then guilt melted to shame.

I brought my hand down to cup his face. "Ares. Tell me." The command was heavy, an anchor in the quiet darkness.

His lip trembled; eyes shining with unshed tears. "I'm trying. I love you, and Ditey, but I'm terrified I don't fit. That when you both realize I don't fit, it'll be too late."

His admission was a pendulum swing to my gut, and anger flared within me that he could feel like that.

My grip turned hard on his jaw, forcing him to look at me as a tear rolled down his cheek.

"You are ours. You are *mine*. Worthy of every ounce of love and then some. I don't need you to be perfect, Ares. I just need you to love me and let me in. Please. There isn't a side of you I wouldn't fight for," I whispered the words to his cheek, pressing kisses over his tears, over his trembling lips.

Long talks and tears had been shed these last weeks. Visions of memory of the trauma he'd endured had me feeling raw and protective of him. This strong, emotionally cut-off god to everyone else showed me his tears. His pain. I'd never take that for granted, and I knew that was what had made Aphrodite so protective of Ares for so many centuries.

"I'm yours," he admitted on a sigh, and my heart soared as he melted against me.

Entwining our hands, I pulled his arm up, the planes of his hard body opening to me as the covers slid down.

"Mine," I growled against his lips, slipping my hand back down over his skin. The scars of battles long past lived like a tapestry on his body, but every single one of them forged him into the god before me.

The god I loved.

I soothed him against me, careful not to jostle and wake Aphrodite. It would break her heart to see him crumbling like this and embarrass him to no end. No, this moment between us was for Ares and me.

I laid kisses over his nose, his cheeks and forehead and lips. "I will love you at your worst. I will love you when you don't love yourself. I will never let you go. You are the beating of my heart."

My words landed against Ares's skin, his tears welling up and spilling down his cheeks as I gently repeated them, chanted like an incantation, imprinting them on his body and shade.

His fingers dug into my skin, his blunt nails nearly drawing blood at the flood of his emotional release. Ares's teeth sank into my muscle, muffling his soft cry, a vulnerability I wouldn't ever forget as he shuddered against me.

I leaned in, sealing his lips to mine, tasting, devouring. His tongue slid against mine, strong but tentative, and I poured everything I could into our connection, the ones we shared with Aphrodite, that felt more and more distinct every day. I licked his lips clean of the salty tears that stained them.

"What happens tomorrow?" he whispered, entangling our fingers together and resting them above our heads. His body angled closer, his thighs cradling my side as he laid his hand across my torso, drawing out patterns over my skin.

Aphrodite adjusted, drawing both our attention, but her hand just came up, searching for him. When her fingers came to rest on his cheek, she sighed, nestling back into sleep.

"We fight for her. For each other," I answered.

We lay there entwined until the sun threatened to peek through the purple darkness. Ares's eyes drooped closed, his breathing mirroring the cadence of Aphrodite, and once they were both gone to a place I couldn't follow, only then did I finally fall asleep.

Hephaestus

CHAPTER 35

The sound of the gathered crowds bloomed through the coliseum. Aphrodite squeezed my hand gently, and Ares was calm on the exterior, but I could see the subtle lines of tension in the way he positioned himself between us and Achilles. The large board of trials stood to his left and, again, Achilles offered the bag to Hades, who, for his own reasons, looked exhausted.

"If you would, Your Grace." Achilles flicked his eyes toward Hades, who'd dipped his hands inside to pull a puck free.

Hades walked to the trial board and slid the puck in between the two middle nails before letting it go. It plunked and plopped downward, bouncing on all the spikes and changing the course of direction with each hit. It settled into a slot at the bottom with three snakes.

Hades sucked in a breath.

Bad sign.

"The second trial will be the Lernaean Hydra!" Achilles boomed, and the crowd went wild.

My heart sank into my stomach, and I prayed to the Fates that I'd be the one to draw the puck. Ares had more skill in battle, but I wasn't sure I could stand seeing either of them take on this thing.

The Lernaean Hydra had long been defeated, a massive creature with a single body and multiple deadly heads. Hercules had dispatched it to the Underworld as part of his failed trials, and its shade rested in the Sea of Monsters.

Ares tensed as Achilles opened the drawstring pouch once more. He plunged his hand inside, and I could see his eyebrows knit together in determination, as though he could *will* the challenge puck to himself.

Aphrodite reached in next, and then me. The clay was cool in my hand as I turned it over, the red paint shimmering under the dark lighting. My head shot up to Ares, who smiled triumphantly, blue paint stained against his puck. His glory was short-lived when Aphrodite opened her palm to reveal blue as well.

Two had been chosen.

I was to watch the two I loved most in the cosmos take on one of the deadliest beings to reign in the Sea of Monsters. The story of Hercules's feat was told far and wide, but also greatly exaggerated. He *did* defeat the hydra, a legendary accomplishment, but he had a sword forged by me, arrows made from the light of Artemis, a helm from Athena for strategy, and the favor of Zeus upon him, who'd sent a Pegasus to him at the very last moment and turned the tide of the battle.

We were three barely divine gods suffering from Bond sickness.

Ares looked at me before shifting his gaze to Aphrodite.

"We can do this," he stated, no fear in his voice. He was staying calm for Aphrodite, but I could see the way his nostrils flared. The roar around us was deafening, the shades haunting spectators to our possible demise.

"She shouldn't have to compete again. I haven't yet," I protested, but Achilles frowned.

"Fates choose the participants, Your Grace. Please, take your place." He gestured to the manacles on the ground, and I cursed, kicking the dark earth.

Aphrodite took my hand. "Hey, hey. Look at me. It's gonna be okay." She pressed her forehead up to mine when I finally let her drag my head down.

"I'm useless here," I mumbled, and Ares crowded in, wrapping his arms close around us.

"You're not. I'll be able to focus a little more if I only have to focus on one of you at a time. Knowing you're safe will help. I've got her, Hephaestus. Trust us." His words were so sincere, I knew he meant them.

My lips crashed into Aphrodite's, swallowing her moans. I broke apart reluctantly, and Ares grabbed my face gently.

"I'll come back to you. We both will," he promised, and I grimaced at the thought that one or both of them might not, but that was the reality of what we were doing. It seemed so cruel that we had spent centuries in agony and finally found a way to love and grow, only for us to willingly be thrown to the Hydra.

Ares leaned down and dropped a searing kiss on me before he stepped back and gestured to Achilles, who surveyed the scene appreciatively.

I walked to the manacles and allowed him to latch them around my wrists. The metal bolts slid home, and I tugged once, testing them with a curse. They were well-made, infused with power.

Ares took Aphrodite's hand, and they walked together to the side of the arena with Achilles.

I was out of earshot now, alone with only Hades, who also looked tense.

"This is going to kill them," I said, voicing my fear now that they were far enough away not to hear.

Hades crossed his arms, letting out a sigh.

"It was the Trial I was hoping for least. It's been known to be a favorite first Trial of hers, for the clearance rate alone," he said, the corners of his mouth pulled down in a frown.

"What's the survival rate?" I asked, pushing past the lump that had formed in my throat.

Hades turned his eyes back to their retreating forms.

"Zero," he admitted bitterly, and my throat constricted.

There had to be a way out of this.

I watched Ares step into the chariot pulled by the shades of two great stallions and reach a hand back for Aphrodite to join. They trotted to the middle of the arena, and we waited. The crowd had gone silent as the dead.

Ares disembarked from the carriage and reached for Aphrodite, who pulled with her a shield and sword.

We had all donned our traditional armor for this Trial, opting for the extra protections. Ares was in his full regalia, shining bright. His armor was powered and fueled with the lifeblood of all whose blood he'd spilled over the centuries. Aphrodite looked radiant in hers as well. The gold chest plate hugged her tightly, allowing ease of movement. She wore a black bodysuit under it instead of her usual pink chiton, the better to run and leap and not snag or give anything a way to snatch her up. A bow slung across her shoulder, along with a quiver full of moonlight arrows. Artemis had insisted.

Hecate had braided Aphrodite's long hair intricately on her head, and the only jewelry either of them wore was the glinting bracelets that bound them to me. They looked determined, no sign of fear.

I could feel Ares pulling the power from the air around him, ramping up his blood. He paced back and forth, wearing a furious path into the sand.

Aphrodite stood behind him, silent and stoic, pale eyes searching the arena for signs of movement.

The air to the back of the enclosure shimmered, blurring completely before our eyes. When the mirage refocused, an impossibly large lake stood, placid and dark in the middle of the arena, feet from where they stood. A large mountain radiating heat jutted up from the side of the lake, jagged and glistening with salt water. The ground below us transformed as well, sand giving way to dark bedrock. I could feel the tremble of the fires of the Asphodels move beneath us. My forges were fed from these same fires.

This was seafloor, tectonic plates. The trial had transported the Hydra's home *here*. Horror washed through me at the realization.

A slight ripple floated across the still waters, pulling all our attention back to the dark lake. One, then two, before a tidal wave built slowly, lapping the shore with churning waves.

Ares stepped farther back, sunk low into his fighting stance. He put his body between Aphrodite and the water, and she matched his stance.

With little more warning, the surface of the water broke apart with a mighty roar that bounced around the stone, shaking the marrow of my bones. The Hydra rose from the Sea of Monsters, its thick heads writhing and coiling against each other as it ascended from the depths.

I counted nine heads, on necks as thick as tree trunks and teeth that jutted from its skeletal maws in sharp, yellowed points.

This was not the three-headed Hydra of old, no. This was the shade of the Hydra in the form it had met its end, after Hercules had already cut off several heads and they had regrown. The once–deep blue skin shone black, slick with seawater and marred with bouts of rotted flesh. Soulless black eyes assessed the scene as two monstrous legs pulled it from the depths toward the shore, sending great storm surges over the banks.

Ares and Aphrodite backed up, still standing in calf-deep water from the tide.

The heads snapped their teeth, the shock waves from the pressure pulsing around them.

I glanced at Hades, the blood in my veins ice. His lips pressed into a thin line, keen eyes calculating what he was seeing. I strained against the restraints, groaning from the effort.

The screeches and roars of the Hydra swallowed up the grunts from my efforts. The heads pushed forward, snapping toward them and putting Ares on the back foot. The two thick feet of the Hydra dug into the sand, hauling its massive body almost completely out of the water. Two more back feet could be seen from this angle, and a long, sharp tail with spikes along the back ridge swayed with each step.

They studied each other, Ares and the creature. I watched Ares's jaw set, fire of a challenge shining in his dark eyes. The Hydra *almost* seemed hypnotized by him, stilling so only the lapping waves were moving.

Ares cracked a psychotic grin, and then, all at once, they lunged.

The God of War discarded his shield and grabbed his dagger in his offhand, and I knew then he was about to do something reckless. Ares let out a cry that shot through me and jumped, closing the distance between him and the sea beast. His body flew through the air, sword raised, and I watched as time slowed. It took forever for the momentum to fade, and he landed with a wet smack on the leg of the Hydra, plunging his sword in like a foothold.

His muscles bulged with the effort of holding on as the beast screamed, stomping backward toward the sea.

I rushed forward, panicked. If that thing got him under the water, there would be no getting him out.

He swung his dagger up and plunged it through the Hydra's decayed flesh, repeating the motion until he'd almost reached the first neck. The Hydra snapped at him, sharp teeth grazing his skin as he writhed and kicked to keep moving.

Aphrodite stepped closer, baiting the Hydra. She'd picked up the bow Artemis had given her and notched an arrow, and after a calm and steady breath, she aimed and let loose the arrow of moonlight that found purchase in the eye of a head focused on Ares. Aphrodite wasted no time celebrating her victory, instead rapidly notching another and shooting beams of light, always aiming for the eyes.

I didn't dare let myself get complacent, but the way they worked in tandem to take out the Hydra was methodical. They just might have this.

Ares shimmied up the neck of the nearest head and straddled it between his powerful thighs. He sunk his dagger into the top of its head, past the hard scales in a crunch we could hear from here. The head slumped, writhing and flexing its powerful muscles. Ares held on tightly, riding it down like a raging bull as it crashed into the shore. He pulled the dagger from it, dodging between uncoordinated strikes from the remaining eight snarling heads.

Ares backed up, baiting it onto more solid ground, as Aphrodite continued her assault. Silver arrows jutted from several eyes and nostrils; some stuck through the scales on its skin. It lunged for her, dragging itself fully out of the water before three heads descended on her.

Ares intercepted, again, leaping and jamming his dagger into the side of its face as he maneuvered closer to those teeth than I'd like. His boot found leverage on the bottom jaw of the Hydra's open mouth, wide from a roar, and Ares found himself standing directly in the mouth of one of the heads.

My heart stopped.

The Hydra clamped its jaw shut, and Ares reached up, crossing his forearm. He let out a yell as a yellowed fang sunk deep into him, protruding straight through the flesh of his arm. Ares pushed upward, battled the downward pressure, and with a mighty thrust, impaled the sword in his non-injured hand through the soft palate of the Hydra.

Another scream. More thrashing.

Ares leapt from the corpse of the snake that took a bite from him, landing hard enough to do serious damage. He had taken the fang with him, and it stuck from between his bones menacingly. He faltered once, but turned, long sword raised this time, ready to fight. They had two heads down, seven more to go. As long as they didn't sever a head, no more would grow.

The Hydra stalked toward them, thrashing its feet into the bedrock, dragging the lifeless appendages that were once fierce heads behind it.

An arrow shot from Aphrodite took out the other eye on an already injured snake, felling it. The Hydra screamed and snapped, pulling its body toward her.

Ares surged forward again, and I saw their plan. Keep it on land. Use Ares as bait so Aphrodite could take it out from afar with arrows.

Two heads lunged at Ares at once, catching him in a crossfire. He almost managed to slip through, but the long necks twisted at the last moment and wrapped tightly around him. They coiled swiftly, and I saw the veins in his neck bulged from the pressure. The uninjured arm holding his sword spasmed, and his weapon tumbled to the ground with a dull thud. The heads entwined with him rose to taunt him, long forked tongues tasting the air around him.

Salivating.

Tasting the fear.

At once, two arrows in rapid succession soared through the air, taking out the eyes of one snake, and Ares wrenched the long, sharpened tooth from his forearm and plunged it into the eye of the other. He pulled the tooth free and stabbed again, repeating the gesture until he was covered in ichor and blood and eye fluid.

Two more down.

The two necks crashed to the ground, knocking Ares's head against the ground with enough force to send out a shock wave. It knocked Aphrodite off her feet and sent her bow flying.

Ares was unmoving and unresponsive to Aphrodite's screams, and I strained forward again, the metal manacles cutting rivers of blood down my wrists from the strain.

"Hades, let me out. *Now!*" I commanded, and he looked torn. I knew he wanted to help, but there were rules in the Underworld.

"I don't give a fuck what it costs, you let me out of these fucking chains, or I will raze this realm to the ground," I swore, fury laced in my tone.

"Ares, get up, baby, please." Aphrodite's voice cut through me.

Ares groaned as he tried to lift his body from the churned ground, the mud and muck coating his greaves. He grunted as his arms gave out, and the God of War collapsed in on himself, breathing hard, bleeding freely.

The Hydra dragged him and the tangled bodies underneath it in its fury to get to Aphrodite.

I saw Ares's head lift, and the vice grip in my chest loosened just a fraction. He disentangled himself and stood, scooping up his discarded sword. He was facing Aphrodite, eyebrows set as he assessed his next course of action. He was still dazed from the impact, because he didn't hear the whooshing air behind him and didn't register the shadow.

"ARES! ON YOUR SIX!" I screamed, desperate for him to hear me.

He turned in surprise, sword outstretched, and five millennia of war and fighting instincts overtook him in his stunned form. His swing was deadly. Precise. The cool metal sliced through the fleshy neck of the Hydra, arcing up with force. The head dropped at his feet, eyes wide and forked tongue lolling out of its mouth.

"*FUCK, NO, NO, NO!*" he yelled.

The Hydra let out a scream that shattered glass and cracked a crevice in the middle of the arena. I could feel the magma flowing from the tectonic plates under us, pressing closer to the top. The beast took several steps back, stumbling as the severed head writhed and split into not two or three but *four* new heads.

Four snarling, snapping, drooling heads with nothing but blood in their eyes. Ares deflated, limping to Aphrodite, scooping her up to retreat. This was bad, and we all knew it.

The force of the wave that knocked Aphrodite over had more effect than I'd thought. I could tell by the way she clutched her chest, feel the drain coming from the Bond.

She was spent, and Ares knew it too. I could tell in the way he held her, shielded her. He was running on fumes, too, injured arm and crushed ribs from the impact and pressures of strangling necks.

The Hydra stalked toward them, confident as it swayed, despite the corpses dragging in its wake.

Hades turned to me; eyes narrowed.

"Will you survive if they don't?" He asked, and I looked at him with all the sincerity I could muster.

"No," I replied, honestly.

Hades swore, turning away from me, worrying his hand through his dark hair. He turned to me abruptly. "It's possible these chains have links made by the hand of the God of the Forge," he breathed, staring at me pointedly.

I glanced down at the chains binding me, adrenaline spiking. My hands traced the links, searching for one with my stamp, my power. I found it in the connecting link. My hands would still be bound together by a four-foot chain, but I'd be free of the ground. I wrapped my fingers around the link and willed it to listen, to *yield*. My hands warmed, and it responded happily, answering the call of its master. The link melted in my hands, freeing me.

Achilles looked down but otherwise made no move to stop me.

I scooped up a few long pieces of iron and set off like a shot across the coliseum grounds.

The Hydra didn't notice me, or if it did, I didn't register as a threat. It continued its slow and deliberate path toward Ares and Aphrodite, so certain of the easy meal it was yet to enjoy. I saw Ares's eyes widen as he backed them up against the wall of the mountainside.

The Hydra dragged its dead behind it like tassels, and I slid forward, lining up an iron spike on an unmoving head and reaching for my hammer in its hook at my waist.

I drove the spike home—once, twice, three times. I rushed forward, driving in two more spikes in the corpses. On my fourth and final approach, the Hydra faltered, tethered to the ground by its dead compatriots. It turned and roared, and I felt a small sense of relief that I'd managed to trap it. But the beast huffed and turned back to Ares and Aphrodite, pinned between the rock and its approach. With a sickening heave, it pulled, and the heads began to split around the spikes from the force and the rot.

I looked at Ares, who'd come to the same realization I had. He grabbed Aphrodite and hurled her up the mountain as high as he could, using the rest of his waning strength. She grabbed at the edge and scrambled up the ledge, far higher than any mortal would have been able to ascend.

I watched the rest of Ares's power drain from him. The God of War had given the last of what he had to get her to safety.

The Hydra would have a hard time climbing up that hill.

No, it would go for the easy kill. *Him, rather than her.*

Ares looked at me through the gore and dripping blood of the Hydra.

"I love you. Take care of her." His voice echoed on the wind.

In moments, the last of the spikes would give and he'd be eaten. I couldn't let that happen.

Frantically I searched for something to stop its approach. The magma under the tectonic plates called to me, feeding from my rage and helplessness. I let out a howl of rage and rushed forward, striking the ground behind the Hydra with layered blows.

My hammer drove deep into the ground, shaking the very bedrock. The earth rumbled as I willed the magma to come to me, to eat through the plates, to *obey*. Chips of earth flaked away until I could see the river below, like water that raged under a frozen lake. Power rippled through my muscles as I struck, again and again. In the distance, I heard Ares yelling, Aphrodite, too, but all I could focus on was the sound of metal striking the stone.

The Hydra surged to Ares, ripping free of the last spike, and I threw every ounce of power I held, called in every boon the Fates ever owed me, and sent my hammer once more into the earth. The stone crackled apart on a hissing, steaming fissure, wedging a path to the beast. Bright orange and yellow light engulfed the back legs of the Hydra as it fell into the cavern of magma below, and for a moment, I was triumphant.

The crack spread.

Swallowed the floor of the coliseum.

The Hydra. And, I realized too late, me.

Aphrodite dropped back down to Ares, and he held her back from the unstable floor as she fought, tooth and nail, to get to me, but there was no time.

"I love you both," I whispered as the world below dropped out around me in a hundred-foot radius, but seeing them safe was enough.

Death was swift.

I felt no pain.

Ares

CHAPTER 36

Hephaestus plummeted through the cracked bedrock in front of us with love in those brown eyes and acceptance in his posture. We were safe, and that gave him peace, but the tether that bound me to him ripped my heart from my chest as he fell.

Aphrodite clawed at me, crying and screaming in wails that shook me to my core, but I locked my arms around her, desperate to keep her safe. It was the last thing he had charged me with, and I wouldn't ever fail at it again.

This was my fault.

Through the shock, my mind assessed the aftermath of the battle, critically picking apart all the ways in which I'd fallen short, like a good soldier would. We were immortals, with limitations. Being enveloped by lava, burned apart from the inside out, wouldn't allow him time to heal.

Aphrodite wailed in my arms, collapsing as she struggled to get to the hole where his body had disappeared.

I felt nothing but numb.

It was cold now.

The bracelets Aphrodite and I wore cracked once with a devastating pop and slid to the ground, bounding away against the bitter stone. Hephaestus was dead, and he had taken all the warmth in the cosmos with him.

Achilles reached us with Hades, Hermes close behind. Tears stained Hermes's usually jovial face, and he rushed to Aphrodite. He held her, hands brushing over me as well, but the instinct to remove him from my person was gone.

I didn't care if he touched me. It didn't matter anymore.

Aphrodite slumped down between us, the swell of her heartbreak fracturing the air. It leaked from her like her life's blood, unstemmed and free-flowing, the pain a bone-deep sorrow that permeated the Asphodels.

The shades had been dismissed, and an eerie silence settled over the coliseum, save for the wails of Aphrodite that sliced through my skull.

Hermes held on to her, speaking softly as she cried in my arms.

Hades, Achilles, and Hecate were in deep discussion, and Medusa and Hygieia were knelt down with Dionysus, silent tears streaming down their cheeks.

Thanatos blinked into being feet from us, shaking his head. "I can't find him, Hades."

His cockney accent pierced through me, and I stiffened. I wanted his body, wanted *proof*. I needed to know if his shade made it.

What happened to gods once we died the True Death was a mystery even to us. Other creatures could dwell in the Underworld. Medusa had when she was murdered by Perseus, as had several others. But what happened to those of us born of divinity was unknown. We didn't end up in any realm of the Underworld, that was certain. Hades or Thanatos would know.

"He's the God of the Forge, could he survive that?" Hermes asked, hopeful, but Hades shook his head slowly.

"He's beyond the veil for me. I can't feel his spark." His eyes cast to me, pain etched into every line of his features. "I'm sorry."

I stood, lifting Aphrodite with me.

Hermes backed up slightly, giving me space.

"Take her," I instructed, handing Aphrodite's shaking body over.

He nodded, and she sunk into him, clinging to his shirt.

I separated from the crowd as blood rushed through my ears. The numbness gave way to the only emotion I ever truly felt at home with—*rage*. I paced back and forth, tension ramping up in my shoulders. My breaths labored, erratic, as I fought for control.

I marched over to the chariot and lost myself in a tidal wave of rage. I lost myself in the destruction I dealt, kicking, splintering the wood and metal through my fingers. I tore it apart in my grief, in my anger, and every moment we spent together flashed through my mind. Tears fell in hot streams, and I punched, bloodying my knuckles. I hurtled a wheel across the coliseum, relished in it smashing into the stone wall with a crunch. I pulled a sword from a corpse on the ground and paced.

Achilles approached me slowly, hands up.

My grip tightened. I leveled my blade, inches from his neck, stopping him short.

"*Where the fuck is he?*" I demanded, and Achilles shook his head. "*WHERE?!*" I screamed, face red with blood and grief and soot.

"Lord Ares, please, lower your blade." A strong female voice I didn't recognize rang out clear as a bell behind me.

I turned to see a small woman in a dark sheath dress, barefoot with long fire-red hair staring me down. Her features were delicate, but her eyes were sharp as steel. I lowered my blade and pushed back from Achilles.

"Who are you?" I asked.

"I'm Melia. I believe you have been seeking an audience with me," she answered, looking over each of us.

Achilles stepped forward, slightly to her right, in a protective stance.

Aphrodite stormed over to us, pushing right up into Melia's space, and hissed, "Where is he?"

Melia cocked an eyebrow at her.

Aphrodite was a mess in her bloody armor, but she looked every bit as menacing as I did.

"He's dead," Melia answered simply, gesturing to the large cavern glowing beneath us. The nonchalant way in which she said it, as though it were the most obvious answer in the cosmos, set my blood on fire again.

"Where is his *body*?" Aphrodite demanded, her voice a venomous tremble.

"I have it," Melia answered.

Aphrodite lunged, but Hades stepped in and placed a hand on her shoulder to guide her back.

My blade came up on instinct at the contact, and Hermes raised an eyebrow to me. I lowered it a fraction.

"Give him back," I ground out, barely controlling the rage inside. I was seconds away from giving into my baser desires.

"No," she replied flatly, and Aphrodite exploded before I could.

"*No?*" she shrieked, face contorted with rage. "*NO?* Have you no fucking respect? We are his partners, his Bondmates. He deserves a proper burial. He deserves to be with people who love him. Give him back, or I swear I will shred your shade to pieces and scatter it across the cosmos, do you fucking hear me?" Aphrodite finished, chest heaving.

Melia studied her curiously. "Weren't you seeking for a way to break your Bonds, Lady Aphrodite? Seems to me now you don't have to choose, and you get the mate you originally chose, without the dead weight," Melia mused, her face bent into a sneer.

Aphrodite started to move, but I stalked forward, raising my sword again before she could.

"Watch your fucking mouth, woman," I spat. "You're underestimating my penchant for committing gratuitous violence. Speak about Hephaestus like that again, and you *will* gain firsthand knowledge."

Melia looked between the two of us with a curious expression. Something had come to light behind her eyes, and she moved closer to Aphrodite. "Explain, please."

"I wanted to break the Bonds, not because I didn't want to be with them, but because we've got a corrupted Bond, and it may kill us all," Aphrodite answered, lifting her chin defensively.

Melia studied her, then turned to me and asked, "If I told you I could swap your places, would you do it?"

"Absolutely," I said, without hesitation.

She arched her eyebrows.

"No, it will be me who takes his place," Aphrodite answered, crossing her arms. We locked eyes in a silent war neither of us were willing to give in on.

"*No*. She asked me. I will go instead," I reasoned, and Melia's eyes sparked.

"You're really both volunteering to swap with him? Even though it means True Death?" she asked, and we both nodded, still looking at each other.

"There is no world for me without both of them," I answered, and Aphrodite softened.

"Nor for I," she breathed.

"And the Forge God? Would he say the same?" Her eyes pierced through me, as Aphrodite and I both spat, "Yes."

Melia lifted one of her crossed arms to grip her chin and settled into deep thought. All was still, and the tension stretched between us for far too long. She clapped and turned to face us. "I've made a decision. Lord Hephaestus cheated in the second

Trial. That makes his fate mine alone to do with as I will. In lieu of accepting a sacrificial swap, I'm going to allow him to compete in the third Trial, *alone*. If he succeeds, I will release him. If he does not, he stays dead."

Her words were final, and she offered no space for comments or questions. She turned to Hades, who nodded and opened a shadow portal. She stepped through, Achilles hot on her heels.

She turned an expectant eye on the two of us.

"Coming?" she asked, and we nodded, following after her.

The portal closed around us, and for the first time in an hour, I breathed. We had a chance.

He had a chance.

Hephaestus

CHAPTER 37

My body bounced slightly, moved by the shake of something soft underneath me. Soft light pushed through my closed eyes, and the bouncing intensified.

"Dad! Dad! Wake up!" a small voice trilled.

I cracked my eyes and ran my fingers across my eyes, brushing the sleep from them.

AJ jumped once more, folding his legs as he landed on the soft mattress and rolled onto my center.

"Alright, bud, I'm awake, I'm awake." I put my hands up in surrender.

He rested his tiny hands on my chest, tapping out a beat.

I grinned and kissed him lightly on the forehead.

His dark brown eyes stared up at me, and he scrunched his nose in distaste. "Dad, I'm not a baby, you don't gotta kiss me on the forehead," he protested, wiping it off.

"Is that so? Too cool for me now, kiddo?" I shot him a look of mock offense, and he giggled, rolling onto his back and crossing his hands behind his head. The shit-eating little grin sent a bolt of shock through me. He was so much like his namesake sometimes.

I lifted him easily and threw him over my shoulder like a sack of potatoes, his tiny echoing squeals of delight filling the rooms and bouncing off the hallway.

"Dad, put me down! I'll take it back, you can kiss my forehead!" he conceded, but I was having none of it.

We trudged through the studio, and I heard music coming from the open door. We looked at each other wearing matching mischievous smiles and snuck quietly through the door, watching Aphrodite as she twirled and leapt through the air. She looked so incredibly beautiful. AJ leaned into me, just as awestruck by her as I was.

It had been seven years since the Trials. I'd died, and Ares had made a deal, in his grief, to swap places. I begged and pleaded for the Oracle Melia to swap us back, but she insisted it was a onetime thing. We were broken for a long time, after that. Aphrodite was crushed and I was just a shell of who I was. We learned to live with the pain of a ghost and vowed to live, as he wanted.

A few years later, AJ had been born, and he'd saved us, given us real meaning. He acted so much like Ares sometimes, it was hard to not think he was still here, some small part at least.

We still lived in the city, and he went to Magnolia Park with his "cousins," Melinoe and Zagreus. He and Zag were thick as thieves, in the same grade and never giving us a moment's peace. I played music with the GorgonKnots, and Aphrodite taught dance.

We settled into life.

We raised our son.

We missed Ares.

The music faded out, and Aphrodite dropped her pose.

AJ clapped rapidly, and I joined in, his tiny smile wide and authentic.

Aphrodite spun toward us, and I caught her, planting a kiss on her lips.

AJ let out a groan and rolled his eyes.

"Ew, get a room," he admonished, utterly grossed out by his parents and any public displays of affection.

I chuckled and let him lead us into the kitchen.

"What are we doing today?" Aphrodite asked, pulling out AJ's chair at the table so he could settle in.

He hopped up, and she walked to the cabinets to pull out cereal and milk from the fridge. She sat his bowl of Apple Jacks in front of him, and he dug in with his Hot Wheels spoon.

"Let's go to City Park!" he exclaimed excitedly, stuffing his face full of sugary cereal.

Aphrodite put a mug of coffee in front of me, and I thanked her with a kiss before she settled into her seat with her own piping hot mug. She took a long sip before lowering her mug.

"Okay, but I thought you wanted to go to Auntie Hecate's today? They're going to visit Auntie Artemis at the preserve," she said, and his ears perked up.

"Think she'll let me shoot today? I wanna get good with the bow!" he asked, excitedly, and I smiled. He was already so adept at most weaponry, and he adored the forge. Aphrodite wore a bangle he'd crafted for her just a few weeks ago under my bracelet.

AJ shoveled more Apple Jacks into his face without swallowing and almost choked.

I leaned forward to smack his back gently, and he grinned.

"Ares James!" Aphrodite chided, and he shrugged sheepishly.

"Thanks, Dad." He smiled and went back to his bowl.

We spent the day with our friends, our family. AJ begged for a Lucky Dog for dinner, and then we came home for bath time. AJ laid in bed, snuggled tight between the covers in his X-Men pajamas.

"Dad, I love you. Can you send Mom in to read tonight though? Please?" he asked, and I smiled.

"Sure, bud, I'll get her." I stood and crossed the room before stepping into the hallway where Aphrodite waited. He used to want her to read for him all the time, but he'd been on a Dad kick lately. She wasn't taking it well.

I smirked when I saw her leaning against the wall, chewing on her thumbnail.

"Tag out," I said, and she grinned, pushing off the wall. "I'm gonna pop up to the roof and get some air. I'll be back when you're done?" I asked, and she nodded, leaning in for a kiss before pushing past me and heading in to read to our boy.

I took the stairs to the roof and popped the hatch door, stepping into the crisp autumn air. It was one of those rare Octobers where New Orleans actually experienced a fall, and I reveled in it. I walked over and propped up on the ledge, looking out over our city.

We had a good life and a kid I'd die for. Seven years, though, and we'd yet to go a day without thinking of *him*.

The wind shifted and wrapped around me. Muscle memory was a wild thing, and in that moment, the smell of fire and black powder flitted over me. It was easy to pretend he was here with us.

Large hands wrapped around my torso, pulling me against a strong chest. I balked, spinning out of the grip my body was already responding to, but my mind refused to believe.

Ares stood before me, looking as stunning as the day they'd taken him from us.

I lunged forward, tears pricking the back of my eyes, crashing into him. I sobbed into his shoulder while he smoothed my hair with gentle hands and soft whispers.

"Shh, shh, I'm here," he soothed, pulling my face up to look at him. He was here, in the flesh. I needed to tell Aphrodite, but before I could think more, I crashed my lips to his in a searing kiss.

"How?" I choked out, and he smiled, still holding my head in his hands.

"I've come to collect on the deal. Seven years. I can swap places with you for seven more," he whispered, and I sighed, exhaling hard. I hadn't really remembered the deal that had gone down, it was part of the magic of Melia.

"So in seven years we will swap again? Does Aphrodite know?" I asked, and he shook his head.

"No, you insisted we keep her out of this loop. Catch me up on what I missed?" he asked, and I kissed him again, a true smile on my face for the first time since we'd lost him.

"We have a son. His name is Ares James. We call him AJ," I said through tears.

Ares's eyes grew wide.

"Persephone and Hades have two kids now. Aphrodite is teaching dance at the center." I rattled off random facts, and he listened intently, brows knit together.

"You can't leave the kid, Heph. He needs a father," he reasoned, gently, casting his eyes down. The stipulations of Melia's deal were coming back to me now. I had to willingly go, and when the time came, so would Ares.

I grabbed his face, bringing it back to me.

"And he'll have one. *You.* You're going to do amazing. Now, how much time do we have? I know you want to see Aphrodite, but I need to tell them goodbye, and I want to spend a little time with you too. I missed you so much." I leaned into his chest.

"You're just going to swap? Just like that? Fuck this happy little life you've built? The kid, the wife?" he asked, and I pulled back, confused.

"To give you a chance to live? Absolutely. I love you, and I love them. They need you too. This was the price. How could you think I'd leave you to that fate? I agreed to the deal, Ares. I have no regrets, except that you and I are so limited on our time," I confessed.

Ares disentangled himself from me and began pacing. There was tension in his shoulders as he looked me up and down, like he was deciding if I was bullshitting him. There was something in his walk, in the way he carried himself that seemed . . . *off*. Something cold sliced down my spine, and in moments, I'd drawn the dagger I kept strapped in my boot and raised it high.

"Who are you?" I demanded, and not-Ares turned to me, expression bewildered.

"What are you talking about?" he asked, stepping forward.

I raised my blade higher, circling to put myself between him and the door to my home.

"Ares would have already tried to see Aphrodite. He'd have insisted we go to her immediately, to be together. Whoever you are, this is a cruel fucking joke."

Not-Ares paused his pacing and faced me head on.

"Damn it. You really would have traded?" he asked, and I nodded. He waved a hand over his face and torso, and a red-headed woman replaced his form.

She sighed. "Fair is fair. Congratulations, Lord Hephaestus, on completing the third Trial."

She snapped her fingers, and I woke up in my bed. Everything ached.

Everything.

The door to our room stood ajar, and I swung my feet over the bed and padded down the hallway.

Ares was seated on the couch, eyes dead, stroking a crying Aphrodite's hair.

I stopped in the hall and cleared my throat.

"Hey," I croaked, my throat scorched. Their eyes flicked to me for a millisecond before they were both up in a hurry, kissing and holding and crying into me.

"What happened?" I rasped, and a voice rang out from across the room.

"I can answer that."

Aphrodite

CHAPTER 38

Melia sauntered over and hopped her ass up onto our counter with a flourish, and I had to resist the urge to maim her.

Hephaestus was pressed up against Ares and me, and he felt so solid. It'd been three days since the second Trial, and after Hephaestus had died, this bitch had told us to "sit tight."

I hated her.

Ares kept us both so tight to him, I worried he may strangle us, but honestly, I didn't mind much.

"Hephaestus completed the third trial. Per our bargain, he has been returned. He won't retain memories from that time, as to keep his mind from becoming confused. I am here now to pay a debt. I'm afraid I cannot tell you directly how to break your Bonds. I did make great strides before my death, but I did not complete the task. I can, however, fix whatever this is." She motioned her finger between the three of us, and I scowled.

"How, if you can't break the Bonds?" I asked, annoyed. If we'd completed the task, we were owed our prize.

Melia hopped down and walked toward us.

Ares stiffened.

"Oh, be easy, Muscles. I called in a favor: a very old and very powerful boon. Hera will perform a proper Bonding, *for the three of you*. It will heal the corrupted Bonds. You will be as one, should you wish it. This is all I could offer you." She shrugged, in a take-it-or-leave-it manner.

I glanced at the boys, who looked unsure.

"What do you think?" I asked, and Hephaestus turned to me.

"I would like that very much, but I also understand your reasoning behind wanting to break them. Bond or no Bond, my love will not change," Hephaestus answered, kissing me lightly on the temple.

"Same for me," Ares offered. "You already belong to me. I belong to you. I am good with merging the Bonds."

I looked at Melia and nodded.

"Set it up," I answered, and she dipped her head low.

"It will be done," she said, and with that, she was gone.

*

OCTOBER 31, 1997

Cherry blossoms lined the aisle in our private garden, the bluest skies I'd seen in forever above us.

Hermes held my hand, guiding me in my deliciously ridiculous heels toward Ares and Hephaestus, who waited for me at the raised dais. The large slabs of trees held our gathered family, quiet and intimate in our company.

"You look beautiful," Ares murmured, sending his words for my ears only on the wind.

I blushed, the red staining the tips of my ears while his eyes devoured me.

I wore a classic white chiton, cinched to hang over my shoulders with armor Hephaestus had fashioned for us. Delicate spindles of gold spun around my torso, a stark contrast to the white gossamer underneath. My hair was down, loose in curls, the way they both preferred it. My only jewelry was the bangle on my arm.

Ares wore his traditional red himation, sharp against his golden skin. His gauntlets were forged by Hephaestus, and his horses were featured, as well as the crest of a wave for me.

Hephaestus's deep ore armor hugged his lithe frame, simple and elegant in its beauty.

The both of them looked so stunning that the rest of the room fell away.

I passed Hades and Persephone, seated in the first row, and smiled at the beautiful dark-haired baby cradled in Persephone's arms.

Hermes kept me steady until we drew close enough for the boys to collect me. They shook his hand before taking each of mine, and Hermes fell back to sit next to Hecate. Her hair was twisted, long and swaying, tipped in a blue hue that popped against her deep brown skin. She smiled at him lovingly as he stretched his arm across her shoulders.

Medusa stood off to the side, her angelic voice wafting through the space as she sang in the old tongue, a ballad of love and strength for all.

Ares squeezed my hand, and Hephaestus brought my other to his lips.

A portal opened at the front, and Hera stepped through.

I bristled slightly, but forced myself to calm. It wasn't as though I didn't *know* this was coming. Hera was the only one who could perform a Bonding, and this one was unconventional, to say the least.

She looked at Hephaestus with adoration but spared as little a glance for Ares and me. Melia had traded in a favor in exchange for her presence here, and though details had been vague, it was surely something to do with the task that got Melia killed in the first place. There would be other times to sort that out, to dig into the mystery of why Hera did anything she does.

Right now was about us.

"We are here to witness the reunification of three eternal shades, and the strength of the . . . *unconventional* Bond they share. A Bonding is the most primal and sacred of our ceremonies, and one that should not be reversed or broken, in this realm or any other. The vows you take today shall be unbreakable, immutable. It is a contract of love and devotion, but also of love and respect. If the three of you agree to these commandments and are willing to honor this commitment, please make the physical bridge," Hera instructed.

We each placed our right hands together, ensuring we were each touching the other two.

Hera lifted her hands high, drawing on her power. She brought them together in a thunderclap before placing her hand on top of our joined ones.

A soft sting shot through me where our Bondmarks were. Hephaestus gave out a small hiss, too, and we watched in fascination as the golden thread that had settled into the tattoos on our skin retreated to our hands, binding our wrists in three distinct golden threads.

"Do you wish to be Bonded to one another, from now until the death of the cosmos?"

Three resounding, enthusiastic yesses rang out between us. Murmurs of quiet laughter rumbled through the crowd, and Hera shot them disapproving looks.

"You may now speak your vows, should you so wish it. Then place your hand over the position in which you will bear your mark to reforge the Bond. Hephaestus, you may speak." She nodded, and the God of the Forge shifted excitedly.

"Aphrodite," he began, and I brought my eyes to him. "I have loved you for a thousand lifetimes. You have shown me what it is to let someone see my light, and to trust them to love me when it's dimmed. I'll never grow tired of growing with you, learning with you. I *choose* you." He placed his hand over the soft flesh on my chest, just under my collarbone. A new place. A new beginning for a new mark.

"Ares," he said, and I felt my core tighten at the intensity of his gaze. "You were such a surprise in my life. Centuries wasted on things that didn't matter when we could have been exploring the world together. I don't regret a single moment of it though. If we didn't have the pain, I wouldn't know *this* good is worth it. And it's so fucking good." His voice dropped suggestively, causing Ares to flush as someone, probably Helios, let out a whoop of praise from the crowd.

I laughed, and Hephaestus pressed on. "I love the way you love our girl. I love that you push me. I choose you. *Always*."

I placed my hand on Ares's chest. "Ares, I have loved you for my entire existence, and you have been there to push me into being more every step of the way. You trust me to save myself when I trip, and you love me so deeply that, sometimes, I worry it will swallow you whole. You are such a deep spirit, protection so rooted in the fabric of who you are. More kind than anyone could know, my God of War. I love you. I choose you."

I slid my eyes to Hephaestus, who'd sucked his bottom lip under his teeth. His eyes fire that sent a bolt of electricity straight to my core.

"Hephaestus, my God of the Forge. You have stoked the fires inside me in a thirst no drink can quench. You see through the parts of me I'm not proud of, and you love them anyway. Publicly, in the light. You are warmth and kindness and everything that makes this cosmos turn. You're our own private sun, and every day, I will choose you. *We* will choose you."

Ares placed his hand over Hephaestus's chest, completing the circuit. "I have no specific words for each of you, but instead, I make you this vow, together. I will protect you in every way I am able. I will love you, and I will ravish you. Seriously, the way you two look right now, you're lucky I haven't thrown you both over my shoulder and told everyone to beat feet—"

Another giggle shot from the crowd, but an admonishing glare from the Goddess of Bonds and Marriage had Ares clearing his throat.

"I love you. That doesn't mean much when I come from a place of war and destruction and ruin. But what love I *do* have, I give to you freely. You take up all the space in my life, and I will never put you below anything else. This Bond that we share was forged in a crucible, in fire and fury, and it will not be tempered. I will gladly burn for you both, if you ask it of me. I, too, choose you both. Every day."

A hot tear slid down my cheek.

The golden threads of our Bonds lit up brightly, melding together and slipping down each of our outstretched palms, settling on the exposed flesh of our chests. It burned, but not in an unpleasant way.

I looked on in awe to see the shape of a flame and sword crossed together as our new union solidified. It clicked within my chest, heralding a swell of emotion coming through the Bond from both of them.

"What is done shall not be undone. Peace and happiness to you all. You may kiss . . . whomever you'd like," Hera finished with a noncommittal wave.

We fell together in a tangle of smiles and tears, kissing and laughing through the joy and applause from our gathered.

Ares broke away momentarily to address the crowd. "You can all head to the reception. We'll see you in an hour or so." He winked, and several laughs could be heard as the God of War dragged us through a portal Hades had waiting.

"Best day ever." I beamed.

"Best day *yet*."

Aphrodite

CHAPTER 39

My hands gripped the metal Master between my fingers, cool to the touch as I looked at my God of the Forge, strapped naked to the bed, waiting for my instruction.

Ares's hands, warm and comforting, wrapped around my waist, goose bumps erupting in their wake across my skin as his chest pressed to my back, every hard line of his body pure sex.

I shivered, quaking under his touch in anticipation.

"Just relax, Little Goddess. You're in control, so just tell us what you want and watch the power you wield over us," he whispered into the shell of my ear, and I arched, pressing against the hard cock resting against the cleft of my ass.

I'd wanted this, begged for it even, to see how it would feel to top properly, but now that it was happening, I didn't know what to do. Where to even begin.

Ares tilted my chin, exposing the column of my throat as he stared into my eyes, waiting.

I swallowed thickly and gripped the Master tighter. "Take the Master and work it onto Hephaestus. Then kneel on the bed and wait for my instruction," I husked, channeling every ounce of dominance Hephaestus had ever used on me.

Ares smiled and pressed a kiss to my temple before taking the golden cock from my hands and sauntering over to our Bondmate.

I flooded as this sword of violence tempered at my command, sank a knee onto the bed and then *crawled* across the covers.

I pressed my thighs together, watching the way Hephaestus's abs constricted in anticipation, the lust-blown pupils swallowing all the honey brown of his irises as he tracked Ares's movements.

"Such a pretty cock, baby," Ares whispered, dropping a featherlight kiss against the glinting bars of Hephaestus's piercings before maneuvering the golden ring of the master around his balls.

Hungrily, I watched as Ares began to stroke both shafts, and Hephaestus threw his head back, whimpering at the sensations bolting through him. The chains keeping his arms held aloft rattled as he writhed, and the smooth gold of the Master was replaced by delicate skin.

I smirked as Ares licked across both tips of Hephaestus's cocks, then sat back on his haunches obediently.

Fuck.

This was power that I'd never felt, new and bolstering, as I stepped toward the bed.

"You look so good tied up like this. Presented for us." The words purred from my lips, and Hephaestus's eyes blazed while his gaze raked over my naked body.

"Plenty of room for you both to ride, Little Love." He smirked, thrusting his hips up so his dual cocks smacked into his abdomen, smearing the tight skin with pre-cum.

"Ride?" I cocked my head to the side, sinking my teeth into my bottom lip.

Ares groaned, his eyes flicking from me to Hephaestus like he was starved.

"Now that is a good idea. Ares, baby? Straddle him, face forward. Line up, but don't sink down until I say," I commanded.

He moved gracefully, welcoming Hephaestus into the cradle of his thighs before slicking his palm over his mouth, gathering the spit there, and reaching between them.

"*Shit*," Hephaestus grunted as Ares lined the crown of his cock up against his hole, his body a taut line as he waited for my command.

"One inch," I instructed.

They both groaned as the God of War sank down, enveloping Hephaestus's crown.

"Squeeze, Ares."

Ares's head fell back, his eyes rolling as he tipped his hips and lowered a fraction, gripping the tip of Hephaestus's cock in what must have been a vice. The Master was thick and heavy, rubbing against Ares's hard shaft with every slight movement, both of them leaking.

For me.

For each other.

Fates, I wanted to taste it.

"More." The command was obeyed instantly, and Ares's legs started to shake from the angle of his body, the stretching of the most intimate parts of him.

"Give him another rung of your ladder, baby."

Hephaestus's eyes moved to my hands, tracking the way they glided over my breasts, pinching my nipples just the way he liked to do. His hips slammed up, causing them both to cry out, filling Ares completely with his cock. I watched him plant his feet and fuck up into Ares, defiance burning in his eyes. Hephaestus topped even from the bottom, and he was challenging me, the way I always did him.

"Tsk, tsk," I muttered, closing the distance between us as Ares's fucked himself down onto Hephaestus, the sounds of flesh on flesh making me dizzy with want.

"Stop." My command was firm, and Ares groaned but stilled his hips, pinning Hephaestus down so he could no longer move. "I see you're intent on being a brat today, and that's okay. I'm well-versed in how to play like that."

I crawled onto the bed, situating myself right next to where their bodies were joined. Their cocks were thick and beautiful, everything I'd ever desired, and weeping. Leaning down, I began stroking them together, frotting them against one another before sucking them into my mouth. I ignored the burn and stretch of my lips around them, instead focusing on the otherworldly sounds coming from their lips.

"Fucking Fates, Ditey," Ares groaned as I swirled my tongue along his crown, spitting over the two of them.

"You think that is a punishment?" Hephaestus teased, his voice a rough grunt. "Suck his cock, Little Love, and I'll make him see the cosmos."

I moaned around them, then popped off, shuttling my hand up and down them both as I stared at Heph's twinkling eyes. Ares's hips stuttered, and I could see the subtle movements from Hephaestus, knew firsthand the exquisite torture that cock could unleash. His eyes flicked to Ares's face, twisted up and panting, and I saw his own need becoming overwhelming.

"So fucking desperate to come on my cock, hmm," he whispered, unable to stop himself, but I knew he needed Ares to come just as badly, needed to see him fall apart first.

I grinned. "Ares, get off."

The growl that ripped from Hephaestus was primal as Ares ripped his ass away with a whimper. He strained forward, his nose nearly touching mine as Ares untangled his legs and sprawled out, breathing hard.

"Rude," Ares huffed, and I blew him a kiss.

I grabbed both of Hephaestus's cocks and dragged my fingers over them slowly, teasing that nerve just under the tips, carefully dragging the skin over his piercings and grooves. Slowly, I sped up, ignoring the burning gaze of Heph's eyes as his cocks cried for me, slickening my strokes.

"Don't," he whispered, voice low and dangerous as it clicked in his mind what I was doing. He hated coming first. It was his first mission to drag the orgasms from our bodies, kicking and screaming sometimes, before he even let us touch his cock. But now? So on edge?

"Poor baby, is this too much? You too close?" I taunted, relishing in the way his breathing hitched, his muscles tensed. "I bet you're hanging on for dear life right now. I can feel how badly you want to make a mess on me, baby."

Hephaestus swore, pulling his hips back, running from me.

I scooted my body down, slowing to a languid pace, and felt Ares settle next to me on his stomach. I looked over with a grin and released the Master, watching as he gripped it tightly around the base and spit on it. I licked up the side of Hephaestus's barbells, and he shuddered beneath our touch.

"First one to make him come fucks his ass," Ares wagered, and then we both moved, licking and slurping and sucking on his cocks, making a mess between us. We moved in tandem, and I looked up to see Hephaestus's eyes nearly crossed from the pleasure, lost in absolute rapture as we took him to the back of our throats.

Ares's hand wiggled between Hephaestus's thighs, fingers glistening, and I moaned in protest as he sank a finger inside of the God of the Forge's tight hole, massaging up to that soft spot that had Hephaestus's body shaking.

"Cheater!" I shouted around a mouthful of cock and piercings, but Ares's just grinned as cum erupted over his lips first, then warmth filled my mouth as Hephaestus shook apart on a cry. He was sloppy and wet, and Ares wasted no time in urging me up to straddle him.

It was a pleasant consolation to see a blissed-out Hephaestus. Our perfect, commanding god, lost for control.

A DARK FATES NOVEL

Prometheus

I glanced around the crowded hall at the brethren gathered, eyes constantly sweeping, searching for any sign of Zeus. This was a bad idea, to allow myself to be seen amongst so many gods, but the fire message I'd received had been a little too enticing to ignore, and that also had me wary.

Voices hung in a low murmur around me, and I tightened my fist against the top of my thigh, forcing my body to calm.

Ares, Aphrodite, and Hephaestus looked radiant as they swayed together on the dance floor. I couldn't have been happier for them, but at the same time, a three-way Bond, unheard of before today, painted a different target on their backs. One I knew could and would be used against them, if the opportunity ever presented itself.

All around I saw pairings on divinity, and I both envied and remained cautious at their happiness.

At their boldness to declare it for anyone to see.

Love was a weapon; one used to carve out hearts and shades and livers.

Hermes walked over with two long-neck bottles in his hands, offering me one before taking the seat next to me.

I grabbed it gratefully and popped the top, tipping it back before scanning the perimeter. Again.

Hermes chuckled.

"He's not here. Ares would kill him if he tried, Prometheus," he assured, but it did nothing to quell my anxiety. Centuries of hiding and decades on the run had ingrained the inability for me to trust anything or anyone into the very marrow of my bones.

I glanced around with exactly zero subtlety.

"So what is this thing you needed to speak about?" I asked.

Hermes dropped his fingers to his lips and cut his eyes.

"Just because *he* isn't here doesn't mean his bloody spies aren't. Come, let's find somewhere more private."

I stood with him, following the God of Thieves across the crowded dance floor. Hermes maneuvered through them with ease, laughing and dancing and singing in tune, winged converses in perfect step. He was so graceful that I almost *didn't* see the small doorway he sauntered through.

Almost.

I followed him inside to find Hades and Hera in deep conversation with a red-haired woman who definitely didn't belong in this realm. A shade, judging by the look of her. A powerful one, based on the aura emanating in arcs around the room.

I stopped short at the strange company, assessing exits that didn't exist. One door in, one door out. *Damn it.*

"What's all this about?" I asked, pausing without taking another step deeper into the room.

Hermes chuckled as he blew past me to drop a drink in Hera's hands. She thanked him, and I raised my eyebrow at their civility. Last I'd heard, Hermes was on an Olympian shit list after abdicating his duties while Olympus fell, to throw in with the Death Gods. Seeing the Queen Goddess didn't bode well—where she was, he usually followed.

"Revenge. On Zeus. We need your help," Hera stated.

My defenses immediately rose, every self-preservation bone in my body weary of her words.

"What kind of revenge?"

"The kind where we ruin his life for all the people he's fucked up. Are you in or are you out?" Hera's chin lifted, her words cold and calculating, but there was a fire in her blue eyes, a raging inferno laced with pain and misery I didn't understand. Something had happened to the goddess, and by her own reputation, it had to be shade-crushing to have her turn on her Bonded.

A dull ache, one that lived near constant in my lower side twinged.

Hades, Hermes, and Hera waited for my answer, and the shade's eyes narrowed as she assessed me.

I took another swig of the amber liquid and swallowed around the lump in my throat. "Count me in, then."

Acknowledgments

Book Three. What a ride. I have to be honest: This one scared me, partly because it is so close to my heart, but also because it is so close to so many of my readers. I hope the expansion on the Hephaestus/Ares/Aphrodite lore gave you so much comfort (and, if we're honest, the need for a cold shower).

First and foremost, I must thank my team, but most especially, Brandy for sticking with me on this one. For the three-a.m.-breakdown phone call when she read *that* part with Hephaestus. Thank you for being on my side, in my corner, in the passenger seat for all my crazy shenanigans.

To the rest of my team, for safeguarding me and giving me space to crash out, under the most bizarre conditions.

To Rachel, for her incredible insight during the developmental stage for Trad, and my agent, Amy, for fighting and advocating for me. I am forever grateful for the incredible humans in my world, who keep my wheels spinning, who support me endlessly. I couldn't love you more if I tried, but I've got no problem trying. <3

To Janessa, as always, for knowing this world nearly as well as I do.

And to Snow, for your talent, for bringing the Dark Fates to life through your art and vision. We are so glad that you're ours.

The next installment is one of my favorite books, with our sassiest couple. We'll see y'all in Atlantis by way of New Orleans in *Of Myths & Muses*!

Don't miss the next installments in the epic Dark Fates series

JULY 7, 2026

DECEMBER 1, 2026

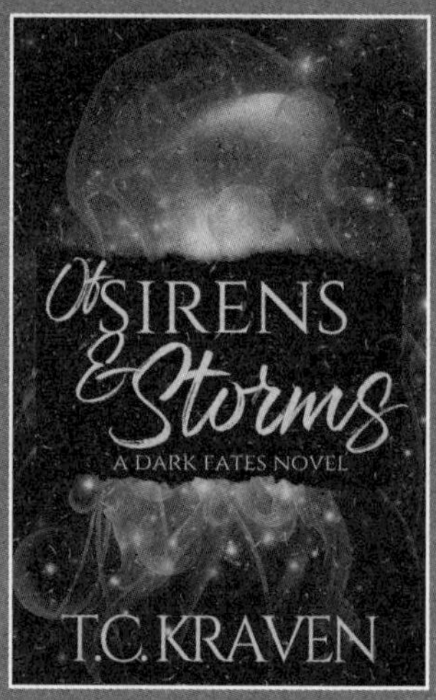

Available wherever books are sold.

But wait, there's more . . .

BLOOD & BEDLAM, a brand-new title by T.C. Kraven and the first in the NOLA After Dark series, publishes Fall 2026

DIVERSION BOOKS